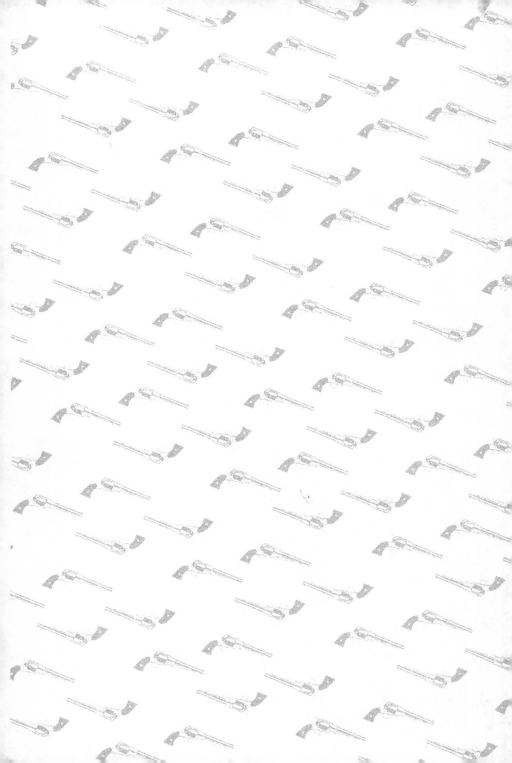

R. S. KELLY

A MAN
OF THE TERRITORY

R. S. KELLY

A MAN
OF THE TERRITORY

John Wesley Anderson

Honoring the Past *Shaping the Future*

Circle Star Publishing
Colorado Springs, Colorado

Published in the United States of America by
CIRCLE STAR PUBLISHING
P.O. Box 60144
Colorado Springs, Colorado 80960

Anderson, John Wesley
R.S. Kelly A Man of the Territory / John Wesley Anderson
First printing June 2019
Library of Congress Control Number: 2019905864

ISBN 978-1-943829-21-7

PRINTED IN THE UNITED STATES OF AMERICA

Circle Star Publishing is an imprint of Rhyolite Press, LLC

Cover design and book design/layout by Donald R. Kallaus

To the Men and Women of the
El Paso County Sheriffs Office
—past, present and future . . .

Books by John Wesley Anderson

Ute Indian Prayer Trees of the Pikes Peak Region

Rankin Scott Kelly, First Sheriff, El Paso County, Colorado Territory

Native American Prayer Trees of Colorado

R. S. Kelly, A Man of the Territory

Contents

Chapters

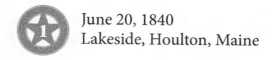 June 20, 1840
Lakeside, Houlton, Maine

He didn't mean to kill him. But there at his feet lay the body of his sister's fiancé.

"I think you done killed him Kelly!" his friend Morgan said as he bent over the motionless man at Kelly's feet. Neither teen-ager had seen a dead body before, but from the endless flow of blood pouring down both sides of the man's face, and from the mangled cartilage that had once been the young man's nose, the boys were convinced no one could survive such carnage.

"But, but, I didn't mean to," Kelly stuttered as he glanced from his blood-covered hands to his sister swimming frantically to shore from the small overturned rowboat out on Houlton Lake.

Turning to face his sister, Kelly began pleading, desperately asking his sister for forgiveness as she emerged from the water. "I'm so sorry Katherine," he said, as she gathered her wet dress in her arms, then ran and dropped to the ground at Emitt's side.

"Emitt, Emitt, please dear Lord, please let him live," Katherine Kelly prayed as she knelt over him, gently stroking his hair. She looked up to search her younger brother's eyes. "Rankin Scott Kelly, what have you done?"

Hearing his older sister use his full name reaffirmed the severity of the trouble that had befallen him. As Kelly looked down at the almost unrecognizable face of the man his sister was betrothed to marry, he tried to replay in his mind what had happened. Only moments ago, he and Morgan were casually walking along the shoreline of the small lake near his home in Houlton, Maine. They were enjoying a warm midsummers day, while his sister Katherine, her fiancé Emitt, and another girl were out on the lake in a small rowboat. Emitt stood up and starting rocking the boat from side to side.

SPLASH!

Kelly gasped then held his breath, anxiously counting as three heads slowly emerged from the water. He knew Katherine could swim, his father insisted all three of his children learn to swim after their mother had drowned. He watched Emitt swimming to shore, leaving Katherine and the other girl to fend for themselves, both clinging to the hull of the overturned rowboat. Kelly knew Emitt had just been showing off, but leaving the girls behind was a cowardly thing to do.

"Emitt! Go back out there and help them!" Kelly shouted, pointing to the girls still holding on to the overturned boat.

"They're fine, you little cow patty," Emitt said, rising up out of the water and walking the rest of the way to shore, where Kelly and Morgan were standing.

"Come on Katherine! You can do it!" Kelly shouted, encouraging his sister and the other girl as they pushed away from the overturned boat and began swimming toward shore.

Emitt laughed, pushing Kelly aside, as he turned away from

the shoreline.

"You're a scoundrel!" Kelly shouted, making a fist with his right hand. Then he grabbed the older boy's arm with his left hand and spun him around to face him.

"Who you callin a scoundrel, you little twerp," Emitt said menacingly, as he pulled his arm aggressively free of Kelly's grasp, then leaned his face into Kelly's, almost inviting a punch or so it seemed to Kelly, the shorter of the two by several inches.

Kelly's first blow, an uppercut, connected squarely with Emitt's chin, snapping the young man's head back with surprising swiftness and force. Recovering, Emitt pushed Kelly hard in the chest with the palm of his open hand, forcing the young teenager to fall down into the wet mud at the water's edge. Kelly, unhurt, was up immediately, swinging with both fists at Emitt's midsection. Emitt, not accustomed to fighting, slapped Kelly twice across the side of his face with an open hand, while laughing aloud, infuriating the younger boy all the more.

A strong punch by Kelly's fist to Emitt's stomach bent him forward, forcing the air from his lungs and silencing his laughter. Then at precisely the same moment when Emitt's head was bent forward, Kelly brought his right knee up with all the force he could muster, a fighting technique Uncle Doug had taught him while pretending to, "fight wild Injuns." Kelly grabbed the back of Emitt's head, forcing it downward, just like Uncle Doug had taught him to do. Emitt's nose collided violently with Kelly's bony knee. The resulting effect was the crunching sound of cartilage as Emitt's nose broke. Kelly and Morgan were sickened to see how Emitt's nose had been splayed, lying openly across both sides of his face. Blood spurted forth with what seemed to the two boys an unstoppable torrential flow.

Kelly watched as Emitt fell over backwards, landing in the wet mud with a thud. Taking advantage Kelly jumped on and straddled the older boy's chest. Then, using his knees, Kelly pinned Emitt's arms down to his side just like Uncle Doug taught him to do last summer. Instantly, Kelly began pummeling Emitt's face with both fists as Emitt struggled. After countless blows from each fist, Kelly realized Emitt was no longer struggling. Surprisingly enough Emitt was not moving at all. When Katherine had made it ashore she pushed her younger brother away from her fiancé's body, gasping in horror as she saw the extent of Emitt's injuries to his face.

The fury Kelly had unleashed had startled him, sickening him to his stomach as he slowly backed away from the scene.

"I best run and get the marshal," Morgan said.

Kelly looked into his sister's eyes as she looked up from the crumpled body of the man she was supposed to wed and mouthed, "I'm so sorry Katherine." And then he turned and ran away.

"Rankin!" Katherine shouted, standing now, she shouted louder, "Rankin Scott Kelly!"

Those were the last three words Kelly would hear his sister or any family member say.

For the next three days Kelly wandered the foothills near his home and spent two sleepless nights in a cave. He repeatedly weighed his slim options. He could turn himself into the law, where he would most surely be hanged for a murder he had not intended to commit, or he could be the coward now and simply run away. There were no excuses, Kelly knew, no justifiable defense for what he had done. He rationalized to himself, more than once, that perhaps he deserved to die for his unintended crime. Kelly had never seen a hanging before, but imagined the terror

4

one would feel as the thick rope was placed around their neck and what's worse, the shame his family would experience from his heinous crime and public execution. Truth be told, like most fourteen year olds, he was simply afraid to die.

With only a fifty cent piece in his pocket, a birthday gift from his Uncle Doug, fourteen year old Rankin Scott Kelly turned and ran away from home, never to return again.

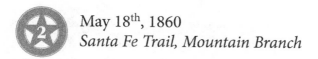 May 18th, 1860
Santa Fe Trail, Mountain Branch

It had been nearly twenty years since Rankin Scott Kelly ran away from Houlton, Maine, yet he habitually looked over his shoulder to make sure he wasn't being followed by the law. Kelly started using his middle name, Scott, fearing someone who knew about the murder in his hometown might recognize the less common name of Rankin. When using his name on documents he often used just his initials R.S. Kelly and would allow his last name to be spelled either Kelly or Kelley. But here, as he rode further west on the Santa Fe Trail, he began to feel as if he might finally slip into obscurity in the vastness of the American West.

Kelly's dapple gray mare nickered as she nodded her head toward the lone Indian rider on the mesa ahead. "I see him," Kelly whispered softly, reaching down to pat the right side of her neck assuredly. Then he slid his Hawken black powder rifle out of its tan leather scabbard attached to the underside of his horse's saddle. Kelly's .53 caliber muzzle loader was a work of art, with an octagon rifled barrel, beautifully finished walnut stock and double set brass triggers. But more importantly it was deadly accurate, even at this range of 300 yards. From experience Kelly knew he could easily knock the rider off his mount, or should the Indian come at him head-on, a shot from his rifle would be even more certain of hitting its mark with each step the rider took to close the distance. Kelly hoped it wouldn't come to that; he'd already had enough killing in his thirty-three years of life to last him a lifetime.

Resting the brass butt plate of the heavy buffalo gun on his right thigh, Kelly cocked the rifle with his thumb then gently nudged Marengo, his twelve year old mare, into a slow canter. Kelly placed himself between the Indian on the near hillside and the wagon train on the trail a quarter mile behind him. From years spent fighting hostile Indians, followed by his military service during the bloody Mexican-American War, Rankin Scott Kelly had long ago made his peace with his Creator. Truth be told, he was simply no longer afraid to die. Kelly's friends claimed his knack for surviving countless deadly encounters was his "luck of the Irish," although he knew luck would only carry a man so far. Besides, Kelly explained whenever his friends brought up his heritage, "I'm only half Irish." Kelly didn't remember much about his mother, for she had died when he was only three, but it always gave him a sense of belonging to know his mother was Canadian-English.

Luck, or more likely God's will, was the only way most men could explain how a bullet or an arrow could claim the life of the man riding right next to you, while leaving you unscratched when the fighting was done. Whenever he faced danger, Kelly drew courage remembering the faces of the brave soldiers he fought alongside in Mexico, during the siege of Vera Cruz, but he tried to forget the faces of the soldiers he had killed during the Battle of Cerro Gordo. He remembered the confidence General Winfield Scott placed in his troops, even the Irish volunteers like Kelly. Where Kelly had been born, in what had once been part of Canada, most Americans referred to General Scott as the Hero of the Aroostook War. But General Scott was better known to his men as "Old Fuss 'n Feathers," a nickname he had earned in far-away Mexico for his extraordinary attention to detail, never leaving anything to chance. Like most of the American soldiers who survived the Mexican-American War, Kelly knew that had it not been for the tenacious leadership of their U.S. Army's officers and dedication of its soldiers, the war in Mexico would not have been won and the Treaty of Guadalupe Hidalgo would never have existed.

The Treaty of Guadalupe Hidalgo opened up the American West. It secured for the U.S. all the land that extended from the Arkansas River south to the Rio Grande River and west to the rugged coastline of the Pacific Ocean. The Mexican-American War resulted in the Mexicans losing half their geographical area and positioned the Americans to begin to fulfill what they felt was their Manifest Destiny, becoming one Nation from Sea to Shining Sea. That Treaty, and the discovery of gold, is why men like Kelly were now headed out West, to fulfill their dreams and seek out their destiny. The only thing that stood in the way of these early pioneers, such as Kelly, were the hundreds of thousands of Indians who already lived in the American Southwest, most of whom were also prepared to die to protect their people and preserve their cultural way of life.

When he was nineteen Kelly enlisted as a private in Company B of the 1st Pennsylvania Infantry. He fought under General

9

Robert Patterson, a seasoned veteran from the War of 1812. General Patterson was a tough old Irishman who possessed the leadership experience and bloodline necessary to lead the unruly Irish volunteers, most of whom were "fresh off-the-boat" immigrants, direct from Ireland. The U.S. Army's victory over General Santa Anna's much larger force was also attributable to the military skill brought to the battlefield by the West Point graduates, including Captain Robert E. Lee and Lieutenants Sam Grant, Pete Longstreet, George Pickett and Tom Jackson. What these young officers had learned was the glory days of deploying Napoleonic tactics on the field of battle had drawn to an end. Unfortunately, for thousands of Mexican soldiers and their families, General Santa Anna had not learned this lesson nor was he blessed with the advanced weaponry the young West Point graduates deployed to full advantage. To defeat General Santa Anna's larger army, desperate to defend their homeland, General Scott had drawn upon the finest military men and weaponry the U.S. had ever brought into battle.

As for Kelly, he simply accepted that when a man's number was up, his time on this earth would be at an end. Until then, he was not one to ever back down from danger. With that pre-destined premise etched deeply into his character, Kelly gently urged Marengo into a slow gallop, advancing to meet the lone mounted Indian on the ridge ahead. Kelly was an accomplished rider, who never wore spurs, and was always suspicious of men who used them, especially to excess without regard for the horse. Hoping for peace, prepared for a fight, Kelly allowed Marengo to lope along at a leisurely pace; the two of them, horse and rider, gliding gracefully across the tall yellow-green prairie grassland. Each graceful stride of his horse closed the distance between the two men and their individual fate.

The rhythm of Scott Kelly's beloved mare at an easy gallop always thrilled him, as horse and rider moved forward as one. He felt the soft rush of the cool breeze against his sunburnt face, welcoming the relief from the hot summer's day. Kelly rarely wore a hat while riding and now enjoyed the sensation of the wind flowing through his long blonde hair and short cropped beard. It was at times like this that Kelly felt most alive, closest to God or whatever that divine Spirit was that decided the fate of a man and of nations. As Marengo loped effortlessly along, she too was increasingly aware of the potential danger that lay now less than a hundred yards ahead, on the crest of that bluff to their right. Kelly gave Marengo her reins, and she began to slow to a trot then a cautious walk, not wanting to be lured into an ambush.

Drawing nearer, Scott squinted his sterling blue eyes to where he could more clearly see the Indian riding a beautiful roan horse. The man was very muscular yet shorter than most of the Plains Indians he had encountered over the past four weeks, scattered along the western portion of the Santa Fe Trail. The wagon train Kelly was part of had headed west departing from Johnson County, at the eastern edge of Kansas Territory. After a month on the trail they camped two nights at Bent's Fort, the only trading post they had come across. At the Fort, Kelly noticed most of the Plains Indians were nearly as tall as he was, standing just over six foot, noticeably taller than this man he was approaching. This lone imposing figure sat motionless holding a shield in his left hand, a lance in his right. The Indian sat proudly astride the young roan stallion, snorting loudly, drawing in the wind deeply into his massive lungs, attempting to catch a sniff of Marengo to sense if she was in heat and in need of servicing.

The Indian turned his head from watching Kelly and raised his lance skyward. Kelly was now close enough to see that it was adorned with two eagle feathers, indicating this warrior had two confirmed kills in battle. The warrior dipped the point of his lance to the west and instantly nine other unseen Indians rose up from the tall buffalo grass, effortlessly mounted their ponies, and rode off toward the snowcapped mountains to the west. The lone mounted Indian who remained sat patiently for several more seconds watching Kelly, before turning slowly to ride away to the northwest beyond the bluff. Pulling Marengo to a halt, Kelly heard the sound of hoof beats riding hard up behind him, announcing that his reinforcements had arrived.

"Think they're a looking for trouble?" William Booth, the Wagon Boss asked, reining up alongside Kelly on the right. Two other riders, Ambrose Furnoy and Robert Finley, pulled up alongside Kelly's left.

"No, I kind of got the sense he was just wanting to get a good look at us," Kelly replied, decocking his Hawken rifle.

"Could ya tell what tribe they was a from?" Ambrose Furnoy, the closest rider on Kelly's left asked, almost out of breath.

"No, but they didn't look overly tall, so I don't think they was Cheyenne or Arapaho," Kelly offered, nodding as the last of the nine mounted Indians rode over the hill out of sight, their chief taking a different route further to the northwest.

Joining Kelly and the three riders as they watched the Indians ride away, was George Smith who blurted out, "Jesus H. Christ, Kelly! You just gonna take them all on by yurself?" George had also ridden up from their wagon train, but had struggled with his brown mule for several minutes before it finally agreed to join the other riders and their better trained horses.

12

"Didn't figure I'd have to George," Kelly replied as he slid his Hawken back into its sheath, "I knew you gentlemen would be up soon as you had a mind to."

"If'n they wasn't painted up none, I don't suspect they were Dog Soldiers," Robert Finley confirmed.

"How can you tell fer certain?" George Smith asked, nervously watching the horizon for the Indians to make sure they weren't trying to outflank them on left. George was the only one among them who had yet to share the belief that their danger had passed.

"Well," Kelly offered, trying to suppress a grin, "I'll tell you how you'd a knowed for certain they was Dog Soldiers," Kelly said. "If you looked up and saw me riding past you a hell-bent for leather toward the safety of the wagons, like I was being chased by a ghost, then you'd a knowed for certain we'd stumbled across us some real Dog Soldiers."

The other men laughed aloud with George, all knowing full-well Kelly would have never backed down from a fight or turn his back on a friend during a fight, even if it were with almost a dozen fearsome Dog Soldiers. Throughout the West the Dog Soldiers were known as the bravest warriors from the Cheyenne and Arapaho tribes. Many a campfire war story retold of skirmishes with the Dog Solders. Their War Chiefs' leadership position was distinguished in battle with a red sash. One end of the red sash was tied around his waist and the other was tied to his war lance. Whenever the Dog Soldier's War Chief dismounted and drove his lance into the ground it meant he would not retreat from that place. Tribal honor dictated the War Chief could not pull his lance from the ground himself, as this is where he was intended to die.

The five men remained quiet for several minutes, allowing the tension of the anticipated fight to fully dissipate, and their horses to catch their breath. Ambrose Furnoy was the first to break the silence, stepping down from his horse and unbuttoning his pants to relieve himself. Ambrose turned away from the other four men facing toward the Spanish Peaks, two tall mountain peaks off to the southwest that had once been in Mexico. "Seein' these Injuns up close here I'm a wonderin' if'n maybe we mighta made a mistake in not takin' the Smokey Hill Trail or maybe we should a followed the South Platte Branch off the Oregon-California Trail."

"Well there's no turning back now Ambrose," Finley said, "sides, I hear they done changed the name of the Smokey Hill Trail to the Starvation Trail to keep folks like us from using it to reach Denver City. Heard tell of three brothers who set out and only one made it, had to eat his other two brothers just to stay alive."

"I heard that story too, don't know if'n it's true, but those Injuns ridin' off over yonder are sure enough real," Ambrose said as he looked around nervously. "I don't want no Dog Soldiers to be a chasin' us."

Booth interjected, "We'll double the guards at night and keep an eye out for another wagon train to join up with before taking the Chico Basin Cutoff. I never been chased by no ghost or Dog Soldier, but I'd like to avoid both those experiences all together if'n we can. From what I been told when a Cheyenne or Arapaho warrior takes the oath to become a Dog Man, they accept that their fate has already done been decided; they will die in battle. The only unknowns are when and where, everything else is already a foregone conclusion."

"Maybe they wasn't Dog Soldiers," Ambrose Furnoy said, buttoning his fly and turning back to where the Indians had disappeared over the near horizon, "but they still had us outnumbered

14

more than two to one. Why do you suppose they rode off like they done?"

"Well," Finley replied, "if'n I was to take a guess, I'd say maybe they got a look at that there mule George here is a ridin' and didn't want to run the risk of it breeding with one of their ponies."

All the men laughed at the joke, sensing their immediate danger was now passed.

"I heard when they becomes Dog Soldiers," George offered, wanting to impress the other four men with how much he knew about fighting Indians, "they swear an oath or sumpthin' not to ever sleep with a woman ever again."

"Guess that might explain why they'd be so mean," Ambrose offered with a smile as he turned and repositioned his gun belt square across his hips and then tightened the cinch on his horse before climbing back up into the saddle.

"Then you think they wasn't a war party?" Finley asked seriously of his friend Kelly.

"No," Kelly answered, watching a big green fly land on one of the fresh buffalo patties that littered the grasslands around them, "I suspect they was a following the same tracks I'd been following earlier," nodding to the fresh buffalo chips on the ground. "Probably just a hunting party out looking to bring down a buffalo or two to feed their hungry families."

"Well, we best be getting the wagon train moving back toward the trail running along the Arkansas River there before nightfall," Booth directed, turning his tall black horse around.

As the other four riders turned to head back toward the wagons, Kelly said, "I'll be along shortly, just want to take a look over that there hill to see where that lone Indian rode off to and maybe see about killing a buffalo or two to feed our hungry tribe as well."

"You might want to keep an eye on those storm clouds gathering over yonder," Booth suggested, pointing to the Spanish Peaks off to the southwest. "I aim to make camp under some big cottonwoods down by the Arkansas, before the rain starts, if a storm does come up on us; always hard to tell this late in the spring."

Kelly raised his right hand to the side of his right eyebrow, a silent salute to the authority of their elected Wagon Boss. The other riders waved over their shoulders as they rode back toward the wagon train. These five men knew one another well, having started out together over a month ago, following the Santa Fe Trail westward. As had become the custom on the trail, as soon as they had gathered up a sufficient number of wagons to mount an effective defense if attacked, all the wagons headed west. There were about fifty men, women and children in this wagon train, all intent on making a new home in the Pikes Peak Region, but what was special about this wagon train is that it contained the components of what was to become the first sawmill in that part of the western Kansas Territory.

This sawmill was owned by Robert Finley, and a few of his business associates, who had convinced Finley to relocate their sawmill further out west. They told him of an abundance of virgin timber waiting to be felled and cut into lumber to build houses, churches and businesses. More lumber would be needed to support the growing number of miners or perhaps someday, for the railroad ties on which the coming railroad tracks would be laid. These railroads would one day connect the east coast to the west, and untold wealth waited along the way for those willing to work hard and take the risks required to build the infrastructure needed to settle the American Southwest.

Their wagon train had been on the trail for over a month, and while it was still only mid-June, the grass closest to the trail had already been well-grazed, forcing the next wagons to venture off the main trail to feed their hungry teams. Horses were faster than oxen, but they could not pull as heavy a load and had to stop along the route to graze. Oxen, like the ones that pulled the covered wagons hauling Finley's steam powered sawmill, could not only pull a heavier load; but could graze along the trail without stopping, as long as there was grass tall enough for them to feed on. Kelly, an experienced teamster, as well as a good stonemason and carpenter, agreed to help Finley relocate his sawmill out west, to the western Kansas Territory, a land destined to soon become its own territory.

Robert Finley was an experienced town builder. He had helped survey the town of Olathe, in Johnson County, where all wagon trains leaving from Independence had to make an important decision: take the right fork for the California-Oregon Trail or the left fork choosing the Santa Fe Trail. The Santa Fe Trail was less traveled and more dangerous, but it led more directly to the Pinery, the black forest east of Pikes Peak. The oxen they had chosen were Devonshires, prized oxen whose arrival in the New World could be traced back to the earliest days of the pilgrims. Oxen are by definition, any castrated, mature, male cows that have been trained to work. Other early settlers who had headed out West had also selected this breed of cattle for the same three reasons the pilgrims brought them to the New World; they could pull a heavy wagon, be butchered for their choice beef and they also made wonderful milk cows as their milk was rich in butterfat.

As Kelly watched the wagon train continue west on the Santa Fe Trail, he stopped on top of the mesa and stood upright in his stirrups to stretch and glance back over his shoulder across the vast yellow-green sea of buffalo grass. He watched to make sure the other four men had made it back to the safety of the wagon train. Then as he leaned forward to urge Marengo on, he paused and smiled at the warble of a meadowlark watching from just off the path ahead. As they neared the beautiful prairie bird, with the black V visible across her yellow breast, she extended her right wing painfully and hopped off, mimicking the actions of a wounded bird hoping to lure the perceived threat away from her nest of baby birds. The thought of the baby birds ducked down in a nearby nest, as they were trained to do so as to not attract a coyote or another four-legged threat, made Kelly smile. Their mother, pretending to be injured, drew another smile from the rugged carpenter turned cowboy. Playing along, Kelly turned Marengo to follow the mother bird until she felt they had reached a safe distance away from her nest then she withdrew her wing and flew gracefully away in a wide arc, landing somewhere behind them hidden in the tall grass. Kelly admired how the Lord had given even the smallest of animals the natural skills for survival. Man, however, Kelly had learned long ago, was a different kind of animal.

At the crest of the mesa Kelly looked down below the slope of the hillside to see a dark mass stretching before him on the prairie. The distant buffalo herd easily numbering in the hundreds, if not the thousands. Moving slowly, yet purposefully, toward the large Bison herd in front of him, Kelly withdrew the Hawken .53 caliber rifle once again from its leather scabbard, scanning the herd for a choice young buffalo. He hadn't ridden more than 150 yards when he noticed a large bull pawing up the dust ahead, as if he was about to charge another bull. Drawing closer Kelly noticed a broken lance sticking out of the side of the huge beast, which was causing him to be so enraged. Glancing ahead to where the bull was preparing to attack, he saw the beautiful roan horse the Indian he had seen earlier had been riding. The roan was lying down on its side, kicking the dirt while struggling to regain its footing. Trapped beneath his horse was the Indian Kelly had seen minutes ago on the mesa top. The horse was obviously injured and in distress. Kelly urged Marengo into a gallop, steering to their left while closing the distance between them and the downed horse and rider. He guided his swift mare to where the Indian and his horse were positioned in a straight line between them as the raging buffalo started its last deadly charge toward the downed horse and rider. Dismounting and resting the heavy Hawken rifle over the saddle of his horse, Kelly cocked the hammer and the double set trigger as he took aim down the long octagon barrel. Aligning the round brass bead of the rifle's front sight between the V-notched rear sight, Kelly focused the rifle sights on the up and down motion of the buffalo's massive head charging down on the helpless rider, trying desperately to free himself from underneath his crippled horse.

"Steady now," Kelly whispered to Marengo, as both horse and man held their breath. Kelly squeezed the hair-trigger at precisely the right second to take the shot over the top of the downed Indian and horse, striking the buffalo directly between the eyes, dropping him to the ground in a huge cloud of dirt and dust. The massive weight and speed of the charging bull plowed a furrow into the ground, coming to rest within fifteen feet of the downed Indian. Kelly noticed the Indian had withdrawn a knife to defend himself from the charging beast. Kelly swung up into Marengo's saddle without using the stirrups, then raced to where the Indian struggled to free his leg from under his injured horse. Kelly, dismounting, saw the white bones protruding from the roan horse's bloody front legs; an injury the likes of which the animal clearly could not survive.

"Good thing I came along when I did partner," Kelly commented, kneeling next to the Indian to search for any injuries and not expecting a reply.

"I was just tryin to lure him in closer," the proud Indian replied in nearly perfect English, then holding up the knife in his right hand, added, "so as I could finish him off with my knife."

Kelly's jaw dropped, before realizing the Indian was teasing with him. "Here," he said to the man still trying to quiet his injured horse, rolling the weight of the horse partially off the Indian's leg. "See if that helps," Kelly said as he lifted. The Indian on the ground grimaced, but finally managed to pull his right leg free from under his injured horse.

Kelly stood, shook his head sadly from side to side, then withdrew his Colt revolver from its tan leather holster and walked purposely around to the front of the horse's head.

"No," the Indian said firmly, limping toward Kelly and pushing his gun hand toward the ground, "not our way."

Kelly watched the touching yet tragic scene unfold before him. As the Indian bent over his horse's head, he whispered something softly into the horse's ear that Kelly could not hear and may not have understood if it had been spoken in Ute. Then while the Indian held his horse's head with his left arm and covered the animal's eyes with the fingers of his left hand, the Indian brought his knife up in his right hand, looked toward the sky, then reached under the animal's sweat covered neck, slit its throat in one fluid motion, and placed his mouth directly in front of the horse's muzzle, drawing the roan's last breath into his mouth.

The Indian paused for a few minutes longer, obviously in prayer, holding the head of the beautiful stud until it stopped struggling and slowly bled out on the ground. The Indian finally stood; stepped back favoring his right leg, then looked down at the knife clutched in his right hand. Slowly he drew the sharp edge of the knife blade across the palm of his outstretched left hand, cutting the palm of his left hand and then mingled the horse's blood from the blade of the knife with his own.

"I promised him we will meet again in the afterlife, where I will ride him for eternity," he said, solemnly explaining to the stranger standing next to him. "The Ute do not have a word for good-bye; we accept that we will see you again, either in this life or in the next."

"I'm sorry for your loss," Kelly said, "He was a beautiful horse."

"I captured him this last spring; he was intended to strengthen the bloodline of our herd. Obviously the Creator has something else in mind."

Kelly thought for a moment, then walked over to Marengo, unhitched her saddle, lowering it to the ground, and then removed her bridle before telling her softly, "get baby." Marengo looked back toward where the wagons were last seen, and then galloped off to the south. When Kelly looked back he saw the Indian had begun to field dress the buffalo. Kelly withdrew his 10 inch Green River knife from its sheath tucked into his right boot, then walked over and knelt down beside the Indian to help him dress out the buffalo while the meat was fresh.

Pointing to the bullet hole directly between the buffalo's eyes, the Indian commented, "Good shot."

"Just lucky," Kelly replied, "I was aiming over his head just trying to scare him off."

Glancing to his left, Kelly saw the Indian had caught his joke, then watched as the Indian removed the buffalo's tongue, cut off a slice then offered it to him first before taking a bite himself.

"No thanks," Kelly replied, "I had raw buffalo tongue for breakfast."

The Indian shrugged his shoulders, grunted, then bit off a generous piece of tongue and began to chew, obviously enjoying the delicacy.

"Guess you missed the joke," Kelly said as he resumed field dressing the carcass in front of him.

"Got joke," the Indian replied slowly, "just not funny," he said, taking another bite of the tongue.

"Probably an acquired taste," Kelly suggested.

"Buffalo tongue?" the Indian asked, swallowing the piece of the bloody animal tongue he had been chewing.

"No," Kelly replied, "my sense of humor."

The stout Indian smiled, "My name is Ouray, but most whitemen just call me Arrow."

"Pleased to meet you, Ouray," Kelly replied.

"You not call me Arrow?"

"I'm not like most whitemen," Kelly answered without a smile.

Ouray grunted softly in acknowledgement, and then the two men returned to their butchering chores.

Kelly watched in amazement as Ouray skillfully quartered the buffalo, following the techniques no doubt handed down to his people from one generation to the next for thousands of years. He helped Ouray roll the carcass over to the other side, realizing that although Ouray was shorter than he was by several inches, this Indian was incredibly strong and very swift with a blade.

"What tribe do you claim?" Kelly asked.

"I am Ute," Ouray replied proudly. "My father was Jicarilla Apache, but my mother was Ute, we live there," pointing to the west, "in the Shining Mountains. What is your tribe?"

"Guess I hadn't thought of it as a tribe, but I suppose I belong to the Lawrence Party right now," Kelly answered, looking down at the expertly cut quarters of meat that lay before them.

"You in search of the yellow metal, like all the others?"

"No. We're making our way to Colorado City, built just last year near the mouth of your Ute Pass. You know of Colorado City?"

"Been there, many times; never could understand your white-man's obsession over the yellow metal."

"Me either," Kelly replied with a smile, standing up to see Marengo running toward him, her beautiful white three year old colt running beside her. Ouray also stood up now to see the pair of horses coming to a stop where this tall cowboy beside him was standing.

"There are just some things money can't buy," Kelly offered nodding at the beautiful dapple gray horse and colt standing nearby in the tall buffalo grass. "He was such a beautiful colt, just didn't seem right to geld him," Kelly explained cleaning the blood from the blade of his knife.

"Yes," Ouray replied in agreement, "that would have been a waste."

Kelly wiped his bloody hands on the buffalo hide, then walked over to pet Marengo as her colt followed behind him, playfully rubbing his head against Kelly's back. He obviously had spent a lot of time with them to develop such a deep affection for both horses, and more importantly they of him, Ouray observed respectfully. The young horse was now full grown. Kelly patted the powerfully built shoulders of this magnificent stud horse that had a noticeably whiter coat than its mother. Kelly led the colt by the mane over to Ouray's dead horse and reached down, removed its hackamore, and slipped it over the colt's head. The Indian's braided yucca hackamore fit like a glove. Kelly led the colt to Ouray.

"He's yours now; he will be in need of many mares and doesn't belong penned up in a corral. He will make you and your tribe a fine stud, he will strengthen your bloodline," Kelly said, handing the reins to Ouray.

Ouray, surprised at the generosity and maturity of this young stranger standing beside him, reached out to accept the reins. To refuse such a gift was likely to offend this man before him but more importantly possibly offending the Creator above them, who had just moments ago reclaimed the spirit of the horse he was riding and had now brought this stud horse to him and his people. Ouray warmly embraced the horse's neck, whispered something into the horse's ear, and then stared off quietly into the distance at the gathering storm clouds. A moment later he turned to face Kelly once again, then nodded in gratitude.

"He's a fine horse. Towaoc," Ouray explained, "is the Ute word for thank you. I will name him Thundercloud."

"What be your name?" Ouray asked.

"My name is Rankin Scott Kelly, but my friends just call me Scott."

"Then I will call you Scott," Ouray said as he stood looking to the southwest toward where several dark storm clouds were gathering above two prominent peaks off in the distance.

Kelly followed with his eyes to where Ouray had been watching the clouds continuing to build. "What is the name of those two mountains over yonder?" he asked.

"The Spanish call them 'Dos Hermanos'...two brothers. We call them 'Wahatoya.'"

"Brothers, in your language?" Kelly asked.

"Breasts of the World..." Ouray replied with a smile; the two men laughed together sharing the humor as if they were both still fourteen year old boys.

Ouray collected his personal belongings, including his broken lance with the two feathers attached to the tip, slid his shield over his left forearm, and then effortlessly mounted Thundercloud bareback. Ouray pointed his broken lance to the dressed-out buffalo, "I will send two men to fetch our half, the other half and the robe are yours, along with this," he said as he tossed Kelly the knife with the blade folded neatly into the handle.

Catching the folded knife, Kelly looked down at the handle, rubbing his thumb across the ornate crest and noticed one of the standing lions was missing.

"It belonged to my great-grandfather, Five Eagles Soaring," Ouray explained. "It was given to him by a brave Spanish Conquistador."

As Thundercloud pranced around, getting the feel of his new rider, the stud reared up on his back legs, pawed the air with its front legs and snorted loudly at Marengo, as if saying fare-well to his mother. Then Ouray, without a word of goodbye, simply nodded toward Kelly and said, "I will see you again," then turned Thundercloud to the southwest and galloped gracefully off toward the distant Shining Mountains. Turning Marengo back toward the Santa Fe Trail, Kelly cracked a smile thinking, "Yep, I can kinda see why the Ute might call 'em Breasts of the World.

Then again, maybe I've just been too long out on the trail. Come on girl, we gotta get that buffalo meat into camp, we got our own hungry tribe to feed."

Kelly drew in one more deep breath, filling the expanse of his broad chest with the purest air he believed he had ever inhaled. Kelly thought he could smell rain and glanced once again to the southwest, as his piercing blue eyes caught the flash of jagged white lightning tracing over the Spanish Peaks.

"Looks like a storm's a headed our way," Kelly said softly to Marengo, nudging her forward gently with his knees. "We best be moving on."

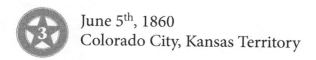 June 5th, 1860
Colorado City, Kansas Territory

At Jimmy's Camp on the Fountaine qui Bouille, Scott Kelly helped Robert Finley hitch the six oxen to their wagon one last time, and then turned to his friend. "You're sure you don't mind if I ride on ahead into Colorado City and meet up with you later in a few days out there by the Pineries?"

"Not at all," Finley replied, "Booth wants to keep the wagons together starting out here on the Jimmy Camp Trail, til we make camp tonight on Black Squirrel Creek. Fortney will ride on over the Divide tomorrow to Denver City escorting the rest of the wagons. George and I'll establish us a base camp in the Pineries and then I'll start scouting around for a good place for us to build the sawmill. Sides, it'll be good for us to learn what news you pick up in Colorado City about the gold diggings. By the way Scott, while you're there you might ask if the widow Lucy Maggard is taking on any new boarders. It might feel mighty good to have a roof over yer head and sleep in a real bed whenever you're in town, plus" Finley added with half a smile, "I hear she's a great cook and ain't hard to look at either."

"Sounds like you already got plenty of news on your own without me going to town, but after eating George's cooking and looking at the back end of an ox for the past six weeks, anything's bound to be an improvement," Kelly replied as he climbed up and settled into the saddle astride Marengo. "Let's go girl," Kelly said to Marengo, as he waved his hand in farewell to those on the wagon train getting underway on the trail leading toward the northeast.

Robert Finley also gave a wave of goodbye to Kelly, "See you in a couple days partner. Keep yer powder dry."

George Smith also waved toward Kelly, then added, "Don't do nothin in town I wouldn't do!" His farewell remarks were punctuated with a cackle that seemed to reverberate as an echo under the canopy of the huge cottonwood trees.

Kelly watched as the covered wagons headed northeast on the trail toward the Black Forest and then steered Marengo to the muddy water's edge, allowing her to pick her own path across to the right bank of the creek. William Booth had told him that this creek had been named by the early French fur trappers, Fountaine qui Bouille, meaning the Fountain that Boils. The name, Booth implied, came from the mineral waters that flowed from several natural springs near the standing red rocks that Kelly could see jutting skyward off in the distance to the northwest. Without a doubt, the most breathtaking sight now before him was the majestic snowcapped Pikes Peak towering above the green foothills to the west. Kelly followed the old Indian trail north along Fountain Creek.

"Looks like a mighty fine place for a man to build himself a ranch," Kelly said to Marengo, patting her on the side of the neck as he eyed the tall cottonwood trees along the creek. "Come on girl, time we go see if Ms. Maggard needs another boarder."

After a short ride along the trail winding to the west, Kelly found they were soon approaching the southern outskirts of Colorado City. Kelly observed a well-used ford crossing the creek and nudged Marengo into the knee deep clear water. He allowed the mare to drink her fill, and then he reached down into the water and scooped up a palm full of the finest crystal clear water he had ever tasted. Patting Marengo again on the side of her gray neck, Kelly said softly, "Don't know that we've ever tasted anything quite as sweet as that, have we 'ole girl?"

Marengo nickered in reply as she lifted her head, letting him know she was finished drinking and ready to go on ahead. Kelly turned the reins as they easily ascended the opposite bank of the creek and made their way into Colorado City. Entering the fledging small town with the one main dirt street, they passed a small hand-painted wooden sign which read, "Colorado Avenue", identifying the main road into Colorado City, established the year before as a mining supply town. Along both sides of Colorado Avenue Kelly observed where an optimistic land surveyor had staked out lots for future houses and cross streets; obviously someone had taken the time to carefully survey and plat out this townsite that was barely one year old.

There were only fifty or sixty log buildings, consisting primarily of a handful of businesses intended to supply the miners up in the mountains, along with a few dozen smaller log cabins for the people who were building this new town. Behind most of the crude cabins stood a tiny outhouse and other small outbuildings, including a few barns and crude corrals for the livestock. Kelly smiled and nodded at the few people he saw busily walking along

29

the main dusty street. He paused near what appeared to be the center of town and asked a rugged old prospector loading mining supplies on a pack mule for directions.

"Excuse me friend," Kelly asked, "could you point me the way to Maggard's Boarding House?"

"It's just ahead there young man, on the north side of this here street," the old timer replied, obviously not wanting to waste valuable time in useless chatter; time away from his trip down from the mountain for supplies. Kelly was still just thirty-three years of age, but didn't really think of himself as a young man anymore, not since the war in Mexico. Yet, compared to the old prospector who Kelly guessed was well into his seventies or perhaps even his eighties, thirty-three would seem rather young.

"Much obliged," Kelly replied as he nudged Marengo ahead gently with his knees. In the next block Kelly observed a one story log building with a covered front porch. He headed that way since it looked like the only building large enough to accommodate people like himself looking for a room and perhaps a decent meal. Dismounting, Kelly wrapped Marengo's reins loosely around the hitching post in front of the rustic building and loosened the cinch on her saddle. Kelly stepped out in front of the building and read the small newly painted sign attached hazardously at an angle above the door, which read "Maggard's Boarding House." Knocking first and then ducking through the narrow doorway, Kelly looked inside but didn't see anyone in the main room.

Announcing himself with a friendly hello, he waited for a moment for a reply and then stepped into the adjoining kitchen following the delicious aroma of coffee and freshly baked biscuits that made his mouth water. Noticing a red and white checkered cloth carefully covering what looked to be a pan of about a dozen freshly baked biscuits, he stepped closer to the kitchen table before noticing movement beyond the greenish tinted wavy glass window panes. He noticed a slender attractive woman, which he guessed to be in her mid-forties, standing outside hanging up a tan colored bed linen on a clothesline.

Kelly stepped out the back door toward the woman who had her back to him. As he approached he could hear her softly humming a tune with which he was familiar but just couldn't place. He found the moment slightly awkward, yet pleasant and stood quietly listening and watching her slim figure which he thought was like that of a dancer. The woman held a wooden clothes pin in her mouth as she hummed. Her long silky black hair hung down across her broad shoulders. She held the corners of the bedsheet out at arm's length, momentarily pretending it were a dancing partner as she reached up to fasten the bedsheet to the clothesline sagging slightly above her head. She slid behind the bedsheet, and then her humming stopped as she held still in silence for a moment or two, before peaking slowly around the bedsheet, smiling and somewhat embarrassed from being caught doing something silly.

When the woman turned to face him, Kelly noticed she had a darker complexion with a narrow streak of silver running through her long black hair that added to her beauty rather than distracted from it, but what he noticed most was her mischievous smile that would stop most men dead in their tracks.

"I hope I didn't startle you madam," Kelly said, somewhat embarrassed that she had caught him staring at her from behind.

Smiling back she said, "I was afraid you might have been someone else," she offered as an explanation, as she continued to take the measure of this tall handsome stranger who had just ridden into her life.

"Who might that be?" Kelly inquired as he slowly looked over his shoulder, worried he might have missed someone when he walked outside, having been distracted by the slim figure of the most beautiful woman he had seen in months, perhaps years.

"Well, he calls himself Colorow," the lady replied as she picked up her empty wicker laundry basket. "He claims to be Ute, but he seems much too big for one of the Mountain People. I think he might be more Cheyenne or Comanche, but whatever he is he has an uncanny knack for arriving at my back door just as I pull a fresh batch of biscuits from the oven. I worry that he might be interested in more than just my biscuits."

"I can see where he'd be tempted," Kelly said before adding, "by your biscuits I mean...I smelled them in the kitchen, your biscuits and..."

She smiled, tucked the wicker laundry basket under her left arm as she confidently approached the handsome stranger, held out her right hand, looked him square in the eye and said, "I'm Lucy, Lucy Maggard."

Kelly took her small right hand in his, taking notice of the firmness of her handshake, then said, "My friends call me Scott, Scott Kelly." He shook her hand, noticing how it seemed she held his hand a bit longer than a casual handshake, as if she was taking his pulse, which he felt was beginning to rise.

"Well Scott," Lucy said warmly, slowly releasing his hand, "how would you feel about coming inside for a cup of coffee and trying one those biscuits?"

"That would suit me right down to the ground, Mrs. Maggard," he replied, ever the gentleman, despite his wandering thoughts to the contrary.

"Please call me Lucy," she smiled as if she shared his thoughts as they started toward the cabin. "Here," she said, handing him the clothes basket, "hold this, I have some fresh butter in the ice house."

He watched her lift the heavy wooden door, which he observed had once been the side boards of a wagon, with one hand while she gathered up her skirt in the other, so she didn't trip as she descended the four or five steps that led to the small underground storage area. Kelly recalled from his time in eastern Kansas Territory how many settlers filled these underground ice houses with ice during the spring to keep things cool throughout the summer months. They also doubled as tornado shelters. Out here in the west he suspected they were more often used as shelters from Indian raids. Lucy emerged from the cellar, balancing a tin cup in her hand and a small package cradled in the crook of her arm.

She accepted his outstretched hand assisting her up the last step, brushed a cobweb away from her face and nodded a polite thank you as she handed him a small round pad of butter wrapped in tan colored wax paper. She lowered the door again and started toward the back door to the boarding house, offering him the tin cup that she had carried up the stairs.

"I thought you might like some cold buttermilk to go with your biscuits."

"That sounds wonderful," he said, holding the door open to the kitchen before following her inside her modest log home.

"Please sit down Scott," Lucy offered, as she hung the empty laundry basket on a hook behind the kitchen door and then opened a kitchen cabinet to remove two coffee mugs and two matching China plates. He watched, trying not to allow her to catch him staring at her body, as she poured the steaming hot coffee and placed one cup on the table in front of him. She served Kelly two buttermilk biscuits, herself one, plated delicately on two small China plates. Kelly noticed the plate she kept for herself had a small chip in the rim. These China plates, he thought, were likely two of her most cherished possessions from home and he genuinely appreciated the thoughtfulness of her kind gesture.

Lucy sat down in a kitchen chair across the table from him, slid the yellow pad of butter toward him with a smile, and then looked him in the eye intently, "Tell me about yourself, Scott Kelly."

"Well," he began, "there's not much to tell. I was born in Canada, my mother drowned when I was still young and I was raised mostly by my older sister, Katherine. My Father was from Ireland. He was a stonemason and a carpenter and taught me and my older brother John to build most anything, whenever he was around, my dad, that is. I found myself headed out here to the American West it seems, trying to make my way best I could on my own. Did a little time in the military, down Mexico way, then signed on to help Robert Finley and some of his business partners relocate a steam powered sawmill from eastern Kansas to here. He's out scouting abouts at the Pineries to find a place to set up. People say this here Pikes Peak Region is set to bust open at the seams and folks are going to need cut lumber to build their businesses, and houses, and churches and schools."

"Well, they got that right. How many people were on your wagon train?"

"We had about fifty men, women and children, twenty wagons, with about fifty head of cattle and a few horses. William Booth is the Wagon Boss, he's leading most of 'em on up over the Divide on to Denver City. Some's a going on to California or Oregon after that. Me, Finley and a couple other men are staying here to build the first sawmill in these parts. Robert Finley's the one who told me to look you up, said I might find a room and a hot meal with you whenever I was to be in town."

"Well we have both and will be delighted to have you stay here whenever you need a roof over your head." Lucy looked down at the crude boards she had placed over her dirt floors and laughed. "Lord knows we could use a sawmill here bouts. These boards here used to be the floor of our wagon when we left Westport last summer."

"Who'd you come out with?" Kelly asked as he finished off his last bite of his second biscuit before washing it down with the last of his buttermilk.

"Started out to Denver City with my son Jack and two of my three daughters, Catherine and my youngest girl Felicia Ann. My husband David was killed by bushwackers back home in St. Joseph, Missouri. Most folks back home thought we was just a little too outspoken as abolitionists, some even accused my boarding house of being on the freedom train circuit, harboring runaway slaves on their trek north to Canada seeking freedom. We hadn't ridden a full day outta St. Joe when word caught up with us on the trail that after we left they burnt my house plum down to the ground, just to make sure we wouldn't be coming back."

"We'd heard most folks hereabouts have northern leanings," Scott mentioned casually, knowing how tempers were easily inflamed on both sides of the burning issue of state's rights and slavery in the Territories.

"That's certainly true, most folks hereabouts are loyal to the union, least here in Colorado City. Not so much tho in Denver City. The Russell brothers are from Georgia, as you may have al-

35

ready known, and one of our town's founders W. Parke McClure, who serves as Denver City's postmaster, makes no bones about being loyal to the Southern cause," Lucy replied before taking a small bite of her biscuit before changing the subject. "Tell me then," Lucy asked inquisitively, "is there a Mrs. Scott Kelly and children traveling with you or back home, Mr. Kelly?"

"No," Kelly answered, staring down into his empty tin cup for an answer, "guess I was always just too busy to find much in the way of romance."

"Well then, I hope things slow down for you here, after you get your sawmill up and running. Meanwhile, won't you dine with us this evening Scott? I have a nice honey cured smoked Virginia ham that I have been saving for a special occasion, with mashed potatoes, brown gravy and maybe we'll even have some biscuits if Mr. Colorow doesn't show up and eat them all."

"I'd be honored ma'am, I mean Lucy." Kelly stood, preparing to leave, "Tell me, do y'all have a blacksmith here in town or is there somewhere as so I could bed down my horse?"

"Certainly, we have a wonderful blacksmith, Xavier Bent; he used to be one of William Bent's slaves down at Bent's Old Fort, before Mr. Bent set him free. I heard tell when the military wouldn't pay the price Mr. Bent was asking for his first fort down on the Santa Fe Trail, he tried to blow it up so as no one else could make use of it. Then he sets his three slaves free, including Xavier who came here last year to set up his blacksmithing business. He does very good work and he's an honest man. You'll find him down by his barn and corrals further on down Colorado Avenue here, just a couple blocks west to 28th Street and over one block to Pikes Peak Avenue. Street's aren't well marked here, but you'll find him easy enough."

"Thank you Lucy, I'll be looking forward to supper," Kelly said with a wide smile, as he turned and started through the doorway, bumping his head on the top of the door frame. "Ouch," he said, rubbing his forehead, "guess I'm a little taller than whoever built that door."

"That'd be me," Lucy said with a smile, "and yes you are."

"Guess I better learn to duck," Kelly said as he smiled at her one last time, admiring her spunk, and walked out onto the covered front porch.

Marengo nickered at him in recognition. Kelly untied the reins and rubbed her forehead, "Come on girl, let's us go see if we can buy you a new pair of shoes."

Kelly led Marengo west along Colorado Avenue, reading the hand painted signs on the buildings as he passed: Meyers Mercantile, Doctor Garvin Home/Office and Tappan Brothers Outfitters, and then he turned right at 28th Street. Just as he rounded the corner, he heard the faint yet familiar ping of a hammer striking against an iron anvil sing out from inside the unpainted wooden barn on the corner. The pinging sound of the heavy hammer grew louder as he approached the front of the blacksmith shop. It was surrounded by a sturdy wooden four rail corral. Walking in through the open double set of wooden doors, wide enough to accommodate the width of a wagon, he listened to the measured rhythm of the hammer connecting purposefully against the heavy metal anvil, "tap, tap, bam, tap, tap, bam."

The blacksmith's powerful shirtless back was turned away from the door where Kelly stood, patiently waiting for the man to finish taking advantage of the hot metal to forge whatever it was he was fashioning on the anvil. As Kelly's eyes slowly adjusted to the dark interior of the barn, the sweat covered sheen of the man's taut black skin came into focus, revealing multiple overlapping elongated welts and thick scars that had once cut deep into his flesh, confirmation of his harsh years as a former slave. The man was powerfully built; a body chiseled no doubt from years of hard labor. It was difficult for Kelly to guess his age, at first thinking them to be about the same age in their early thirties, but then realized the man was likely closer to his late forties.

The blacksmith finished hammering on the anvil, straightened his back and lowered the metal object into a bucket of water. A hiss of steam echoing from inside the wooden bucket announced the metal object had cooled sufficiently to allow a closer inspection. As the man held the object up to catch the light streaming in the barn door, Kelly could see the object he was working on was a perfectly shaped horseshoe and he knew at once he had come to the right place.

"Excuse me Mr. Bent," Kelly said in greeting.

The blacksmith turned squarely around to face Kelly, and eyed Marengo standing patiently behind him. With a kind smile he replied, "Please, call me Xavier. Whenever I hears someone says Mr. Bent I always look around outta habit for my former master."

"Very well then, Xavier it is," Kelly said as he reached out to shake the man's hand. Kelly noticed the man hesitated before taking the leather glove off his right hand, then wiping his palm across his pant leg before accepting and gripping Kelly's outstretched hand. Kelly wasn't sure if the man was unaccustomed to shaking hands with a white man or if he was simply extending him the common courtesy of not shaking hands while wearing a glove or shaking hands with a sweaty palm. Whatever the case Kelly couldn't help but notice the firmness of his handshake and the toughness of the calloused hand of the blacksmith that felt almost as if he was still wearing a thick leather glove.

"I'm pleased to make your acquaintance, Xavier. My name is Scott, Scott Kelly. This here filly is my Marengo, and I promised her a new pair of shoes once we got here after six weeks on the Santa Fe Trail. Think you could make good on my promise?"

"Well, let me see here," Xavier said softly, approaching Marengo's right front quarters with an outstretched palm held close to her nose so she could catch his scent before patting her softly on the shoulder and whispering something soothing in her ear. He bent over to lift her front hoof as Marengo adjusted her weight naturally, waiting patiently for him to remove a hoof cleaning tool from his back pocket to scrape the muck from the inside of her hooves. Kelly watched as the man repeated the process with the other three hoofs, carefully inspecting every horseshoe nail on each horseshoe before returning to her right rear hoof for a closer inspection.

"Well," the blacksmith finally announced, as he returned her right rear hoof to the ground, "I think we can find something in her size, but here, let me show you one thing we may want to address while she's here," he said as he knelt down and pointed his right index finger to the middle of her right rear hoof. "See this here little crack," pointing to a small fissure Kelly had been keeping an eye on for the past few days, "if this pretty little filly belongs to me, I'd file a shallow horizontal furrow just above where this here crack starts to keep it from spreading up any further, and if'n you can leave her with me a day or so I'd like to coat that there hoof with an adhesive concoction an old Cheyenne medicine man taught me whilst I was blacksmif'n down at Bent's Old Fort. He'd showed me how to mix up pine pitch in boiling water and add beeswax and ash from a gone out campfire to whip up into this tacky glue-like mixture, and that'll help heal up that little gap afore it widens into maybe a bigger gap."

"Well, nothin's too good for my Marengo here. We've been together the last ten years or so, since she was about three I'm guessin." Kelly explained, "This here's about the best friend I've got in this here whole world, isn't that right girl," Kelly said as he rubbed her head. "I'm hoping we'll get another ten years together at least, maybe longer," recalling how Ouray seemed certain he'd be riding his roan horse throughout eternity in the afterlife.

Seeing how comfortable Marengo was with Xavier, and having already judged the skill level of this well-trained and experienced blacksmith, Kelly handed over the reins and began to remove her saddle. "Sounds good to me, I think she wouldn't mind a day or two enjoying the easy life while I go off exploring these hereabouts. What'll you charge for your services?"

"How's fifty cents for two days board, including all the grain and hay she can eat, plus two dollars and fifty cents for trimming and fitting her new shoes sound to you?"

"Sounds more than fair, Xavier" Kelly said, shaking hands once again and sealing the deal, before sliding his rifle from the saddle scabbard and untying the saddlebags from the back of the saddle. Kelly turned to Marengo and said, "I'll see you in two days. Enjoy your life of leisure old girl, you've earned it." Leaving his saddle behind, Kelly threw his saddlebags over one shoulder, his Hawken rifle over the other, and headed back toward Maggard's Boarding House.

When he arrived at Lucy's he found she had made up a fresh bed in what he suspected was her best guest room. "If you have any clothes that need laundering just leave them there on the floor by the foot of the bed and I'll be happy to see to them this afternoon."

"I'd be most grateful," Kelly replied, leaning his rifle in a corner and pushing the door partially closed so he could drape his well-worn saddlebags over the small room's only chair, "if it's not too much trouble."

"No trouble at all," she replied, smiling.

"I was thinking I might take me a walk up the creek here aways, to the Soda Springs and maybe take me a bath before making my way over yonder afterwards to those standing red rocks I seen off there to the north," he said pulling back the burlap curtains to look out the window to see if the standing red rocks were visible from his bedroom window."

"Those rocks are called the Garden of the Gods. The Utes put up a small village along Camp Creek a few weeks ago." Lucy commented then added, "Oh, and I hope it's alright, but I invited Doc Garvin and Mr. Beach to join us for supper this evening. M.S. Beach is another of the town's founding fathers who helped stake out this townsite last year and he also helped name the Garden of the Gods."

"Well I'll be lookin' forward to meetin' them over dinner this evening," Kelly said as he started for the front door, then turned back toward Lucy. "By the way, I've found myself constantly humming that tune you were humming earlier, when we first met out by the clothesline there, and it's been driving me crazy that I can't remember how I'd might know it or what its name is; can you help me out here?"

"Surely. That bothers me too when I'm trying to recall a tune or words to a familiar song but can't quite seem to remember how it goes entirely. It's a varsovienne; a slow, graceful dance in three-quarter time, that originated in Warsaw, Poland about twenty

41

years ago. It's very similar to a waltz. It goes like this," Lucy said as she put her arm out to Kelly and clutched him in a dance posture. She leaned her slim hard body lightly against his broad chest and began to sing softly, *"put your little foot, put your little foot, put your little foot right here,"* moving them gracefully around the bedroom floor.

"That's where I know this tune from," Kelly replied in recognition. "My sister Katherine used to sing it sometimes when she was trying to teach me how to dance, when I was maybe four or five."

"She certainly did a good job in teaching you," Lucy remarked as she looked down at his feet while she continued to hum the tune; both of them enjoying the moment. Lucy, still humming, closed her eyes as she continued to dance across the small bedroom floor, lost in the arms of a strong man's firm embrace.

Suddenly, the bedroom door burst open and in walked a young girl of about twelve, trying to braid her red hair. "Oh, sorry mom, I didn't know you, ah, had company," she said realizing she had embarrassed both her mother and this handsome stranger.

"It's alright dear," Lucy explained as she backed away from Kelly's embrace and smoothed out the front of her dress. "This is Mr. Kelly; he's new here in town and will be staying with us from time to time. Scott this is my youngest daughter, Felicia Ann.

Kelly, trying to mask his reddened face, reached out his hand to say in greeting, "it's nice to meet you Miss Maggard." He bent down to kiss the back of her hand. "It's not hard to see where you get your beauty," he said smiling at Felicia Ann, and then back at Lucy as he awkwardly backed into the hallway to make good his escape from an embarrassing moment. "I'll be back in time for dinner ladies," he said making his way partially down the hall before hearing the girl trying unsuccessfully to suppress a snicker, then followed by a burst of outright laughter coming from Lucy's youngest daughter.

Lucy shouted from the bedroom, "Don't forget to..."

Bump, "Ouch!"

"Duck your head," Lucy concluded, a second too late. Lucy turned back to her daughter and began to braid her long red hair.

"Sorry mom, I thought you was alone making up the bed," the young girl snickered again while placing both hands over her mouth.

"It's not what you think young lady," Lucy admonished, trying unsuccessfully to recover herself from what certainly looked like a compromising position in the bedroom. "Come on now, I could use your help peeling potatoes for this evening's supper," Lucy said, trying to change the subject.

A half hour later, Kelly found himself at the headwaters of the Fountain That Boils, or at least that is what he understood the English translation meant from the French term, "Fountaine qui Bouille". He knelt over a large smooth stone to taste the soda waters that squirted up at least three feet in the air from somewhere far beneath the ground and flowed into a small natural pond which poured into what was the beginning of a crystal clear stream.

Kelly observed several perfectly shaped arrowheads shimmering up at him from the bottom of the clear pond, then he walked around to see that many of the branches on the nearby trees had been decorated with feathers tied to the lower limbs, evidently by the local Indians as offerings to their Creator. This place, at the foot of Pikes Peak, was no doubt a sacred place and he assumed had been for a long time before the French or the Spanish ever stepped one foot into these majestic mountains. Kelly then walked on a short distance to the north, following another old Indian trail a mile or two, passing a massive balanced red rock which had no doubt been there for thousands if not millions of years.

Kelly followed on further down the trail, deeper into the Garden of the Gods, northwest of Colorado City, where he thought he heard drums off in the distance. He walked on through perhaps the most beautiful rock formations his eyes had ever beheld. From there he made his way east, crossed a shallow creek and climbed up a nearby bluff to watch an Indian village below. Smoke curled skyward from the six tipis laid out neatly along the narrow creek, which wound gently downstream in front of the majestic white and red rock formations. He watched the Indian children below happily playing a game of kick ball, which he had been told was called "shinny". The older Ute women were nearby and looked to be telling stories while tanning three buckskins, but it was the ever-present vista of Pikes Peak that dominated the majestic landscape, a mountain Kelly hoped to explore once he became more settled.

Judging from the position of the sun approaching the mountain's skyline to the west, Kelly guessed it was late afternoon and he didn't want to be late for what was certain to be the best meal he had eaten in several months. He walked south down the mesa top and soon came across the dirt street known as 28th Street, which served as the main road into town from the north. As he neared Pikes Peak Avenue he was accosted by three happy school children; a younger boy and what looked to be his two older sisters, who he guessed were maybe five or six years of age.

"Hey mister," the oldest girl began, "you wanna buy some apples?"

"I just might," Kelly smiled, then asked, "how much you asking for them?"

"Depends," the boy answered, holding up a basket. "You wanna buy a whole basket or just half a basket?"

"How much you want for half a basket?" Kelly asked.

"Five cents," the third child answered, not wanting to be cut out of the deal.

Kelly reached into the front pocket of his pants and felt around for a nickel. "Here you go," he said handing the coin to the oldest girl while the other two siblings quickly selected the best apples and dropped them into the small wicker basket on the ground beneath their makeshift table.

"I'll check 'em to make sure they ain't got no worms in 'em," the young boy offered earnestly.

"Thank you, I wouldn't want to bite into one and find a worm," Kelly acknowledged with a chuckle.

"You know the only thing worse than biting into a big ole juicy apple and finding a worm in it, don't ya mister?" the younger girl asked.

"What?" Kelly asked sincerely, allowing them the privilege of finishing off what he felt was a well-rehearsed joke, no doubt used on most all their paying customers.

"Finding only half a worm!" all three children shouted gleefully.

"Thanks for the apples," Kelly laughed as he cradled the flimsy basket of apples in one arm and waved goodbye with his free hand and headed toward Xavier's blacksmith shop.

Marengo recognized him coming toward her from over a block away and ran to the edge of the corral, extending her head over the top rail to greet him, still chewing on a mouthful of hay.

"Well," Kelly said, "you're probably too full to want one of these," he said to Marengo playfully as he selected a delicious apple from the basket, then set the rest of the bushel on the ground. Extracting the blade from the knife handle, admiring again the ornate crest on the handle of the knife Ouray had given him, he cut the apple in half, placed one half in the palm of his hand which he extended beneath the top rail of the fence where Marengo could reach it. She nickered in appreciation, accepting the apple, all the time watching the other half in Kelly's left hand. Kelly wiped the apple juice off the blade on his pant leg before sliding it back into the leather holster he had made and attached to his gunbelt.

"Yes, this half's for you too," he said, feeding her the other half before continuing on into the barn. He spotted Xavier polishing a saddle propped up on a saddle tree near the back side of the barn. Kelly picked out two juicy apples as he approached the blacksmith.

"Thought I might share in the bounty," Kelly said with a smile as he placed the apples on a nearby workbench. "Not sure where the kids picked them, but they sure know how to close a sale."

"They'd likely be the Fosdick's kids, two girls and a boy over on 28th Street. I can't walk past their occasional lemonade stands either, even after seeing the boy a stirring the sugar off the bottom with his bare hand," Xavier said with a chuckle, before applying more saddle soap to his rag to resume his task at hand.

"That my saddle?" Kelly asked, somewhat taken aback at how nice it looked.

"Yup," Xavier acknowledged, "I kinda figured it could use a little lubricating after so many weeks on the trail." He continued to rub the saddle soap into the leather with a rag as Kelly watched over his shoulder.

"Looks like new," Kelly said.

"Better than new," Xavier commented. "This one here's all broke in like and fits you and that little filly out there like a glove. She should be ready to ride by around noon tomorrow."

"Sounds great, I'll drop by then, afore she gets so used to the good life here with you she won't never want to leave. How's about I settle up my account with you now," Kelly offered, "What do I owe ya?"

"Three dollars, just like we agree," Xavier replied.

"That was just for the shoeing and board. What about your work restoring my saddle?"

"That's on the house," Xavier said, "can't have a pretty little lady like Marengo there going around being seen with new shoes and wearing a dusty old saddle, can we now?"

Kelly pulled four silver dollars from his vest pocket and placed them on the workbench by the apples. "Much obliged. Dinner's on me for you and your missus."

"Oh, I ain't ever been married," Xavier laughed at the thought. "Not that I wouldn't be interested in having me a family some-days. You may a noticed already, but us men outnumbers the women folk here bouts some twenty to one, and when your skin's dark as mine, well the pickin's can be ever more slim."

"Well, you keep treatin all your customers as good as you've done me, you'll soon be so rich the women folk will be beating on your barn door with a stick begging you to get hitched."

The two men shared a laugh. "How'd you find your way out here to Colorado City?" Kelly asked as he felt the soft leather on his beautifully reconditioned saddle.

"Mr. Bent freed me 'bout the same time he did my Uncle

Dick and Aunt Charlotte. They wasn't really my relations, but theys' bout the only kin I'd ever know'd. Uncle Dick taught me blacksmifin and his wife Charlotte was said to be the best cook west of Independence, Missouri. I only had a first name, Xavier, but when I left the fort with Uncle Dick and Aunt Charlotte, they tolds me I was gonna needs a last name too, so I done what a lotta other freed slaves done did and took on Mr. Bent's last name. I stayed with Uncle Dick and Aunt Charlotte for a spell, helped them build a small homestead down in da Beulah Valley there, south a El Pueblo a piece, but they's a whole lotta secessionists talk down that aways, and folks keep looking at me a wonderin if I was truly a freed slave and not some runaway with a bounty on his head."

"I can see where's that'd be a problem," Kelly acknowledged. "You find folks here abouts have a little friendlier view toward the north?"

"That's what's been my experience since I gots here last year," Xavier acknowledged, "some more so then others. Mrs. Maggard, she's a proud abolitionist, and don't shy away none from speaking her mind, and there's da editor of our weekly newspaper, Mr. Benjamin Crowell. He's a good man and has written several pieces I done read supporting Mr. Abraham Lincoln for President, sayin how he'd be holdin the Union together and hinting at maybe doin' away with the sins of slavery. But not everyone's as like-minded as Mrs. Maggard and Mr. Crowell," Xavier thought before continuing to speak. "I thinks most of the town fathers are just focused on making a go of things here, keepin' they heads down' til all this secessionists talk blows over, except that Mr. Parke McClure fella. There's a Southern man for you if'n there ever was one. Fortunately, we don't see much of him here 'bouts, since Vice President

Breckinridge done appointed him postmaster up in Denver City."

"That's good to know," Kelly replied as he reached down to pick up a grey barn cat that had rubbed up against his pant leg. "Who's this?"

Xavier chuckled, "I's call him Ole Fuss n Feather, after he done got caught in Mrs. Maggard's chicken coop last fall. Since then he hangs around here mostly, not sure who he belongs to, guess he kinda belongs to all of us. Looks like he's adopted you too. Funny how animals are sometimes a better judge of a man's character than another man."

Kelly stroked the top of the cat's head gently, and then handed the old barn cat over to Xavier noticing how the cat rubbed warmly up against the big man's chest. "That's kinda been my experience too," he acknowledged as he picked up the remaining basket of apples. "I'm hoping a few of these find their way into one of Mrs. Maggard's pies." As Kelly reached the doorway he turned to say, "I'll drop by tomorrow around noon to fetch Marengo." With that Kelly left Marengo at the blacksmith's shop and headed south on 28th Street toward Maggard's Boarding House. On the way Kelly stopped along Fountain Creek for a quick bath, all the while thinking about what he was sure would be the best home cooked meal, and a good night's sleep, he'd had since leaving Johnson County in eastern Kansas six weeks ago.

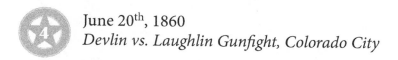

June 20th, 1860
Devlin vs. Laughlin Gunfight, Colorado City

As Scott Kelly rode east out of Colorado City, he could not remember a more enjoyable dinner or better night's sleep than what
he found last night at Lucy Maggard's boarding house. The ham
dinner she fixed for him and her other dinner guests was wonder-
fully delicious. In addition to Doc Garvin and M.S. Beach, Marcus Foster, another carpenter who had recently come to town,
also joined them for dinner. Doc Garvin and M.S. Beach were
bachelors who lived in the log cabin they built, one of the first
buildings in the fledging little town of Colorado City. The young
Doc Garvin also used the cabin for his medical office whenever
there was a need, which was rather frequent in most supply mining towns, like Colorado City.

Kelly recalled how Marcus Foster was fairly quiet during
dinner, but everyone laughed at M.S. Beach's many stories,
especially the one he told of how he and Rufus Cable named the
Garden of the Gods. The previous year they had camped there in
front of the standing red rocks where Kelly had spotted the Indian

village. Beach explained that he, Anthony Bott and a few other men had tried to establish the town of Eldorado the previous year in 1858, but it didn't take on their first attempt. He and Rufus Cable returned from Denver City the next year to stake out the town of Colorado City, two miles further west, which took hold in the summer of 1859. After driving the survey stakes into the ground laying out the town straddling Fountain Creek, two miles long east to west and one mile wide north to south, they spent the night on what other pioneers had named Camp Creek in front of the red rocks.

While talking about the beautiful setting of the red rocks at the foot of Pikes Peak, M.S. Beach couldn't help recalling how this place reminded him of his homeland in Germany. M.S. Beach had casually commented to Rufus Cable how this setting would make a wonderful beer garden. Cable seemed rather offended and chastised him saying, "Beer Garden! Why, this place is suitable as a garden for the gods!" As soon as M.S. Beach concluded his story he let loose a righteous full-belly-laugh, adding, with tears in his eyes, "and so the name stuck. That's how the Garden of the Gods got its name!"

Everyone Kelly had met so far welcomed the business the Finley Mill would bring to the Pikes Peak region. Although he had yet to meet Rufus Cable or Anthony Bott, he liked M.S. Beach and Doc Garvin right out of the gate. However, of the seven original town founders, the one he was continually warned about in not talking politics was Parke McClure, apparently a harsh outspoken southern sympathizer. Since McClure had been appointed postmaster in Denver, he didn't spend a lot of time in Colorado City, but he did have political connections which included the Vice-President of the United States, John Breckinridge. Beach explained that Breckinridge was a Democrat from Kentucky who took a strong states' rights stand against any interference with slavery. When one of the mining supply towns west of Denver City wanted to be granted a U.S. Post Office, McClure suggested that if they named the town Breckinridge their post office application was more likely to be approved than not. It worked.

Kelly didn't enjoy talking politics, but absent those two topics, he had enjoyed the previous evening's casual conversation and dinner immensely. Kelly's mouth almost watered as he thought about Lucy's delicious ham dinner, with the creamy mashed potatoes with thick brown gravy and Lucy's homemade biscuits and hot apple pie. This morning, after Lucy had fixed him fried ham and eggs for breakfast, she put a generous slice of thick ham between two biscuits for his lunch, which she wrapped in wax paper and tucked into his saddle bags with a smile. "See you next time Mr. Kelly," she said as he rode away. The thoughts of Lucy's warm hospitality, and warm embrace when he held her in his arms in the bedroom, still stirred him deep inside. He also appreciated the warm dinner conversation and how she had skillfully engaged her male companions to make each of them felt as if they were the star performers of the conversation, but then the best part he thought was her mischievous smile. Kelly could not remember a night where he'd sleep better than he had last night and woke up wishing Lucy had slipped into his bed in the night. Perhaps next time...

"Must be the crisp mountain air," he said to Marengo, redirecting his thoughts as they crossed to the left bank of Fountain Creek. On the other side he stopped to allow Marengo to chomp for a few minutes on the tall green grass. Kelly looked back over his shoulder at the glistening white snow glimmering brightly off the top of Pikes Peak standing behind them. "You know girl, a fella could get kinda used to this city life and who wouldn't want to spend an eternity at the foot of that majestic mountain?" Kelly said as he leaned forward in the saddle, "but for now, we best be going, daylight's a burning."

Marengo whinnied as if in agreement. Perhaps she was thinking about all the hay and apples she had eaten the past two days. The horse and rider began an easy lope toward the treeline of the Black Forest off on the horizon to the northeast. Two hours later, Kelly found Robert Finley in the Pineries, right where he said he'd be camped along Black Squirrel Creek where it intersected with the Jimmy Camp Trail. Finley had found a suitable location on the left bank of Black Squirrel Creek, where he and George Smith had unloaded the wagons. Kelly helped the other men reassemble the 12-horse steam powered sawmill and soon they were chopping down tall Ponderosa trees in this pristine virgin forest. They used the oxen to drag the fallen trees to the sawmill and within a few days had a stack of boards ready to be hauled into Colorado City.

Robert Finley wiped the sweat from his brow with a red handkerchief, and then turned to Kelly to ask, "You ready to be the first man to haul a load of cut lumber to Colorado City?"

"Sounds good by me," Kelly replied, thinking of Lucy and enjoying the smell of the freshly cut lumber stacked neatly onto the ox drawn wagon they had driven west on the Santa Fe Trail.

"You might wanna take your rifle," Finley offered, surveying the treeline on the south side of Squirrel Creek where it opened up to the grassland. "George said he spotted five mounted Indians camped over yonder when he was tracking a deer he'd shot, but never found."

"That seems to happen fairly regular with George, shooting a deer that always manages to run off somehow," Kelly replied with a chuckle. "Good thing he's better with an ax than with a gun, otherwise we'd been just as well off leaving him back in Johnson County."

Finley laughed, "I'm glad you and Lucy hit it off and thanks again for sharing your lunch yesterday. Don't know when I've had a better ham sandwich. George tells me he's been on the prowl for some turkeys he got his eye on for our supper, but if we're counting on his good marksmanship for supper, I'm suspecting he and I will be eating beans again."

"Lucy told me how all the townsfolk and ranchers are planning a big barn dance out at Judge Stone's place for the Fourth of July; you thinking you and George might wanta go join in the festivities?" Kelly asked, as he picked up the whip to start the oxen.

"Wouldn't miss it," Finley replied as Kelly started off, "but I'm warning you here and now, I'm wantin to have at least one dance with Lucy Maggard. George has no rhythm at all and sides, he's always steppin on my toes!"

Kelly laughed as he waved goodbye, the tune he had heard Lucy humming repeating in his head again, "Put your little foot, put your little foot, put your little foot right here." Thinking again of how he had held her against his chest as they danced in the bedroom gave him even more to look forward to as the pioneers around Colorado City prepared to celebrate America's 84th birthday.

As Kelly walked alongside the three pair of oxen pulling the heavy wagon west toward Colorado City, he let Marengo run free alongside the narrow trail, allowing her to graze on the tall green grass. He had placed her saddle on top of the lumber toward the front of the wagon where he could reach his rifle quickly if needed. He slept the night underneath the wagon, Marengo tethered nearby. He had planned his arrival in Colorado City for noon the following day and although their trip was unexpectedly hot, it was uneventful.

As Kelly drove the oxen past the Garden of the Gods, he glanced over by Camp Creek to where he had seen the Indian village a few days ago and noticed that they had moved on. He assumed they were Ute Indians, as Lucy had mentioned, and he sensed the joy that seemed to radiate from their small encampment. He thought again of Chief Ouray, a memory that accompanied him all the way into town and wondered where he and Thundercloud were now; somewhere over there, no doubt, riding through the Shining Mountains. He glanced over his shoulder at Marengo, who now was tied behind the wagon as they approached the small rustic town. He wondered if Marengo was also missing Thundercloud and might be imagining where he was as well; or do horses think that way?

"Whoa," he said to the oxen team drawing them to a halt on Cucharras Street which ran parallel to and a block south of Colorado Avenue. This is where he intended to unload the lumber and hopefully find some paying customers. After turning the oxen out to graze and water down by Fountain Creek, he took off his shirt and knelt down by the cool water to wash the sweat off. He kept his shirt off as he began unloading the wagon. He had about half the boards unloaded, stacked neatly on the ground, when a man walked up to examine the lumber.

"Howdy friend," the potential customer began, extending his hand; "name's Laughlin, James Laughlin, but my friends just call me Jim."

"Pleased to meet you Jim, name's Kelly," he said with a firm handshake, allowing the other man ample time to inspect the cut lumber on the ground and the other boards yet to be unloaded from the wagon.

Laughlin lifted a four foot 2x4 board from the back of the wagon and eyed along the length of its edge for straightness. "Nice to see we got a real sawmill here abouts, you set up out at the Pineries?"

"Yep," Kelly replied, "What you needin to build?"

"House is needin an extension, so my wife tells me since we have another young'un on the way, but me, I'd like a larger barn to bring the horses and cattle in at night so as they don't disappear with such regularity."

Nodding his approval, Laughlin handed the 2 x 4 to Kelly, then continued to inspect the lumber stacked on the ground and in the back of the wagon. Kelly watched patiently and spotted Lucy walking toward him from the creek with a wooden bucket in one hand and a tin cup in the other. Even with a bucket full of water in one hand Kelly couldn't help but admire her graceful stride and square shoulders as she placed the heavy bucket on the ground between them and smiled warmly. He had often wondered how old she was, although he knew it would be impolite to ask. He ventured a guess she was probably ten to twelve years older than he was which put her around forty-three or forty-five years old. Still, she was remarkably well preserved, Kelly thought, admiring her fine figure and not for the first time. Things might work out okay; especially if a man doesn't mind being mothered a bit from time to time.

"Thought you might be gettin a bit thirsty out here in the hot sun, Mr. Kelly," she said with a smile, dipping the tin cup into the bucket, then handing it to Kelly. "Afternoon, Mr. Laughlin, how's your family?"

"Afternoon Lucy," Laughlin replied as he reached up to tip the brim of his hat down toward her. "Josephine said to thank you for the eggs."

Kelly finished drinking the water, then reached over to pick up his shirt which had been draped over the wagon wheel. He'd caught Lucy glancing at his chest while he drank, which made him wish they were alone and not standing here in the presence of another man.

"Thank you Lucy, that hit the spot," Kelly said with a smile, handing her back the empty tin cup. He put on his shirt, buttoning it up from the bottom, and then turned back toward his customer. "You suspect Indians or rustlers are responsible for your missing cattle and horses?" Kelly asked.

"Likely both; end results the same, and with no law to speak of out here in the western most part of the Kansas Territory. There's not much chance of gettin any of my livestock back. How much you want for what lumber is left there in the wagon?"

"How's twenty dollars sound to you, delivered," Kelly offered.

"Sounds more than fair," Laughlin said, sealing the deal with a handshake.

"Jim," Lucy asked, "are you and Josephine planning on comin to the Fourth of July barn dance out at Judge Stone's ranch? I'd like to see her again before the baby arrives."

"We'll be there, unless she isn't feeling good. Baby's not due till the end of July so hopefully she'll feel up to it. I hear Judge Stone's niece Lizzy will be visitin them this summer."

"Yes," Lucy acknowledged. "Now that she's done graduated

from Oberlin College back east, she's maybe going to be moving out this way..."

"MEOW!" came the loud shrill of a cat in distress interrupting Lucy midsentence. The three of them turned to see where the noise came from and soon a loud hiss reaffirmed the cat was somewhere close to Colorado Avenue. Kelly spotted Ole Fuss 'n Feather, scurrying across the street toward Xavier's Blacksmith shop. He was running away from a surly looking cowboy who had obviously been drinking heavily at one of the town's many saloons on the south side of Colorado Avenue.

The drunken cowboy spotted the three of them standing by the wagon, pointed his forefinger and started walking their way, as he shouted, "You there, Laughlin! I'll be havin' a word with you!"

"And I'll be having a word with you Devlin, when you're sober," Laughlin responded.

"I hear you been askin all over town about my whereabouts. Well here I am, what's it you want?" the drunk cowboy sputtered as he stopped a few feet in front of Laughlin.

"You know damn well what I want Pat Devlin, the money you owe me from the sale of those cattle up in Denver City, but I'll not be talking to you when you're drunk," Laughlin replied firmly.

Kelly could detect the smell of split beer and stale tobacco on the drunken man's breath as he spoke loud enough that bystanders across the street could hear him.

"I done told you Laughlin," Devlin said menacingly, "money's all gone, spent on a good time up Denver way. Them Denver whores don't come as cheap as these Spoiled Doves around here abouts," he concluded glancing back toward the saloons on the south side of Colorado Avenue.

"You best be makin this right Devlin," Laughlin said.

Devlin turned back, and reaching for his gun, lunged toward Laughlin.

Kelly reacted quickly; bringing the 2x4 he was holding to separate the two men and said firmly to Devlin, "He ain't armed."

Devlin glanced down at the board Kelly was holding and noticed he wasn't armed either. He turned his focus back on Laughlin and looked him square in the eye, "And you best be getting yourself a gun, for the next time I see you I aim to shoot you dead on the spot."

With that, Devlin backed away from the piece of lumber Kelly was holding and spit on the ground before staggering away back toward the alley behind the saloons. Kelly also noticed that Xavier Bent, with his hammer in hand, had come up behind the drunken cowboy and had watched cautiously as Devlin staggered away. Kelly nodded his head in appreciation toward Xavier, who returned the silent acknowledgement – it's good to know who you can trust and who you can't out here in the West.

The next afternoon, out at the Finley Sawmill, Robert Finley helped Kelly finish stacking a second load of cut lumber to be delivered to Colorado City.

Finley smiled as he looked at his friend, "Heard you got to meet the charming Pat Devlin last time you was in town."

"Yea, he's a piece of work," Kelly replied, "I think he'd a shot Laughlin dead if Lucy and I hadn't been there. Too many witnesses I reckoned."

"Well, best watch your back Scott, and please let Lucy know to expect two more guests for the Fourth of July. George is getting so excited about the barn dance out at Judge Stone's he's even talking about taking a bath!"

Kelly chuckled as he cracked the whip above the heads of the lead oxen, Tom and Jerry, heading the team west toward Colorado City. As they crossed Monument Creek, a few miles northeast of the Garden of the Gods, Kelly looked off to the north at Laughlin's 160 acre ranch below the tan colored bluffs that the locals referred to as Pope's Bluff, where he had delivered his last half load of lumber. He wondered if Laughlin might be interested in buying a second half load of lumber.

Kelly hoped Laughlin was all right. He seemed to have a loyal wife in Josephine, who would be soon giving birth to their second child, a child who would need a father there to support and protect his family. From what Laughlin had told Kelly after being threatened by Devlin, he always made it a habit to avoid trouble and in fact he didn't even own a gun. With the likes of Devlin hanging around, it looked to Kelly that this trouble wasn't going away on its own.

As the team of oxen drove past the entrance to the Garden of the Gods, Kelly saw that several tipis had been erected along Camp Creek near where the Ute camp had been. These tipis didn't have the blackened tops like the Ute tipis had and he suspected these Indians might be Cheyenne or Arapaho, or both since they often camped together. The Garden of the Gods, he had been told by the locals, was the only place where the Indian tribes all met in peace, except for the constant warring Comanche. Comanche, which meant, "He who wants to fight me all the time," was a name given them by the Ute years ago. This hostile sentiment also sounded like how Devlin now felt about Laughlin.

Just as Kelly turned the wagon's oxen around the corner of Pikes Peak Avenue, to head them south on 28th Street, he heard the unmistakable boom of a shotgun blast. The oxen startled, but

Kelly quickly steadied them as he looked south down 28th Street toward Colorado Avenue to see where the shot had come from. Just past the alley he spotted the gray cloud of gun smoke hanging a few feet above the ground where Jim Laughlin was standing holding a shotgun and looking down at the man withering in pain at his feet. Kelly jumped from the wagon and ran to where he could see the wounded man lying in the street was none other than Pat Devlin. The wide shotgun blast had hit him square in the chest, but he was still alive.

A crowd was beginning to gather and Kelly recognized among them was M.S. Beach. He came over and picked up Devlin's Colt revolver lying on the ground and handed it to another man. Beach tore open Devlin's shirt to reveal where he had taken both barrels to the chest. M.S. Beach turned and said to the other man, "Rufus, run down to my cabin and fetch Doc Garvin and then get Judge Stone, he was down at Maggard Boarding House a few minutes ago talking to Lucy."

Kelly looked at the other people beginning to gather and recognized Xavier Bent standing next to a clergyman, whom he believed to be the Reverend Howbert. Within minutes, Lucy came running up 28th Street with a distinguished looking older gentleman Kelly assumed was Judge Stone, who was quick to take charge.

"You men," Judge Stone ordered, pointing at Rufus Cable and Anthony Bott, "carry that injured man over to Doc Garvin's cabin." Then he nodded toward the Reverend Howbert, "Reverend, you better go too...looks like your services might be needed as well."

Kelly stepped back as the two men picked up Devlin. Without looking away from the dying man, Laughlin handed Kelly a double barrel shotgun. Kelly held the shotgun, with the barrel pointed upward, and recognized immediately from the feel it was a quality firearm.

"A Hollis & Sheak, 12 gauge, nice piece," Kelly said to Laughlin, adding, "I thought you didn't own a gun."

"Bought it just this morning down at Meyers Mercantile," Laughlin replied. "It's for sale if'n you're interested," then added, "Only been fired once. I'm expectin' I won't be needin it anymore."

Both men watched as Devlin's limp body was carried around the corner toward Doc Garvin's log cabin on Colorado Avenue.

"How much you want for it? Kelly asked.

"Oh, I'm thinking maybe a half load of fresh cut lumber," Laughlin replied.

Kelly smiled, "sounds like a good deal all the way around. I'll drop by in a day or two to deliver the rest of your lumber Mr. Laughlin."

Jim Laughlin turned toward the corral behind the blacksmith shop and began to walk away. He turned his head to look back over his shoulder toward Kelly, "I'll be out at the ranch if'n anyone's looking for me."

Later that evening Judge Stone gathered Scott Kelly, M.S. Beach and Anthony Bott together at Maggard's Boarding House. Lucy poured each man a cup of coffee as they gathered around the dining room table.

"Thank you gentlemen," Judge Stone began, "for sitting as jury for the El Paso Claims Club, in the case against James Laughlin for the murder of Pat Devlin."

"Has Pat Devlin died?" Anthony Bott asked.

"No," M.S. Beach replied, "but Dr. Garvin assures me it's just a matter of time."

Judge Stone started the proceedings, "It's my understanding that each of you know about the shooting of Pat Devlin by James Laughlin?"

"Yes, sir," all three men replied.

"And it is my understanding," Judge Stone continued, turning to Kelly "that Mr. Kelly here witnessed Pat Devlin make it clear he intended to shoot Mr. Laughlin, to whom he owed money?"

"Yes, sir," Kelly replied.

"Mr. Kelly," Judge Stone continued, "it's my understanding that you witnessed Mr. Laughlin shoot Mr. Devlin."

"I heard the shot, sir. Got there on the run just seconds afterwards, while the smoke still hung in the air," Kelly replied.

"And what were your impressions of Devlin, Mr. Kelly?" the Judge inquired, as Lucy looked on, still holding the coffee pot anticipating refills would soon be required.

"Well sir, I can't say for certain Devlin wouldn't have shot Laughlin the first day I seen him, but that was my impression. He was in a drunken way then, and he started arguing."

"And Laughlin handed you the gun he'd used to shoot Devlin?"

"Yes sir, a double barrel shotgun. He said he had just bought it that morning and hoped he wouldn't be needin it again. Said he'd be at his ranch if anyone was lookin for him."

"Dead or alive," Bott commented, "that Devlin was no damn good."

"Never has been," Beach added.

"Well," Judge Stone concluded, "if you gentlemen would take a few minutes to discuss this case as a jury, I will wait outside for your verdict."

"Judge," Kelly inquired, "I'm a little unclear here. I thought the El Paso Claims Club was organized to settle disputed mining or land claims, or maybe convene if I claimed the mule

Beach sold me was not his to sell; how then are we deciding if a man is guilty or not of murder?"

"Good question," Judge Stone acknowledged, "in the absence of any other recognized legal authority, any Claims Clubs organized in the Territories can be convened to hear criminal cases, such as if that mule Beach sold you was stolen from Mr. Bott. Claims Clubs could meet to decide if Beach was responsible for stealing the mule and selling you stolen property. This is considered a criminal case."

"Yea," Bott added, "the El Paso Claims Club has tried more than one horse thief and we have strung up several horse thieves from the hanging tree down there by Fountain Creek; but I'd prefer we used someone else's name in your hypothetical mule-stealin scenario."

"Well," Judge Stone concluded, "if there's no further questions, I'll be waiting outside for your verdict."

"If you wouldn't mind some company while you wait," Lucy added, "I thought I might sit with you on the front porch. Help yourself to more coffee gentlemen."

Out on the front porch Judge Stone and Lucy sat in matching rocking chairs she had brought with her from eastern Kansas. "Judge, I understand your niece Lizzy might be making her way out here after she's finished with college at Oberlin? I would so love to see her again."

"Well, how nice of you to ask Lucy. I did extend Lizzy an open invitation to come stay with us after she finishes her schooling later on next year."

"We're all so proud of our college girl," Lucy beamed.

"In her last letter," Judge Stone added, "she wrote that there's nothing a newly degreed Archeologist loves more than getting her hands into some fresh dirt!"

Lucy laughed along with Judge Stone. Both sat rocking back and forth on the front porch, sharing thoughts about the continuing efforts in Washington D.C. to establish the Colorado Territory. Waiting patiently for the three men inside to decide the fate of another man.

The creak of Lucy's front screen door opening announced to Judge Stone that the jury had reached their decision.

"Gentlemen," Judge Stone asked, "have we come to a verdict?"

Kelly was the first to speak, "We have sir."

"What say you?"

"Not guilty sir," Kelly replied, "Laughlin appears to have announced himself, Devlin turned around and went for his gun. Laughlin had the right to defend himself."

"This town is better off without the likes of Pat Devlin," M.S. Beach added.

"Then we are adjourned," Judge Stone announced, as he stood to face the three men. "I thank you gentlemen for doing your civil duty. And thank you madam for your generous hospitality. Goodnight," he nodded at Lucy.

It had taken less than twenty minutes for the three person jury to find Jim Laughlin not guilty of any crime, deciding unanimously that he had acted in self-defense. Two weeks after Jim Laughlin was found not guilty of murder, Pat Devlin finally died. Scott Kelly, along with a few other men from town, helped bury Devlin's body in an unmarked grave on the hill north of town. Pat Devlin was the first man ever killed in Colorado City. What affect, if any, that one of the three men on the jury, Rankin Scott Kelly sat believing he was at the time wanted for murder himself, will never be known.

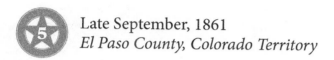 Late September, 1861
El Paso County, Colorado Territory

It was autumn of 1861 when Marcus Foster, a handsome young man in his mid-twenties, joined Scott Kelly and a third man on an elk hunt in the mountains southwest of Pikes Peak. Foster, like Kelly was a carpenter by trade, and was but one of over a hundred thousand people to participate in the Pikes Peak Gold Rush. Although the dreams of finding gold, coupled with the adventure of hunting elk, were a large part of the allure, Kelly was equally interested in exploring the far western portion of El Paso County, now being organized at the heart of the newly established Colorado Territory.

The three men reined in their horses at the top of a ridge, stopping long enough to take in the grand view as well as to rest their mounts.

"Magnificent view," Marcus commented. "El Paso County might be just the kind of place where a man might wanna settle down and build hisself a home and raise a family."

"This high up might be a bit of a challenge," Kelly replied. "Most miners, here abouts anyway, spend the winters down in Colorado City, then head back up here in the Spring."

"I had no idea El Paso County was so big," Marcus said, sweeping his outstretched arm across the expanse before them and pointed to the eastern horizon, "extends all the way from here to that Indian Reserve out there on the high plains. From what I seen on the proposed Colorado Territorial map the papers published, except for El Paso and Pueblo Counties that bump up against the Cheyenne and Arapaho Indian Reserve, the other eastern counties will run all the way to the Kansas border."

"Not sure the politicians knew how big this land was either, when they drew up the boundaries for those original seventeen counties that will make up the Colorado Territory a couple months back," Kelly said, then added, "Supposedly they took into consideration how far a man could ride a horse in a day to reach every part of the county."

"It'd take a pretty good rider to cover all this land in a day," Marcus commented.

"And a pretty good horse," Kelly added, as Marengo nickered, as if in agreement, causing the three men to chuckle good-naturedly.

"You two notice that bent tree over there?" the third man asked.

"Must be from the heavy snows they get up this high," Marcus suggested.

"No," Kelly said, "that's a Prayer Tree. The Ute bent them that way to point toward Tava, Sun Mountain, their most sacred mountain. We call it Pikes Peak. They used the trunk of the tree as an altar of sorts, to direct their prayer toward the Creator. That one there, with the two ninety degree bends I'm told is a burial tree, but the more common one is a trailmarker tree. Once you know what to look for you can find them all over what the Ute

68

knew as the Shining Mountains. Many of those Ponderosa trees are hundreds of years old."

"What's that rocky point sticking up over there?" the third man asked.

"Mt. Pisgah. It might be as good a place as any to head," Kelly said, leaning forward in the saddle and allowing Marengo to pick the safest route off the ridge into the tree-lined meadow below.

When the three riders reached the southernmost edge of the meadow, they couldn't help but be amazed by the color of the aspen trees, most having already turned a blazing shade of yellow accented by their white trunks and the blue sky above Mt. Pisgah. The three men dismounted, took the saddles off their horses, and then tethered the horses together with a long lead rope to allow them to graze. Kelly closed his eyes and listened to the gentle rustle of the aspen leaves quaking quietly in the breeze. Drawing his heavy .53 Hawken black powder rifle, with its distinctive octagon barrel from its leather sheath, Kelly hoisted the long gun effortlessly over his right shoulder and led the way up a narrow foot trail that meandered toward the top of the pyramid shaped mountain peak above them.

As the three men reached the summit they saw they were not alone. Lying on his stomach, outstretched over a large boulder about 75 yards away was an Indian man dressed in tan colored buckskin, peering through an extended brass spyglass down into the valley on the opposite side of the mountain. Sensing danger, Marcus brought his rifle into a ready firing position and positioned his thumb on top of the hammer.

Kelly reached over and gently placed his hand on top of Marcus's rifle, pushing the barrel down toward the ground before walking over to where the Indian was laying. Kelly continued to approach the Indian, stopping just short a few yards behind the Indian before speaking.

"You tryin' to lure another buffalo up here so you can finish him off with your knife?" Kelly asked the Indian leaning over the rock.

Without turning around to acknowledge the three white men approaching him from his blindside. "No. I traded my knife off to some dumb cowboy for a stud horse," Ouray replied, still looking intently through the handheld brass telescope.

"You sure it wasn't a gelding?" Kelly probed earnestly, looking over Ouray's shoulder to the scene unfolding below; several mounted Indians were trying to bring down a large buffalo bull that had been separated from the herd.

"Very sure," Ouray said looking up at Kelly for the first time and then acknowledged the other two hunters. "That stud horse of mine has tried to mount every mare in South Park," Ouray stated proudly, pointing off to the jagged snowcapped mountains to the southwest. "Come next spring, you'll see there'll be hundreds of little Thunderclouds running all across these Shining Mountains."

Ouray looked back through his brass spyglass one last time, then collapsed the extended telescopic barrel into its handle, slowly shaking his head in disapproval. With a heavy sigh, Ouray said, "If you wish it done right, you must do it yourself."

Kelly chuckled as the other two white men looked on, somewhat dismayed by the conversation between these two men who they were beginning to guess were not strangers. Ouray stood up, glanced at the faces of Kelly's two companions, and then looked off in the distance without saying a word.

Kelly asked, "Are you looking for somethin' in particular?"

"Someone," Ouray replied, before adding, "There is someone I am always looking for."

Then without a goodbye, Ouray whistled loudly as Thundercloud whinnied from out of sight below in acknowledgement. The three white men watched in amazement as Ouray turned and ran effortlessly down the steep slope of Mt. Pisgah, bounding gracefully downhill like a deer and while still running leaped midstride from a large boulder onto the back of the magnificent white stallion who had stepped out from the trees and backed itself up to the rock awaiting its rider. After Ouray had landed perfectly on the back of his waiting horse, he looked back up at Kelly and nodded his head before galloping off to join the other Ute hunters in the kill.

Kelly looked over at the other two men, both standing speechless at what was perhaps the most extraordinary feat of athleticism and horsemanship they had either one ever witnessed.

Marcus was the first to recover, "Good God Almighty! Have you ever seen such a sight?"

The third man watched as Ouray and Thundercloud galloped into the trees and out of sight, then replied, "Can't say that I ever did. But Kelly, I couldn't help but notice that stud down there looked an awful lot like your Marengo."

"He should," Kelly said, "that was her last colt and I guess that'd make me the dumb cowboy that traded him for this," Kelly acknowledged with a smile, retrieving Ouray's knife out of its belt holster and flipping it open with the flick of his wrist.

"Well, I kinda figured you two musta met somewhere's before," Marcus commented, "the way you bantered back and forth, but wasn't that rather odd he didn't say good-bye or nothin' as he left?"

"Not odd for a Ute," Kelly explained, "Utes don't even have a word for good-bye."

"That is peculiar," the third man observed, "How can a people with a language of its own not have some word for good-bye?"

Kelly explained as he folded his knife and slipped it back into its leather sheath positioned on the right of his gun belt in front of the cartridge loops, immediately behind his gun holster. "The way I been told is, in the Ute traditions they always accept that they 'will be seein' you again, either in this life or the next.'"

Marcus thought that over for a second, then replied, "I'd imagine there might be a whole lot to learn from a people such as that."

"Reckon so," the third man agreed.

"Yep, I've always thought that to be the case," Kelly replied as he situated his rifle over his right shoulder as he'd done a thousand times before, then turned to march down the mountain to where their horses were tethered. "I suspect we got a lot more to learn from them than they do from us," then paused one last time to take in the raw beauty that surrounded them from the top of Mt. Pisgah.

Marcus walked over and stood next to Kelly, then nodded his head to the distant horizon. "Looks like a storm's a brewin' off there to the east.

"Yep," Kelly replied without looking, "kinda feels like it might be headed our way."

Academy of Music, Cleveland, Ohio

"For heaven's sake, Mother!" Lizzy Hill said to her mother Bessie Hill, an aging southern belle.

"Lizzy! Oh, Lizzy!" her mother replied, laden with hoop-skirts and pulling a handsome younger man by the wrist through the crowded lobby. Stopping to give her daughter a perfunctory hug, "Lizzy, this is the young man I wrote you about. Mr. John Wilkes

Booth, this is my daughter, Miss Lizzy Hill."

John Booth bowed politely while Lizzy sighed heavily; taking notice of the Knights of the Golden Circle emblem consisting of a red cross positioned inside a golden crown on his lapel. "Very nice to meet you, Mr. Booth," she replied. "What do you think of the music?"

"Yankee's seem to have no talent for Verdi's 'Nabucco' it seems, but then again there is nothing as beautiful as your mother's lovely soprano."

Bessie giggled girlishly.

Lizzy responded to Mr. Booth's remarks. "I thought the 'Chorus of the Slaves' was beautiful."

Bessie interrupted the awkward silence that followed. "John is a wonderful performer!"

"Perhaps," Lizzy said, "you should've come to Oberlin, Mr. Booth, and given a master class."

"I wouldn't have thought to bring your dear mother anywhere near a place that allows nigras as students, Miss Hill."

"I see, Mr. Booth," Lizzy acknowledged.

Bessie interjected, "Lizzy will soon be done with her studies there, Mr. Booth. Perhaps she'll get her lovely Southern charm back, then."

Lizzy replied, "I doubt that, Mama, I'll be heading to Uncle Stone's after graduation to study the dig beds there."

Bessie struggled to maintain her smile as she dragged Lizzy away from John, whispering with hostility into Lizzy's ear. "Elizabeth Hill! I have tolerated your insistence to study, but your father is in the ground and you must get seriously to the point of getting home and finding a husband. Now, I was very lucky, indeed I was, to meet Mr. Booth at the theater, and as we only have my former circle of singers to find society amongst us, you must put aside your silliness and grow up."

"Mother! I have no intention of finding myself a husband, back home, or otherwise. The only society for me back home is with Blandia."

"Blandia is gone."

"What?! Mother, why?"

Booth approached the two ladies, then inserted himself into their personal conversation, much to Lizzy's resentment. "Miss Hill, I must tell you that it was my doing."

Lizzy, aghast, turned to face him, "Was it, Mr. Booth?"

"It was. Your poor mother has little money left, my dear Lizzy. She deserves to maintain the lifestyle she's become accustomed to and while you have been up here with these Yankees, learning about bones and such, your mother has need of income."

"So," Lizzy replied, "you, sir, encouraged her to sell the woman who raised me?!"

"I encouraged her to sell her property, as is her right," Booth replied, then paused for effect before continuing, "and I would encourage you, Miss Lizzy, to listen to your mother, leave these Yankees and these darkees behind, and take the hand extended to you, while there is still an offer to take."

Lizzy looked down at Mr. Booth's extended hand, then turned to whisper to her mother, "Mother, this is unforgiveable." Then without shaking Booth's hand, she turned and walked away without looking back.

Maggard's Boarding House, Colorado City, Colorado Territory

Lucy and Kelly sat in the wooden rocking chairs on Lucy's front porch after dinner, drinking coffee. Lucy had a broad smile on her face. Kelly wore a frown.

"Scott," Lucy continued, "you'd be perfect. You were an Indian fighter and a trail boss."

"I wasn't the trail boss," Kelly interrupted.

Not reacting to his nay saying, Lucy continued, "You've already established a repartee with the Ute..."

"One Ute...one time..." Kelly interrupted again.

"You obviously showed sound judgement in the acquittal of Jim Laughlin."

"Three men made that decision."

Still not reacting to Kelly's nay saying, Lucy continued, "I'm just saying I'm not surprised they asked you to be Sheriff, is all. You have far more to give than your skills with wood and rock."

Defensively, Kelly replied, "What's wrong with making an honest day's wage doing a craftsman's work?"

"Nothing," Lucy said, "and Lord knows, when your term is over you'll return to it fulltime. But this is a chance to do something more. Something that shapes El Paso County...If we're going to be the capital of the Colorado Territory, we have to have law and order...That's why we're all here, that's why I'm here, to build a better life and escape the bleeding part of Kansas. When do they want you to start?"

"November," Kelly replied, setting his coffee cup down on the small table between them.

"Good, you still have time to decide."

Kelly, searching for the right words, finally broke the silence and tried to explain, "I'm just not sure I'm the best man for the job, Lucy."

Lucy reached across the small table and took his hand in hers, "If they didn't believe in you, they wouldn't be asking you to serve…I believe in you. I don't know why you're worried about being the 'right man for the job'. What are you running from, Scott?"

Looking down the dirt street, as if looking for a ghost from his past, Kelly studied the dark grey rainclouds building off to the east before he replied. "Everybody has something they worry about, something that makes them feel unworthy, something in their past they're not proud of. I have my reasons for not saying."

Lucy squeezed Kelly's hand firmly, and then replied, "I know you're not saying something Scott. I know you were young and must have seen a lot of blood when you were a soldier and Indian fighting. Men see and do awful things at war, I hear. I know you must've had some hard decisions to make, many I suppose with no easy right or wrong. Listen, I understand what it is to lose sight of yourself. My husband and I…back in Missouri…we were proud Abolitionists and could never believe it was right for one man to own another. But then Confederate guerrillas came and burned down our house, killing my husband inside, and I fled. Does that make me a coward? Now, here I sit, not really a whole woman, like I was as his wife. But these days, since you've been around, I feel like that's in the past, now. I might not be who I was, but that's all right. You protect this town, and we'll stand by you Scott, and I'll be here to take care of you."

Kelly squeezed Lucy's hand, and said, "That means a lot, Lucy. You know, I haven't felt like I had any family for a long, long time." Then Kelly removed his hand from hers.

Lucy replied, "Well you do now, Sheriff Kelly."

Both smiled at each other, as rain began to dance on the tin roof over their heads.

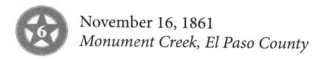

November 16, 1861
Monument Creek, El Paso County

Charlie Stone, the fourteen year old son of Judge Wilbur Stone, rode his buckskin horse along the left bank of Monument Creek, a few miles east of Colorado City, searching for his father's missing cattle. Peering over a patch of tall red willows, and across the wide creek, he spied several men camped on the opposite side. He slipped quietly from his horse, tied the reins to a handful of willow branches, and then crept into the willows for a closer look. Nearing the edge of the creek Charlie cautiously parted the willows with his hands and saw the men were butchering cattle. Charlie suspected these were his father's open range cattle and if so, these men were cattle rustlers, a crime punishable by hanging in the West. He needed to confirm his suspicions before telling his father.

Charlie returned to his horse, made his way upstream to a crossing, then after fording the creek and finding another place to tie his mount, moved in for a closer look. Charlie spotted several cowhides stacked on top of one another, making a pile nearly two feet tall, and saw that the top cowhide carried his family's brand, the unmistakable "Rocking J". He counted seven men total, and then began to realize that while most of the men appeared to be in their late thirties or maybe forties, one or two of the men appeared to be much younger, maybe even teenagers not much older than he was. One of the younger men, who Charlie guessed to be maybe sixteen or seventeen, walked away from the others and knelt at the eastern edge of the creek to wash his bloody hands in the cold water. Charlie weighed the risks, then decided to approach this younger gang member to see what he could learn.

"Mornin' to ya!" Charlie says with a friendly wave in greeting.

Without standing, the young gang member looked around to see that Charlie was alone, "Mornin'..."

"You boys also new around here?" Charlie asked.

"Just passing through," the young gang member replied, while standing and wiping his wet hands on his pant legs.

"Business in Colorado City?" Charlie inquired further.

"Yeah...their cattle," the young outlaw said with a grin.

Charlie laughed at the other teenager's apparent joke, then feigned excitement and admiration while saying, "You rustlers?"

"Best there is! We're the Salt Lake City Jim Gang," the young outlaw claimed proudly, then motioned with his thumb toward one of the shorter men with wildly colored red and brown hair. "That's Salt Lake City Jim over there, you musta heard of us?"

"Hell yeah!" Charlie says, acting impressed, "You been in any shoot outs?"

"What do you think?" the young gang member replied, drawing a Colt revolver out of his belt holster, twirling it over theatrically before slipping it quickly back into his holster."

"Holy Cow! Yer the fastest draw I'd ever seen," Charlie continued with his act, although he was genuinely impressed by the young outlaw's practiced quick-draw.

"One day, when you're old enough, maybe we'll let you join," the young outlaw said.

"Oh yeah?!" Charlie replied, again taking measure of the other teenager who was slightly taller, but couldn't be more than a year or two older than he was, "and would you teach me to fast-draw like you?"

"Sure," the young gang member said, then added, "but now you best get back to your Ma, before she worries."

"Yes sir," Charlie replied, then turned, grabbed his hat and sprinted back north along the left bank of the creek to where he had tied his horse out of sight.

Midmorning, Same Day - November 16, 1861
Lucy Maggard's Boarding House, Colorado City

Scott Kelly walked into Lucy's kitchen with his shining new circle star sheriff badge in his hand, and laid it on the blue and white checkered table cloth next to a steaming cup of hot coffee. "Look what Judge Stone handed me this morning."

Lucy picked the badge up from the table and shined it against her oatmeal colored apron that she had sewn from a flour sack. Then she pinned the badge on Kelly's vest. "Have a seat, Sheriff. I'll cut you a piece of apple pie to go with your coffee! How's your first day going?"

"Been noticing all morning," Kelly replied, as he slid a kitchen chair out from under the wooden table and sat down, "that the first thing a man loses when he gains public office is his first name."

79

Lucy laughed softly, poured Kelly a cup of coffee, then asked, "Is Mr. Finley going to sell his sawmill now that he's been appointed to be our first Treasurer for El Paso County?"

"He's hoping to do both, at least for now since our new County has no money to speak of," but before Kelly can finish his sentence the front door of Lucy's Boarding House slammed open and Charlie Stone burst into the kitchen.

"Mr. Kelly! Mr. Kelly! I mean…Sheriff," Charlie stuttered excitedly, then seeing Lucy quickly snatched his cowboy hat from his head and held it with both hands, trying desperately to catch his breath and contain his excitement.

"Why Charlie Stone, what's got you so riled up this morning?" Kelly asked.

"Cattle rustlers!!!" Charlie blurted out, adding quickly, "It's the Salt Lake City Jim Gang! They done set up camp down on the Monument Creek, just above where it joins up with Fountain Creek! Daddy says they'd likely be the ones who done stole our cattle!"

"Where's Judge Stone now?" Kelly asked.

"He's over at the County Admin Building swearing out a warrant and sent me to fetch you. Come, I'll show you," Charlie said, motioning excitedly with his hat in his hand for Kelly to follow him out the front door.

Half a block ahead and across the street, Sheriff Kelly saw Judge Stone locking the thick wooden door of the small log cabin which served briefly as the Territorial Capitol Building. Now it was the El Paso County Administrative Building. Judge Stone slipped the heavy key, attached to his watch fob, into the front pocket of his vest and then leaned over the hitching rack in front of the building to wait for his son and the newly appointed County Sheriff.

Sheriff Kelly was first to speak, "What do you all got on this guy, Salt Lake City Jim?"

Charlie interrupted before Judge Stone could answer, "Cattle rustlers, Sheriff...and murderers! They set up camp on Monument Creek, must'a been late last night 'cause I rode through there just afore supper and they wasn't there then, and when I went lookin' for our lost cattle this morning at day break, I saw'em – 'bout seven of 'em."

When Charlie paused to catch his breath, Judge Stone finally spoke, "Charlie here managed to talk with one of them and from what I can piece together from exchanging telegrams with a judge up in Arapaho County, it appears they've been stealing our cattle for several weeks now, open range stock, butchering them and selling the meat as if it were buffalo to the Cavalry up at Camp Weld outside of Denver City."

"Why would they try to pass the beef off as buffalo?" Charlie asked as he balanced himself precariously on the hitching post in front of the El Paso County Administrative Building.

"I'm told the Cavalry pays a premium for buffalo meat," Sheriff Kelly replied.

"But couldn't the soldiers tell the difference?" Charlie asked, adding, "Even I know buffalo is leaner than any free range cow."

"From what I understand," Judge Stone answered, looking at Sheriff Kelly, "the army quartermaster is rumored to have a much less discernable palate if he finds a quart bottle of Taos Lightning left behind with the off-loaded meat delivery."

"In talking with Reverend Howbert I can't imagine Major Chivington would approve of their quartermaster's practices," Sheriff Kelly said.

"True enough. I'd imagine a fella paying a premium for beef

instead of bison might just look the other way if 'n he thought they might be stolen too," Judge Stone replied. "Reverend Howbert and John Chivington go way back to the Methodist Conference in the Nebraska Territory."

"Hard to figure why a man of the cloth would refuse a chaplaincy commission in favor of a fighting commission with the First Colorado Volunteers," Sheriff Kelly said.

"I understand Chivington's an uncompromising abolitionist and guess he figures out here in the West a man can accomplish more with a gun than a bible."

"Well, I'd probably have to agree with him on that, and I don't mean to question a man's faith or patriotism," Sheriff Kelly continued, "but doesn't it strike you odd that just a week before Chivington volunteered, he received word from his parents tellin' him his brother had been killed at Wilson's Creek, near Springfield, Missouri, fighting for the Confederacy?"

"Well, I can rightly imagine a man volunteering after learning his brother had been killed, but to join up on the other side, well that does seem a bit peculiar," Judge Stone agreed, scratching the greying whiskers under his chin. "Heard tell Lewis Chivington was a Colonel in the Southern cavalry, served under General Sterling Price, rode alongside Ben McCulloch."

Kelly added, "Ben McCulloch was also at Pea Ridge, fighting under General Albert Pike, where William Bent's boys, George and Charley, took up fighting with the Cherokee Rifles. George was away at the Whiteman's college when the war broke out, then dropped out to fight with his half-brother Charley, 'til he was taken prisoner. George was one of the prisoners exchanged for some of the Union soldiers after swearing an oath not to fight against the North no more. Charley's kinda dropped outta sight, but from what I understand he may have joined up with the Dog Soldiers. Things turned real ugly there at Pea Ridge, the Indians there weren't used ta giving quarter to any enemy and taking scalps was somethin' that came kinda natural to all of them. Understand that controversy cost General Pike his command, or so I'm told."

"Is General Pike related to Zeb Pike?" Charlie asked, looking up toward the purple mountain towering above them a few miles to the west.

"No, not that I can determine," his father answered.

Kelly said to Charlie, "What can you tell me about these seven rustlers Charlie?"

"I only got a close look at the one younger guy that I talked to. Hell, he can't be much older than me," Charlie said, then glanced at his father.

"Charlie Stone, you best not let your mother hear you saying 'hell," Judge Stone admonished, then turned his head and winked at Sheriff Kelly.

"Yes sir," Charlie acknowledged, looking down at the ground, accepting his admonishment for a moment, then remembered, "Oh yeah, this younger fella said they was the Salt Lake City Jim Gang and pointed out an odd lookin' shorter man with wild red and brown hair as the leader of their outlaw gang. The younger fella is really fast on the draw and although he didn't say his name, I seen he had his initials KGC on his holster."

"KGC?" Kelly stroked his dark beard as he thought for a few seconds, then turned toward Judge Stone. "Could stand for the Knights of the Golden Circle. Mean anything to you sir?"

"If it's the same KGC or Knights of the Golden Circle I been hearing whispers 'bout, supposedly they was trying to form a castle, or some such thing," Judge Stone replied after looking around to make sure they weren't being overheard before continuing. "They're a secret society of southern sympathizers, including men like Albert Pike, Ben McCulloch and Sterling Price. The KGC first attempted to annex Mexico, Cuba, the Caribbean Islands and the Bahamas, into the Union so the slave holding South would have more political power in Washington DC than the industrial North. They failed, but have now begun to advocate for the southern states to secede from the Union to form their own country, the Confederate States of America. Some say the KGC has Masonic ties, and they do have three degrees and similar oaths, secret passwords and such, but I've known many a Mason in my life, all equally loyal to the north and most of those men I'd known wouldn't stand for secession talk. But make no mistake Scott, the KGC is made up of some very powerful men. You best take care, Sheriff."

Kelly looked down Colorado Avenue as the darkness of a rain storm began to envelop the small mining supply town of Colorado City. Sheets of rain could be seen just a few miles east of town, blowing in from the yellow prairie. A flash of white lightning jutted across the open plains, followed a few seconds later by a loud crack of distant thunder; a prelude of what was to follow.

Next morning at sunrise
Monument Creek, a few miles East of Colorado City

Sheriff Kelly slowed his gray horse, Marengo, nearing the east bank of Monument Creek, just above its confluence with Fountaine que Bouille. He observed the smoke slowly swirling up from the campfire where the Salt Lake City Jim Gang remained encamped. A coffee pot hung over the campfire, while strips of meat hung drying nearby from crudely made wooden racks. Several cowhides were spread across two flat rocks near the campfire and more hides were stacked nearby measuring about two feet deep. From that distance it was hard for Kelly to tell how many cattle had been butchered, but he estimated at least eight or ten of the local ranchers' range cows had been killed.

Slowly, the seven gang members stirred in the camp as they watched Kelly. The Sheriff nudged Marengo ahead slowly yet purposefully toward the camp. Kelly had crossed the creek downstream so he'd have the sun rising steadily at his back. The double-barreled shotgun Kelly traded Jim Laughlin a half wagon load of lumber for a few months back lay cradled in his arms, both exposed hammers were fully cocked. The Sheriff was also armed with his six-shot 1851 Colt .36 revolver, with a 7 ½ inch octagonal barrel carried in his belt holster, and his five shot 1849 Colt .31 revolver, with a 4 inch barrel in a shoulder holster. Both Colt revolvers were black powder and in his saddle bag he carried an additional cylinder for each handgun already loaded. Most Colts in the West were carried with the chamber directly beneath the hammer empty to prevent the hammer from being accidently bumped, causing the firing pin to inadvertently strike the "cap and ball" causing an accidental discharge. Cowboys often carried their last will, directing whoever found them to notify their family in case of their untimely death, along with a few dollars to be used for their funeral. Cowboys don't leave their debts unpaid.

On this day, Sheriff Kelly carried both revolvers fully loaded, a total of eleven shots, plus two shots from the double-barreled shotgun. From experience he knew reloading during the gunfight was generally not an option. Also carried on the Sheriff's gunbelt, within easy reach on the right side behind his holster, was Ouray's knife, always within the lawman's reach wherever he went. From experience, the Sheriff knew that many gunfights in the West ended in a knife fight. As Sheriff Kelly neared the outlaws, they began to form-up alongside a man Kelly took to be their leader, Salt Lake City Jim. Getting closer, Kelly heard nervous laughter, jokes no doubt made at his expense. He saw smirks forming on their faces as they realized he was a lawman and came alone, one man against seven. Kelly whispered softly to Marengo, "whoa" and patted her gently on the neck.

Horse and rider halted just ten feet in front of the seven men, lined up from his left to his right, the man with the wiry red and brown hair was standing on Kelly's far right. The man was not tall. Kelly looked the man in the eyes and noticed his eyes were slightly crossed and of two different colors; one an unsettling bright blue and the other a wild red brown. Besides being short, the man's back was severely curved, making his arms appear to be two different lengths. He smiled showing all his teeth, they were gleaming white – surreal in their perfection. A .44 Colt Revolver hung in a leather flap holster engraved with the letters "KGC". Kelly noticed this man looked nothing like the younger man on his far left, so they obviously don't share the same initials KGC. The man on the right wore no hat; he looked like a bald boy. The outlaws who followed him were all taller than he was, including the youngest gang member, who Kelly believed to be the quick-draw outlaw Charlie spoke with last evening.

Kelly looked slowly into the faces of each of the seven men, starting from his left to his right, stopping lastly to look squarely into the different colored eyes of the man on his far right, then spoke. "Been hearing you boys have been stealing cattle from our ranchers."

The man replied, "No sir," smiling menacing at the Sheriff, then added, "you musta' heard wrong…"

"You'd be Salt Lake City Jim then?" Kelly inquired.

"Well then, I guess you musta heard something right," the man replied with a broadening grin, then nodded at the badge on Kelly's chest, adding, "Sheriff."

Kelly pointed to the nearby stack of cowhides with his double-barreled shotgun, commonly referred to in the West as a scatter-gun. "Guess'n you wouldn't mind me checking them hides for our ranchers' brands then?"

Salt Lake City Jim just smiled.

Kelly asked, hoping to disrupt the outlaws' thought processes for just a split second as he prepared to dismount and fight on the ground, "Can I ask you somethin' I been tryin' to get an answer for?"

"What's that Sheriff, I'm always willing to help a lawman out with his learnin," Salt Lake City Jim replied with a fake quizzical look on his rugged face as the other gang members laughed at their leader's bravado and cynical humor.

As Kelly dismounted from Marengo, he turned her head, placing her backside between himself and the outlaws lined up furthest to the left, causing them to take a step or two back so they didn't risk getting kicked by the gray horse. Kelly dropped her reins, then took three long sidesteps to his right, so the other six outlaws were all lined up behind their leader, then brought the shotgun quickly up to his shoulder and looked down the double-barrels into the shocked face of Salt Lake City Jim, standing just three feet from the front of the shotgun. Salt Lake City Jim tried in vain to draw his gun, but was way too slow as Kelly pulled both triggers.

Ka-Boom! The shotgun roared to life, throwing hot lead, flames and smoke out of both barrels. The back of Salt Lake City Jim's head exploded, scattering blood and bone, as gray-matter spewed out the back of his skull and across the faces and chests of the gang members who were standing closest to their now nearly headless leader. The remaining six outlaws watched in astonishment as the lifeless body of Salt Lake City Jim dropped to the dirt with a heavy "thud." Kelly stepped quickly to his left, knelt down low to see under the cloud of gunsmoke. He rested the shotgun against the stack of cowhides, quickly drew his six-shot Colt revolver with his right hand and took careful aim at the shiny belt buckle of the outlaw who had been standing closest to Salt Lake City Jim. Kelly saw the man's holster was now empty, his Colt had also been drawn. Sheriff Kelly ducked down lower just as a shot went off inches over his head.

Kelly cocked the hammer of his large frame Colt revolver, lowered his aim two inches below the man's belt buckle, and brought the round brass front sight at the end of the revolver's blued barrel into focus, he slowly squeezed the trigger. Boom! "Draw fast, shoot slow," Kelly repeated in his mind, "Doesn't matter how fast you are if you jerk the trigger and miss what you're aiming at." The heavy lead bullet struck the second outlaw in the pelvis, forcing him to drop to his knees. Kelly looked the man in the eyes and recognized the stunned look of disbelief on his face. Kelly saw the man was still holding his handgun, so Kelly fired another precious round into the man's chest. The outlaw absorbed the shot, but remained kneeling on the ground four feet in front of Kelly, on the other side of the campfire. The wounded outlaw looked down to see the bullet hole smoking from the unburnt gunpowder on his coat and in anger began to lift his revolver.

Kelly's next shot caught the man square in the forehead, between the eyes. The man's lips formed an O, but no words followed. Gunfights happen fast, but are remembered in slow-motion and often remembered afterwards as individual affairs. The second outlaw fell face first into the campfire, sending the steaming hot coffee pot splashing into the air.

Kelly crawled forward quickly, still crouching beneath the smoke screen, as several more shots were fired frantically over his head. He transferred his Colt .36 revolver to his left hand, then picked up the nearest dead man's .44 Colt revolver with his right hand. While raising both handguns over his head, Kelly fired both revolvers as fast as he could in the direction of where the last gunshots were fired from until both revolvers ran dry. The opposing gunfire subsided, as Kelly laid both empty handguns on the stack of cowhides he had been using for cover and drew his five-shot handgun from the shoulder holster under his left arm. The lawman crawled quickly forward on his hands and knees, crouching behind the stack of thick cowhides for cover and listened intently for any sounds to confirm where his adversaries stood.

Kelly heard the heavy thud and felt the impact of a large caliber lead bullet slamming into the stack of cowhides he was leaning against. He smelled and looked up to see the thick gunsmoke overhead was drifting slightly to his left, then cocked his revolver and raised his head up a couple inches to quickly glance over the stack of cowhides to locate where that last bullet came from on his right. Kelly found he was now looking directly into the face of a third outlaw, who was also trying to peer beneath the thick cloud of bluish grey gunsmoke. Before the man could cock, aim and fire his revolver, Kelly shot first. As the lead bullet struck the man in the left shoulder, the outlaw was spun around to his left and cried out in pain, followed by a string of profanity, but he still refused to drop his gun. Kelly fired two more rounds over the top of cowhides toward the bandit; one round managed to hit the other man in the right elbow. The outlaw finally dropped his gun, and then fell backwards out of sight.

Several more shots rang out and Kelly heard the all too familiar whiz of bullets spinning rapidly as they passed overhead. He recognized from the sound they were no doubt being fired from a modern rifled gun barrel. Kelly mentally counted the number of his remaining rounds, two, then knowing reloading is not an option, accepted the fact that he was still outgunned and knew instinctively that he had to end this gunfight, and fast. Reaching behind his holster, on the right side of his gunbelt, Kelly withdrew the folded knife from its leather sheath, flipped open the razor sharp blade and cocked his short barreled revolver in his left hand. Then in one fluid motion jumped on top of the stack of cowhides, challenging his remaining four adversaries.

The tactic worked. Emerging upward through the thick gunsmoke and landing with both feet spread apart on the cowhides, Kelly caught the remaining four outlaws by total surprise. Two of the bandits dropped their handguns and threw up their hands, a third, the youngest outlaw, simply threw up from fear. However, the outlaw closest to Kelly's right stood up and while cradling his right arm with his left hand, attempted to raise and fire his Colt revolver while using both hands. Kelly instinctively slashed out with the sharp edge of his knife, catching the man with a vicious upward thrust. The knife blade cut deep into the man's face just below the chin, then slicing upward across the man's right cheekbone, all the way up to the top of his ear. A single massive spurt of blood arced three feet into the air. The outlaw howled in pain, and finally threw down his revolver, dropped to his knees, trying in vain to reconnect the flap of flesh that hung down exposing the man's white jawbone and yellow teeth.

"Come on boys," Kelly shouted at the four remaining outlaws while standing on top of the stack of cowhides, "Who wants to dance with the devil tonight!"

Two of the outlaws raised both hands higher. The wounded man could only painfully raise one hand but no longer posed a threat, being preoccupied with trying to reattach the right side of his face to his head. The other outlaws watched as their wounded companion used his shoulder to try to hold his face in place. Then he sputtered through the blood said, "We give up, Sheriff, you done got the best of us."

Noticing one of the other outlaws was grimacing in pain, Kelly asked him, "You hit?"

The man slowly reached behind his butt with his hand to feel his right buttocks and returned it to see his hand was covered with blood.

"Did I do that?" Kelly asked.

"No," the outlaw said with disgust, nodding toward the youngest outlaw standing behind him. "My little brother here, Dead-eye Dick, done shot me in the ass!"

Kelly noticed the younger outlaw wiping vomit off his chin with the back of his left sleeve while holding his right arm in the air. He was wearing an empty holster with the initials KGC engraved on the leather flap. The young outlaw had started crying.

"You hit too?" Kelly asked of him.

"No," the youngest gang member managed to say between

sobs, "I done pissed myself."

Kelly looked down from the vomit on the young gun's shirt, to the dark wet stain growing down the young outlaw's tan pants legs, then commented to the youngest of the outlaws, who had started sobbing uncontrollably. "Well," Kelly said, "looks like you might want to consider another line a work young fella. Doesn't look like you got the stomach much for gun play."

Staring down at the blood on his hands, the older brother said, "My blood feels really weird, it's thin, like, like water and I ain't got no feeling in my buttocks."

"Well, that happens. I suspect the feeling will return soon enough," Sheriff Kelly replied, then noticed the other two outlaws with their hands held high over their heads were looking over Kelly's shoulder. The sound of horse hooves splashing through water behind the Sheriff, coming from the direction of Colorado City, announced that help had arrived. Sheriff Kelly, holding his handgun trained on the four outlaws still standing, and the one who had dropped again to the ground in pain, glanced over his left shoulder to see Charlie in the lead, being followed by Judge Stone and three of his ranch-hands, racing across Fountain Creek on their horses.

"Mornin' Sheriff Kelly," Judge Stone acknowledged as he pulled up, handed the reins of his horse over to Charlie before dismounting to take a closer look at the dead and wounded men lying on the ground. "Thought we'd ride over to see if you needed any help, but looks like you got things well in hand." Judge Stone pointed to two of his ranch-hands, "Bruce, you and Rod search those men over there to see if they're hiding any more weapons, then stack their holsters and guns and all the money they got amongst them there on those cowhides." Turning back to Sheriff Kelly, Judge Stone said, "I'm thinking they'll be making restitution to our ranchers for the cattle they done stole." The Judge looked at the empty shotgun and handguns lying on the ground and added, "From the looks of things here we might need to reimburse you Sheriff for all the ammunition you done shot up here this morning."

Kelly holstered his handgun. "Much obliged, your Honor." Kelly then picked up his long barreled revolver and placed it carefully back into the holster on the right side of his gunbelt and collected his double-barreled shotgun.

Judge Stone took note the morning sun and said, "We kinda thought maybe you'd be awaiting for us in town this morning, afore coming out here and facing down these hoodlums alone." The Sheriff and Judge watched as his two ranch hands, Bruce and Rod, began to check to make sure the first two outlaws were in fact dead and started gathering up the surviving outlaw's firearms and stacking them on the cowhides.

"Well, I didn't want to expose anyone else to any unnecessary danger," Kelly said, glancing at Charlie who had, up until that morning, never seen a dead man. "Sides," Sheriff Kelly continued, "I always found that in a gunfight there's usually some men wanting to be there more than others, trick is trying to figure out which ones want to fight and which ones don't."

"These two are dead for sure," one of Judge Stone's ranch hands announced, "and these two are shot-up, that one over there's pretty bad," he said nodding at the one laying on the ground. "This one here's just shot in the ass, looks like a through and through wound, but I suspect he'll live unless he gets lead poising," he added loudly with a smile.

"You fixin to hang these five men Sheriff?" Judge Stone asked.

"Well, with your permission your Honor, I was thinkin' I might drive 'em on up to Denver City and turn them over to Marshall Townsend. I suspect he'll probably take 'em on to the penitentiary over in Fort Leavenworth, but first we may want to pay a visit to Camp Weld and maybe point out to Major Chivington the quartermaster that's been defrauding the government in paying buffalo rates while buying up all this stolen beef from these outlaws. I can't imagine these are the first stolen cattle that been feedin' those hungry soldiers during their training time up at Camp Weld...and unless you have a better idea, I could deliver this meat that's already done been butchered here and bring back any of the money I can get to hand over to you and the other ranchers who lost cows."

"Sounds like a good plan to me Sheriff, though you might just want to turn whatever money you collect to Robert Finley, since he's our County Treasurer now. Then he can make a written report to the County Commissioners to see what plans they might have, I'll make sure they get this cash reported to them as well," Judge Stone said, nodding to the small pile of coins and currency being taken from the outlaws and placed on top of the stacked cowhides. Judge Stone said, pointing to the two newly disarmed and uninjured outlaws, "You two get to loadin that stolen beef onto that wagon."

Sheriff Kelly turned to Judge Stone, "I reckon we ought to bury these two dead men, only decent thing to do I suppose." Then pointing to the two outlaw brothers, ordered, "You there, Deadeye-Dick, stop your bawling and grab a shovel and help your lame ass brother here dig two graves over there by the creek." Then walking over to Charlie, Kelly said, "Unless your dad has something else in mind for you to do Charlie, maybe you can keep them covered with this," drawing the smaller pocket Colt revolver from the shoulder holster and handing it to Charlie. "It's only got two rounds left, but that oughta make do with these two fellas. Don't expect they'll give us any more trouble."

"And if either of you cattle rustlers are thinking of continuing in this line of work," Judge Stone added, "you might just want to dig a third grave while you're at it. You're going to be needing one for yourself soon enough."

"Well," one outlaw replied, "I can't speak for Jeb here but this cattle rustling business don't look near as invitin' as it did half an hour ago."

Grabbing a shovel in one hand and his younger brother who had shot him in the butt in the other hand, stopped and turned back to face Sheriff Kelly. "Sheriff, I got's to know, before all the shootin started, when you was gettin' down from your horse, you said you had a question you wanted to ask us. What was it you was a wantin to ask?"

Kelly replied, looking down at the two bodies of the men he had just killed, "I was just gonna ask if any of you knew when it was time to stop talking and start shooting. Apparently the answer was 'no.'"

Christmas Eve, 1861
El Paso House Hotel, Colorado City

"I really have to hand it to you Lucy," Scott Kelly said as he twirled her gracefully around the dancefloor of the El Paso House, "you and your daughter's family really did a wonderful job with the Christmas decorations, everything looks so festive."

"Why thank you Mr. Kelly," Lucy replied as she beamed at the Sheriff's compliment. "The hotel truly did come out lovely and with Felicia's help in managing the boarding house and cooking, I was able to concentrate all my attention on the finishing touches for the Hotel. With the stagecoach stopping right out front, it seems we'll have a steady flow of customers from now on."

"Especially as word continues to spread about your cooking," Sheriff Kelly said, adding, "the roast beef and trimmings this evening were absolutely delicious."

Lucy smiled up at Sheriff Kelly and embraced him a little tighter, but not so that others would notice. Kelly enjoyed her touch, and even though she was several years older than he was, he marveled at her lean figure as he held her tightly against his chest, both dancers keeping perfect time to the music. The dance was Lucy's favorite, a Varsouvienne, being played tonight by a string quartet made up of Anthony Bott as the viola player, Doc Garvin as cellist, John Brown as violin player one and Xavier Bent as violin player number two.

Sheriff Kelly nodded toward Xavier Bent, the town's blacksmith, as he and Lucy passed in front of the quartet, and said to Lucy, "Mr. Bent seems to be a man of many talents."

"He is a kind and gentle man. He told me he learned to play the violin while living at Bent's Old Fort. I hear the Bent brothers knew how to throw a real fandango," Lucy replied with a knowing smile.

As the tune came to an end, Lucy turned to bow to her partner and joined him and the other dancers in a warm applause for the band. "Care for some punch Mr. Kelly?" Lucy asked, "I must warn you though, I suspect George Smith may have spiked the punch bowl on the left, so you'll more than likely want to drink from the one on the right."

"That sounds like George," Kelly replied with a smile. "Won't you join me?" Kelly asked as he extended his elbow toward Lucy to escort her from the dance floor toward the punch bowl near the back door where Reverend Howbert was speaking with Judge and Mrs. Stone. Three of the band members nodded as they exited outside to take a break. Xavier Bent remained behind with his violin and was joined by the young Irving Howbert.

Irving Howbert began to sing as Xavier played "Lorena", "*The years creep slowly by, Lorena. Snow is on the grass again. The sun is sinking low Lorena. Frost is where the flowers have been. The music sad and low Lorena. Happy sounds have left the day...*"

"Your son has a beautiful singing voice Reverend Howbert," Lucy said admiringly.

"Raised on Methodist hymns," Reverend Howbert replied, "mostly written by Charles Wesley; don't imagine he or his brother John would approve of this tune."

"It is rather daunting," Mrs. Stone agreed, then added, "I read last month where Major Chivington was recruiting a company of volunteers from El Paso and Fremont Counties. Surely you'll stop your son from joining won't you Reverend Howbert?"

"I reminded him he was only fifteen, but he wasn't too happy with me when I finally forbid him from volunteering to serve in the state militia," Reverend Howbert replied, then nodded toward the other side of the room where Majors Tappan and Wynkoop stood wearing their dress blue uniforms. Alongside Major Sam Tappan, were his two brothers, Lewis and George, listened in admiration to what had become one of the most popular songs being sung by men in uniform for both the Union and Confederate Armies.

Judge Stone nodded to the two officers in uniform before commenting, "They do make it seem rather romantic, appealing to a young man's sense of honor and duty to his country, all while both sides of this war claim to be fighting in God's name. I just don't see how the Lord can be on both sides of the killing at the same time, if at all."

"Always sounds more romantic 'til the killin' starts and young men are a dyin'," Kelly replied quietly, his thoughts drifting away to a distant memory.

"Judge Stone," Lucy said, attempting to change the subject and reinvigorate the Holiday spirit, "tell us how your niece Lizzy is doing with her studies back East at Oberlin College?"

"Very well," Judge Stone replied, thankful for a shift from the conversation about the War Between the States. "After the Holidays, she will be starting her final semester in college and I'm delighted that she's accepted my invitation to come stay with us for a while after she graduates. She's had a hard time of it after my brother John died year before last. John was a very dedicated medical doctor, and had become very successful, until the war. I am concerned if things don't change by the time Lizzy graduates, there are not many opportunities for a young female archeologist to advance in her field, most especially back in war-torn Tennessee."

"Well, I'm looking forward to seeing her again," Lucy replied warmly. "I'm sure she will bring a breath of sunshine to the Pikes Peak region when she arrives."

The band finished the waltz and as the dancers began to clear the dancefloor Mrs. Stone commented, "Looks like everyone has saved the last dance for you Sheriff Kelly and Lucy."

Thankful for the courtesy extended them from the other dancers, Sheriff Kelly and Lucy bowed to one another, then to the band, and then to the other dancers assembled around the outskirts of the dancefloor, all encouraging them to accept their invitation. Sheriff Kelly took Lucy in his arms and began the last dance, a Varsouvienne.

"I wish they wouldn't do that," Sheriff Kelly whispered into Lucy's ear.

"It does seem to have become a bit of a custom. That's what you get for being such a good dancer, Sheriff, everyone likes seeing how it's done," Lucy said as she thrilled at being lead around the dance floor to the rhythm of the music.

"Still," the Sheriff added, "while I appreciate their kindness, I just don't like to attract all the attention."

"Well Scott," Lucy replied teasingly, "that's what you get for being such a good dancer and also one of the most eligible bachelors in all the county!"

It was nearing midnight, when the last dance ended. People began to slowly exit the El Paso House Hotel headed for the comfort of their homes, most looking forward to waking up the next morning and spending Christmas with their families.

Sheriff Kelly put on his coat as he turned to bid Lucy a goodnight.

"Would you like to stop by later Scott?" she asked.

"Thank you Lucy, I have to make my rounds, but perhaps I could stop by tomorrow sometime," he replied with a smile.

"You're welcome anytime," Lucy replied, somewhat disappointed in the rebuff to spend the night. Then she brightened with a smile. "We'll be having supper around two o'clock and we would love to have your company."

"Thank you Lucy, I'll look forward to joining you and your daughter's family then," Sheriff Kelly said, as he buttoned his coat and slipped out into the darkness.

When making his nightly business checks of Colorado City, Sheriff Kelly varied his route and times. He did not want anyone with ill intent to anticipate his movements. Most of his time spent doing business checks at night focused on the south side of Colorado Avenue, between 21st and 28th Streets, where the majority of the saloons and brothels were located. As he walked east through the back alley behind Thunder and Buttons, he noticed one of the so-called Ladies of the Evening, sitting on the steps leading upstairs, smoking a cigarette.

As Sheriff Kelly approached he recognized her and spoke softly, "Good evening Rebecca."

"Oh Sheriff," she said with a nervous laugh, "you startled me. I thought you was someone else."

"I apologize if I scared you Miss Becky, I just wanted to make sure you were all right," the Sheriff said kindly as he removed his hat respectfully.

"That's very thoughtful of you Sheriff Kelly," she replied, blowing smoke away from the lawman into the cold night air. "May I ask you somethin' Sheriff? How comes you don't call me Becky Red Stockings, like all the other mens in town do?"

"Guess I'm just not like all the other men," Kelly replied as he sat down next to her on the unpainted wooden stairs.

"Interest you in joining me for a smoke," Becky Red Stockings said with a smile, adding, "or maybe you'd like to come upstairs for a drink or maybe something else?" she offered with a twinkle in her eye.

Sheriff Kelly smiled, noticing and not for the first time, how attractive the young lady beside him was. She was dark complected, with dark hair and eyes, but it was her mischievous grin that caught and held his and many other men's attention.

"That's a right tempting offer, Miss Becky," the Sheriff replied, "but regretfully I will have to decline this evening. Got to finish my rounds."

"Let's see, you don't smoke, you don't drink, you won't come upstairs, so tell me Sheriff, what does a man like you do in his spare time," she said with a smile.

"Well, truth be told," the Sheriff replied with a slight smile, "I don't have much spare time, but if I do, well from time to time I have been known to," pausing for effect, "give in occasionally to a good smoke."

"Ha!" the Spoiled Dove said with a laugh. "See, I knowed all along you wasn't like all the other men in town."

"There are some good men here in town," he replied defensively, mindlessly playing with his hatband.

"Well, I don't know that I've met very many of 'em yet," she concluded.

"Now, can I ask you something?" the Sheriff asked gently as the lady snuffed out her cigarette on the wooden handrail beside her.

"Sure, anything," she replied.

"Where are you from, originally I mean, where's your hometown?"

"Well, I was born in Louisiana, outside of New Orleans, if that's considered a person's hometown I suppose. My mother's name was Anne, with an e, and she was a Negro slave on a sugarcane plantation in St. Bernard Parish, Louisiana. My father was kin to the plantation owner. When my mother was expectin' with me, she was traded to another plantation owner in Alabama, so peoples wouldn't gossip none. I never met my real father, but my mama gave me his last name when she named me Rebecca Anne Toutant-Beauregard. My mother was very beautiful and talented. She taught me to sing and dance and write some afore she died.

She got me an audition at a dancehall in New Orleans and encouraged me to make the most of my talents. I met a handsome young man from Georgia, with the Greene Russell Party. He invited me to join him out West here, but when the War broke out he rode off with some of the other Russell men, back to Georgia to join in the Confederate States Army. Said he'd be back for me in a few months, but I knowed I'd never see him again. Not much else for a woman to do arounds here, she just tries to get by with whatever talents the good Lord done gave her."

The woman stared off into the distance for a few minutes, then turned to look at the lawman, then glanced down to the ground. "I'm sorry, Sheriff, I didn't mean to carry on like that, just kinda poured outta me. No white man ever really asks about me, just more interested in what I can do for them."

"That's quite alright Rebecca, I enjoy your company," the Sheriff said as he noticed a few large snowflakes were starting to fall. The Sheriff stood and turned to leave, then stopped when he noticed her eyes beginning to moisten, and added, "Merry Christmas Miss Rebecca, may the New Year bring you much happiness."

"Merry Christmas to you Sheriff," she said, then added as the twinkle returned to her eye, "if you ever find you need to comes in outta the cold, I'm up the stairs, second room on the left."

The Sheriff nodded with a smile, placed his hat on his head, and then walked on down the alley, noticing the light snow was starting to stick to the ground. He was appreciative of how the freshly fallen snow would make his business checks easier throughout the night, as he'd only need to read the footprints in the snow. Fresh footprints in the snow helped him to separate out someone just coming out back to use the outhouse or someone who might have broken into one of the town's businesses or churches. As the lawman was about to cross 27th Street, he stopped in the shadows of the dark alley and turned back to watch Rebecca playfully trying to catch a snowflake on her tongue.

Just then, the door at the top of the stairs creaked opened, spilling a faint light from inside out into the cold night. The Sheriff watched and listened to another woman's voice shout loudly, "There you are Becky Red Stockings. Come on back in here, girl. There's a customer wantin' to buy himself a special Christmas present. I'm thinkin it might be you, honey child!"

"I'll be right there Miss Laura Belle," the young woman at the bottom of the stairs replied as she stood, glancing down the alley way toward where the sheriff stood watching from a recessed doorway. Then Becky Red Stockings brushed the light snow from her curly black hair and started back up the stairs.

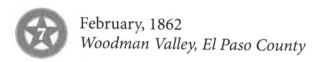

February, 1862
Woodman Valley, El Paso County

"You think'n they might be a war party Sheriff?" young Irving Howbert asked Sheriff Kelly, as the two reined in their horses on top of a high white rocky bluff south of Woodman Valley, cautiously watching the six mounted Indians riding past in single file in the valley below.

"No, but they might be scouting for a war party. That second one from the front, that's Charley Bent. He's called White Hat by the Cheyenne and Arapahoes. He's William Bent's youngest son. You best be lettin your father know what we've seen here, so he can inform the people of his congregation on Sunday to be on the lookout for any Indians who might be up to no good. Looks like they're headed toward the Garden of the Gods, or maybe up the Ute Pass toward South Park," Sheriff Kelly replied.

"How do you know the difference between a scouting party and a war party?" the fifteen year old Howbert asked while trying to settle his pony.

"A war party of Dog Soldiers usually shaves their heads, except for a Mohawk, a strip of hair they wear down the middle of their heads. Then they paint their entire heads blue with two white bear claws running down each side of their faces," the Sheriff replied adding, "they also paint their horses bright colors, usually blue and white, and braid their pony's tails with eagle feathers or other decorations, like ribbons, sticking out so they catch the wind when they gallop into battle. You riding an Indian pony?" Kelly asked noticing how Howbert's pony acted out, watching the other horses pass down below.

"Thinkin' maybe so. He sure wants to join them more than staying up here with us. You think they'll be attacking Colorado City?" Irving asked while pulling tightly on his pony's reins.

"I suspect they're more interested in seeing where the Ute might be encamped," Sheriff Kelly replied. "There was a battle here, in this valley, between the Ute and the Cheyenne and Arapaho a year or two back, before the first settlers arrived. I hear tell the Ute won the battle but at the cost of many warriors on both sides, and I always suspected the Utes buried their honored war dead somewhere near here, not far from where they musta fell in battle."

"These white sandstone bluffs up here sure could'a made for a good place to bury their warriors," Irving said, pointing to a bluff area running along the south rim of the valley.

"You might be right. They'd have a nice view of Tava, their most sacred mountain, that we white folks renamed Pikes Peak. Those tall, white sandstone formations over there, Indians call'em hoodoos, would serve as a natural grave marker indicating the location of where they and maybe some of their horses would have been sacrificed and buried as well."

"Why did they bury their horses with them?"

"So they'd have something to ride in the afterlife," Sheriff Kelly explained. "A Chief killed in battle was almost always buried separately, but close to his fallen warriors, and his horse was generally buried with him, 'cause they knew that being a Chief, he would have a longer way to ride in the afterlife and might need a remount. Sometimes the Ute Medicine Man would plant a juniper seed along the trail that ran nearest the gravesite so those Ute that followed would know where their honored Chief was buried so they could return to offer their prayers or leave him an offering stone whenever they was to pass that way again."

"You think they might attack the Ute village that got set up a couple weeks back, where the Camp Creek joins up with Fountain Creek?" Irving asked.

The Sheriff took one last long look at the six Indian scouts, turned Marengo back toward Colorado City, and then replied, "I suspect being that close to Colorado City, the Cheyenne and Arapaho maybe wouldn't take the risk of attacking those Ute fearing they might have to fight both the Utes and us, but all the same, I think we ought to be headed back now. I'd appreciate it if you'd tell your dad what we seen here. I'll ride on over to the Ute camp along Camp Creek and warn Chief Ouray to keep an eye out for these six riders."

November 26, 1862
Colorado City, El Paso County

"Afternoon Sheriff," the U.S. Marshall said to Sheriff Kelly, "I think we got things well in hand," nodding at the double barrel shotgun Kelly held in his arms.

"Oh, this isn't for them," Kelly replied, looking from the shotgun to the forty-four captured rebels the Marshall and his deputies had captured in Beulah and were escorting through town on the way to Denver City. "It's for them," Kelly said as he nodded to the three men standing in front of the Painted Lady Saloon.

"Isn't that our former Postmaster," Marshall Townsend asked, "Parke McClure?"

"That's him," Sheriff Kelly confirmed, "I don't know who the other two men are, but they been talkin' 'bout ambushing you and your men somewhere between here and Denver City, whenever you least expect it, and setting Captain Joel McKee and his men free."

"That's a bit unsettling," the Marshall agreed.

"Reckon I could try to dissuade them; but I don't want to butt in if you got everything in hand."

"Whatever you could do would be very much appreciated Sheriff," Marshall Townsend replied as he hurried out of town to catch up with his deputies.

After the Marshall, his deputies and their prisoners had ridden out of town, Parke McClure and his two men stepped back inside the Painted Lady Saloon. A few minutes later Sheriff Kelly stepped inside and walked up to where the three men were drinking at the bar.

"Mr. McClure," the Sheriff replied, then waited until the man turned around before he continued, "just wanted you to know I've impounded your horses and saddles for the next 24-hours. You men can get them back at the blacksmith's shop this time tomorrow."

"Well, have you now," McClure said, looking at the badge on the Sheriff's chest. "That's a mighty unfriendly thing you've gone and done there Sheriff."

"Not trying to make friends. Just trying to make sure the Marshall gets his prisoners to Denver City without interruption," Kelly explained as he backed out of the saloon.

Twenty-four hours later Sheriff Kelly dropped by Xavier's blacksmith shop, "Parke McClure and his two friends pick up their horses and saddles?"

"They did," Xavier said, "left about twenty minutes ago. They weren't none too happy with you or me for taking their horses."

"I suppose we best be watching our backs for the next few weeks," Kelly replied to his friend. "Sorry if I got you into my business, didn't mean to put you in harm's way."

"I've been there 'afore," Xavier replied. "Funny thing though."

"What's that?" Kelly asked.

"Well, you said you was a worried about them ambushing the Marshall on his way to Denver City, but when they rode out of town they was well-provisioned and headed south, toward the Santa Fe Trail. If'n you was ta ask me, I'd say they had pressing business at the other end of the trail, back in Kansas or Missouri maybe."

March 18, 1863
Deadman's Canyon, Southern El Paso County

The first known murder victim of the Espinosa Gang was a Mexican Corporal out of Fort Garland. He had been sent along with several other cavalrymen to assist Deputy U.S. Marshall George Austen in the first attempted arrest of Felipe Espinosa and his younger brother Vivian. The two Espinosa brothers had robbed a freight wagon headed from Santa Fe to Galisteo and were recognized by the teamster who lived in the Conejos area not far from the Espinosa's modest homestead. The Deputy U.S.

Marshal had given pursuit of the two Espinosa brothers north toward the rocky tree shrouded mountains above Fort Garland. Unfortunately, the lawman's horse tripped and fell. The deputy marshal's leg was severely injured, but he survived.

The second murder victim of the Espinosa Gang was 56-year-old Franklin William Bruce, who was building a sawmill on Hardscrabble Creek, six miles south of the Arkansas River where he and his wife Ruth had taken to raising their four small children. The Bruce family was formerly from Wisconsin, where Franklin had operated a sawmill, and like Scott Kelly and Robert Finley, decided it might pay better to disassemble the components for his sawmill, load them on a wagon and follow the Santa Fe Trail West in search of a better life.

After watching to make sure Bruce was alone, the two Espinosa brothers crossed the grassy meadow to the stream where Bruce had taken to rebuilding his sawmill, rode up and shot him once through the heart. While Bruce lay on his back, dead or dying, one of the brothers took a knife, ripped open his shirt, and carved a large cross on his chest. They ransacked the sawmill, finding nothing of value, then rode north, crossed the Arkansas River and rode another fifteen miles. After entering El Paso County from the South they arrived near a place called Red Rock Canyon where they spotted a herd of cattle. They separated one of the cows from the herd, cut its throat, then carved out about fifteen pounds of meat which they cooked over an open campfire before rolling out their bedrolls for the night, waiting for a chance to attack their next victim.

The next morning the Espinosa Gang claimed their third murder victim. Henry Harkins was described as a kind elderly man, known affectionately by his friends as Uncle Henry, and was by coincidence an acquaintance of Franklin Bruce. Henry Harkins, along with four other men, was also in the process of building a sawmill and constructing a small crude cabin nearby to be used as a living quarters by the men working the sawmill. These five hardworking men had come to the Pikes Peak Region to strike it rich, but like the 100,000 other souls who had come out West found gold wasn't just laying around on the ground and in mountain streams just waiting to be picked up. Making a living in the West was the hard part; the dying came easy.

March 19, 1863
Xavier's Blacksmith Shop, Colorado City

"Looks like you've got some official business headed your way Sheriff," Xavier told Sheriff Kelly as he looked up while grooming Marengo in the corral.

"Mornin' Gary," Kelly said to the Fremont County Sheriff, as he reined in and dismounted with his deputy from their tired horses.

"Mornin' Scott. This here's my Deputy, Joel McClintock," the lawman replied, as the rugged lawmen shook hands with one another.

"Mornin' Joel. Gentlemen this is Xavier Bent, the proprietor of the finest blacksmith shop in all the west."

"Mornin'," Xavier replied. Sensing the lawmen needed to discuss their business in private, he reached out to take their horses' reins. "Let me tend to your horses. Looks like they could do with some water and maybe a little grain."

"Much obliged, Mr. Bent," the Fremont County Sheriff and deputy replied, handing their horses off to the blacksmith. The Fremont County Sheriff turned to address his fellow sheriff privately. "Scott, afraid we've got some unsettling news. We've

111

been on the trail of two outlaw brothers, Felipe and Vivian Espinosa. They done killed a corporal outa' Fort Garland, then a man down our way on Hardscrabble creek, carved a big cross on his chest. Then they headed up north here to El Paso County, where it looks like they might a shot and killed another man in Red Rock Canyon. You mighta known him, a Henry Harkins. You heard of him?"

"I do know Uncle Henry, he was helping build a sawmill down south, toward Turkey Creek. Know what set these two fellas off?" Sheriff Kelly asked.

"Felipe Espinosa is one of them devout penitents from the San Luis Valley, claims to have had a visit from the Virgin Mary who told him to go kill gringos," the Fremont County Sheriff explained. "The neighbors who found Mr. Harkins' body thought he'd been attacked by Injuns, cause they'd taken an ax or a tomahawk to his head, bloody awful sight, then ransacked the cabin where they'd been staying. We've been following these two outlaw's tracks for a couple days now, all the way from Hardscrabble Creek to where we came across a recently killed steer just south of where Mr. Harkins' body was located. Seems they shot this steer between its eyes, cut out a couple steaks, left the rest of the meat to rot, and then camped for the night before they rode up on Mr. Harkins. Looks like they robbed him and the place, but we didn't stay long enough to inquire what mighta been stolen. Might be helpful to see if anyone in the area there had seen a couple strangers and maybe see about making a list of things that might have been stolen during the robbery."

"Which way was they headed?" Sheriff Kelly asked of the other two lawmen.

Joel McClintock pointed west toward the entrance to Ute Pass.

"They was headed up that way, fore certain, but their tracks got mixed in with all the other traffic comin' and goin' up the pass this mornin.'"

"I'm thinkin, after our horses are freshened up, we'll head up the pass a ways and see if we can separate their horses' tracks out up top there. If not we'll likely head back south down Four-Mile Canyon, toward Canon City and see what we can see." The Fremont County Sheriff concluded by asking, "I don't want them circling in behind us and attacking any of our citizens while we're off on some wild goose chase. What's your thoughts Scott?"

"I'm thinkin I'll ride down to Red Rock Canyon in the morning, ask around a piece, like you said, see if anyone noticed a couple strangers out and about and try to make a list a what mighta been stolen. Might come in handy whenever these two hoodlums get run to ground," Sheriff Kelly replied.

The Fremont County Sheriff turned to his deputy then nodded toward Xavier's barn. "Mind checking on our mounts Joel?" Then turned back to Sheriff Kelly saying, "Best take a deputy with you Scott, these are a couple of mean vermin I'm here to tell ya."

"I'll stop down at Gassenger's ranch, along the Fountain Creek, maybe ask Dan Gassenger if he's available to serve as my deputy again for a couple days," Sheriff Kelly replied as he shook hands with his fellow lawman. "Dan's wife is due here in a few weeks, he'll want to be home afore that. You and Joel take care of yourselves. Honest lawmen are getting hard to replace these days."

March 20, 1863
Red Rocks Canyon, Southern El Paso County

"Whoa," Sheriff Kelly said to Marengo, as he and Deputy Dan

113

Gassenger slowed their horses to a walk, as they approached a small gathering of people in the canyon at the foot of the towering red rocks. As they neared they saw two of the men were placing an engraved white tombstone at the head of a freshly dug grave. The gravestone said it all, "Henry Harkins, Murdered Wednesday Eve, March 18, 1863."

Sheriff Kelly and Deputy Gassenger waited respectfully for the elder of the two men to step away from the grave, leaving the younger man to finish their solemn work. The elder man walked over toward the two lawmen, then while leaning against his shovel spoke deliberately, "Sheriff, I'm John McPherson and that young man over there's my nephew, Murdoch McPherson. These folks here are our family's friends, the Priest Family, and other friends of Uncle Henry Harkins, who we done buried here this morning. Most of us been together since leaving Sparta, Wisconsin."

Sheriff Kelly replied, "Sorry for your loss. How long you been out this way?"

"We crossed the Missouri at Council Bluffs summer of 1860, moving a sawmill out here, following along the Mountain Branch of the Santa Fe Trail. Spent last winter in Canon City. Thought this might be a good place as any to rebuild the sawmill and set up a homestead. We got here just a couple months ago, not sure we'll be staying now. Be worried the women and children might be put at risk while we men are out working."

"It is a beautiful canyon. Trees might not be as big as out at the Pineries, but the winter's aren't as severe and you can reach the markets of Canon City and Pueblo, as well as here in El Paso County. My deputy and I will be joining in on the man-hunt. Anyone see who done this?" Sheriff Kelly asked scanning the tall red rocky walls to each side of the canyon.

"No one saw nor heard anything. We'd been thinking it was Injuns that did it at first, but the Sheriff from down Fremont County way stopped by yesterday. Said they'd been following the trail of two outlaws he called the Espinosa Gang, who'd done murdered another friend of ours, Franklin Bruce, down on Hardscrabble Creek a few days back."

"What all did they take from here?" asked Deputy Gassenger, who had touched a stubby pencil to the tip of his tongue and was starting to take notes on the back of an off-white postcard.

"Near as I can tell," Murdoch McPherson replied, joining his Uncle in the conversation with the lawmen, "after they killed Uncle Henry, they done split open his skull with two axes, spilling his brains out on the ground, then ransacked the cabin, slashed opened my suitcase, strung its contents out on the dirt floor. They took Uncle John's gold watch and chain and his satin vest with the embroidered flowers down the front, and stole Uncle Henry's gold wire rim reading glasses. The killers opened every box and sack, dumping out the contents, then poured flour across the floor all over everything."

"The pocket watch have any identifiable markings on it?" Deputy Gassenger asked while adding to his notes.

"It has my Uncle's initials, JM, engraved on the case and a tintype of his mother, my grandmother on the inside of the case," Murdoch McPherson replied.

The older McPherson spoke again. "After finding Uncle Henry's body, the way it was, we forted up at the Priest's cabin the first night, figuring Cheyenne Injuns was on the warpath again, till we spoke with that Sheriff and his Deputy yesterday as they was riding up from Fremont County."

"Sorry again for your loss," Sheriff Kelly replied to the friends of Henry Harkins who had gathered on this chilly Spring morning to pay their last respects to their departed loved one. "We'll be off to see if we can help run these two murderers to ground." The two El Paso County lawmen turned their horses around and rode back up out of the canyon to the north.

Late Spring 1863
South Abeyta Creek, East of Old La Veta Pass, Huerfano County

Riding east under the green aspen trees, Sheriff Kelly saw two deer had been spooked out from some scrub oak and then spotted a lone rider coming toward him up the narrow trail. He slowed Marengo to halt, waiting on the high ground as the other man approached. The men were soon face to face as the noses of their horses touched. The man appeared to Kelly just as he had been described; light skinned, middle aged, compact in build and dressed all in black, from a black cowboy hat on his head to his black boots. He wore a black coat, black shirt, black pants and black leather gunbelt. The man was even mounted on a black horse and rode a black saddle. His appearance was nearly the exact opposite of Sheriff Kelly, with one exception; the man in black also carried a Hawken big bore rifle, with an octagonal barrel, just like Kelly's.

Kelly knew it was the man he'd been told about down at Fort Garland, even before he was close enough to see his ashen white complexion and looked into his pale blue eyes. The two men's horses stood facing one another for a full minute, while the men took measure of the other from head to toe. Sheriff Kelly spoke first, "You'd be Thomas Tate Tobin."

"I'd be Tom Tobin," the man replied, then nodded to the circle star badge pinned to Sheriff Kelly's coat and said, "You'd be Sheriff Kelly, out of El Paso County. Heard you was down this a way, trackin the last of the Espinosa Gang."

"I am Kelly," the Sheriff acknowledged with the nod of his head, "Spoke with Colonel Sam Tappan, Garrison Commander at Fort Garland, couple days back. Said I might find you out this way. Looks like you might have had more success tracking these men than most," Sheriff Kelly said, nodding to the decaying human foot hanging from a cord worn around Tom Tobin's neck.

"This here's what's left of Vivian Espinosa," Tobin said, stroking the shriveled up foot hanging around his neck. Then while holding up a bloodstained flour sack by its drawstring said, "These here are the heads of Filipe Espinosa and his sixteen year old nephew, Jose Vincente Espinosa. A posse outa Fairplay shot and killed Vivian, left his body to rot along Four Mile Creek. I'd heard Felipe returned a few months later to bury his dead brother. It was he who cut off his brother's foot to wear around his neck so as to never forget to avenge his dead brother. Colonel Tappan hired me to track down these last two of the Espinosa Gang, seems one of their victims was a Tappan brother. Five hundred dollars is a lot of money to a man like me. I'm taking the Colonel their heads so as no one can dispute my claimin' of the reward money."

Placing the flour sack on his lap, behind the saddle horn, Kelly watched as Tobin loosened the drawstring and pulled out a human head by the hair, "this here's Felipe, or what's left of 'em. He was still alive when I took to cutting off his head, told me to 'get on with it, complaining all the while how dull my knife was." Tobin concluded his remarks with a wry smile, then turned the severed head toward Kelly so he could take a good look.

"Well," Sheriff Kelly replied, "that just goes to show you some folks can always find something to complain about."

"The younger fella, Jose looks like he was pretty much dead when he hit the ground," Tobin commented as he stuffed Felipe's head back in the bag, cinched up the drawstring and hung the flour sack back around his saddle horn.

"Heard you carried a Hawken," Sheriff Kelly replied, nodding to the brass butt plate of the rifle butt exposed from the black leather scabbard underslung from Tobin's saddle.

"Appears you carry a big bore Hawken yourself," Tobin acknowledged.

"Folks say you been known to get off four rounds in sixty seconds, I've only been able to manage three rounds in under a minute myself," Kelly said.

Tobin took a moment before he replied, then pulled on another leather shoestring he wore around his neck, "I don't share this with most fellas, but you don't strike me as being like most fellas. See this here leather disc? I made it with six nipples stickin out and I carry a percussion cap pushed down on each one. Then afore I gets ready to shoot, I puts two or three lead musket balls in my mouth, saves a couple seconds between each reload."

"I'll have to give that a try sometime," Kelly said. "Appreciate the tip."

"One other tip you might wanta keep in mind," Tobin said with another slight smile.

"What's that?"

"Ya gotta remember to breathe through yer nose, not yer mouth, otherwise if'n you was to get excited you might swallow one of them lead balls. Can be a bit of a problem next couple days, trying to digest them and all," Tobin replied, finishing his shootin' lesson with a slight grin.

"Sounds like good advice," Kelly acknowledged with a smile. "I heard you was related somehow to them Espinosa's, any truth to that?" Sheriff Kelly inquired, nodding at the bloodstained sack containing the severed heads of the last of the Espinosa Gang.

"Through marriage is all, not like we was blood or nothing," Tobin replied matter-of-factly, before adding, "I'm just tryin' to clear up the family name, some might say."

Tobin pulled out a gold pocket watch from his vest pocket, opened it to check the time, then asked, "Any of your victims lose a watch?"

"If it has the initials JM on the case, I'd say yes," Kelly replied.

Tobin snapped the watch case closed then pulled up close alongside Kelly's horse and handed him the pocket watch, "Violent times we live in now a days. How long you been on their trail?"

"Three weeks," Sheriff Kelly replied, "this time. Went after 'em a couple times afore, first time was just a couple days after they killed one of our citizens in Red Rocks Canyon, friend of the man who owned this watch. He'll be grateful to get it back, kinda a family heirloom, as I understand it. Espinosas' also killed a former citizen of El Paso County, John Addleman, from Colorado City. John was a good man, the son of a U.S. Supreme Court Judge. John was prospecting out of a cabin he built over on the south side of Wilkerson Pass. They came upon him when he was sleepin'. From his footprints outside, I'd say they marched him around barefoot before they killed and butchered him, like some of the rest. Tough bunch, those Espinosas', not an easy gang to track down."

"Or kill, once you done caught up with 'em," Tobin acknowledged with a nod of his head before turning his horse toward

119

Fort Garland. "Good day to you, Sheriff," Tobin said, as he started riding away, the bloodstained flour sack with the two severed heads of the Espinosas' dangling down alongside his saddle.

June 1863
Colorado City, El Paso County

Riding into town from the north, Sheriff Kelly stopped Marengo in front of the four rail corral on the west side of Xavier's blacksmith shop, where he saw his friend walking a horse. "Got a minute Xavier?" Kelly said without dismounting.

"Anytime Scott, what can I do you for?" the blacksmith said with a wide grin as he walked the horse toward the fence.

"Have you heard about Parke McClure?"

"Not since he picked up his horses a few weeks back. Why what happened?"

"I just rode in from Denver City," the Sheriff explained. "Seems when McClure and his two buddies left here, you were correct in thinking he was headed for the Santa Fe Trail. Word spreadin' around Denver is he made it to Missouri where he met with General Sterling Price, who gave him an officer's commission in the Confederate Army. McClure and his two companions were able to recruit sixteen other men with Southern sympathies to be officers and they was a headed back to Denver City to recruit more volunteer enlisted men. Appears they decided to take a shortcut across Indian Country and they were attacked by the Osage."

"What happened to them?" Xavier asked.

"Seems they were surrounded for a few hours and when their ammunition ran low they decided to make a break for it and as they was riding up an embankment McClure's saddle slipped down under his horse and he found himself alone fighting for his life. The other men left him, but 'fore long they was ambushed again and this time all of them but two were killed. Those two men rode back to Fort Arbuckle. The Osage later delivered the severed heads of the other seventeen Confederate officers to the Union Army."

"Why did they cut off their heads?" Xavier asked.

"Apparently, the Osage had been asked by the Union Army to stop the rebels from riding across their reservation once before, but when they did the officers said they didn't believe them and wouldn't pay the reward they had promised. I understand that when they handed over the severed heads of the seventeen Confederate officers, including the head of Parke McClure, they were paid what they were promised without any more questions. I just wanted you to know that you didn't need to keep looking over your shoulder."

"I appreciate you letting me know Sheriff, but that man, McClure, said he recognized me from being Mr. Bent's slave and when he and his friends picked up their horses that you impounded, he warned me that it was legal to shoot runaway slaves. I explained that Mr. Bent set me free, but he just smiled and said sometimes mistakes get made. I expects as long I live this close to Bent's Old Fort, I have's to be a lookin' over my shoulders alls the time. Leastwise till this here war's over. But I appreciates you letting me know about Parke McClure, sounds like he done lost his head over this slavery business."

"Reckon so," Kelly said with a smile, "see you later."

As Kelly rode through town he spotted a familiar looking roan horse tied to the hitching post in front of Lucy Maggard's Boarding House, and saw a familiar looking man sitting under the covered front porch in a rocking chair next to Lucy.

It had started to rain slightly as the Sheriff dismounted and tied Marengo alongside the roan, loosened her cinch, then started up the front steps of the porch as the man stood up to greet him.

Lucy spoke first, "You remember Mr. Stetson here, don't you Scott?"

Mr. Stetson spoke next, extending his right hand, "Sheriff, nice to see you again. We met briefly once the back side of Pikes Peak near Cripple Creek, a few months back. You was out a trackin' that Espinosa Gang."

The two men shook hands, as the Sheriff replied, "I do remember meeting you, John isn't it?"

"Yes, John Batterson Stetson, at your service. I'm from New Jersey, a hatter by trade. Came out to explore the American West here, after the doctor diagnosed me with tuberculosis and gave me only a short time to live."

"Looks like the fresh mountain air and sunshine agrees with you Mr. Stetson," Lucy replied with a smile, holding her hand out from under the tin roof and noticing how the rain was picking up a little.

"Never felt better in my life," the hat maker replied. "I'm headed back to Philadelphia to reopen my hat makin' business, but first I wanted to deliver this one to you, Mr. Kelly."

The hat maker pulled a beautiful light colored grey cowboy hat from a large cardboard box and handed it to Sheriff Kelly.

"You remembered," Sheriff Kelly replied, as he accepted the hat and admired its craftsmanship. "Size 7 ¼," he said, reading the tag on the inside of the hatband.

"Remembered our conversation well, and followed your advice. I decided hard rock gold mining and prospecting was much harder than one might imagine, and so I started talking to the prospectors, like you suggested, asking 'em about the kinda hat they wanted and couldn't find anywhere out West here. They told me they wanted a durable, lightweight, all-weather, fur-felt hat with a wide brim that would keep the sun off their faces in the summer and the rain from running down their backs in the spring. I didn't realize you folks got this much rain out here."

"I've been here five years now," Lucy replied, looking out into the pools of rainwater starting to form in the mud of Colorado Avenue, "and every Spring we have our Monsoon Season, then after a few weeks of torrential downpours, about the time you wish it would stop, it dries up for the next several months. Then you find yourself praying it would rain again."

Listening to the rhythm of the rain beating hard against the tin roof overhead, Kelly noticed the inside of the hatband was engraved and read it aloud, "Custom made for R. Scott Kelly with deep appreciation, John B. Stetson, Silver Belly. What's Silver Belly mean?"

"That's what I named this here particular color of cowboy hat, in trying to match the silver color of the underside of your beautiful grey mare there, Marengo. You named her after Napoleon's famous war horse, didn't you?"

"I did. You're well-read Mr. Stetson," Kelly acknowledged.

"Well, Marengo was a very famous war horse, a grey Arabian imported from Egypt to France in 1799 as a six-year old and he was always known to be the most steady, reliable and courageous mount on any battlefield. Wounded eight times in battle, yet always carried the Emperor valiantly into battle, up until the Battle of Waterloo in 1815, where Napoleon was defeated and Marengo was captured on the battlefield, one of the few survivors. It has been said Napoleon Bonaparte tried to replicate Marengo's dark grey color with his uniform overcoat. That's what I've tried to do here in replicating her color here with the Silver Belly, which I made a lighter color grey, like your Marengo's underbelly there," Mr. Stetson replied nodding back toward Marengo tied to the hitching post a few feet away.

"Beautiful hat, how much I owe you?" Sheriff Kelly asked, as he removed his old hat and placed it on the cardboard hat box Mr. Stetson had given him. He tried on his new hat for size.

"Looks like it fits like a glove. How's five dollars sound to you?" Mr. Stetson inquired.

"Sounds like a bargain to me," Sheriff Kelly replied as he reached into his vest pocket and retrieved a five-dollar gold coin which he flipped in the air toward the hat maker.

Mr. Stetson effortlessly caught it, then examined the five dollar gold coin before saying, "An 1861 Clark Gruber! This will make a fine memento of my adventure out West here. Thank you Sheriff, for your sound advice and to you madam," turning to Lucy with a tip of the brim of his stylish cowboy hat, "for your warm hospitality."

"Sure you don't want to spend the night?" Lucy offered, holding her hand out palm up again from the cover of the front porch to see how the rain was still coming down.

"No thank you ma'am," Mr. Stetson replied. "I want to try to catch the train in Julesburg a few days from now. Might you know anywhere I could stay the night between here and Denver City?"

"Few miles north of here, before you cross over the Arkansas-Platte Divide, if you follow Dirty Woman's Creek, you'll find Mrs. Tom Salem. She runs a stagecoach stop there at Dirty Woman's Ranch and she takes in overnight boarders, least those that don't mind sleeping in the same house with the chickens and pigs."

Noticing the peculiar look on Mr. Stetson's face, Sheriff Kelly explained, "Folks there abouts lose a lot of chickens and pigs at night, if they're left out on their own. There are a lot of foxes or coyotes up that way, but some folks say the local Indians kinda look at the settlers' stray chickens and pigs as a gift or maybe intended as an offering of sorts, like paying rent for the white men settling in on their ancestral homelands."

"Well, pigs or no pigs, a roof over one's head could sure beat sleeping out in the rain," Mr. Stetson replied. Looks like it might be letting up a touch, so best I'd be going."

"Please give my best to Mrs. Salem, if'n you see her," Lucy said.

Stepping out into the rain, Mr. Stetson untied his horse's reins from the hitching post in front of Lucy's covered front porch, put his foot in the stirrup and climbed up into the rain soaked saddle of his roan gelding. Turning his horse, Mr. Stetson tipped his cowboy hat one last time toward the porch, then trotted off on the mud soaked Colorado Avenue toward Denver City.

Sheriff Kelly sat down in the rocking chair next to Lucy. They watched the rain for a few minutes, as it began to taper off into a drizzle. Turning to their right, they noticed Charlie Stone riding an older grey mare east down Colorado Avenue, from the direction of Ute Pass. Charlie pulled up on the horse's reins, stopping abruptly in front of Lucy's boarding house.

"Afternoon Sheriff, Ma'am," Charlie Stone said respectfully.

"Afternoon to you Charlie, you interested in some lemonade?" Lucy offered.

"Mighty nice of you ma'am, but I'm fine," Charlie replied.

"How's Judge Stone and your mother been Charlie?" Lucy inquired.

"Fine! Everybody's fine, just overly busy getting ready for my cousin to make her grand appearance," Charlie replied expressing a little show of frustration.

"Lizzy'll be here soon then?" Lucy inquired further.

"Next stage, ma-am," Charlie replied politely, "leastwise that's what everyone keeps saying."

"You noticed any activity lately Charlie?" Sheriff Kelly asked.

"Charlie your deputy now Sheriff?" Lucy inquired playfully.

"As good as!" Sheriff Kelly replied.

Charlie puffed up his chest with pride, "Actually Sheriff, I did see some rough lookin' men up north a ways, looked to be building a small fort up at the head-waters of Kiowa Creek. Mentioned it to Pa but all anybody's talking about is making the ranch house ready for Lizzy."

"Did you recognize any of 'em?" Sheriff Kelly asked.

"No sir, can't say as I did…one of them has long red hair, and one of the others looks like somebody branded his cheek with a letter D!"

Lucy noticed Sheriff Kelly raise an eyebrow at this piece of information before responding, "Well, if you see anything of them 'round here, you let me know about 'em, hear?"

"Yes sir, I will," Charlie replied, then added with a smile, "nice hat!"

"Thank you, just bought it."

"What ya going do with that ole one of yours?" Charlie asked, nodding to Kelly's worn cowboy hat sitting on top of the cardboard box.

"Don't know, guess a fella can only wear one hat at a time," Sheriff Kelly replied with a grin.

"Can I have it?" Charlie asked earnestly, adding, "Please."

Sheriff Kelly picked up his old hat then tossed it to Charlie, still sitting aside his old horse. Charlie caught the Sheriff's old worn cowboy hat in mid-air and placed it proudly on his head. Lucy and Kelly watched as the hat drooped down over Charlie's ears.

"Looks like you might still need to grow some," Kelly said with a smile.

"Charlie, if you was to ride down to Ben Cromwell's newspaper office there," Lucy offered nodding up Colorado Avenue, "and ask him politely for an old copy from *The Colorado City Journal*, you could stuff some of the newspaper into your hatband for now, until you grow into it in a few years."

"I'll do that ma'am, thanks Sheriff!" Charlie acknowledged as he trotted his pony down Colorado Avenue, tipping his new cowboy hat to everyone he saw on both sides of the street.

Looking past Charlie, a few blocks further east, closer toward the heart of the town, Lucy and Kelly saw the rain had finally stopped and noticed five mounted riders coming toward them, one halting about a block and a half to the east.

"Looks like the cavalry has arrived," Lucy committed.

"One officer and four enlisted men," Sheriff Kelly acknowledged.

"Now, how can you tell that from this distance?" Lucy inquired.

"Officers always stop and tie their horses up across the street from the nearest saloon, then walk across the street to quench their thirst. Enlisted men always water and tend to their horses first, and then they visit the saloon."

As four black cavalrymen rode past, Kelly nodded his head at the sergeant, who saluted by touching two fingers to his hatband, then the four mounted soldiers turned north up 28th Street headed toward Xavier Bent's blacksmith shop.

"Buffalo Soldiers, good men I hear to have around you in a fight," Sheriff Kelly acknowledged, as they disappeared around the corner of the Meyers Mercantile building and out of sight.

"Scott," Lucy began, "can I ask you something?"

"Certainly," Kelly replied.

"When Charlie mentioned one of the men building the fort looked like he'd been branded on the cheek with a letter D, I saw you grimace. Does that D mean something to you?"

Kelly removed his new hat and draped it over his knee, combed his thick blonde hair back with his fingers then replied. "Back during the Mexican-American War, there was a group of Irishmen, not like me, they were fresh off the boat…well, about 175 of those men deserted the U.S. Army and joined up with the Mexicans after they was promised land, money and commissions. They were led by a Jon Riley and called themselves the 'San Patricios', meaning the Saint Patrick's Battalion. Most of them felt that as Irish Catholics they likely had more in common with the Mexicans, most of whom were also Catholics. Many of those soldiers were either killed or captured at the Battle of Cerro Gordo; I was there, at the end, when they ran out of ammunition. Fighting was hand-to-hand."

Kelly was quiet for a moment of reflection, and then continued, "Our Lieutenant, fella from down South named Beauregard, suggested that if we was to take this high ground, called Atalaya Hill, the Mexican's position could be turned. Captain Robert E. Lee was ordered to lead our reconnaissance efforts and later he led the attack. The San Patricios fought valiantly, but when the Mexican officers didn't resupply them with ammunition, or even water, those Irishmen were abandoned on the field of battle to fight against their former soldiers and officers. The battle lasted most of the afternoon, before those that survived finally surrendered, and then afterwards they was court-martialed. Jon Riley and the other leaders were shot dead by a firing squad, another fifty were hanged, but there was a few that General Winfield Scott allowed to live…but they were branded on the cheek with a "D" for deserter. I'll ride over tomorrow with Dan Gassenger to have a look. Don't want Judge Stone's niece being greeted by any unwelcomed ruffians."

Sheriff Kelly and Lucy both stood up from the rocking chairs at the same time. Lucy gathered her long dress and petticoat up in her arms and stepped out into mud six inches deep on Colorado Avenue.

"I have to walk over to invite Mr. Bott for dinner this evening. You'll join us won't you Scott?" Lucy asked as she searched for the best route across the wide mud strewn street. "We're having fried chicken, mashed potatoes and gravy."

"I'd be delighted to join you for dinner this evening and it will be nice to catch up on things with Anthony over dinner, thank you," Sheriff Kelly replied as he watched Lucy jump over one mud puddle to the next before slipping and falling on her rear.

Kelly raced into the street to rescue Lucy and help her up out of the mud. Just as he reached where Lucy was struggling to stand, he too slipped on the slick mud and fell into the muddy water, landing on his butt with a splash next to Lucy. At first she was furious, seeing her mud covered dress. She looked down to see the mud had even poured in over the tops of her button-hole boots. Before either could say a word, the two Robbins boys, George and Franklin raced by on their captured paint pony, splashing more mud over both Lucy and the Sheriff.

"Sorry Ms. Maggard, Sheriff Kelly," George shouted, as he ran past the couple sitting in the middle of Colorado Avenue.

Lucy flicked mud from her fingertips playfully at Kelly, as the two of them began to laugh at one another covered with thick mud. They watched as the Robbins boys turned south down 27th Street and out of sight. George was trying in vain to control his pony with one hand, while trying to hold onto his younger brother riding double behind him, both holding on for dear life.

"Well," the Sheriff said with a laugh, "at least we're not riding a runaway Indian pony."

"Come on Scott," Lucy said, "help me up and if you don't mind inviting Mr. Bott to join us for dinner, I'll head back to my house to start heating water for a couple baths."

"Sounds inviting," the Sheriff replied.

"Shall I heat water for two baths or just one?" Lucy asked with a mischievous smile.

Next Day - June 1863
Stagecoach Road, Northeastern El Paso County

Riding east out of Colorado City, Sheriff Kelly and Deputy Gassenger spotted the Leavenworth Pikes Peak Express stagecoach on the road a half mile up ahead. "Might as well wait for 'em here," Sheriff Kelly said.

Deputy Gassenger agreed, "Horses certainly could use a rest."

"I had dinner at Lucy's last night with Anthony Bott," the Sheriff commented to his deputy.

"Mr. Bott's a good man," Deputy Gassenger commented.

"I'd agree," the Sheriff said, nodding his head as the two men watched the progress being made by the stage. "He told me that Uncle Dick Wooten had set up a toll road over by the Soda Springs and was starting to charge everyone who wanted to travel up the Ute Pass to reach the gold fields."

"Can't image that went over very well with the miners," Gassenger said.

"No it didn't, since the other two roads out'a Denver City are already toll roads. The Ute Pass is the only free access to the gold fields and some of those Irish miners took a dim view on paying another man to pursue their dreams of striking it rich. Apparently they threatened to tar and feather Uncle Dick, then made him a cash offer which they said he couldn't refuse. After some negotiations Uncle Dick accepted their final offer and rode off toward the New Mexico Territory. They tore down Uncle Dick's toll booth and hauled the cut lumber into Colorado City, where they built a new outhouse behind Laura Belle's for the Ladies of the Evening."

"Well, I'll bet the Spoiled Doves were very appreciative to have a new latrine at least," Gassenger said with a smile.

"Yes," Sheriff Kelly replied with a smile, "from the way Anthony explained it, the ladies were most appreciative."

Meanwhile, inside the bouncing stagecoach, the only two passengers sat quietly across from one another. The elderly thin man, with the gold wire rimmed glasses, was holding a soiled handkerchief to his nose while trying to read the title on the book being read by the young woman wearing a satin purple dress and matching bonnet, white pearl necklace, earrings and a shiny Oberlin Class ring on her finger.

The elderly man's curiosity finally got the best of him and he asked the young lady, "My dear Miss Hill, who is that you're reading so intently?"

"Charles Eliot Norton, sir. He's a Harvard Professor. He writes about archeology," the young lady replied, barely looking up from her book.

"Archeology? The so-called science of digging in the dirt?" the older man inquired, expressing some astonishment.

"Yes, sir," Lizzy Hill replied, not wanting to engage in senseless banter.

"What interest could a lovely young lady like you have in digging in the dirt?'

"I appreciate your compliment sir, but this lovely young lady intends to spend her life digging in the dirt searching for the bones of Mesozoic Era reptiles."

"Meso-mo-zo-tic?!" the venerable older man sputtered.

"Gott senge Sie," Lizzy says playfully.

"Young lady, why, that's blasphemy," the older man admonished.

"Isn't it just..." Lizzy said with a smile, as the stagecoach jerked forward suddenly in acceleration. Looking out the window the two passengers saw that four outlaws with bandanas pulled up over their faces were in hot pursuit behind their stagecoach.

"Oh dear," the venerable man uttered aloud, as he and Lizzy heard the first of several shots being fired from the outlaw gang. As the stagecoach began to slow, the two passengers crouched together on the floorboard.

"We don't want any trouble!" they heard the stagecoach driver shout, as the stage came to a sudden stop, being surrounded by the four mounted outlaws.

"Then you'll be throwing down your strong box and mail-pouch," Hank Way, the leader of the outlaw gang demanded.

Seeing the stagecoach come to an unexpected stop and watching as the driver tossed the strong box and mail pouch over the side of the stagecoach, Deputy Gassenger shouted to Sheriff Kelly, who had dismounted to allow Marengo to graze while looking in the other direction, toward Pikes Peak.

Gassenger pointed, and then said to the Sheriff, "Looks like they might be in trouble down there!"

"Let's ride," Sheriff Kelly shouted as he mounted Marengo and rode off at a gallop toward the stage.

Two of the outlaws trained their handguns on the stagecoach driver while the other two outlaws dismounted from their horses. Frank Riley knelt down and started prying open the strongbox while Hank Way jerked open the door on the stagecoach and peered inside.

"Well, well, hello there…" Hank Way said to Lizzy.

"Take whatever you want," the venerable man said nervously.

Hank Way looked Lizzy over menacingly then said with a grin, "Let me think about what it is I want from you, little girl…"

Lizzy looked him in the eye and said in defiance, "You CAN NOT take whatever it is you want FROM ME."

Hank Way grabbed both coach passengers, dragging them out from the stagecoach. The venerable man began to whimper uncontrollably, but Lizzy was aggressively fighting against his grip. Hank Way twisted her hand and attempted to shimmy her class ring from her finger.

Clenching her fists, Lizzy saw the bandana on Riley's face had dropped down below his chin revealing a letter D that had been branded on his cheek. She also recognized a "KGC" emblem, a gold crown with a red cross tilted outwards from its center, on Hank Way's lapel pin. "That's an interesting emblem," she said still struggling to keep her hand closed so he couldn't steal her new class ring. "Whatever does it mean?"

"Never you mind, lil' lady, now give me that ring or I'll cut your damned finger off," Hank Way threatened as he pulled out a long knife from the top of his cowboy boot.

Just then two shots rang out from the approaching lawmen. Hank Way and Frank Riley quickly abandoned their attempted robbery and mounted their horses before turning in the opposite direction of the lawmen and rode off forty or fifty yards. Hank Way was trying to look back to see how many lawmen they were facing. Only seeing the two lawmen, Hank Way turned his horse back and drew his revolver, firing a shot at Sheriff Kelly and Deputy Gassenger. Deputy Gassenger drew his Sharps carbine rifle from his saddle scabbard, jumped from his horse to the ground, and then ran to the stage where he climbed atop the stagecoach roof and fired a quick shot off toward the outlaws. Two of the other outlaws also drew their revolvers and started shooting toward the stage.

Sheriff Kelly shouted, "I'll draw their fire Dan, you stay with the stage."

The stagecoach driver and his two passengers dropped to the ground to hide beneath the stage as Deputy Gassenger reloaded and fired one more shot off quickly in the direction of the outlaws to get their attention, while Sheriff Kelly began to give chase. Hank Way fired one more shot in frustration, then turned to join the other three outlaws riding off in the opposite direction, toward the safety of the tall Ponderosa trees lining Stagecoach Road. After a short chase, Sheriff Kelly recognized this approach could be a good place for an ambush and turned back toward the stage to see if anyone was hurt.

"Everyone alright here?" Sheriff Kelly asked as he dismounted.

"No one's hit, just a little shaken up," Ven Tinsley, the stage-coach driver replied, as he hoisted the heavy strongbox back up to

Deputy Gassenger, who was still on the roof of the stage.

The elderly passenger pulled the dirty handkerchief from his pocket and began to wipe the sweat and dust from his wire rimmed glasses. "Sure glad you and your Deputy came along when you did or this ordeal might of ended with a different story Sheriff."

"I shouldn't have rested the horses back there a piece," the Sheriff replied. "Might have avoided this unpleasantness altogether. You alright, ma'am?"

"Miss," Lizzy corrected with a warm smile, "Miss Elizabeth Hill."

The Sheriff returned the smile, and then removed his hat while offering his hand. "You'd be Judge Stone's niece then?"

"I am," Lizzy replied as she shook the Sheriff's hand firmly.

"Dan will escort you all on into Colorado City," the Sheriff said, as he looked off toward the tall pine trees to the east where the four outlaws were last seen. "Does anyone know what time it is? The Cherry Creek Stage is due at Buzzard's Ranch at 2:30 and if they're headed that way I'd like another shot at catching 'em."

Lizzy opened her purse and flipped open a man's silver pocket watch. "It's a quarter past one, Sheriff."

"Good, I might have time then," the Sheriff replied as he climbed back up into the saddle, nodded at Deputy Gassenger, then tipped his hat toward Lizzy, "Glad you're alright Miss Lizzy. My compliments to your Uncle when you see him." Kelly turned Marengo to the east and galloped off across the prairie grasslands toward Buzzard's Ranch, the next closest stage stop.

Later, Same Day June - 1863
Colorado City, El Paso County

As Sheriff Kelly rode back into Colorado City he saw a familiar looking mule tied to the hitching post next to Dan Gassenger's horse resting in front of the El Paso House Hotel. George Smith was waiting on the front steps, talking excitedly to Deputy Gassenger.

"Any sign of them Sheriff?" Deputy Gassenger asked, as Sheriff Kelly pulled Marengo to a halt.

"No, they haven't been seen at Buzzard's Ranch today," the Sheriff replied. "Sylvester Buzzard converted his tack room into a saloon, been drawing a lot of excitement out at the Pineries since he opened up for business. He's taken to callin' it "Buzzard's Roost", where the men meet up to share information on the Cheyenne and Arapaho. Seems lately there's been a rough bunch of strangers hanging around, arrived about the same time a number of horses started disappearing from the ranches there abouts."

"Seems George also had some excitement out at his place this morning. Tell him George," Deputy Gassenger said to George Smith, who needed little encouragement.

"Well," George began excitedly, "I was fixin' me some bacon and eggs this mornin' when these four rough lookin' fellas walked in all unannounced and made me fix them breakfast while they ransacked my cabin. Stayed almost an hour, took everything I had to eat that they's hadn't already ate for their breakfast. Said I could go get myself more grub, but I heard them talking when they thoughts I wasn't listening. Seems they's been stealing horses and hidin' 'em in a cave during the day and lettin them outs at night to graze. Said when they gets enough of 'em penned up, they'll drive 'em on up to Camp Weld, and sells 'em to the cavalry. These horse thieves says they been building a fort around the opening to this cave to keep the horses in during the day when folks might be out lookin' for their missing horses."

"This fort that you say they're building, is it up near the headwaters of Kiowa Creek?" Sheriff Kelly asked.

"Tis," George replied, "I can lead you right to them if you like."

"We might just do that," the Sheriff said, turning his attention back to his deputy. "Dan, have you seen any of the Colorado Mounted Cavalrymen around town today?"

"Sure have," Dan replied, "I seen that the four horses those colored troops was a ridin' are still over in the corral at Xavier's and two other mounts are tied up in front of the Tappan Brothers Outfitters. I can find a fresh horse at Xavier's if you want me to ride out with you to Kiowa Creek."

"No," the Sheriff replied, looking at the sun starting to dip behind Pikes Peak in the west, "it'll be dark 'for we could get out there. Best you stay here in town, case there's trouble here. I'll see if any of those cavalry troopers are available to ride with me and George in the morning. I suspect if the Army's been buying stolen horses from this gang, they'll want to know about it."

The Sheriff and George Smith rode their mounts east down the main dirt street of Colorado Avenue two blocks, then stopped in front of Tappan Brothers mercantile just as the two cavalry officers and a black sergeant stepped outside with Lewis Tappan and M.S. Beach.

"Gentlemen," the Sheriff acknowledged, as he stepped down from his horse, draped the reins over the hitching post and joined the five men on the boardwalk on the north side of the street. "Seems those four fellas that tried to hold up the stage this afternoon might be stealing horses from some of our ranches to sell to you all up at Camp Weld," nodding toward Colonel Shoup and Major Tappan. "They paid George here an unfriendly visit earlier today and he thinks they'd be holed up at a fort they're buildin' near a cave up at the headwaters of Kiowa Creek. I'm fixin' on ridin' up there first thing in the morning with George to check things out."

"You ain't planning on going out there with just you and George are you?" M.S. Beach inquired.

"Prefer not to," Sheriff Kelly acknowledged, turning to the cavalry officer. "Colonel, you or any of your men available, seein how's they may be sellin' y'all stolen horses?"

"Me and Major Wynkoop here are due at Fort Garland day after tomorrow, for an inspection of the 9th and 10th Cavalry, but maybe we could loan you Sergeant Johnson here and three of his men from K Troop."

"Sergeant," Major Wynkoop replied, handing the sharply dressed Sergeant two boxes of ammunition they had just purchased from the Outfitters. "Mind splitting these up between you and your men? I'll be along shortly."

"Yes sir," the Sergeant said as he saluted, accepting the two boxes of ammunition and walked off toward the blacksmith shop. When the Sergeant was out of earshot, Major Wynkoop took the Sheriff aside from the other men to inquire privately, "You sure you don't mind riding with colored troops?"

"Hell, Ned," the Sheriff replied, "you been a lawman before you was in the military. You know how it is, when the bullets are flying and men are dying, you could care less what color the man next to you is. You just want to know if he'll stick with you and it helps if he can shoot."

"Oh, they'll stick with you alright and they can shoot," Major Wynkoop acknowledged, nodding toward the black Sergeant half a block away. "That sergeant there is Henry Johnson, one of the bravest men I've ever met, and he's probably the best shot with a

Sharp's Carbine in the whole damned army. Those three privates with him were attached to the 54th Massachusetts and all three were wounded at the Battle of Fort Wagner. Confederate General P.G.T. Beauregard reportedly buried the bodies of 800 Union soldiers in front of the Fort, all in one mass grave, including the bodies of Colonel Shaw and their other white officer. At least two of these Buffalo Soldiers would have been awarded the new Congressional Medal of Honor President Lincoln just authorized, if'n they had been white."

"Sounds like they'll do just fine," Sheriff Kelly replied. "We ride at first light."

Next Morning – Late June - 1863
Headwaters Kiowa Creek, Northeastern El Paso County

As the sun rose above the tall pine trees to the east, Sheriff Kelly, George Smith and the four Buffalo Soldiers approached the small log fort under construction at the entrance to a cave on horseback. The few men scattered around the fort slowly made their way inside. Sheriff Kelly, having ridden Marengo hard the day before, was riding a tall horse he had borrowed from M.S. Beach. The six riders stopped their horses about forty yards from the front of the fort and readied their firearms. The three privates were lined up to the left of their Sergeant, who was next to Sheriff Kelly, with George Smith mounted on his brown mule to the right of the Sheriff.

"You in the fort!" Sergeant Johnson commanded, "Lay down your arms and come outside. We'll be havin' a word with you…"

Before the Buffalo Soldier could finish his sentence, a hail of bullets were fired in their direction from over the top logs of the fort's four foot high walls. One of the outlaws' first bullets struck George Smith square in the chest. Hearing the sickening "thump" of lead hitting a body, Sheriff Kelly reached down to his right, trying to keep George Smith from falling from his mule, just as another bullet tore the heel off the Sheriff's right boot and another bullet severed his right stirrup from his saddle. Struggling to maintain his balance, Sheriff Kelly was unable to reach George Smith before he fell to the ground, dead. At the same moment, Sheriff Kelly felt the horse he was riding drop instantly out from under him. The Sheriff instinctively pulled his left boot free from the stirrup just as the horse fell to the ground, landing in the dirt with a thud.

The Sheriff rolled to his right, drew his Colt revolver, and looked up from the ground in time to see Sergeant Johnson motioning for two of his Buffalo Soldiers to make their way to the back of the fort, cutting off any escape the outlaws might have had, and then he watched the Sergeant level his Sharps carbine and heard the crack of his rifle shot. Sheriff Kelly was trying to aim his six-shot revolver at one of the men's heads, barely visible over the top of the logs, just as the Sergeant's bullet hit its mark. Sheriff Kelly saw a red mist appear behind the man's head, as he dropped out of sight behind the wall. Searching for another target, the Sheriff saw no other heads were visible and realized that the shooting from inside the fort had suddenly stopped.

"We give up," one of the men from inside the fort called out.

"Throw down your guns and come out with your hands high!" the Sergeant yelled in return.

The Sheriff managed to stand up, and then glanced down to see the horse he had been riding had been shot square between the eyes.

"Died instantly, must have struck him in the brain," Sergeant

Johnson replied, nodding to the dead horse. "Least he didn't suffer."

"Neither did he," Sheriff Kelly acknowledged, nodded toward the limp body of George Smith.

"Don't shoot!" the four outlaws exiting the fort pleaded, their hands held above their heads as the Sheriff and four cavalrymen approached the fort.

"Who's inside?" Sheriff Kelly demanded.

"Just Bill Waggle, but he won't be goin nowheres," one of the outlaws with longish red hair and freckled pale skin replied. Sheriff Kelly noticed the brass belt buckle on his gunbelt bore the emblem of the KGC.

"What's your name?" Sheriff Kelly demanded.

"They call me Hank Way," the man replied.

"All of you, slowly drop your gunbelts," Sheriff Kelly demanded, while keeping his Colt cocked and trained on the four men. After they complied, the Sheriff turned his attention to the man standing next to Hank Way. The man was wearing a scraggly dark beard, but Kelly had already taken note of the D branded into his check, "Who'd you be?"

"Names Frank Riley," the man replied, staring at the ground.

"Irish," Sheriff Kelly replied, then nodded at the D on the man's cheek and added, "See you been to Mexico."

The outlaw looked up at the lawman, rubbed his cheek, and then replied, "Never been to Mexico, yourself? Sheriff Kelly, is it?"

"Once, long time ago," Sheriff Kelly replied, as two of the Buffalo soldiers began to search and take custody of the outlaws. Sheriff Kelly sat down on a log and gently pulled off his boot, now without a heel, making sure he hadn't been shot.

"Looks like there's still a little luck of the Irish in you Sheriff,"

Frank Riley replied, watching as Sheriff Kelly rubbed his sore heel on his unbloodied foot.

"Looks like you fellas been rather busy since gettin' here haven't you? Sheriff Kelly replied, looking at the six horses being led out from the cave by the other two Buffalo Soldiers.

"If it's alright with you, Sheriff," Sergeant Johnson replied, we'll be taking these four men and these horses with us to Denver City, see what Major Chivington wants done with them. You might want to pick out one of these here horses to ride back to town."

"Sounds good by me, but first these fellas got two graves to dig, while I cut out and saddle one of those better mounts to replace that dead one over there on the ground."

"Mr. Smith have any kin folks here abouts?" Sergeant Johnson inquired, looking up from George's bloodstained body.

"None here that I'm aware of," Sheriff Kelly replied, as he pulled his cowboy boot back on. "Just a few friends."

End of June - 1863
Crystal Peak, Western El Paso County

"Hey! Help me out of this hole," Lizzy Hill shouted to her young, decidedly dirty Chinese male assistant, perched above her on the edge of the meticulously excavated rectangular shaped hole they had dug into the red ground.

After helping her out of the pit, he watched in amazement as Lizzy slapped her gloved hands together, creating a cloud of red dust to appear between them, and then pulled her hair back into a dusty ponytail. The young female archeologist was now the polar opposite of what she looked like just yesterday when she hired him at his father's laundry in Colorado City. When

142

she stopped in the buggy to pick him up early this morning, neither he, nor his father, Sam Wah, had ever seen a white woman wearing pants before, let alone one wearing red suspenders and a man's blue button down shirt, now covered in red dirt.

"Come on, don't just stand there," Lucy said as she knelt over the pile of wooden crates, pointing to the shipping address on the label, which read, "Smithsonian Institute, Washington, D.C." Grabbing the handle on one end of the wooden crate, she tried to reinforce her sense of urgency. "These have to be waiting on the front porch of the El Paso House in the morning when the Leavenworth Pikes Peak Express stagecoach arrives."

"Yes, Mizz Hill," her young Chinese assistant replied, having no notion at all of what a Smithsonian Institute was, but he did know that Washington D.C. was very far away and if he was going to get paid, he understood these wooden boxes needed to be waiting when that stagecoach arrived first thing tomorrow morning.

"You finish loading these last crates and put the tools into the back of the buggy," Lucy instructed, brushing the dirt off her pants. "I'm going up there, for a look," Lucy announced, pointing along the trail that lead up to the top of the nearby hill.

"Yes sir," the young man replied, then saluted. After Lizzy looked at him sternly, "er, ma'am," he added sheepishly with a bow, then corrected himself again, "er, Miss."

"Just have these boxes loaded up by the time I get back," Lizzy replied as she rolled her eyes and started up the steep hillside toward the tall Ponderosa pine trees where she could see the backside of Pikes Peak to the east and the snowcapped Sawatch Mountains far to the south.

As Lizzy climbed to the top of the hill, she slipped quietly into the canopy of the dense forest, her eyes were drawn to a nearby tree bent unnaturally at two ninety degree angles. She walked over and leaned against the bent trunk of the tree and rubbed her forehead, trying to figure out how and for what purpose this unusual tree had been shaped. Tracing the peeled bark pattern above the first bend with her fingers, she determined this deep cut in the bark could only have been made with human hands. Positioned on top of the horizontal portion of the trunk she noticed a small blue stone; Amazonite, she observed without disturbing the rock; assuming it might have been an offering stone. Then Lizzy heard what she thought was someone singing, and looked down from the mysterious tree to observe an Indian squaw standing in the meadow below, with her arms outstretched heavenly, facing Pikes Peak while singing. Lizzy waited for the woman to finish her song before approaching the first Indian she had ever seen up close.

"Hello?" Lizzy said as she approached the beautiful Indian woman, whom she guessed was perhaps fifteen to twenty years older than she was. "I hope I didn't interrupt your prayers."

"My dear one! Hello!" the kindly Indian woman replied, turning toward Lizzy to greet her with a warm smile.

"You have such a beautiful voice," Lizzy said. "My mother also has a beautiful voice."

Chipeta smiled. "Is your mother with you?"

"No," Lizzy replied, "we have not been together for some time. I was wondering if you might know why that large pine tree up there is bent so?"

"That's the Holy Woman's tree. It is a prayer tree and was shaped like that a long time ago by my people. It points the way for us to know where to go to visit the spirits of our ancestors."

Lizzy waited for the woman to continue, "My name is White Singing Bird. I am wife of Chief Ouray, you may call me Chipeta," she said, looking back down into the meadow below.

"I am Lizzy and my assistant and I are on our way back to Colorado City," then following Chipeta's gaze into the meadow below, asked "Do you look for something?"

"For some...one," Chipeta explains.

"Might I be able to help you?" Lizzy offered.

Chipeta smiled warmly at the young woman's generosity, "Yours is a kind offer, but no, this is a personal quest my husband and I are on, but for your kindness I say Towaoc, which is the Ute word for thank you."

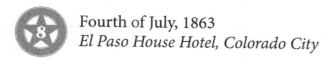

Fourth of July, 1863
El Paso House Hotel, Colorado City

As the second waltz came to an end, Lucy gracefully bowed to her favorite dance partner and said, "Thank you, Scott; you do so take my breath away."

"I don't know about that Lucy," Sheriff Kelly said with a smile. "I believe you could go all night and I'd still be struggling just trying to keep up with you."

Lucy leaned in to whisper in her partner's ear so as not to be overheard while squeezing his muscular forearm, "I don't believe you would ever have any trouble keeping up with me," she said softly, before adding, "Oh, how I do miss the barn dances we used to have out at Judge Stone's ranch, and the buggy rides back to town afterwards. Funny how those two gray horses of your's always seemed to get lost on the way home. You would have thought as many times as we rode out to Judge Stone's ranch together, they could have found their way back to town on their own."

"Well, horses can sometimes have a mind of their own," Kelly replied quietly, scanning the room to see if anyone was eavesdropping in on their personal conversation.

Lucy released her embrace and looked around the room at the happy setting, "Oh look Scott, here come Judge and Mrs. Stone now. Won't you join me in welcoming them?" Lucy asked as she led Sheriff Kelly by the arm over to greet Judge and Mrs. Stone. There were perhaps twenty or so other couples who had already gathered for the small town's annual Independence Day Dance. There were a few unmarried men at the dance in addition to Scott Kelly; however, Mrs. Lucy Maggard was the only unaccompanied woman to dance with that evening. Being attractive and an excellent dancer meant that Widow Lucy Maggard's dance card would be filled up all evening; except for the dances she set aside for the man she had her eye on, Scott Kelly.

"Good evening Judge Stone, Mrs. Stone," Lucy said warmly as she and Sheriff Kelly greeted the newly arrived couple, "I was just telling the Sheriff here how much I miss the old days when we used to all meet out at your ranch for those wonderful barn dances."

"Those made for some memorable nights, that's for sure," Judge Stone acknowledged with a laugh. "Good evening Lucy, Scott. Been meaning to thank you Sheriff for rescuing my niece on her way into town the other day. That Hank Way Gang sounds like a mighty rough bunch."

"Just glad Dan and I arrived when we did," Sheriff Kelly replied humbly.

"Why Judge Stone, where ever is your niece?" Lucy asked intently, peering over their shoulder into the open doorway. "I thought Lizzy was coming with you this evening?"

"She'll be along shortly," Judge Stone said with a slight smile, turning to his wife, "seems she and Charlie decided they needed to bring a second buggy, just in case us older folks got tired later and needed to leave a little early so we could get our rest."

Mrs. Stone laughed, "Guess that's another way of them saying, 'We're both old enough now to start staying out late on our own.'"

The two couples shared a laugh before Judge Stone became serious in wanting to speak to Sheriff Kelly, "Have you heard anything from Governor Evans in Denver City since you turned that Hank Way Gang over to the federal authorities there at Camp Weld?"

"No, not a word and that silence is what troubles me," the Sheriff replied quietly, scratching the back of his neck, "I am a might concerned we could see that outlaw bunch up this way again."

"Why?" Lucy inquired, "They are in the custody of U.S. Marshall Townsend now and certainly they will be in jail at Camp Weld or in the federal prison at Fort Leavenworth for some time Scott."

"Or conscripted..." Sheriff Kelly replied.

"Is that even an option?" Lucy asked, "After all the horses they stole and they killed poor George Smith."

"The longer this War Between the States goes on," Judge Stone answered, "the less particular either side is going to be about the character of the men they put in uniform."

"Can't image that if any of these men deserted the U.S. military in the past, they'd hesitate for a minute in deserting the Union army anytime in the near future," Sheriff Kelly replied, peering out the window into the darkness, as if looking for a ghost from the past.

"That man that Lizzy saw with the D branded on his cheek," Mrs. Stone inquired, "what's the story on him, Scott?"

"Said his name was Frank Riley," Sheriff Kelly replied, turning his head back from looking out the window before he continued, "I don't know if it's the same man, but there was a Francis Michael Riley who was one of the deserters from the U.S. Army during the Mexican American War. Many of the San Patricios were killed fighting against their former comrades, but Francis's brother, Jon Riley, was executed by firing squad on General Scott's orders down in Mexico. About half of the 150 of the Saint Patrick's Battalion that were taken prisoner were hung outside of the walls of the castle of Chapultepec in Mexico City, but over a dozen were given the option of being branded with a D on their cheek for deserter. I'm bettin this Frank Riley was one of 'em."

"Come on, Scott," Lucy said, tugging on Kelly's elbow, "nothing you two gentlemen can do about any of that unpleasantness now. Let's enjoy another dance and I'll keep an eye out for Lizzy so I can properly introduce the two of you when she arrives."

As the next dance came to an end, the three-person band took a break and Lucy glanced toward the hotel's double doorway, "There's Lizzy and Charlie now. Come on Scott, let me introduce you to Lizzy."

As Sheriff Kelly turned toward the doorway it seemed to him as if the entire ballroom had suddenly lit up, radiated by the beauty of the young woman being escorted inside by her younger cousin, Charlie.

"Welcome Lizzy," Lucy said, giving the younger woman a warm embrace. "I'm so glad you were able to join us this evening," then she turned toward Charlie, wearing a new blue suit, blue tie and sporting a fresh close-cropped haircut instead of his hand-me-down cowboy hat that Kelly had given him. Lucy said playfully, "but I don't believe I have met this gentleman before."

"Aw, Ms. Maggard," Charlie said, turning a little red in the face, "you know'd it t'was me all along. Mamma made me take a bath in the stock tank and Lizzy done shampooed my hair with some kinda rose petal stuff and cut my hair down to where there's almost nothing left to comb. I'm a gonna have'ta stuff more newspaper in my hatband just to keep my hat on my head."

Everyone laughed along with Charlie, then Lucy released Sheriff Kelly's arm and turned to Lizzy, "Lizzy Hill, may I introduce you to Scott Kelly, our Sheriff? Scott Kelly it's my pleasure to introduce you to Miss Lizzy Hill, a most recent graduate of Oberlin College."

Stunned by her beauty, Kelly found himself somewhat speechless and uncertain how to respond. Lizzy, sensing his uncertainty, held her hand out just a few inches below his chin, making it easy for him to follow her lead by grasping it, then kissing the back of the softest hand he believed he had ever held.

"Miss Hill and I met briefly a few days ago out on Stagecoach Road," Kelly replied, finding himself reluctant to release her warm hand from the grip of his rough hand.

Lizzy looked up into Kelly's eyes with a smile that he felt would melt his heart. "I was uncertain if you would recognize me from our first encounter. After the ten-day road trip from Independence, Missouri, in the back of that dusty stagecoach, and with the shock of being held up at gun point, I must have looked a fright."

"I've never seen anyone as beautiful as you were then or are right now," Kelly replied honestly, as Lucy interjected with a question.

Shifting her attention from Scott to Lizzy, Lucy asked, "I was just trying to remember how old you were the last time I saw you in Kansas City. You were accompanying your father while he was

151

attending a medical conference."

"That would have been in the spring of '56, I wasn't much older than Charlie is now, and I just turned 23 this year," Lizzy replied. "I so enjoyed dinner that evening with you and your husband. I was so sorry to hear about his passing."

"Missouri trash," Lucy uttered under her breath with distain, before commenting, "this war over succession has cost so many lives and, sadly, there's no end in sight. Please accept my condolences on the passing of your father, I know the two of you were particularly close."

"That we were," Lizzy said with a heavy sigh. "Although he was only my stepfather, he loved me like I was his natural-born daughter. I never met my real father, as he went to sea when I was only eighteen months old and never returned. When mother became a widow for a second time…well, I'm afraid mother has not been the same since. I believe Papa's influence over her was apparently much stronger than any of us ever realized."

Trying to lighten the mood, Sheriff Kelly interjected, motioning toward a long table toward the back of the room, "Would either of you ladies care for a glass of punch?"

"That sounds lovely," both ladies replied, but before they reached the table where the punch bowl was located the three-man string band struck up the next song.

"Oh," Lizzy said excitedly, "The Tennessee Waltz, it's one of my favorites!"

"Then Scott," Lucy said encouragingly, "you must ask Miss Hill for her first dance of the evening."

"I'd be honored. Miss Hill?" Kelly asked, extending his elbow toward the beautiful young lady at his side.

"That would be wonderful!" Lizzy replied with delight, taking the Sheriff's extended arm and bowing politely to her partner.

As Lizzy and Kelly joined the other couples twirling around the hardwood dance floor, Lizzy began singing the words to the Tennessee Waltz, "I was dancing with my darling to the Tennessee Waltz, when an old friend I happened to see..."

Lucy stood by the punch bowl next to Charlie and finished the words to the song in her head, "...I introduced her to my loved one and while they were dancing my friend stole my sweetheart from me." Lucy stood at the punchbowl watching Lizzy enjoying the dance with the Sheriff, then felt a sudden stab of jealousy as she watched the couple share a laugh. As the band played on, Lucy finished the rest of the words to the song silently in her mind, "I remember the night and the Tennessee Waltz, now I know just how much I have lost; yes I lost my little darling the night they were playing the beautiful Tennessee Waltz."

"Please excuse me, Ms. Maggard," Charlie said, spotting a pretty blonde girl about his age standing alone across the dance floor as the next tune began.

Lucy pushed Charlie's shoulder encouragingly, "Go, and enjoy yourself, Charlie, while you're young." Lucy watched him make his way cautiously across the dance floor to ask the pretty girl with the blonde hair to dance, realizing that Lizzy was ten years older than Charlie and Scott was twelve years older than Lizzy. While she poured herself a glass of punch, Lucy finished the math in her head. I am twelve years older than Scott, which makes me easily old enough to be Charlie's grandmother.

As Lucy sipped her punch, she smiled politely watching Scott and Lizzy finish the dance and then slipped off to the opposite side of the dancefloor, where they could talk without being interrupted. Lucy thought to herself, "Well, that's an interesting development." Then the Widow Maggard downed the glass of bland punch, finding herself alone and wishing George Smith was still with them, for he was always one who could be counted on to spike the punch.

After a few more dances together, Lizzy and Kelly found their way outside to catch some fresh air and strolled casually south across the lush green grass away from the lights of the El Paso House Hotel, into the moonlight. As they neared the bubbling waters of Fountain Creek they could hear the gentle flow of the water over the smooth river rocks that lined the crystal clear creek, and enjoyed the smell of the fragrant wildflowers that lined its banks.

"What did you study back east, Miss Hill?" Kelly asked Lizzy, as they paused under a cottonwood tree.

"Archeology," Lizzy replied proudly, "I've started a dig up on Crystal Peak."

"You're in Ute country up there," Kelly said, turning his head west toward the entrance of Ute Pass. "But you should be safe thereabouts. The Ute are a peaceful people."

"That's what my uncle tells me. I've only met one Native person, named Chipeta. She seemed very nice, and I've seen their bent trees and tipis. I bet you've met all kinds of Indians, not to mention a few cattle rustlers from what I hear."

"Hasn't been much law out here in the West," Kelly acknowledged, finding himself being drawn into the gaze of her beautiful brown eyes. "I've met my share of characters all right, Indians and outlaws alike. With the Wars, from Indian or Civil…well, there are a lot of characters to meet out here of all kinds; good and bad. I met Chipeta's husband, Chief Ouray a couple times. He struck me as a decent man. We made a trade the first time we met—my horse for his knife."

"Must have been a nice knife," Lizzy replied, then added with a laugh, "or an old horse."

"I think it was pretty old, the knife that is, not the horse," Kelly replied with a chuckle.

"Well, I have a gift for you...something to say 'thank you'. It's the least I could do, I guess it's like a trade – my life, for ...this," Lizzy said as she retrieved a man's pocket watch from her small purse and placed it into Kelly's hand. She wrapped the silver chain carefully around Kelly's wrist and then held the watch up for him to see in the moonlight.

"Why Miss Lizzy, it's beautiful, but I don't see how I can accept such a precious gift."

"It was my stepfather's. I couldn't help notice how you needed a watch a couple days ago and I wanted to give you something special. Somehow I feel he would be proud knowing you are carrying his watch, and I know he would have done something to thank you for saving his little girl from certain harm. Thank you Sheriff Kelly," Lizzy concluded as she closed Kelly's hand around the pocket watch, leaned against him on her tiptoes and kissed him softly on the cheek.

"Thank you, ma'am, I will treasure it and this moment always, but please call me Scott."

"Very well Scott, but only if you call me Lizzy," she said with a twinkle in her eye.

Resisting the urge to take her in his arms and give her a proper kiss, ever the gentleman Sheriff Kelly replied, "I suppose we best make our way back inside," and reluctantly led the way back to the hotel.

When they returned to the dance, Lucy was nowhere to be seen.

Two Weeks Later
Crystal Peak, Thirty Miles West of Colorado City

Lizzy and Kelly sat next to one another, under the shade of two tall pine trees, enjoying the majestic view of Pikes Peak from the west.

"It looks like such a different mountain from this side," Lucy replied.

"We are quite a bit higher up here," Kelly commented, noticing the markings of a bear claw on the trunk of one of the nearby Ponderosa trees.

"So sweet of you to come visit me, Sheriff."

"Well, there's been news of a 'wild woman' up here, had to check it out," Kelly replied playfully, as he removed his hat and placed it on the soft grass to his side.

Lizzy reciprocated with a gleaming smile, "Well! You've found me," Lizzy replied, brushing the dirt off the knees of her jeans, "covered in a lot of dirt."

"You are an original, Miss Lizzy Hill," Kelly replied with a wide grin.

"And you are everything I'd ever hoped to find in a brave sheriff here in the 'Wild West,'" Lizzy responded playfully, teasing his blonde hair and scooting closer to him across the tall green grass, then leaned up against him.

Kelly wrapped his arm around Lizzy's shoulder, pulling her closer to his side. Cupping her chin with his left hand he raised her mouth toward his, before saying softly, "I've been wanting to do this ever since the night of our first dance, but I have been struggling in trying to find the right words..."

Lizzy pressed her index finger softly against Kelly's lips, "Shhh, no need for words Scott." Then she kissed him passionately with an open mouth, and pulled his lean body down next to her, on the cool green grass in the shade of the tall pine trees.

Three Weeks Later
First Methodist Church, Colorado City

"That was a powerful sermon Reverend Howbert," Lizzy commented as she walked out of the church and paused on the front steps to shake hands with the minister.

"Hard to go wrong quoting John Wesley when speaking out against the slave trade," Reverend Howbert replied. He repeated from memory the opening line of his sermon read from one of Wesley's monologues, "Liberty is the right of every human creature."

Lucy finished the quote from memory, "as soon as he breathes the vital air."

The Reverend smiled, inhaled deeply a chest full of clear mountain air and exhaled slowly as he released Lizzy's hand, "You are a breath of fresh air, my child. Go with God and enjoy the rest of your Sunday, Miss Hill."

Lizzy smiled and nodded toward the Reverend as she opened her parasol and walked gracefully down the front steps of the church onto Colorado Avenue. She spotted Sheriff Kelly across the street, waiting under the shade of a tall silver oak tree with a matching pair of beautiful gray horses hitched to a buggy. She smiled, lifted the hem of her dress so it would not drag in the dirt as she crossed the unpaved street toward the awaiting buggy.

"Good morning Miss Lizzy," Sheriff Kelly said as he removed his hat, "I wondered if I might have the pleasure of offering you a buggy ride back to Judge Stone's ranch."

"Why, I would like nothing better, Sheriff Kelly, especially if you were to take the long way home," Lizzy replied with a wide smile. "Just let me inform my aunt or uncle inside I will be going with you and will be meeting them later at home." Lizzy turned around to see her aunt and uncle standing on the front steps of the church shaking hands with Reverend Howbert. She ran over and spoke to them for a minute. They waved as Lizzy crossed the street and watched as the Sheriff helped Lizzy into the buggy.

"Scott," Lizzy asked as he climbed into the carriage next to her, "have you seen the new stained glass window Reverend Howbert received last week?"

"No, but I hear it is beautiful," Sheriff Kelly replied as he steered the team of gray horses eastward down Colorado Avenue.

"He's going to have it installed this week. I heard it was you who handed Reverend Howbert the money to purchase that window. But no one else even knows who that anonymous person is who paid for it."

"Well, that's not entirely true," the Sheriff replied as he looked up and tipped his hat to the young lady looking down from the second story window of Laura Belle's brothel. "The woman or man who paid for the stained glass window certainly knows."

"Well," Lizzy replied looking up in time to see a darker complected woman blow smoke from a cigarette out the open window before stepping back into the dark interior of the room, "whoever it was they certainly have good taste. When I was leaving the church I stopped to look at the window on display toward the back of the church and I noticed that stained glass window was handcrafted by Louis Comfort Tiffany and shipped all the way here from Tiffany and Company, in New York City. The shipping and handling costs alone must have cost a small fortune."

Turning the carriage south onto 26th Street from Colorado Avenue, Sheriff Kelly guided the two gray mares carefully into Fountain Creek, stopping long enough to allow the pair of horses to drink their fill from the cool mountain stream. Lizzy sat close to Sheriff Kelly, leaning against his body as they enjoyed the cool shade cast by the tall cottonwood trees.

"Have you always wanted to be a Sheriff?" Lizzy asked casually.

"No, I came out here to use my skills at being a stonemason and a master carpenter," Kelly replied, "just wasn't anyone else around these parts to take on the job of Sheriff."

"My uncle told me you are a very skilled carpenter, but I didn't know you were also a stonemason."

"Other than being a teamster, I mostly did work as a stonemason to make my living," Kelly replied, enjoying their conversation. Naturally uncomfortable talking about himself, the Sheriff continued somewhat reluctantly, "I built the first lime kiln here in the Pikes Peak Region and fired the first bricks right over there," Sheriff Kelly said, pointing his buggy whip toward the white colored sandstone bluffs a mile up Bear Creek and off to the west.

"Will you run for reelection when your term in office is up?"

"No, I'm expecting someone will have come along by then, wanting to run for Sheriff."

"It is an important office, especially out here in the West," Lizzy acknowledged. "Where did the term Sheriff come from anyway?"

"It's an English term and comes from combining two English words; shire, which is a group of ten or so townships in England and the word reeve, which was the man appointed by the king to enforce the laws and collect taxes in that part of the kingdom. Whenever a crime was committed the shire reeve would assemble a posse of citizens to track down and apprehend whoever was

159

responsible. When the pilgrims came here from England they brought that office with them and as Americans came out west, the office of sheriff emerged as the region's top law enforcement official."

Lizzy noticed a tall young man about fifty yards upstream hopping gracefully from one rock to the next, crossing Fountain Creek northwards toward the small cluster of buildings that made up Colorado City. Lizzy watched as the young man, who appeared to be about her age, paused midstream atop a rock to wave at her and Sheriff Kelly riding the opposite direction in the buggy.

"Who is that young man?" Lizzy asked Kelly, as they waved their hands in return and Kelly touched the rump of both horses gently with his whip.

"That's Marcus Foster," Kelly replied, "He's a carpenter, been staying at the El Paso House Hotel while working with me on the Stockbridge building."

Lizzy watched the young man as he continued to cross the narrow stream by jumping from the top of one round rock to the next before safely reaching the other side.

It was late summer and the grass was belly deep to the horses in places along the narrow two lane trail winding southward toward the sprawling Stone Ranch at the foot of Cheyenne Mountain. Kelly held the horses' reins in one hand and draped the buggy whip casually over the left side of the carriage, allowing the tip of the long whip to brush gently across the top of the tall grama grass. Lizzy adjusted her parasol above her head and placed her left hand on top of Kelly's right thigh. Her touch thrilled him in ways he had never felt before. He turned the buggy gently up the Stone's long driveway leading toward their ranch house and out buildings, regretting this Sunday's afternoon ride would too soon come to an end.

Stopping his team of gray horses in front of Stone Ranch house, Sheriff Kelly stepped down from the buggy and walked around to the front of the team of horses to tether them to a wooden hitching post under the shade of an elm tree. After seeing to the horses, Kelly walked around to the side of the carriage and extended his arms upward as Lizzy stood up. She leaned toward him, allowing him to take her by her narrow waist and lift her effortlessly from the horse drawn carriage and place her gently on the ground.

Lizzy twirled her parasol casually over her shoulder as she turned and slowly walked toward the Stone's large red barn. Pausing for a moment, before the open wooden barn doors, she said with an innocent grin, "Charlie went camping with Mr. Robbins and his boys, up in Eleven Mile Canyon, and my aunt and uncle were stopping by Meyers Mercantile after church. Looks like we might be alone for a little while," she said with a smile before starting inside the barn, and then nodded her head telling the handsome lawman it was okay to follow her inside.

Four Months Later
Christmas 1863, Judge Stone's Residence, Colorado City

Lizzy and Kelly sat next to one another at the dinner table, holding hands beneath the white table cloth. Charlie was sitting across from them, with Mrs. Stone at one end of the table closest to the kitchen. Judge Stone was sitting at the head of the long table, to their right, all enjoying a warm conversation over a delicious Christmas dinner. The home had been decorated gaily for the Christmas Season and the engaging conversation at the dinner table had been lively and varied.

"So glad you could join us this evening, Scott," Mrs. Stone said, as she and Lizzy stood to clear the dinner dishes and fetch dessert.

"No place would I rather be, Mrs. Stone, thank you again for inviting me," Kelly replied sincerely, smiling at Lizzy as she brushed her leg purposely against his as she leaned against him to remove the china dinner plate.

Mrs. Stone added, "I ground fresh coffee and Lizzy made us a delicious pecan pie for dessert."

"Sounds wonderful," Kelly replied earnestly.

"And I helped papa churn vanilla ice cream to put on top of Lizzy's pecan pie," Charlie added with a sense of pride, then leaned forward resting his elbows on the table, "Do the coin trick again Sheriff!"

"Charlie Everhart Stone!" Mrs. Stone admonished, "You take your elbows off the table, we're not finished with dinner yet."

"Yes mother," Charlie said, somewhat embarrassed he had been scolded in front of the man he looked up to more than any-one, outside of his father, of course.

After Mrs. Stone and Lizzy had left for the kitchen, Kelly, who was always amused by Charlie's sense of wonder and excitement in watching the only magic trick the Sheriff knew, said, "Okay Charlie, but just this one time before the ladies return with the dessert."

Kelly smiled at Judge Stone as he pulled the silver half dollar from his right vest pocket. Kelly stood the coin on edge, balanc-ing it upright on the table while placing his left index finger on top of the coin and then extended his right index finger above his left. "Now, watch carefully."

"I will, I promise," Charlie said, leaning almost over the top of where Kelly was holding the coin upright on the table, balancing it with the tip of his left index finger.

"One," Kelly counted, as he stroked the underside of his right index finger across the upper surface of his left finger. "Two, keep watching," Kelly said, again rubbing his right index finger across the top of his left finger which still held the coin in place. "Three!" Kelly said, only this time he extended the tip of his right thumb slightly outward so it lightly touched the edge of the coin causing it to spin rapidly as he lifted his left index finger off the coin.

"Wow!" Charlie said in amazement, "How do you do that!"

"Told you, it's magic," the Sheriff said with a laugh, as Charlie watched the half dollar spin like a top, slowly losing momentum and landing face up on the white table cloth.

Charlie picked up the silver coin and read the date aloud, "1840! Wow! That's really old. Com'on Sheriff," Charlie pleaded, handing the heavy silver coin back to Kelly, "please tell me how you do that!"

"Maybe when you're older," Kelly replied, and then added, "If you listen to your mother and father and keep doing well in school."

"Aw, all right," Charlie replied with a heavy sigh, "I will, but I'm already at the top of my seventh grade class in reading and math."

"How many are in your grade, Charlie?" his father asked, seeming to know the answer.

"Well, there's only the two of us, but even Irv Howbert will tell you how good I am at math, and he's in twelfth grade and about the smartest kid in the whole school. He's going to graduate in the spring and says he's going to go off and join the Union Army and fight them rebels, if'n there still is a war on."

"Well, come on you gentlemen," Mrs. Stone interrupted, returning from the kitchen with a blue metal coffeepot in her hand, "I'm sure there's more pleasant things to talk about during Christmas then the war. Now who's ready for coffee?"

Both Judge Stone and Sheriff Kelly pushed their coffee cups forward as Lizzy placed a hot piece of pecan pie in front of everyone. "Now," Lizzy inquired, "who wants ice cream on top?"

"I do, I do!" Charlie repeated excitedly, holding his pie plate up off the table.

As Lizzy dished up ice cream, Kelly slipped the silver half dollar back into his right vest pocket and traced the outline of the coin instinctively with his right thumb. With his left thumb, he felt the presence of the heavy silver pocket watch Lizzy had given him that night at the dance at the El Paso House Hotel. It was always reassuring to Kelly to feel Uncle Doug's birthday coin and know that the pocket watch was tucked safely away in its rightful place. Kelly thought, for the second time that evening, of his own family back in Maine, listening to the chatter around the Stone's dinner table, wondering if Uncle Doug and his family were enjoying Christmas dinner with his father and brother John and sister Katherine.

It had been twenty-three years since Kelly had last seen his family, since the day he killed Katherine's fiancé Emitt. Kelly played with his fork, wondering if the law was still looking for him and if Katherine had ever found someone else to marry and if she had any children of her own. Reflecting on his past, Kelly found he had lost his appetite. The lawman watched as Charlie finished his pecan pie and stared across the table at Kelly's untouched dessert.

"Aren't you going to eat your pie Sheriff?" Charlie asked, watching the ice cream melt slowly down the slice of the hot pecan pie.

"I musta' filled up too much on the ham and sweet potatoes," the Sheriff answered, "Think you could help me out here?" He asked, sliding his pecan pie topped with ice cream across the table toward Charlie.

"Sure!" Charlie answered with delight, and then paused long enough to see if his father was going to object, before asking, "Is it okay Papa?"

"I guess so," Judge Stone replied. "Why not, it's Christmas after all," he added with a smile, watching his growing son devour a second piece of pie as if he hadn't eaten all day.

Half way through his second dessert. Charlie looked up across the table at Kelly, "Think you'll catch those Hank Way boys 'fore New Year's, Sheriff?"

"No!" Lizzy interrupted, taking her seat at the table next to the Sheriff before adding playfully, "He won't, because he'll be too busy spending time with me! There's a thick blanket of fresh snow on the Peak and I'll be cold and bored without his company."

Squeezing her hand beneath the table, Kelly added, "You heard the lady Charlie. Guess they'll just have to wait."

Kelly smiled at Lizzy, as Judge and his wife watched with approval at the obvious love and affection Kelly and Lizzy had developed for one another. Charlie noticed his parents smiling at the happy couple, and then rolled his eyes, as he focused on finishing off the remaining bit of crust from his second piece of pecan pie.

"You were certainly right to worry about Colonel Chivington offering them conscription in lieu of prison time." Judge Stone commented, "Those boys served two whole days at Fort Garland before robbing the paymaster and stealing off with the fort's payroll and four good government horses and saddles."

Kelly shook his head.

"I can help you, ya know!" Charlie offered. "When you go after 'em I can scout for ya."

"Well, I appreciate your offer Charlie," the Sheriff replied, "and as soon as you turn seventeen, with your parents' approval, I intend to deputize you."

Charlie puffed up his chest with pride as his family reacted to the sheriff's promise; Judge Stone reached over to pat Charlie on the shoulder.

Lizzy got up from her chair, then taking Kelly's hand, said, "Now that you've given Charlie a promise of a Christmas gift, I have something of a promise to give to you, Scott Kelly."

Holding Lizzy's hand, Kelly rose up from the table and followed her outside, as the other three watched the happy couple leave the dining room and head toward the front door, stopping long enough to put on their warm winter coats. Kelly helped Lizzy put on her coat first, then put on and buttoned his heavy wool topcoat as they stepped out into the dark.

Out on the front porch, Lizzy walked them casually to the end of the porch where she turned and leaned into Kelly, feeling her way with the palms of her hands across his firm stomach in the dark, as she pulled his pocket watch from his right vest pocket. She held the watch in her hand, then popped it open, just as she had done dozens of times before and looked at its face for a moment.

"You must miss your father," Kelly said.

"I do. He believed in me," she replied almost in a whisper, remembering how her stepfather always made her feel safe and loved.

"You should have his watch Lizzy. It's too dear a gift to have given to me…"

"No…he would have believed in you too, Scott."

Lizzy opened the back of the watch to a compartment empty of a photo. She pulled a small round tin type photo from a pocket in her skirt, and placed it carefully into the compartment. Then, turning it around to show Kelly, he saw it was a picture of Lizzy taken the day of her graduation from Oberlin College.

"As I do," she added softly, closing the watch and returning it to his vest pocket.

Kelly leaned over and kissed her warmly as the snowflakes softly began to fall.

Late afternoon Mid-winter 1864
Front Steps El Paso House Hotel, Colorado City

Lizzy and Kelly stood patiently waiting on the front steps of the hotel. Sheriff Kelly checked the time on his pocket watch. They smiled and nodded to Doc Garvin as he approached them from across the street, coming to a stop beside them on the wooden steps stage passengers used when arriving or departing the twice daily stagecoaches.

"Anything wrong?" Doc Garvin asked the couple waiting beside him.

Lizzy replied first, "The Pikes Peak and Leavenworth Express is late. I was expecting a letter from the Smithsonian yesterday."

Turning his attention toward Sheriff Kelly, Doc Garvin asked the lawman, "You expect they ran into some trouble?"

"Ven Tinsley's drivin' today. Not like him to be late..." Sheriff Kelly replied, looking again north up 28th Street, the direction where the stagecoach would normally have appeared a half an hour ago. Stepping down from the front porch onto Colorado Avenue, Sheriff Kelly tightened the cinch on Marengo's saddle, then commented to Lizzy and Doc Garvin, "Maybe I ought to ride out and see if everything's okay."

Just as Kelly started to untie Marego's reins from the hitching post, the rattle of an approaching stage could be heard coming toward them down 28ᵗʰ Street, slowing to stop on Colorado Avenue in front of the El Paso House Hotel. Everyone around the front of the hotel cleared the way as the stagecoach came to a full stop.

"Whoa!" Ven Tinsley, the stagecoach driver commanded to his team of six heavily lathered horses, "Glad you're here Sheriff, Doc Garvin. Ran into some trouble out there in the Black Forest, this side of Buzzard's stage stop. Four outlaws. Two of my passengers fought back from inside the coach, they shot one of the outlaws off his horse. One of my passengers was killed during the shootout. His wife got his gun and picked off another one of 'em."

Kelly and Doc Garvin looked inside the stagecoach to see a wide-eye woman holding the body of her bloody, dead husband in her arms. Lizzy took in the woman's expression, one of shock and immense grief. Lizzy entered the stage instinctively to comfort the other woman.

Ven Tinsley climbed down from atop the stage to stand next to Sheriff Kelly, "I may have wounded another one of them before they rode off to the east." Ven removed his hat and wiped the sweat and dirt from his forehead with the dirty red bandana he wore around his neck, before adding, "They left two of their gang lying dead on Stagecoach Road. Just rode off and left them lying there in the dirt."

"Did they take the mail pouch?" Kelly asked.

"Yeah," Ven replied, "I threw it down before the man got shot by one of my passengers. Mail pouch was still lying on the ground beside that outlaw when I drove away."

"Were there any dispatches for Fort Garland?" Kelly inquired further.

"I believe there were two or maybe three," Ven replied.

"Why?" Doc Garvin asked Kelly, "You thinking they wanted to intercept the mail?"

"I'm thinking someone maybe didn't want those dispatches to reach the Garrison Commander at the Fort..." Kelly replied as Doc Garvin entered the coach to confirm the man was dead and the woman inside covered in blood was not wounded.

"Ven," the Sheriff said, "can you tell me anything more about the two guys that got away?"

"Well," the stage driver replied, stroking his bearded chin in thought, "they was all wearing bandanas over their faces, but the pair that rode off were rough looking white men. Neither of them was youngsters, and the guy that seemed in charge had long red hair and was a riding a roan mare. The other robber, the one I may have wounded, was on a black horse, a gelding I believe."

Speaking tenderly, the Sheriff turned his attention to the blood covered woman still clutching her dead husband in her arms, "Ma'am, I'm Sheriff Kelly. We're all so sorry for your loss. Know I will do all I can to bring those last two outlaws to justice."

The woman appeared shell shocked, and at first Kelly didn't think she had heard him, but as he turned to mount up she turned her head to speak directly to Sheriff Kelly, "You find those bastards, Sheriff. You find 'em and you kill 'em."

Lizzy put her arm around the woman, but was taken aback when the blood covered women lifted her right hand to show the Sheriff that she still held her husband's .44 Colt revolver, "You kill them Sheriff, or so help me God. I will."

"You'll have my help," Lizzy added as she gently removed the

169

loaded revolver from the other woman's grip and handed it butt first to Ven Tinsley.

"I'll find 'em ma'am. You have my word," Sheriff Kelly replied.

Later that afternoon
Stagecoach Road, East of Colorado City

Sheriff Kelly pulled back on Marengo's reins, then stood up in the stirrups attempting to see further down the road. Although he was still at a considerable distance, he could see the bodies of two outstretched men lying on the ground being searched by two other men; one was holding the reins to a black horse and the other man's horse was a roan.

Sheriff Kelly drew his large Colt revolver and pointed Marengo's head toward the outlaws. When the outlaws saw him riding toward them at a gallop, at about a hundred yards to the west on Stagecoach Road, the outlaw with the long red hair shouted, "Come on Frank, dammit, just grab the damn mail pouch and let's git!"

Frank Riley draped the U.S. mail pouch over his shoulder and climbed up into the saddle of his black horse, and then followed his boss off down the trail at a fast gallop.

Although Marengo was past her prime, she was still one of the fastest horses in the Colorado Territory. In a pursuit, it was just a matter of time before she overtook the other two horses. Kelly gave Marengo her reins, allowing her to pick her path and pace as they closed in on the bandits. The horse and rider had been together since Marengo was a colt. They thought, slept and moved as one.

At two hundred and fifty yards distance Frank Riley's horse began to falter and the man began to panic. The outlaw fired his

170

first shot from his revolver wildly over his left shoulder toward the lawman, hoping the shot would scare him away. Seeing that this Sheriff wasn't one to scare easy, Riley aimed and fired two more rounds as his horse began to slow to a trot, throwing off his aim. Riley kicked and cursed his tired black horse, causing it to speed up momentarily, but only for a short distance; then the horse was played out. Riley fired another shot from his revolver over his shoulder toward Kelly, who still had not returned his fire.

"Four," Sheriff Kelly counted the outlaw's shots to himself, suspecting the man's revolver still held one or possibly two live rounds yet to be fired. Marengo was also beginning to tire; having covered nearly three quarters of a mile in the pursuit, but still she would not give up the chase. Kelly knew he had to narrow the odds and took careful aim over the top of Marengo's head, timing the shot with his horse's long stride, aiming carefully at the center of the outlaw's shoulders.

"POW!" Kelly's shot rang out, Riley's head snapped back violently as the bullet struck him square in the back, between the shoulders, and exited the front of his chest just below his chin. The black horse bucked wildly to the side, pitching its rider out of the saddle and dumping him onto the side of the road. The body of Frank Riley landed in the dirt with a thud. Kelly watched as the outlaw's lifeless body hit the ground and although he had seen many a dead man fall, he slowed Marengo long enough to confirm this outlaw was dead. Kelly knew from experience that he couldn't risk leaving an enemy at his rear; but, this man wouldn't be going anywhere. Kelly took note of the mail pouch lying in the dirt next to the dead man with the letter D branded on his cheek. Looking back down the road to the east, Kelly could see the second outlaw was getting away and knew he couldn't expect

171

Marengo to carry the extra weight of the mail pouch if they had any chance of catching up with Hank Way.

"Looks like you robbed your last stage, Francis Michael Riley," Sheriff Kelly said aloud, then turned to focus his full attention on the man riding off in the distance on a fast roan horse; the leader of this notorious outlaw gang. "Come Marengo," Kelly said as he reached down and patted Marengo on the right side of the neck, "one down, one to go." Marengo nickered in agreement and took off down the trail in pursuit of the outlaw and the roan.

Hank Way had seen Riley getting shot out of the saddle, but that hadn't slowed his attempt to escape for an instant. "There is no honor among thieves," Kelly thought to himself, watching Hank Way ride away, leaving the three bodies of his now depleted gang behind him, dead on Stagecoach Road.

The roan the outlaw was riding was a strong horse, probably stolen, and much younger than Marengo. Though the two horses seemed fairly evenly matched in speed, Kelly adjusted his pursuit strategy, intent to close the distance between them by changing the race to one of endurance. He knew Marengo was growing more tired with the passing of every quarter mile, so he pulled back on her reins to allow her to walk a little to catch her breath, hoping Hank Way would do the same. The strategy paid off as the outlaw turned in the saddle, then also slowed his horse to a fast walk. The two riders continued east, breaking out of the treeline and emerging out onto the tall prairie grasslands, but still at a distance of about three hundred yards apart.

Whenever Kelly felt Marengo was ready, he allowed her to break into a steady gallop, closing the distance between them and the other horse and rider. Even at her age, Marengo was still the most game horse Kelly had ever ridden, always ready for the chase. Having hunted antelope in the eastern part of El Paso County, Kelly felt he had an advantage over the outlaw who may not know the terrain as well as he did. Two miles to the east stood the Homestead Ranch, nestled into the opening of a horseshoe shaped bluff lined at the top by pine trees. A natural spring flowed from beneath the sandstone colored bluffs where Kelly planned to stop to water his fearless mount. Beyond the Homestead Ranch, at a distance of about fifteen miles stood the Paint Mines, a geological formation of multicolored sandstone pillars, some as tall as twenty to twenty-five feet above the ground.

Kelly knew that the paint mines in eastern El Paso County were located about 35 miles east of Colorado City, and were popular with the Indian tribes of the region who used the pigments in the soil to paint their horses and tipis. Kelly scanned the horizon in front of them for any signs of tipis or smoke from campfires, for if they ran into any Indians out this far on the plains, he would have to hope they were friendly Ute and not the Cheyenne or their constant ally, the Arapaho. The Cheyenne had declared war earlier that year against the white man, who had continually trespassed across their land designated as an Indian Reserve, with a never-ending procession of wagons filled with violent men who abused their horses and shot buffalo for sport.

The Cheyenne and Arapaho Indian Reserve extended west from the Kansas state line until it butted up against the eastern border of El Paso County, but knowing exactly where that boundary was located out on the plains was difficult to determine, for the Indian who lived there or Whiteman who didn't care. Kelly knew the Homestead Ranch was still located a good twenty-five miles from the Indian Reservation. What he didn't know was if any of them had left the Reservation to hunt for the diminishing herds of bison. The Ute also came down out of the mountains in the west to hunt the massive bison which provided a major food source for them as well, and the thick buffalo hides were coveted for their tipis, far outlasting elk hides.

As predicted, Kelly watched the trail ahead as the roan horse smelled water from the spring on the Homestead Ranch, and headed straight for water despite his rider's every attempt to steer him further out onto the plains. Hank Way nervously watched as Kelly closed the distance, then the outlaw began kicking the roan horse viciously with his spurs and whipping it with the ends of the thick leather reins. Finally, the roan horse gave into the commands of the rider and reluctantly pulled his head away from the cool water and climbed the bank on the opposite side of the spring breaking into a slow gallop continuing to the east.

Kelly allowed Marengo to gauge how much water to drink, noticing how she was continually looking up to see how much distance the other horse and rider were gaining. Marengo seemed to drink just enough to quench her thirst and emerged quickly from the spring to renew their pursuit. The distance between the two horses and riders narrowed, from two hundred yards to one hundred and fifty yards, to one hundred yards. The roan was failing. Marengo seemed to catch her second wind and evidently felt the time was now to accelerate and overtake the other horse and rider, now less than fifty yards in front of them. Hank Way turned in the saddle and blindly fired a shot from his revolver toward his pursuers. Kelly saw the smoke from the Colt revolver and heard the whiz of the bullet as it passed overhead.

Kelly drew his Colt revolver from its holster, but held his fire as Hank Way wasted another shot which hit the dirt several yards in front of Marengo. Now, at thirty yards, Kelly could smell the black powder still hanging in the air from the outlaw's last shot, as he and Marengo continued to close the distance. Kelly admired how Marengo had never flinched from gunfire or ducked at the bee-like sound of bullets whizzing past them over the years that they had spent together chasing down outlaws and fighting hostile Indians.

"Okay girl," Kelly said to the very best friend he had ever known, "time to end this." Kelly knew now at twenty-five yards, even at a gallop he would almost certainly hit his mark. The lawman clenched the reins between his teeth, leaned forward over the saddle horn and while taking careful aim at the outlaw in front of him, cocked the single action Colt and gripping the revolver with both hands, he began to squeeze the trigger slowly just as he had done hundreds of times before. Kelly saw the smoke ring from the outlaw's revolver and knew in an instant that something was terribly wrong. Instead of hearing the whiz of the bullet passing harmlessly overhead, he felt and heard the sickening thud of hot lead striking bone.

For just a moment it felt to Kelly as if they were flying; then in an instant Marengo's muscular body went limp. There was no sound. He could no longer hear the familiar sound of Marengo's hoofbeats pounding against the ground. Everything was now in slow motion. Marengo's body seemed to slowly crumple beneath Kelly's legs. Sadly, this sensation was all too familiar as Kelly had felt this before, when another horse was shot out from under him, the day George Smith died. But this time it was different, this time it was Marengo and the shock and grief of what was happening sickened Kelly to his stomach and slowed his reaction time to a crawl.

Instinctively Kelly tried to pull both of his boots from

the stirrups, but when Marengo's limp body plowed into the ground Kelly's left leg became trapped under the weight of her collapsing body. Horse and rider struck the ground hard, then seemed to bounce along a few more feet as a result of their speed. Kelly's body was thrown forward out of the saddle, but his leg remained trapped under his beautiful gray horse, and as he hit the ground a second time his head impacted the ground violently and the force knocked the wind from his chest and the Colt revolver from his hand. The heavy pocket watch was ejected from his left vest pocket and the silver chain snapped in half. When the pocket watch landed in the dirt a few yards away the impact on the ground broke the watch face, popped open the case and Lizzy's tintype photo flew out and landed a few feet away face down in the tall buffalo grass.

Hank Way had not seen Kelly fall at first and didn't realize his last shot had hit Marengo squarely between the eyes. When he finally looked back it took him several seconds to spot Kelly lying in the dirt and by that time he had ridden another fifty or sixty yards away. Pulling his roan horse to a halt, the outlaw turned his horse around and slowly began walking back to the where the helpless Sheriff was lying trapped beneath his dead horse. A menacing grin began to spread across Hank Way's dirt covered face, exposing the outlaw's yellow teeth.

While only semi-conscious, Kelly was still alert enough to sense he was in a bad way. He struggled again to free his left leg out from under Marengo. It wouldn't budge. He looked down the trail and saw Hank Way was still almost sixty or seventy yards away but closing in on him with gun in hand. The Sheriff spotted his Colt revolver lying in the dirt just a few feet out of reach, then he rolled over on his back and tried to pull his rifle from its scabbard, but it was pinned under the full weight of Marengo. Not fully aware he had suffered a concussion when his head had struck the ground, Kelly lay on his back and fought to remain conscious. He looked again down the single track trail to the east to gauge how much time he had before Hank Way was on top of him; he had only seconds to live. Although Kelly was lying on his back and looking upside down at his adversary, it appeared for a moment that the outlaw had stopped in his tracks. Just then Kelly's world closed in around him and he blacked out.

Mid-July, 1863
Eastern El Paso County, Colorado Territory

"Where the hell did you come from?" Hank Way said with a sneer to the Indian who had appeared on a white horse standing on the trail between him and the lawman he intended to kill.

Two more Indians rode up behind the first and stood stoically awaiting the command of their chief on the spirited white horse.

"Go ahead, you sons-a-bitches," Hank Way cursed as he turned the tall roan horse and galloped away, "you didn't earn the kill, but go ahead and claim his scalp! I got better things to do than waste my time killin' the likes of the three of you savages."

The chief dismounted and approached the downed horse and rider. After confirming the horse was dead, and the rider was still alive he paused, looked skyward momentarily in prayer, and then turned to the other two Indians. The chief nodded toward the lawman on the ground pinned beneath his horse, said something in Ute, jumped on the back of the white horse and with his heals urged the majestic white stud forward in pursuit of the man on the roan horse, "Come Thunder Cloud, this white man will soon learn a new definition for savage."

Hank Way was almost a quarter mile away when he looked back toward the west to see he was being followed. After a mile he was alarmed to see the lone Indian on the white horse was still following him, remaining just out of range for a shot. Almost an hour later the outlaw had estimated they had covered at least eight if not ten miles, yet the lone Indian still maintained a constant distance between them, of about eighty to one hundred yards. Whenever he sped up, so did the Indian. Whenever he slowed to walk, so did the Indian. The roan was one of the fastest horses Hank Way had ever ridden, but that white stallion behind him had no trouble keeping up with them at any gait. The sun had not yet set behind Pikes Peak across the plains on the western horizon, but Hank Way knew he wouldn't last the night with this Indian on his trail, allowing his adversary the luxury of choosing the time and place to attack.

Although Hank Way had only ridden out this far east from Colorado City once before, he remembered the multicolored sandstone columns at the Paint Mines and decided that maze-like terrain might make for a better place to try to ambush his pursuer. Anything would be better than trying to make a stand out here on the open plains.

"Come on, damn you," Hank Way commanded as he brutally kicked the tired roan horse beneath him. The roan had given his all for it's rider, but had finally started to become overly winded while they were still a couple hundred yards from the Paint Mines. Soaked in lather and foaming at the mouth, the roan slowed from a trot to a walk, then staggered to the side trying desperately to catch its breath. "You ain't done yet," the outlaw shouted, as he drew a ten-inch knife from a sheath on his belt and stabbed the knife handle deep into the side of the roan. The horse let out a painful shriek, and then inhaled a chest full of air through the gaping stab wound in his side that had penetrated deep into its right lung. The dying horse gave into the merciless kicking of its brutal rider and started loping again.

At the entrance to the Paint Mines the roan finally gave out and dropped to the ground. The outlaw dismounted, drew his revolver, saw the Indian on the white horse was drawing closer, kicked the horse in the side and shouted at the dying animal writhing with pain on the ground, "I ain't wasting a shot on you to put you out of your stinking misery." The outlaw turned and headed off into the tall mushroom shaped sand stone formations ballooning up ahead a few yards to the east.

When the white horse stopped beside the dying roan, it knelt down on its left front leg to allow the Indian rider to dismount easily by swinging his right leg gracefully over the horse's neck. The roan's eyes were wild with pain and fright, struggling to understand what he had done wrong to disappoint his rider, laboring to catch his breath, struggling desperately to survive. The searching eyes of the roan gelding met those of the white stud and after they nickered back and forth to one another the roan finally stopping struggling. The stout Indian withdrew his knife from its leather pouch and bent his knees down on the horse's neck to hold him to the ground.

As Chief Ouray slit the roan horse's throat he whispered soothingly into its ear, "Do not fear my brother, you will be ridden by better men than that red-haired demon in the afterlife." As the roan exhaled his last breath, Chief Ouray bent over the horse's open mouth and inhaled the horse's last breath deeply into his own lungs. As he exhaled, Ouray offered a prayer skyward to the Creator, asking him to accept the spirit of this magnificent creature and reject the spirit of the evil creature that was soon to follow.

Chief Ouray stood, wiped the horse's blood from his knife blade on the back of his bare forearms, and then slipped the knife back into its leather pouch hanging from his belt. Ouray walked back to Thunder Cloud, retrieved an unstrung bow and two arrows from under the horse blanket and started walking purposefully toward the entrance to the sandstone Paint Mines.

Hank Way saw the lone Indian advancing, then hid cowardly behind one of the pastel colored columns waiting to ambush his pursuer. After waiting for what seemed an eternity, the outlaw peered out from around the multicolor stone formation and fired a shot in the direction where he had last seen the Indian standing stringing his bow, but when the smoke cleared the Indian was nowhere to be seen. Within an instant of the outlaw hearing the zing of the arrow flying through the air he felt the shooting pain radiating from his right shoulder. Hank Way ducked back behind the sandstone column, then instinctively reached up and jerked the arrow out of his right shoulder. He looked down and knew he shouldn't have reacted so impulsively, as he saw the arrowhead was no longer attached to the wooden shaft of the arrow. The projectile point was still embedded deep into the muscle of his right shoulder. It hurt like hell.

Realizing he could no longer lift or aim his heavy Colt .44 revolver in his gun hand, Hank Way shifted the handgun to his left hand then turned to run deeper into the Paint Mines, seeking a safer place to hide. He had only run a few yards when the second arrow struck him in the back of his left thigh, just above the knee. Cursing in pain, he started limping, resisting the temptation to pull the second arrow out for fear of losing another projectile point from its shaft, knowing that it would make it much harder and more painful to remove. No longer able to run, the outlaw dropped to the ground and began crawling to hide behind the closest rock formation.

From experience Chief Ouray and Hank Way both knew that the purpose of shooting a man or an animal with an arrow was not to kill instantly, but to cripple. If the wounded animal or person didn't bleed out, then the killing would be done up close and personal. Hank Way found he was losing a great deal of blood from the wound in his leg and untied the sweat soaked bandana from around his neck to fashion a crude tourniquet just above the wound in his left leg. Clutching the revolver in his left hand Hank Way peered around the sandstone column, spotted the lone Indian advancing toward him and fired a shot with his left hand. The shot went wild to the left and struck a sandstone column behind the Indian, who didn't seem to notice or care.

"Don't think I can hit you, do you!" Hank Way shouted as he held the revolver up unsteadily again with his left hand and pulled the trigger. Click. Click. The outlaw's handgun was empty. He threw the empty revolver hard as he could, left-handed at the Indian and then crawled along the ground, leaving a trail of blood across the hot sand. The blood trail was easy to follow, making it impossible for Hank Way to hide. The outlaw was dragging his left leg behind him now and had begun sweating profusely. His mouth was dry and felt like it was full of cotton. He stopped to wipe the sweat that was dripping down his red bushy eyebrows, stinging his red eyes. Hank Way blinked twice, then he opened his eyes and found himself face to face with a lizard. The lizard raised its head and turning toward Hank Way, squirted blood from his eyes. The outlaw screamed and then began to whimper.

The Indian was now standing just a few feet behind him, on the opposite side of the rock formation, but Hank Way found that he could crawl no further. Chief Ouray withdrew his tomahawk from his belt, cautiously walked behind the rock where the outlaw was lying and bent over Hank Way. The outlaw curled himself into a ball and began to cry uncontrollably as Ouray grabbed his long red hair from behind. The whimpering did not last long. The body of the leader of the Hank Way Gang lay lifeless in an expanding pool of blood seeping slowly into the hot sandy soil beneath the multicolored sandstone formations of the Paint Mines in eastern El Paso County of the Colorado Territory.

Three Days Later
Black Forest, El Paso County, Colorado Territory

When Sheriff Kelly first heard the singing he thought it must be an angel; surely he had died and gone to heaven. He had never heard an angel sing before, but imagined this must be how an angel would sound, singing in heaven. The woman's voice was faint and he struggled to make out the words, but could not. Curious to see who or what could produce such a beautiful sound, Kelly slowly opened his eyes. As his eyes began to adjust to the dim light, he noticed a slight wisp of gray smoke escaping heavenwards through a round opening ten or twelve feet above his prone body. Kelly recognized he was inside a tipi and felt the weight and familiar smell of the heavy buffalo robe pressing down on his chest and realized he was lying on the ground. The soft singing continued and Kelly now understood it was coming from outside.

Looking to his right, he recognized the butt of his Colt revolver sticking out of his leather belt holster. The tan leather fringed rifle sheath, that was holding his Hawken rifle, laid on the ground just beyond, yet had been purposely placed there well within his reach. Understanding there would be no need for firearms in heaven, Kelly accepted the fact that he was apparently still alive and evidently in the company of a friend.

Looking to his left he noticed his circle star sheriff's badge was still pinned to his vest, which had been neatly folded and was laying on top of his blue flannel button down shirt, and it too had been neatly folded and was lying on top of what looked like the black pants he last remembered wearing. He lifted up the thick hide of the buffalo robe to find he was completely buck naked, except for a white bandage wrapped around his left knee. He tried to move, but discovered a sharp pain that shot up instantly from his swollen left knee. Kelly tried to bend his left knee but the pain caused him to involuntarily let out a quiet moan of pain. He felt sick to his stomach and soon realized he had a splitting headache, and that's when he reached up and felt that a bandage had been wrapped around his head just above his ears.

Kelly realized the singing had stopped and saw the flap used to cover the opening of the tipi was being pulled open. He watched as an Indian woman wearing tan buckskin clothing bent over and walked into the tipi, followed by three adorable white puppies. The puppies playfully jumped on top of the buffalo robe and licked Kelly's face excitedly. The woman smiled and shooed the puppies outside. One of the white puppies snuck back in and laid down beside the injured lawman. Chipeta knelt beside Kelly and began adjusting the bandage around his head.

"You must not move too quickly," Chipeta said softly in English.

"I know you, you are Ouray's wife Chipeta. Now I understand

why the other Utes call you White Singing Bird," Kelly replied as the Indian woman gently brought a cup of hot tea up to his lips.

"Here, drink this, it will help settle your stomach," she said, cradling the back of his head.

"Thank you," Kelly said as he sipped the bitter tea, "How long have I been here?"

"You have been asleep for three days. Here, please try to drink more tea, you must have some nourishment," Chipeta said, helping Kelly lift up his head to drink from the wooden cup.

"Many thanks for your care ma'am, I hope I have not been a burden."

"Not at all. The man you were chasing is dead. You can rest, and heal..."

Kelly laid his head back and closed his eyes. The white puppy rested its head across Kelly's right ankle and went to sleep.

Several hours later Kelly awoke to the sound of the familiar crackle coming from a fire outside. It was dark and hurt to move, but he managed to put on his pants before he stood. He put on his flannel shirt, leaving it unbuttoned and draped a blanket around his shoulders. As he hobbled outside into the cool air, he found Ouray and Chipeta sitting around a campfire playing with the three puppies, their exhausted mother not far away. Chief Ouray stood to help Kelly into a comfortable sitting position next to the warm fire.

"Thank you both for all you've done," Kelly said, noticing Ouray's lance that was leaning up against the door of the tipi had a fresh bloodied scalp attached.

Ouray saw Kelly looking at the scalp with the long red hair hanging from his lance point and spoke, "You have fierce enemies my friend...and many."

"These are dangerous parts," Kelly acknowledged, adding, "for all of us. I often wonder if all of these outlaw gangs are out here just on their own, or is there something more sinister behind all this that we just can't see."

"I do not pretend to know the white man's ways, especially during this time of war that seems to us as anything but civil, but I do know that greed does not need a cause," Ouray replied.

"We have something to give you," Chipeta said with a smile, trying to lighten the mood. "I have something that is yours," she said as she handed Kelly his silver pocket watch.

Kelly gratefully accepted the pocket watch, then held it in the palm of his hand so he could see it more clearly in the light of the fire, "Much obliged, ma'am."

"It was broken," Chipeta explained, "but I have fixed it, the best I could – the watch chain is braided hair from the horsetail of your Marengo and her son, Thunder Cloud."

Kelly opened the pocket watch to find Lizzy's photo was gone. The crystal face was cracked and the hands fixed at 2:36, the exact moment his Marengo had died. He stroked the horse-tail braid with his thumb and forefinger, then held the horsehair under his nose trying to hang onto the memories he shared with his beloved mare. He closed and clutched the watch Lizzy had given him quietly in the palm of his hand. A heavy sigh escaped his chest as his eyes welled up with tears. One of the white puppies nuzzled against him and he reached down to pet the fluffy white puppy lying next to his leg.

"Thank you," Kelly said, after several minutes had passed.

"You have lost your old gray friend, but you will ride her again, in the afterlife," Ouray acknowledged. "I will remember her always. Her son Thunder Cloud has served me well. He has had many children of his own, now. You will have your pick of my horse herd."

"That's very generous," Kelly acknowledged in gratitude. "I only have this to offer in trade," Kelly replied as he handed Ouray the knife he had once traded him for Thundercloud.

Ouray accepted the knife, unfolded the blade and rubbed his thumb crossways against the blade. "It is still sharp," Ouray said with a smile. He held the knife up to the fire, noticing it now had both of the two lions missing from the ornate handle. "Towaoc," he said using the Ute word for thank you. Then the great Ute chief said, "It is a good trade."

Two Days Later
Black Forest, El Paso County, Colorado Territory

Ouray held the horse's reins steady as Sheriff Kelly lifted Marengo's old saddle up and placed it on the back of his new horse. "You chose well, my friend," Ouray said to Kelly as he patted the spotted gray horse on the neck and handed the reins to the lawman. Kelly accepted the reins, then placed his left leg gingerly into the stirrup and climbed painfully up into the saddle.

"She is a fine horse," Kelly replied as he watched Chipeta approaching with a tan hide bag, drawn closed at the top with a leather cord. She wrapped the cord around Kelly's saddle horn. He watched as the face of one of the white puppies popped up excitedly out of the bag.

"He chose you," Chipeta explained.

"What's his name?" Kelly inquired of Chipeta.

"That is up to you," Chipeta replied.

"I will call him Sam," Kelly replied as he looked down and smiled down at the puppy looking up at him with sad brown eyes.

Tipping his hat to Chipeta and with a nod of his head toward Ouray, Kelly said, "Towaoc. I will not forget your kindness." Kelly turned his new horse toward the small town at the base of the purple mountain in the distance to the west.

By the time Sheriff Kelly rode into Colorado City, his left leg hanging down from the stirrup had gone completely stiff, and his knee was swollen and beginning to throb. Turning onto Colorado Avenue, Kelly spotted Judge Stone's buggy parked in front of Sam Wah's Laundry and saw Charlie Stone helping Lizzy load a bundle of clean laundry into the buckboard. Lizzy dropped the bundle she was carrying on the ground and started running toward Kelly as he gingerly began to dismount from the saddle. He winced in pain as his left boot touched the ground, and hopped to balance most of his weight on his right leg. He stood up straight as he could and turned to smile at Lizzy as she threw her arms around him in a loving embrace.

"Oh, Scott," Lizzy cried, failing to suppress her tears of joy. "I have been so worried about you, and look you're hurt, again," she said as she placed his left arm over her shoulder to help him walk.

Charlie rushed up and took the reins of his new horse. "Here, Sheriff," Charlie said, "I'll take your horse over to Mr. Bent's; but hey, where's Marengo?"

Kelly looked down at the ground, "Afraid she didn't make it home this time," he replied, now it was his turn to fight back the tears. Lizzy tightened her embrace around his midsection.

"I'm afraid I broke your father's watch," Kelly said to Lizzy, pulling the silver pocket watch from his left vest pocket by the braided horsehair chain Chipeta had made from Marengo and Thunder Clouds tails.

"Oh Scott," Lizzy said, "we can always replace the watch, I'm just so sorry about Marengo."

Going unnoticed, the widow Lucy Maggard was looking through the thick glass window of the general store across the street. In seeing Lizzy and Kelly's embrace, Lucy stepped back from the green wavy glass as her smile faded slowly away.

As Charlie led Kelly's horse away toward Xavier Bent's corral, the white puppy named Sam popped his head up out of the top of the tanned hide bag and looked around at his new home.

Sunday Morning One Month Later
Creekside, Colorado City, Colorado Territory

Sheriff Kelly gently steered his team of grey horses up the right bank of Fountain Creek as Lizzy leaned over the side of the carriage to confirm that the white dog was still running playfully alongside.

"He's gotten bigger," she said to Kelly. "Why did you name him Sam?"

"His eyes remind me of Ulysses Grant," Kelly replied with a smile, "best quartermaster we had in the whole Union Army down in Mexico. Sam was the nickname they gave him at West Point and the name stuck with him; if he's half as good a General as he was a quartermaster, the country will be in good hands."

Leaning her head against Kelly's shoulder, Lizzy said with a heavy sigh, "I'll be so glad when all this fighting is done. It's good to have you up and about Sheriff."

"Good to be up and about, Miss Lizzy," he replied, as Lizzy kissed him softly on the cheek.

"I'd appreciate it if we could avoid those kinds of nasty characters in the future, Scott."

"I wish that was a promise I could make, my lovely," the lawman replied honestly.

Lizzy looked away, deep in thought, and then spotted Marcus Foster approaching the creek crossing from the south.

"Morning Marcus!" Lizzy shouted as the young man waved back.

Kelly looked to see Marcus wave and waved back, then asked Lizzy, "Has Marcus been doing good work for you and your Uncle out at the ranch?"

"He has!" Lizzy replied, "He's a hard worker and a good man. I appreciate you asking him to check in on me whenever you're away, and he keeps Charlie out of my hair. The storage building Marcus built for my fossil collection is nearly full already. I might have to ask him to expand it. Maybe someday I can donate the fossils and Native American artifacts I've collected to start a history museum in Colorado City. I can't tell you how satisfying it is for me to write Mama and tell her how successful my archeological research is going here in El Paso County."

"She must be very proud of you, I know I am," Kelly said uncomfortably, not accustomed to handing out praise lightly.

"And I of you," Lizzy replied, "I think she's more hopeful about my frequent mentions of you than being proud of my work, but I suppose she's a woman of her place and time. Always hearing wedding bells in her head and thinking of grandbabies and such."

Kelly smiled at the idea of he and Lizzy getting married and starting a family, as Marcus Foster faded into the thick green leaves of the towering cottonwood trees lining Fountain Creek. Lizzy placed her hand on his thigh, giving him a gentle squeeze. The thought of Scott being pleased when hearing about her mother liking him appealed to Lizzy and she was certain Kelly's rugged good looks would not be lost on her mother. Lizzy believed her mother would likely accept Kelly as being more than ten years her senior, but worried that her mother might eventually say something to embarrass her about marrying a man beneath her station in life, Kelly being a lawman and all.

"How much longer is your term in office?" Lizzy asked.

"It comes to an end in March 1865, same as President Lincoln's," Kelly replied.

"That seems like an eternity from now. Can I be honest with you, Scott?"

"Always."

"I don't think I can bear the thought of another term, or another sleepless night, Scott, not knowing if you're ever coming home, if you're alive or lying dead out there somewhere. I want to wish you goodnight, every night," Lizzy said as she looked up, and Kelly leaned over and kissed her gently on the lips.

"I know what's going on, Scott. I know about the two men the Cheyenne and Arapaho killed on Husted Mill Road, Edward Davis and Job Talbert. Amanda Husted had introduced me once to her brother Job and told me about how helpless she felt watching him die...I know about the Hungate family being murdered north of the Black Forest in Douglas County. I know Governor Evans has been putting pressure on Colonel Chivington to end this problem with the Indians. I heard Anthony Bott, Robert Finley, John Brown and young Irving Howbert are volunteering in Company G, accepting a one hundred day enlistment...and I know that many once peaceful Indians are now Dog Soldiers."

"Those Cheyenne and Arapaho declared war on the white man, Lizzy."

"I know that for every Indian warrior killed there will be retribution – you know there will be, against every white person along the Front Range…and soon. Its all the more trouble for you and the other sixteen Sheriffs here in the Territory to deal with, you must see that, Scott. I never intended to run into marriage, a family, but since I met you I can't think of anything else…but I don't want a violent, fearful life. That's no way to raise a family."

"Whoa," Kelly said to the team of horses, pulling the buggy to a halt before turning to face Lizzy sitting on the buckboard next to him. "I know Lizzy. That's why I'm saving my nickels—to purchase 160 acres from Juan Peralta on Fountain Creek. When my term is up, I'm intending to be building a ranch…a ranch for us to raise a family on."

"Scott!" Lizzy said with excitement, "You serious?!"

The kiss that followed eliminated any doubt that the lawman was serious about marrying the beautiful young woman sitting beside him and hanging up his gun and badge forever.

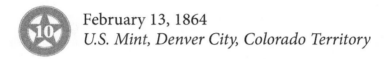 February 13, 1864
U.S. Mint, Denver City, Colorado Territory

"Where is Mr. Clarke?" Mr. Blaine, the superintendent of the Denver Mint asked the young clerk sitting next to the empty desk of James Clarke.

"He told me Saturday he was going into the country to spend the Sabbath," the young clerk replied, "Maybe something happened to him."

"Maybe," Mr. Blaine commented, as he made his way into the adjoining vault room and knelt down to spin the dial and open the safe. "Holy Mother of God!" the Mint superintendent exclaimed, after cracking open the heavy metal door to discover most of the cash and several gold bars were missing.

Hearing the superintendent's verbal distress, the young clerk rushed into the vault room and bent over Mr. Blaine's shoulder, peering inside the open safe to see that only packages of United States Treasury Notes of small denomination were left. Looking around the interior of the room the young clerk tapped his boss on the shoulder and then pointed to a nearby window that opened to the alley in back of the mint. The window had been propped open with a pencil.

"Have you spoken to Mr. Clarke?" Mr. Blaine asked the young clerk.

"Not since Saturday, sir. He'd bought a saddle and bridle and was very proud to tell me about them."

"Does Mr. Clarke own a horse?" Mr. Blaine asked of the young clerk.

"Not that I know of sir, but that didn't occur to me at the time. He was so proud of his news, he bought me a drink. Last I saw of him he was riding up F Street on a rented horse, Saturday night."

Two Days Later
Beach's Cabin, Colorado City

Judge Stone and Sheriff Kelly were sitting around the potbelly stove enjoying their morning coffee when M.S. Beach burst through the door with a copy of the Rocky Mountain News. "Judge, Sheriff, have you heard the news?" M.S. Beach asked in his thick Scottish brogue, holding up the front page of the newspaper so the Judge and Sheriff could read the bold headlines. "U.S. Mint Robbed in Denver," M.S. Beach read aloud as he plopped down on an empty chair and spread the newspaper out on the small wooden table. "I picked up the paper as it arrived just this morning on the Cherry Creek Stage from Denver City," Mr. Beach explained, taking a sip of cold coffee from his blue metal cup.

"Listen to this," M.S. Beach said as he read from the top of the first page, "February 13, 1864: U.S. Mint in Denver 'robbed' of over $36,817.05 (in gold bars, coins, currency, etc.) by James D. Clarke, who has lit out for parts unknown. The daring robbery was committed by a clerk at the bank. Denver City is stirred to its profoundest depths. According to several sources, young Mr. Clarke was said to be a 'bright and shining light in religious as well as social circles' who had recently donated money for a pew at the church and the last man to be suspected of such a disreputable act."

"Jim Blaine must be beside himself…" Judge Stone commented.

"Wouldn't you be?" M.S. Beach, asked not looking up from the newspaper.

"I would indeed, Mr. Beach," Judge Stone replied, "please, do tell us more."

M.S. Beach continued to read, "A Mr. Blaine immediately took steps to overtake him, in which he was heartily seconded by the Military Commander in the District. If the young scamp succeeds in getting away, it will be because he has more accomplices than is now supposed. Although a passably good horseman, it is hardly probable that he is physically capable of running a successful race with the boys of the 'First' even with all the advantage of his start. The 'boys' can ride two miles to his one, and have the advantage of a thorough knowledge of the country which Clarke cannot have, and with relays of horses as well as of men, if he took the direction of New Mexico, as was supposed, the news of his flight is already two hundred miles in advance of him."

"I suppose that means he's headed this way…" Judge Stone commented.

"Could be he's headed to Mace's Hole, south of the Arkansas in the Beulah Valley," Sheriff Kelly speculated aloud to the other two men, adding, "that's where Marshall Townsend captured those 44 Rebels that he marched through town here a ways back. Do we know anything else about this character?"

"What else could we possibly know?" Judge Stone asked.

"I was thinking about the company he might be keepin," the Sheriff replied.

"What are you thinking, Kelly?" M.S. Beach inquired.

"I've just been noticing...I'm wondering if there's not more to this than just a simple robbery," the lawman replied.

""Like a conspiracy?" the judge inquired with a wrinkled frown on his forehead.

"Like the KGC," the Sheriff answered, "I been hearin' ever since the Battle of Glorieta Pass, down in the northern New Mexico Territory, the South is finally beginning to realize they ain't likely to win this war, so the KGC's been burying caches of arms and gold to fund a second Civil War...one with a likely different outcome."

"Well fer shit," M.S. Beach replied, then spit tobacco juice toward a brass spittoon on the wooden planked floor before finishing his comment, "ain't there been 'nough killin' already!"

Judge Stone looked Kelly squarely in the eye and then asked the lawman who had earned his trust and respect, "How long you been suspectin' this?"

"Seems to me, Hank Way and his gang got away from the military mighty easily," Kelly said.

"You're thinking this goes that deep?" Judge Stone acknowledged, stroking the whiskers of his long grey beard.

"Holy shhhiiii..." Beach began.

As Judge Stone interrupted, "Thanks M.S., I think we get the picture."

Later that same afternoon
Finley Sawmill, Black Forest, El Paso County

Sheriff Kelly tied his horse to a hitching post in front of the sawmill with enough slack in the reins so his horse could drink from the wooden water trough. He removed his hat, ran his fingers through his thick blonde hair and casually looked around at the dozen or so men doing various jobs at the sawmill. He spotted Marcus Foster delimbing some large Ponderosa's with an axe, which had been his former job when he wasn't delivering lumber.

"Marcus!" the Sheriff shouted with a friendly wave, "got a minute?"

"Sure Sheriff," the younger man replied with a smile, "thanks for putting in a good word for me with Mr. Finley. I appreciate the work. Robert Finley's an honest man to work for," Marcus replied as he stuck his axe into the stump of a fallen tree.

Marcus pulled off the leather glove from his right hand before shaking hands with the Sheriff. "Anything I can do for you Sheriff?" he asked, as the Sheriff led the way down a narrow path into the nearby forest where they would be alone.

"Actually, Marcus, there is," the Sheriff began, somewhat unaccustomed to asking anyone for a favor.

"Happy to do anything, Scott...I think," Marcus said.

Kelly smiled, then began deliberately, "Got a bit of a manhunt on my hands..."

Marcus interrupted and said, "Scott, ya know...I've never been a soldier, or a lawman...my father was a preacher, a hunter and a farmer. I know how to use a gun but I never killed no one."

"It's not like that," the Sheriff replied assuredly, "I'm not sure how long I'll be gone, but wondered if you might keep an eye on the Stones for me again? Keep Charlie from following me...Keep Lizzy from getting too full o' fear."

"I can do that...I'll take care of them, Scott."

"Much obliged Marcus. You're a good man and I know I can

199

count on you here when I'm gone," Kelly concluded as the two men turned around and headed back toward the sawmill.

Later that Evening
Arkansas Platte Divide, Northern El Paso County

"Hello the camp!" the man driving the buggy hailed, wanting to avoid getting shot entering a camp after dusk uninvited.

"Hello yerself," the man standing said as he stepped out from behind the thick pine tree and uncocked his lever action rifle. "Might you be Mr. Blaine's son, from the U.S. Mint?"

"That I am," James Blaine Junior confirmed, "you must be Mr. Evans. Been told I could locate you up here near the headwaters of Cherry Creek, minding to your cattle."

"Man's gotta stick close to his herd with all the thievery goin on these days, with the Indians and what not. Coffee's not too bad, step on down and join me if'n you wants," Mr. Evans replied.

"Thank you for taking a moment to talk with me," Mr. Blaine Jr. said, before adding, "This here gentleman is Mr. Crocker."

"Glad to know both you gentlemen, come pour yerselves a cup and I'll tell you all I knows," Mr. Evans replied, pulling a flask of whisky out from under a bedroll. "Don't have no cream or sugar to offer, but this Taos Lightnin' might sweeten your coffees if'n you like."

"Appreciate your hospitality," Junior replied, accepting the coffee but passing on the liquor. "It surprised us all. Mr. Clarke was a church going man and all. He came to us highly recommended. Father trusted him completely."

Mr. Evans replied, "Tempted by gambling, women, and drink is what they're a sayin' in the papers."

"That is what they're saying," Junior confirmed, before continuing. "You say this man you met fit his description."

Mr. Evans nodded his head up and down slightly, then went on to explain, "Called himself Jim Jones, was armed to the hilt! Had a Mr. Maine with him. When I asked him what made him go armed so heavily, he replied he had had use of firearms once before and now he always went prepared for the worst. He also said he had cattle on the Fountaine qui Bouille and he was hunting some steers that had strayed."

Mr. Crocker spoke up, "Did Mr. Maine seem to know this story?"

"To be honest," Mr. Evans replied, "he helped him tell it. Mr. Maine claims Mr. Jones professes sympathies for Mexico and was just promoted a Lieutenant Colonel. Mr. Maine did seem to believe the story, but this Jim Jones was a jumpy sort a man. He looked nervous, sore, and sick – not sure he was used to hard country travelin. He matched the description in the paper in every particular. I had a lot of time to ask him questions – they camped the night."

Mr. Crocker continued the questioning, "Did they say which way they were headed?"

"Mexico," Mr. Evans recalled with certainty. "I recall Clarke saying he was meeting with his brother – a Confederate Army Colonel in the Calvary, in Mexico. Not sure what a Confederate Colonel would be doing in Mexico...Unless they's mixed up with the Knights of the Golden Circle somehow...They struck out next morning for the old Santa Fe Road. By nightfall they would've reached Wyte's down near Cotton's homestead."

Junior shook Mr. Evans hand, and then replied, "I appreciate your help Mr. Evans."

"You should seek the help of Sheriff Kelly," Mr. Evans offered, then added, "He found those Hank Way boys...more than once. I'm sure he could help you too."

"Much obliged," Junior replied, tossing the remnants of the coffee grounds from the bottom of his cup into the fire. "We best be turning in, we'll be off first thing in the morning."

Next Morning
Judge Stone's Ranch, El Paso County

Lizzy heard the knock on the door and was surprised to find Marcus standing on the front porch, "Mr. Foster! Did you leave something behind?"

"No, Miss Hill," Marcus replied as he removed his hat before continuing. "I'm sent by Sheriff Kelly to pay a call on y'all and let you know he'll be working on a case for the next few days, but I am here if you need anything atall."

"A case? What kind of a case, Mr. Foster?"

"I'm afraid that's all I know, Miss Hill," Marcus explained, wringing his hat in his hands, before adding, "But he was a bit concerned that Master Charlie might follow him."

Lizzy nodded her head and they both exchanged a bit of an eye-roll.

Lizzy chuckled, "For good reason. Come on in, let's see if we can't find my young cousin who can't wait to become one of Sheriff Kelly's deputies."

Lizzy and Marcus walked through the house, past the elegant dining room and through the kitchen door in back of the house. "Charlie! Charlie!" she shouted with no reply from wherever Charlie may have been hiding. As they walked toward the barn she glanced toward Marcus and asked with a smile, "Were you the kind of boy who looked for trouble, Mr.

Foster, like my dear cousin Charlie?"

Marcus smiled back, then replied, "Ah, no Miss...my parents were strict Quaker parents, come out here from the South, leaving the society of slave-owners behind. My father kept all us kids busy with hard work and learning scripture, sun up to sun down. Didn't leave us kids much time for making trouble."

"Well," Lizzy replied with a smile, "That might be just the cure for Charlie. CHARLIE!"

Lizzy and Marcus walked through the large barn in search of her younger cousin, shouting out his name every few minutes. Finally, as they walked out the back door they located Charlie, behind the barn, trying to rope a rabbit.

Later that Evening
Wyte's Camp, Fountain Creek, Southern El Paso County

Jim Blaine Jr., Mr. Crocker and Mr. Wyte were huddled in conversation when they saw Sheriff Kelly ride in on horseback.

"Sheriff!" Mr. Wyte called out, as the lawman stepped down from the saddle. "This is Mr. James Amos Blaine of the U.S. Mint. He just arrived to inquire about a visitor we had. Called himself 'Jim Jones' but looked a whole lot like this Mr. Clarke they've been writing about in all the Denver City papers."

Sheriff Kelly reached to shake Junior's outstretched hand, "Mr. Blaine. I've only just heard of the Mint robbery, but we might have a lead. A couple men bought a pony and tried to hire an ox team to bring in some saddles. They're at a camp a few miles away. Could be Mr. Clarke?"

"Could we go take a look in the morning?" Junior asked the lawman.

"We'll ride at first light," the Sheriff replied.

February 19, 1864 – Six Days since the Robbery
Cotton's Cabin, Williams Camp, Chico Basin, Southern El Paso County

Sheriff Kelly forced the flimsy wooden door open and burst into the one room cabin with his gun drawn. He found two men inside, eating bread, molasses and bacon for breakfast. One of the men matched the description of James Clarke, the other Mr. Maine.

Placing his hand on James Clarke's shoulder, Sheriff Kelly announced, "You are my prisoner." The sheriff pointed his gun toward the second man, "You're not going anywhere either." The sheriff searched both men carefully, relieving them of any weapons and whatever money they had in their possession that may have been embezzled from the US Mint in Denver.

Jim Blaine Junior stepped inside the log cabin to find Clarke trembling, "That's Clarke alright. I'd recognize him anywhere, although he does look a little rough for wear."

Clarke looked up from the table at the Sheriff and asked quietly, "Could you give me leave to finish breakfast?"

"Best hurry," Sheriff Kelly advised, after draping the robber's gunbelt over his shoulder, "while we're hitching the team. Afterwards we'll be taking our leave back to Denver City."

Blaine Junior said, "I'll keep an eye on him, Sheriff," knowing the Sheriff was anxious to search the men's saddlebags and other possessions outside for any clues of the robbery or the KGC. "Here," Junior said, handing the robber a copy of the COMMONWEALTH newspaper, "thought you might like to read what folks are saying about you up Denver way."

Jim Clarke took a few small bites of bacon and then pushed his breakfast plate away to concentrate on the newspaper article from

Denver City. When he was finished he said, "Well, some of that is true and some ain't. There certainly wasn't any 'wine and women'... I'd only taken to gambling about two weeks before all this happened. Within twenty-five minutes of the time I went to the Mint, leaving town hadn't even occurred to me. I had tried to borrow money to replace what I'd previously taken from the safe, and then came to the conclusion that it might be much better to be proven a big thief than a little one. If I got away, I might as well get it all as having nothing. I am sorry to have deceived Superintendent Blaine; your father was always decent to me. I had the key to the safe with me. Sometimes I've felt...thoughtful and gloomy about matters...and things in general..." Clarke ended his ramblings with a subdued laugh.

When Clarke's laughter faded off into reflective thought, Jim Blaine Jr asked him, "Thinkin' now it wasn't worth it in the end then?"

"It was for a greater cause," Clarke replied, before his words trailed off altogether.

Mr. Crocker entered the cabin, noticing Mr. Clarke's appetite had failed him. Within a few minutes Sheriff Kelly stepped back into the cabin, holding a gold bar wrapped in a handbill displaying the initials KGC in bold lettering – followed by the words: "Knights of the Golden Circle – Confederate States of America". The Sheriff unwrapped the gold bar, handed it to Junior and placed his hand on Clarke's shoulder, announcing it was time for them to leave. "Let's go."

February 21, 1864
U.S. Mint, Denver City, Colorado Territory

A fairly large crowd had gathered in front of the Denver Mint as Mr. Crocker pulled the horse drawn buggy to a halt. Mr. Blaine Jr. had ridden from Colorado City in the back seat next to James Clarke, while the Sheriff of El Paso County rode alongside on his gray mare. The Denver City's Daily Commonwealth ran the headline, "THE MINT ROBBERY! CAPTURE OF CLARK!" The morning newspaper reported the following story:

"He (Clarke) assumes the name 'Jim Jones'. He professes sympathy for Mexico: Claims to be a Lieut. Colonel! He trembles when arrested and confesses all. Enticed into gambling by nice suppers. The excitement of the past week culminated yesterday, on the arrival in town of Mr. (James) Amos Lane, Mr. Crocker, Mr. Kelly, Sheriff of El Paso County, and James D. Clarke, the absconding Pay Clerk of the United States Branch Mint in this city. The party drove up to the mint in front of a large, well-dressed and remarkably jocular assembled crowd. None others but employees of the Mint were admitted, and for two hours the crowd continued to increase. At the end of that time, Clarke was taken to his new quarters on Larimer Street. He is very much altered in appearance, through exposure and exhaustion, so that his old acquaintances did not recognize him at first glance. The story of his capture is nearly as follows:

"On Tuesday afternoon about five o'clock, Mr. (James) Amos Lane, son of the Superintendent of the Mint, in the company of Mr. Crocker, a freighter, left Denver in a buggy, having heard that a horse answering the description of the one rode by Clarke had been seen at the head of Cherry Creek; the two stopped the night at Mr. Slyer's about fifteen miles from Denver; starting early the next morning, they reached the place where the horse had been seen, but could find no further trace of it. They then concluded to pursue their search, and went on to the lower mill and thence up the Creek. At Kerr's Mill they found that the person answering Clarke's description had been leading a horse and that he had afterward hired Mr. Maine to guide him down to Mexico, and that he had furnished Mr. Maine with money, with which to buy a pony. The stranger had said that he was lost – that he had a brother in the Mexican army whom he wished to join, as he had just received a Lieutenant Colonel's commission – that the reason he had left the main road, was that Col. Chivington had forbid his going..."

"Shortly after leaving Kerr's Mill, they (Blaine and Crocker) met a Mr. Evans who told them that a young man answering Clarke's description had stayed at his camp on Monday night. Mr. Evans' camp is just over the 'Divide' (in El Paso County), where he is herding cattle. Mr. E (Evans) had asked him a great many questions, such as 'What made him go armed so heavily?' To this Clarke said he had had use of firearms once before and now he always went prepared for the worst. He also said he had cattle on the Fountain qui Bouille and that he was hunting some that had strayed. He gave his name as Jim Jones. Of course Maine helped this story along. Maine appears to be an honest sort of fellow and probably believed the story of the Mexican Colonelcy."

The newspaper article continued, "The weather was very cold, snow was falling, and as there were no other stopping places that they could reach that night Mr. Blaine Jr. concluded to stay over, until morning, at Mr. Crosby's. The weather was clear, but cold, next morning, when the pursuit was renewed before sunrise. A saddle which Mr. C. (Crosby) furnished was put into the buggy, at this point. Thinking they could make better headway, they struck for the old Santa Fe road. By night they reached Wyte's near Cotton's having traveled about sixty miles that Thursday, but heard no additional things."

"They had been at Wyte's but a few minutes when Mr. Kelly, Sheriff of El Paso County came in. He had only just heard of the Mint robbery, but had heard of a couple men who had bought a pony, and tried to hire an ox team to bring in some saddles which were at the camp a few miles away, their ponies having strayed. The next morning, Friday, accompanied by the Sheriff, they started early and struck the trail of their suspicioned individuals, and in two hours came to a little cabin where Clarke and Maine were eating breakfast."

"The Sheriff first went into the cabin and laying his hand on Clarke said, 'You are my prisoner' while Messrs. Crocker and Lane remained outside for a few minutes. When Mr. Blaine went in, Clarke was trembling violently, but asked leave to finish his breakfast. In a few minutes his appetite failed him, and the party, now numbering five persons was enroute to Denver."

"At Cotton's, the Sheriff went off to get a team, and then Clarke began to ask if there were bills out, and if his description was given – what the papers had said about him, & etc. It was not, however, until he reached Colorado City, that he saw the Commonwealth, containing a full account of the robbery, which he read through without remark; but upon laying the paper down, he laughingly said – 'Well, some of that is true, and some isn't.' What he objected to, was the 'wine and women' portion of the account, and the story about the letter to the prisoner from his sister in Pittsburg; averring that he knew nothing upon which such a story could be based. [A dozen persons have seen these letters, and their genuineness has been doubted]."

The newspaper continued, "He said that he had only commenced gambling about two weeks before, and that up to within twenty-five minutes of the time he went to the Mint, the thought of leaving town had not occurred to him; that he had tried with all his might to borrow money to replace what he had previously abstracted, and then came to the conclusion that it might be much better for him to be proven a big rascal than a little one – that if he got away, he might as well get it all as having nothing. He said that he was sorry Supt. Blaine had been deceived in him. He had the key of the safe with him. Sometimes he was thoughtful and gloomy, and at other he would laugh and joke about matters and things in general."

"The Superintendent, Mr. Blaine Sr., went down to Colorado City last Saturday, but took the Coberly route, while his son and party came by the stage route. Of course, he heard the good news at Colorado City and was expected home by stage last night."

"We are not able to state exactly how much money was recovered, but the major part of it was in the saddle-bags. Of course it is easy to trace the amounts he has dispensed of, even if he were not so willing to tell. It was current on the street yesterday that the bar of gold, worth nearly $3,000, worked through the saddle-bag within a mile of town, and that it has not been recovered; this is all conjecture, we imagine."

"The short stages which Clarke made, shows that he had not well calculated his own powers of endurance. Riding horseback is rather a trying business to a raw hand, and Clarke has proved that a guilty conscience and a brandy bottle are not the best companions on a cold night."

"The horses, which strayed away from the camp of Clarke and Maine, on Tuesday night, of course the captors did not stop to hunt for. It seems Clarke became both sick and sore. On the way from the camp, to the cabin where they were arrested, Maine complained about carrying the saddlebags which contained the greenbacks, but Clarke made him do it – as it contained his commission and valuable correspondence."

"Maine is temporarily committed to jail, as of course, his testimony is required. A preliminary examination will be held in a day or two, perhaps; but a trial will not be had until the March term of the U.S. District Court."

"Most of these particulars we obtained directly from Mr. Blaine, who though wearied, very kindly yielded to the natural desire of the public to the particulars. We congratulate him most heartily upon his share in the capture of the thief."

"Mr. (James) Amos Lane expresses himself under great obligations to Messrs. Slyer, Evans and Crosby for their kindness and valuable assistance; also to his companion, Mr. Crocker and Sheriff Kelly."

"Upon leaving the Mint for the jail, Mr. Clarke said to Mr. Eckfeldt, who assisted Deputy U.S. Marshall H. Hunt in conducting him; 'Walk faster Marshall – there is a good deal more excitement about this thing than I expected – I don't want all these chaps starting at me!' But the crowd kept pace with him, some leading the way, others bringing up the rear, until the jail was reached and he was placed in a felon's cell."

"Inside the jail, the interest was about as great as elsewhere, for as soon as the other prisoners were made aware of the accession to their numbers of so distinguished a member of their fraternity, they put their mouths s to the diamonds of the cell doors, and in all sorts of phrases, welcomed him with a sort of fiendish jocularity that must have been very gratifying."

"'Poor Fool!'" say some – 'he might have known he would have been caught;' just as if the great punishment would not have been to have escaped the clutches of his pursuers – and to have lived a life of perpetual fear, the great crime forever weighing upon his conscience – starting at his own shadow – frightened at the rustling of a leaf, trembling against at the storm; or worst still, as he went on in a career of crime hardening his heart to still more serious deeds, and perhaps adding that of murder to the catalogue."

The newspaper articled concluded, "But who can measure the anguish of the mad youth who plunges headlong into a career of crime – who can imagine the full terror of the wail of the soul which, self affrighted at its own falls, cries inwardly 'Lost! Lost!' Young men of Denver! Think of it! Which road are you traveling? Remember 'Jim Clarke."

The Next Morning
Kitchen Table, Judge Stone's Ranch, El Paso County

"Well now, that's quite a story," Judge Stone remarked, after reading the newspaper account to Mrs. Stone, Lizzy and Charlie.

"Hoorah for Sheriff Kelly!" Charlie shouted, and then stuffed the last two bites of his pancakes in his mouth at the same time with his fork.

"And here comes our hero now," Mrs. Stone commented as she peered out the kitchen window and smiled to see Sheriff Kelly riding up to the front of the ranch house on his new gray mare.

"All right!" Charlie yelled excitedly as he jumped up from the table and raced out the kitchen door to greet the lawman out front.

Lizzy was all smiles as she hung up her white apron on a hook behind the kitchen door and straightened her hair.

Sheriff Kelly, being led inside by Charlie, removed his Stetson cowboy hat and turned to look at the large white dog that had followed him to the Stone Ranch. "You stay out here, Sam," Kelly said as he shut the screen door and said to the Stone family gathered in the kitchen, "Sorry for interrupting your breakfast."

"Please join us," Judge Stone offered, sliding out a kitchen chair from the table with his foot.

"Scott, would you care for a cup of coffee?" Mrs. Stone inquired, pouring her husband a refill as Lizzy took the seat next to the handsome lawman.

"Yes, please," Kelly replied as he pulled a folded piece of paper from his vest pocket.

"Tell us all about it, starting with how much of a reward did they pay you?" Charlie asked excitedly.

"Now Charlie," Mrs. Stone admonished softly, "you know it's not polite to ask others about money," even though that was the one question everyone gathered around the kitchen table wanted to know the most.

"That's alright Mrs. Stone," Sheriff Kelly said with a wide smile, "It was in the paper that the Mint had offered a $1,000.00 reward for the capture of James Clarke, which they gladly paid, but what was unexpected was they paid me an additional $1,000.00 for the cash and gold bars I recovered in the possession of Clarke and Maine and turned back into the Mint. That accounted for $29,000.00 of the just over $36,000.00 that had been stolen from the safe. Guess they hadn't expected to ever see any of that money again."

"Wow!" said Charlie, "You got more money than Bert Meyers got beans!"

"Charlie Everhart Stone," Mrs. Stone scolded gently, suppressing a laugh along with the other adults, "now, we'll not be talking that way."

"Had, more money," Kelly said as he unfolded the paper he

had been holding and placed it face up on the kitchen table.

"Scott Kelly," Lizzy said with a curious frown, "what have you been up to?"

"I just paid $1500.00 cash to Juan Peralta this morning for his two 80 acre adjoining parcels of prime pasture land down on Fountain Creek. Tomorrow morning I aim to start laying the foundation for the new barn. Charlie, you up for making a little extra money? Sure could use your help," the lawman asked.

"I'll help you Sheriff!" Charlie shouted, then turned to his father, "if'n it's okay with you pa."

"If you get your chores done around here first, I guess I'd be okay with that arrangement," Judge Stone replied as he picked up the deed on the kitchen table and began to read, "This is the old Peralta boy's property. That family's been in the San Juan Valley for five generations – all the way back to the Spanish Conquistadors. I heard tell when Juan's grandparents were born in the San Luis Valley they were Spanish citizens, then they became Mexican citizens, and then they became U.S. citizens and never left the Valley."

"They certainly seem to have mastered the art and science of irrigation," Sheriff Kelly replied with admiration. "The ditch they dug on those two eighty acre sections effectively waters the entire ranch out of Fountain Creek and the water rights extend all the way across the width of the creek from the west bank to the east bank. It's good land with rich soil. Crops will grow high; the stock will grow fat and happy."

Lizzy kissed Scott happily on the cheek.

Mrs. Stone leaned over and whispered into her husband's ear, "Can a wedding be far off?"

The Stone's smiled at one another, then Judge Stone remarked to the Sheriff, "I won't be at all surprised, Scott, if El Paso County asks you for a second term as Sheriff. You've done a fine job son."

Kelly noticed a look of concern growing on Lizzy's pretty face, then turned toward Judge Stone to reply, "Well, that's mighty nice to hear, Your Honor, especially coming from you, but serving a second term is not in the plan." When the lawman looked back toward Lizzy, the frown of concern on her face had diminished some, but had not entirely disappeared.

"Charlie, do you think you could check on Sam for me? I hope he's still where I left him on the front porch," the Sheriff asked.

"Sure," Charlie replied, and then turned to ask of his mother, "May I be excused?"

"Certainly, Charlie," his mother replied as she and Lizzy stood up to clear the breakfast dishes from the table, smiling at one another acknowledging Charlie's extra attention to showing good manners in front of Scott Kelly.

A few minutes later, Lizzy and Scott found themselves sitting alone on the front porch swing, enjoying the morning breeze and watching Charlie trying to teach Sam how to fetch a stick. Kelly was still basking in pride and self-satisfaction in having purchased one of the finest ranch properties in El Paso County.

"You know Scott," Lizzy began, "I'm very proud of you."

Still grinning, Kelly responded, "And I'm very proud of you, too. How many young ladies can say the Smithsonian Institute named a fossil after them? Quite an accomplishment I'd say."

"They better name it after me, even though I'm not a man," Lizzy replied only half in jest, "I did find it after all!"

Turning serious, Lizzy turned to face Kelly then asked, "Can I be honest with you, Scott?"

"Please," the Sheriff said, looking her in the eye.

214

"You serving as Sheriff is probably the best thing to happen to El Paso County. I know that. And I know my Uncle is right, but... when I met you it was a few rustlers and horse thieves – now its murderers, bank robbers...Dog Soldiers. I want a family Scott. I never did before, but now, I do. You changed that. I want to be able to wish you a good night, every night for the rest of my life... but I just can't wake up every morning not knowing if I will open my eyes to find you lying next to me or not. I need to know you are here, with me, to protect me and our family."

"I don't intend to sign on for another term Lizzy...I've had two horses shot out from under me already. I think I've had enough. 'Sides, Bert Meyers has been campaigning for two months already, buying every registered voter in the County a cigar."

"Easy for him," Lizzy replied, "owning a mercantile and all."

Kelly laughed, "Bert's even bought himself a new Colt revolver, but don't worry Lizzy; I'm a carpenter and I didn't come out West here to become a lawman."

Lizzy smiled bravely as the Sheriff lifted her mouth gently to meet his, then kissed her fully on the lips. She reciprocated with sincere pleasure and a dream of what their lives together would become; building a beautiful ranch, with horses and puppies and a happy family.

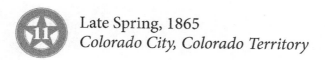
Late Spring, 1865
Colorado City, Colorado Territory

The Sheriff stopped and knocked on the front door of Laura Belle's brothel, tipping his hat politely to the few townsfolk who were walking about that chilly evening. Looking down at the fully grown white dog sitting by his right boot, Sheriff Kelly explained to the dog, "Ya' see Sam, you gotta do that sometimes to keep up appearances, you have to let folks know this here visit is official law business; we can't be starting rumors that we was here on any personal business."

The dog looked up at the Sheriff, cocked his head to the side, listened intently to the lawman's every word, then wagged his bushy tail and turned his large head back toward the heavy wooden door, waiting patiently for it to be opened.

The Sheriff and his furry companion heard some movement inside, followed by muffled voices, and then a few seconds later Laura Belle, the proprietor of the most successful brothel in town, opened the heavy wooden door.

"Evening Ms. Belle," the Sheriff began, removing his hat,

"heard you wanted to talk to me."

"Yes, Sheriff," Laura Belle replied, "so good of you to stop by. Won't you please come in?"

"Mind if my deputy here comes along?" the Sheriff asked, nodding down at the white dog sitting beside him, "He's become my shadow as of late."

Laura Belle smiled, "By all means, Sam is always welcome. My, he has grown."

"Well," the Sheriff replied as he stepped inside with Sam at his heels, "just don't make the mistake of feeding him or you'll never get rid of him."

"Would you feel comfortable if we talk in my sitting room?" Laura asked, glancing up the narrow stairs, "Might prove a bit more private."

The Sheriff nodded, glanced up the stairs to where a few curious heads had ducked out of sight. Kelly smiled and followed Laura Belle to her private quarters in the back lower level of the narrow two story brick building.

When the door to her private suite was closed, she motioned for the lawman to sit on the red velvet coach positioned against the far wall. "May I get you or your deputy anything?" Laura Belle asked sincerely.

"We're both fine, ma'am," the Sheriff replied, and then asked, "Trouble with one of your girls?"

"Yes, regretfully so, with one of my best girls," Laura Belle began, as she sat in a wooden rocking chair near the end of the sofa, adding, "I believe you may know her, Becky Red Stocking?"

"Yes, we have met a few times. Hope she's feeling all right."

"Well there is a small problem. But rather than talk about her, if you don't mind, may I fetch her so the two of you can speak in private?"

"By all means," the Sheriff replied.

Smiling thankfully, Laura Belle stood up and made her way to the door, then looking over her shoulder said, "I'll be right back Sheriff," and closed the door.

The lawman remained seated, patiently waiting with his canine who had laid his head down across the top of the Sheriff's cowboy boot. Kelly glanced around the room and noticed a well-worn King James Bible lying beneath a painted gas lamp on the table beside the rocker. Within a few minutes the door slowly opened and in walked Becky Red Stockings.

"Good evening, Miss Rebecca," the lawman said as he stood to greet the lady.

"Good evening, Sheriff," Becky replied as she made her way to the rocking chair and sat down, uncomfortably holding her protruding belly. "I so appreciate you taking time to talk with me," she said, as Sam walked over and placed his head on her leg, waiting to be petted.

"I see the two of you have met," the Sheriff said with a smile.

"I think Sam knows everyone in town," Becky said with a smile, teasing the hair on top of the white dog's head.

"Sheriff," the pretty young woman with the dark complexion began, "I know this isn't law related, but you see, Miss Laura and I don't know who else to turn to. As you may have noticed, I'm in a motherly way. She lifted her hand from her belly, revealing a bulge that looked about the size of a small watermelon under her dress.

"I can see where that could pose a problem," the Sheriff acknowledged.

"Business, being what it is," Miss Becky replied, "well, Miss

Laura has to give my room to one of the more productive girls, and I gots no place to go."

"Don't suppose you'd know who the father is," the lawman asked, already knowing the answer but thought that option had to be eliminated before going further.

"No," Miss Becky replied quietly, "suppose he could be any one of two or three dozen men; miners, cowboys or possibly even one of the more respectable married men of the town."

"I been noticing where business has picked up considerably, ever since the men dug the tunnel under Colorado Avenue from the Anway Hotel to the back room here at Laura Belle's."

"Yes," Becky agreed, "with the Cheyenne on the warpath the militia men thought the towns folk that were forted up at the Anway Hotel needed an escape route in case of attack. The upright logs they built for the stockade walls are susceptible to fire and the men didn't want the women and children to get trapped inside; at least that's the story they told their wives. Those German gold miners digging the tunnel tried to convince Major Wynkoop that their coming up in Laura Belle's back room was a mistake, a miscalculation from failing to convert meters to feet caused them to be a little off while measuring the distance from the fort to that little stone armory they built down by the creek where they cache their powder."

"I can see where asking a group of lonely miners to dig a tunnel under a brothel might not end exactly where one had intended," the Sheriff replied with a smile.

"I was there when that first miner popped his head up out of the ground, wearing a latern attached to the front of his head, and said with a big grin on his face that as long as he was in the neighborhood, could he please maybe buy a piece of pie? That began kinda of a code for the men folks who emerged from that hole in the ground, all of them wearing smiles on their dirty faces, and asking for a particular kind of pie. 'Apple pie,' meant they wanted to be with a more experienced girl. If they asked for 'cherry pie" they wanted to be with a less experienced, well a less-used girl. If they wanted to be with me, the only colored girl here in Laura Belle's stable, they asks for a 'brownie" and if they wants a white girl to joins us, they asks for a scoop of 'vanilla ice cream' on top. One man, you'd know him if'n I was to mention his name, showed up one night a couple months back and ordered a brownie with two scoops of vanilla on the side, said he was celebrating striking it rich selling a crop of potatoes. He was so drunk he done passed out soon as he gots into bed, but not until after he done paid Miss Laura."

"I think I do know who that might have been," the lawman said, "Tried to tell me and his wife he'd been robbed by some Mexicans down by the Seven Falls, but I don't think either of us believed his story."

"Some of the churchwomen tried to make the men fill in the tunnel, and they told them they would, but that never happened," Miss Becky commented. "Seems like the most righteous church going men are some of our more frequent visitors, and many of the most pious women of the town were formerly Spoiled Doves themselves."

The Sheriff kept his thoughts to himself as Miss Becky continued, "Sunday mornings I like to sit with my window open so I can hear the singing coming from inside the church and I reads the Bible my mama gave me when I was a little girl and being baptized. I only been inside the church across the street once; I done snuck in when no one was around, just had to see what the stained glass window looked like with the sunlight streamin' in, all them pretty colors blending together. It's so beautiful, so calming."

"Do you have any family anywhere?" the Sheriff asked, returning to the business at hand. "I can get you a stagecoach ticket as far as Julesburg; from there you could catch a train to just about any northern city back east."

"That's very kind of you Sheriff," the young woman replied, then looked down at her hands clasped in her lap. "You see, I don't really have any family. The plantation where I was born, well that belonged to the Beauregard family and was located in the deep South, and I hear may have been burnt down during the War. Not sure where my older sister ended up, if'n she's still alive. 'Sides, not sure riding in a bumpy stagecoach is what this little one needs right now."

"Well, first things first," the Sheriff replied, "You know that little house I built off 24th Street there, down by the creek? You can stay there long as you need to."

"But where are you going to stay?" Miss Becky asked.

"Well, when I'm out at the ranch, which is usually on the weekends, I stay in the barn and when I'm here in town I can bunk over at Xavier's Blacksmith Shop.

"He seems like a nice man, although I don't know him, ah professionally if you know what I mean. I only done seen him from my window walking horses down the street. You can tell a lot about a person the way they treats an animal," she replied, adding thoughtfully, "but I wouldn't want to put you out none, 'sides, what would the townsfolk say?"

"Well, some folks do love to gossip, so we might as well give them something to talk about," the Sheriff said with a smile.

"When would you like to move in?"

"The sooner the better I suppose," the young woman answered, then explained as she started to tear up, "you see Sheriff, this happened once before. I got this way last year and I didn't know I was expecting at the time. She was my first baby. I didn't know to listen to what my body was tellin me, I think she must have been about six or eight weeks from being born when I lost her. I named her Anna. You're the only other person alive who knows that part. Broke my heart, it did, to put Anna's little body in that tiny wooden box and buried her all alone up there on the hill, beyond where you men buried that Devlin fella. She's lying there still, in an unmarked grave. Miss Laura was kind enough to give me a couple weeks off to recover; physically, not sure I can ever recover completely. You ever notice that little angel in the corner of the stained glass window you ordered for me for the First Methodist Church?"

The Sheriff nodded, wishing now that he had paid more attention.

"Well, that little angel's for her, so as I don't forget her," Miss Becky said as tears ran down her cheeks, while more tears began to well up in the rugged lawman's eyes.

The Sheriff struggled to speak, but eventually cleared his throat and finally said, "Well, please tell me, when do you want to move in?"

"Next day or so, I expect," Becky repeated, then added as she patted her belly softly, "Not sure when this little one here plans to make an appearance."

"You can move in tonight if you wish."

"I gots a little money hidden away; can I pay you room and board or you can let me know if there's any other way I can earn my keep?"

"You will be my guest, as long as you wish, no strings attached. I will leave the front door unlocked and I will bunk over at Xavier's." Then looking down at Sam who had fallen asleep on Becky's foot, the Sheriff chuckled softly, adding, "Guess we'll let Sam decide where he'd rather sleep, but I'm guessing I'll be bunking alone."

As the Sheriff started to stand, Becky reached over and placed her hand on top of his and looked him in the eye. "Thank you Sheriff, for keeping your promise not to tell nobody it was me who paid for that Tiffany stained glass window over at Reverend Howbert's church. I just didn't want its beauty to be tarnished in any way if'n he or any of the church going folks was to have ever found out it had been paid for by someone the likes of me. I'd always be afraid someone might throw'd a stone through it if'n dat they knowed where da money come from."

"Miss Becky," the Sheriff said as he rose from the sofa, still clutching her hand in his, "you're correct, some people can be quick to throw stones, but we have all done things we regret in life, myself included. Reverend Howbert once told me it wasn't what happened yesterday that mattered as much as what you do today and what you'll do tomorrow that matters in the eyes of the Lord. I know you will make a wonderful mother and it has been my great honor to get to know you and be in your service." He bent over and kissed the back of her hand. As the Sheriff started to leave, he paused for a moment at the door to see if Sam was coming with him, and then added, "I'm sure Sam would agree, you can stay at our place for as long as you want."

When the lawman and his dog stepped out onto the street, he didn't need a watch that worked to tell him it was well past nine o'clock, and on a Saturday night he knew things would sooner than later get lively on the south side of Colorado Avenue. Just as the Sheriff and his furry, four-legged deputy approached Meadow Muffins, on the northeast corner of 25th Street and Colorado Avenue, they heard glass breaking from inside, followed by a gunshot, followed by an outburst of raucous laughter.

"Come on Sam, looks like we'll have to put off moving our stuff over to Xavier's for the moment." The Sheriff and the big white dog crossed the wide dirt street to the north. It served as the main east west street running through the small town.

Stepping up onto the boardwalk, the Sheriff noticed several wooden slats from a water barrel that someone had disassembled to repair were leaning up again the side of the brick building. Pausing for a moment to select one of the three foot long slats, the lawman selected a board about four inches wide and thirty-six inches long, then slapped the sturdy piece of lumber against the outside of his tall right boot, nodded his approval and stepped inside. Sam followed closely at his side. The cigar smoke was thick and the stench of spilt beer and hard liquor rested heavily on the stale air inside the dimly lit saloon.

The enthusiastic piano music was overly loud, which compensated somewhat for the old piano being more than a little out of tune. A half dozen miners, wearing faded blue overalls, and cowboys in work clothes were crowded around two green felt covered poker tables positioned to the right of the double-hinged swinging doors. Four more cowboys stood drinking beer at the bar. The mirror behind the bar had been shattered. The bartender, Rollie, a rugged-looking man from Tucson, Arizona, wearing a black derby and white apron, was standing at one end of the bar cleaning broken glass out of a beer mug with a dirty yellow towel.

The Sheriff recognized the four rugged cowboys drinking at

the bar as ranchhands from the Three Eagles Ranch in Southern Douglas County. As the lawman and his dog walked up behind the four cowboys, the piano music stopped abruptly and everyone inside the bar turned their attention toward where the lawman and his dog stood. The four cowboys, hearing the music stop, turned around to see the lawman holding the wooden slat in his hand. The biggest and most rowdy of the four intoxicated cowboys leaned back, resting his elbows on the bar behind him, and glared at the Sheriff with discontent.

"What do you want, tinstar?" the intoxicated cowboy asked with a slur.

"I want to know which one of you gentlemen is going to pay Rollie here for that broken mirror, or are all four of you going to chip in to pay for the damages?" the Sheriff said, pointing with the piece of lumber toward the broken glass behind the bar.

The drunken cowboy slowly reached down with his right hand and slipped the tie-down leather strap from around the hammer of his revolver. "Or what?" the drunken cowboy asked with a sneer, "You goin' ta hit me with your little stick?"

The Sheriff waited for the other three cowboys to finish laughing before he replied, "Oh, this isn't for you, it's for him," he said nodding down at Sam who was showing his teeth and growling quietly at the cowboys, saliva foaming at the corners of his wide mouth.

Sam took a half step toward the cowboy who had his right hand down by his handgun. Slowly the cowboy raised his hand a few inches above his beltline, as Sam inched slowly forward, staring at his crotch.

Nervously the drunken cowboy lowered his non-gun hand down to cover his crotch and asked, "What's the matter with him?"

"Don't rightly know," the Sheriff replied, "Doc said it might be rabies or something. All I know is his training ain't been going so good. He's taken really good to the attack part, but the trouble is he always goes for the crotch and I can't ever get him to release his bite. That's why I carry this here stick, to whop him atop the head. That usually works but there's just no guarantee."

As if on cue, Sam inched forward again, then growled viciously and shook his head a few times causing several white clumps of thick foam to scatter across the dirty barroom floor, while a long string of drool wrapped completely around his large black nose.

"Last time this happened, it was a cowboy from the JA Ranch there in Castle Rock. You might'a knowed him, he was from Waco...called himself Waco Curly Phil and always wore a big bushy black beard?"

"Can't say I ever met him," the cowboy replied nervously. "What happened to him?"

"Well," the Sheriff explained sincerely, "it t'was a pretty sad affair, Sam here lit into his manly parts and wouldn't let go. By the time I found something to smack him over the head with, well the damage was already done. They tried to nurse him back to health out there on the ranch. He even saw a doctor a couple times up in Denver City, but his voice never returned to normal; it always remained about two octaves higher than it had ever been before. Curly Phil just couldn't handle all the teasing and finally he left the JA Ranch, bounced around a couple other ranches down in the New Mexico Territory, but couldn't find work anywhere and finally gave up cowboyin' all together and joined a travelling Wild West show."

"What did he do there?" one of the other three cowboys asked, as he sipped the head of foam off his warm beer.

"Well," the Sheriff answered slowly, "they dressed poor old Curly Phil up in a green tutu and billed him as The Bearded Lady from Waco."

"HA!" the cowboy who had asked the question laughed, as he spit beer out of his mouth on to the floor and the other two cowboys roared with laughter. "Come on Curly Phil," the cowboy said as he slapped the first cowboy on the back, "Let's call it a night."

"Okay, okay Sheriff," the suddenly sober cowboy agreed, as he stood up and unbuckled his gunbelt, "There's no need for violence."

"You know Curly Phil," another of the cowboys chided in using this cowboy's new nickname, "you might not look half bad wearin a tutu!"

"You shut up," the sullen cowboy replied, "you men wouldn't a been so brave neither if'n it was your family jewels that mangy mutt was a staring at."

"Grrrr," Sam growled lowly, forcing the cowboys to finish handing over their guns.

"Rollie," the Sheriff asked, addressing the bartender, wiping the wooden bar with the same dirty bar rag, "any idea how much it's going to cost to replace that mirror?"

"Last time it got busted it cost us sixty dollars, including shipping from Independence, Missouri," Rollie answered.

"We ain't got that kind of money on us," the more sober of the four cowboys replied.

"Well, now that you boys have finished handing over your firearms and gunbelts, you can decide whatever money you want to leave with Rollie here as a deposit," the Sheriff said. "When you get the rest of the money together you can have Mr. Johnson come in from the ranch to pay for the broken mirror and he can collect your firearms. Agreed?"

Begrudgingly the four cowboys chipped in and handed Rollie $12.50 and then walked outside single-file, followed by the Sheriff and his four-legged deputy. The Sheriff and Sam stood in front of Meadow Muffins and watched as the four cowboys mounted their horses and rode peacefully out of town. As the off-key piano music started back up inside, the lawman leaned the wooden water barrel slat back against the brick wall where it had been, next to the other pieces of milled wood, and started walking across Colorado Avenue back toward his cabin near Fountain Creek.

"Laying it on kinda thick back there, weren't you partner?" the Sheriff said, intending to collecting his things to spend the night at Xavier's blacksmith shop. As they reached the gaslight that stood on the southeast corner of Colorado Avenue and 24th Street, the lawman glanced down at the huge white dog, and in the dim light it appeared almost as if Sam was laughing.

Mid-December, 1865
Xavier's Blacksmith Shop, Colorado City

"That's about the prettiest baby girl I've ever seen," the Sheriff announced to Xavier.

"I'd expect so, her mother is sure one to look at," Xavier commented to Kelly as he prepared to turn in for the night. "You sure you're going to be warm enough out here?" the blacksmith asked of his friend, pitching another large lump of coal into the hearth as he prepared to go inside his small adjoining house. "The nights are gettin' longer in da past month since you been stayin' out here in the shop, and days only be gettin' colder from here on til February."

"I'd be warmer if that dang dog of mine hadn't done deserted me. Sam's decided he'd rather be spending all his time with that little girl and her mother," the lawman mused as he sat down on a bale of hay and pulled off his boots, preparing to turn in for the night.

"Seems to me you done got a right smart dog there." Xavier teased, "I only seen them from a distance, but after spending the last four or five weeks with you while you been stayin' over ta here, I knowed who I'd rather be spending my time with."

"Some friend you turned out to be," Kelly laughed, then added, "and here I was about to extend you an invitation on behalf of Miss Becky and Miss Lizzy to have dinner with us tomorrow evening at my former house."

"Seriously?" Xavier asked, "You mean dat Kelly or you just poking fun at me again?"

"I'm serious. Miss Lizzy was over at my place today, helping the new momma in giving her baby a bath, and I walked in on the two of them schemin' on how's they was a fixin' to invite two handsome fellas over for dinner tomorrow evening." Seeing how he now had his friend's full attention, the Sheriff went on good-naturedly, "Naturally, I assumed they was a talkin' about me and Sam, but to my surprise they said the other man was you that they wanted to invite to dinner."

"Me? Really?" Xavier said with astonishment.

"I know," Kelly went on teasingly, "surprised me too!"

"Come on Kelly, you serious?"

"Yep. They said they was wonderin' if you would rather have ham or fried chicken. I told 'em I'd done seen you eat afore and you never came across to me as being all that particular."

"Boy now, either ham or fried chicken sounds wonderful to me. Can't say when I remembers the last time I sat down and done had a home cooked meal. But what's do I bring?"

"I asked if we could bring anything and they said just to bring ourselves," Kelly replied.

"Well," the blacksmith replied looking around his shop, "I can't just show up empty handed. Maybe I can think of something to bring the baby. What do they need?"

"I don't know," the Sheriff replied, "everything I guess. When Miss Becky showed up at my place it looked to me like the only things she owned was a couple small bundles of clothes, an old Bible and a rocking chair."

"A rocking chair? Say, that gives me an idea," the blacksmith commented, his words trailing off as the big man walked toward the back of his workshop.

The next evening Sheriff Kelly answered the knock at the door of his small house in Colorado City finding Xavier standing out on the front porch holding a small wooden cradle. "Good evening Mr. Bent, won't you please come in?" As the big man entered the front room, he removed his hat as Miss Becky stepped forward holding her baby proudly in her arms. "Miss Becky, may I introduce Mr. Xavier Bent. Mr. Bent, may I introduce you to Miss Rebecca Anne Toutant-Beauregard."

"Miss Becky, I am honored to meet you," Xavier said shyly with a slight bow.

"Mr. Bent, I have so been looking forward to meeting you. May I present my daughter, Kelly Anne," Miss Becky replied holding up her baby and pulling back the corner of a blanket so the big man could see her daughter's smiling face.

"Oh my, she is about the most precious thing I ever done laid eyes on Miss Becky," the big man said beaming with delight, then holding up the handcrafted wooden cradle he added, "I made her something that I thought you might could use."

"Why, it's beautiful Mr. Bent." Miss Becky said. "Here Lizzy, would you mind holding Kelly Anne while I properly accept Mr. Bent's gift?"

"With pleasure," Lizzy said happily, holding the baby naturally in her arms.

"Oh look, Lizzy," Miss Becky said admiringly, as she pointed to the little headboard. "It has a rose carved here, and look here, it rocks. I just love it, Mr. Bent!" Miss Becky stood on her tiptoes and kissed Xavier on the cheek. "Would you like to hold her?"

"I'd love to, but I's be afraids I might drop her," Xavier said.

"Here," Miss Becky said, pulling Xavier by the arm to guide him over to sit in the sturdy rocking chair. "You sit here," and accepting her baby back from Lizzy she handed the little girl to the big man sitting in the rocking chair. "She loves to be rocked."

Xavier pulled the blanket gently away from the baby's face and began to rock slowly as Kelly Anne smiled, then reached up and took hold of his thick calloused finger. "Would you look at that," Xavier whispered, "she's holding my finger."

"Come on, Scott," Lizzy whispered, pulling Kelly gently by the arm, "I could use your help in the kitchen."

Mid-Summer, 1866
Colorado City, Colorado Territory

The Sheriff and Lizzy stood in the small chapel alongside Xavier and Becky, holding Kelly Anne in her arms, as Reverend Howbert performed a simple wedding ceremony followed by a baptism for the baby. The light from the church's lone stained glass window poured softly into the small chapel.

Two weeks later Xavier pulled the buggy to a halt in front of the El Paso County Office Building where Sheriff Kelly sat on the front porch whittling on a stick. Sam sat next to him, his head resting on top of the lawman's boot, staring intently at the stick.

"Whoa," the big man said to the mule team.

"Good morning Mr. and Mrs. Bent," Kelly said as he stood, dipping the rim of his hat toward the lady and handing Sam the stick. "We're going to miss the three of you around here," the law-man said stepping down from the wooden porch to help Becky and the baby out of the carriage.

"We will miss you too Scott," Becky said warmly, and then turned to her husband, "We will be right back dear, just need to pick up a few things for the trip at Meyers Mercantile."

"Looks like marriage agrees with you, Xavier," Kelly replied to his friend. "I never seen you look so happy."

"What's not to smile about, a beautiful wife and a new family? We'll be getting a fresh start out in Oregon." said the town's former blacksmith, then added, "I expects marriage might agree with you too, Mr. Kelly."

"Suspect so," Kelly replied with a smile, "just gotta get through these last couple months here in office, then who knows, maybe someday Lizzy and I might just be visiting you all out there in Oregon."

"I'm sure da women folks will be writing one another, so we'll let you know where you can reach us once we done get settled in," Xavier said as he adjusted the tie-downs on the rocking chair loaded alongside their other belongings in the back of the carriage.

"Sounds like Albert Boone, Daniel Boone's grandson, was happy to buy out your blacksmithing business," Kelly said.

"Made me a fair offer," Xavier commented, patting his vest pocket, "Seems Albert's got his eye on Henry Fosdick's daughter,

Linda, but she's only thirteen. Fosdick said he'd enjoy having him as a son-in-law, but they'd have to wait 'til she's a little older."

"I understand Henry is platting out another township east of El Pueblo down on the Arkansas, he's gonna name the new town Boone," Kelly said.

"Well, Mr. Fosdick is a man who knows his surveying business," Xavier commented. "I studied the Fosdick Plat he drawed up pretty carefully before I built my blacksmith shop and corral over on 28th there. I'm no expert but I'd say it's a work of art."

"You gonna open another blacksmith shop up there in Oregon?" Kelly asked, noticing Sam wagging his tail in seeing Becky and the baby walking back toward them.

"Thinkin' that's always an option, but first I have my mind set on building dis little lady here a home, with a rose garden," Xavier said, smiling broadly at his new bride and baby.

"Surrounded by a white picket fence," Becky said, smiling back at her new husband before stopping next to Sheriff Kelly. "Here, Sheriff," Becky said handing Kelly Anne to her namesake, "mind holding the baby for a second while I find a place for these things to ride in the back?"

Xavier helped Becky position the package safely in the back of the carriage, then helped her up into the buggy. "Here," Kelly said to Sam, holding the baby down toward Sam, "better tell Kelly Anne good-bye."

Xavier smiled, then climbed into the wagon as Sam sniffed the baby being held carefully bundled in the Sheriff's arms, and then picked up the stick in his mouth.

"We're going to miss you, little darlin'," the lawman said as he handed the baby over to Becky.

"So long, Sheriff," Xavier waved as he started the mule team off out of town, "we best be going now, the Pacific Ocean is awaitin.'"

Sam looked up as the wagon started to pull away out of town and suddenly dropped the stick he was chewing on, cocked his head once to the side, whimpered loudly, then ran in front of the wagon and began jumping and barking excitedly.

"Whoa," Xavier said to the mule team, pulling the carriage to a sudden halt. "What's the matter with him?"

Sam ran around to the side of the buggy where Kelly Anne was being held by her mother, then ran over to the Sheriff, barked once, then ran back over to the other side of the wagon.

Kelly walked over to the side of the wagon where Sam was now sitting with his head hung low. "Guess he figured out you all were leaving," the Sheriff said. "He and Kelly Anne been together since the day she was born. Guess it must be hard for him to see her go."

"Hard for us too," Becky replied, as Sam let out another whimper. "He's such a sweet dog, and I always felt safe whenever he was close by the baby."

The Sheriff looked down at the sad dog, then up at Xavier. "Think you could handle a little more weight?"

"If you think you could handle parting with him," Xavier replied with a look of concern.

The Sheriff picked up the big white dog and placed him in the wagon on the floorboard between Becky and Xavier. "Looks like he chose her," Kelly commented, noticing how Sam's mood had shifted almost instantly from one of extreme sadness to sheer delight as if realizing he was now part of the Bent family.

Xavier started the mule team up again and as Kelly watched the carriage pull away, Sam jumped up onto the seat to glance back toward him standing in the street. Kelly waved goodbye. Sam barked one last time, as if to say "good-bye" and then turned back toward the front of the carriage. His bushy, white tail wagged happily from side to side. The Sheriff walked back to the front of the small County Building, sat down in the chair and watched until the carriage rode completely out of sight. It was still early morning and as Kelly looked up across the street to where he had heard a commotion, he noticed a colorful chicken being chased by three excited puppies, two black and one white.

As the trio of puppies started to round the corner from Colorado Avenue onto 24th Street the white puppy pulled up from his poultry pursuit and glanced across the dirt street to where the lawman sat alone on the front porch of the small log County Building. The puppy trotted across the wide street, sat down on the wooden porch and stared up at the Sheriff.

"What do you want?" Kelly asked as the white puppy stared up with big black eyes. "I don't have nothin' to eat," the Sheriff explained as the dog looked back across the street to see that the noisy chicken had made good on his escape, at least temporarily. The white puppy stood up, moved over alongside the Sheriff's chair and plopped down on the wooden porch, resting his head on the lawman's boot.

"Swell," Kelly said aloud, as he looked down to see the white puppy close his eyes to nap. Mindlessly, the lawman reached over and slowly pulled his watch from his vest pocket, opened the case and ran his thumb across the broken crystal on its face. He glanced down at the time, the hands still fixed at 2:36. Kelly slowly snapped the silver watch case closed, stroked its horsetail braided chain for a moment, felt the slight weight of the puppy's head resting across the top of his boot, closed his eyes and tried to imagine the various colors of blue in the Pacific Ocean. Kelly slipped the broken pocket watch back into his left vest pocket, tucked safely opposite Uncle Doug's birthday coin.

Late Fall, 1866
El Paso House Hotel, Colorado City, Colorado Territory

Kelly glanced around the dining room before hanging up his hat on an empty peg on the hat rack next to a new black cowboy hat. It was fairly late in the evening and most of the stage passengers had already had their dinner. Anthony Bott was sitting alone at a table toward the back of the small dining room and motioned for the Sheriff to come join him at his table.

"Aspens are sure pretty this year," the Sheriff said to Anthony Bott as he sat down to join his friend for dinner, purposely selecting a chair where he could watch the front door.

"Sure are," Bott replied, "turned early up high this year."

"Noticed that," Kelly agreed, the two men comfortable with one another and small talk. "You get yourself a new hat?"

"I did," Bott replied proudly, "one of them new Stetsons, like yours only black."

"I saw that," Kelly replied, "you get it at Meyers Mercantile?"

"No, over at Tappan Brothers Outfitters," Bott replied, as he put the menu down. "Think I'll go with the prime rib. What you in the mood for tonight?"

"That sounds good to me," Kelly replied, as he smiled politely at Amanda, Lucy's daughter, as she took the men's order for dinner and returned to the kitchen.

"I understand John 'Prairie Dog' O'Byrne was in town again last night," Kelly commented. "Heard he and his team of elk, Thunder and Buttons, caused quite a stir with the church going women again."

"They did cause a ruckus," Bott said with a smile, "trouble with training elk to pull a buggy is that they only have one speed; full out! Heard Prairie Dog John raced up Colorado Avenue, pulled up in front of the Painted Lady, had a snort or two, and then picked up Eloise at the Green Turtle and raced up Pikes Peak Avenue toward Manitou Springs. Some says they were last seen a headed north toward the Buck Snort Saloon, up in Jefferson County."

"That's a fairly long trip, especially at night."

"I'd wager a prime rib dinner they made it okay," Bott said with a smile.

"No bets," the Sheriff said, thinking what Prairie Dog John and Eloise might have looked like pulling up in front of the Buck Snort Saloon in the moonlight in a carriage being drawn by two fully antlered elk.

"You heard from Xavier?" Bott asked.

"Lizzy got a postcard from Becky; it was postmarked Salt Lake City. Said things were going well and they hoped to be seeing the Pacific Ocean in a few weeks."

"That sounds exciting," Bott replied. "You ever want to visit the west coast?"

"I have thought that it might be nice to see the ocean, even thought some 'bout buying a ranch in the San Joaquin Valley someday," Kelly replied, then added, "not sure Lizzy would ever care to live anyplace else."

The two men continued their casual conversation, and then just as their dinner arrived, Sam Wah, wearing his traditional Chinese garb, rushed in the front door of the hotel.

"Sheriff," he began, spotting the lawman and running up to their table, "you come quick! That Frenchie gunslinger, Salingo, drink too much, on opium pipe all day. Now he over at Laura Belle's causing ruckus. He crazy!"

The Sheriff stood up, placed his napkin on his chair and started toward the front door.

"Watch yerself Scott," Bott warned his friend, "that Johnnie Salingo is supposed to be one of the fastest guns in the West."

"Please ask Amanda to keep my dinner warm and save me a piece of pie," the Sheriff replied as he glanced out the window and then followed Sam Wah outside.

Everyone in town knew Sam Wah's laundry had an opium den in the basement, which was not illegal in the Territories. The lawman walked alongside Sam Wah as the two men started up Colorado Avenue toward Laura Belle's. Sam Wah, taking two steps to the lawman's one, encouraged the lawman to go faster as he sensed Laura Belle was in real danger. When they were about thirty yards from the brothel, the front door burst open and the gunslinger staggered outside pulling Laura Belle by the wrist.

"Come on, you whore!" the drunken man cursed, twisting her arm behind her.

"Stop, Johnnie," Laura Belle pleaded, "you're hurting me!"

"I'll show you what real pain is, you filthy bitch," Salingo said menacingly, as he drew his Colt revolver from its holster.

"You best wait over there," Kelly said to Sam Wah, pushing him aside before challenging the gunslinger. "Salingo! You unhand her!"

"Who's going to make me?" the gunslinger threatened as he pulled Laura Belle up to her full height in front of him.

Seeing he didn't have a clear shot, the Sheriff shouted to the gunslinger, "You always in the habit of hiding behind a lady?"

"Lady!" Johnnie Salingo shouted back, "I don't see no stinkin lady!" Tossing Laura Belle aside, the gunslinger started to raise his revolver as the Sheriff went for his holstered Colt.

Three shots went off in rapid succession; the first one from the gunslinger, the next two from the lawman. Kelly never heard either gun go off, but saw the puff of smoke from Salingo's shot and felt the punch in his right side. Kelly's first shot hit Salingo square in the chest, the second struck him between the eyes. The gunslinger fell over on the porch and then slid face first down the wooden steps, banging his chin hard on each of the wooden steps. He never felt any pain. Johnny Salingo was dead before he hit the ground.

Sam Wah ran onto the street where the Sheriff was standing, and then in astonishment asked, "He miss? Salingo's supposed a famous gun fighter!"

The Sheriff holstered his revolver, took two steps forward, clutched his right side, blood streaming out between his fingers, and said, "He didn't miss." Kelly's vision began to close in around him. Laura Belle let out a scream as the lawman fell to his knees. The Sheriff's vision closed in from all sides, and then faded to black.

/

Late Fall, 1866
Pikes Peak Region, Colorado Territory

The Sheriff felt a tugging pain on his right side and slowly opened his eyes to see Doc Garvin changing a bloody dressing from the gunshot wound. "Sorry Scott, I know this must hurt," the doctor said to his patient.

"How long I been here Doc?" Sheriff Kelly asked as he winced again in pain.

"Try to lie still, if you can," Doc Garvin said, "I'm just about finished. You been in and out of consciousness for about twelve hours now; bullet exited out your right side. I don't think it hit anything vital, just have to worry about infection for the next week to ten days. I think the wound track is pretty clean now. I took advantage of your being out to swab it pretty good when they first brought you in, but you'll just have to stay in bed here a couple days so I can keep an eye on things."

"Thanks, Doc," the Sheriff replied as he struggled to sit up and look around the room, noticing his silver coin laying on the end table with a bullet hole pierced through its center.

"I pulled that half dollar out of your vest pocket," Doc Garvin explained, helping his patient sit up by propping a pillow behind his back. "I can't tell if that coin being in your pocket helped you by deflecting the bullet outward before it entered your ribcage, but at least the bullet and the coin both stayed intact. Would have been a mess if it would have come apart...luck of the Irish I guess."

"I'm not feeling very lucky at the moment," Kelly replied as he laid his head back on the pillow and stared up at the beige tin ceiling tiles above the bed.

"You are lucky enough to have two visitors waiting all morning to see you," Doc Garvin said with a smile as he opened the door and motioned to the two people waiting anxiously on a wooden bench in the narrow hallway. "Don't stay too long, he still needs his rest."

Lizzy and Charlie walked quietly into the room with worried looks on their faces. They naturally gravitated one each side of Kelly's bed. Lizzy carried a cup of tea with her and set it on the end table next to the bullet-pierced coin.

Charlie was the first to speak, "How you feelin', Sheriff?"

"Much better, Charlie," Kelly said with a forced smile.

"I been helping Deputy Gassenger keep an eye on things while you're laid-up here," Charlie said, trying to be helpful.

"Mighty nice of you Charlie, thanks," the Sheriff said.

"And I washed the blood off your coin, but I'm not sure your trick will work with a bullet hole through the middle like that," Charlie said as he glanced at the coin on the nightstand.

"Thank you Charlie, everything's gonna be okay," Kelly said as the teenager nodded.

"Doc Garvin says you needs your rest, so I'll leave the two of you alone for now, but you send word if you need anything. I'll go fetch the buggy, Lizzy."

Charlie left the room, closing the door behind him, leaving the lawman and Lizzy alone. Kelly was the first to speak, "I'm sorry Lizzy, I know this is hard on you, too, but I'll recover."

"I'm not sure I will," Lizzy said, holding his right hand with a sorrowful look on her face. "Every time I see you hurt like this, every time you get hurt I feel your pain. Every time I witness all this bloodshed, well, I'd be lying if I said it doesn't take its toll on me; it does."

"Term's almost over, Lizzy," Kelly said squeezing her hand. "Just a few more months 'til the election."

"Can't you just get out now, Scott, before it's too late? Haven't you already done enough, suffered enough?" Lizzy pleaded, with tears welling up in her eyes.

"I made a commitment here, Lizzy, when I pinned on that badge. I have to finish what I started. I just can't turn my back on these people who put their trust in me to keep them safe," the Sheriff said, then looked around the room hoping to change the subject. "Say, would you happen to know where my clothes went, would you?"

"Sam Wah has your clothes." Lizzy explained, "He felt so bad that you got shot, said he could mend the bullet holes in your vest and shirt and would try his best to get all the blood out if he could. There was a lot of blood."

"Not his fault this happened," Kelly replied. "Any idea where my guns and other things might be?"

"Doc Garvin said he locked everything up that you had on you in his rolltop desk," Lizzy replied. "Here, try to drink some of this tea, it's not hot anymore but you need fluids." After the Sheriff took a couple sips, Lizzy said, "Unless you need anything right now Scott, I'll let you rest. I'm going to head back out to the ranch. I'll check on you again tomorrow."

"Thanks Lizzy," the Sheriff said, "I'll be good as new in no time."

"Not sure I will, Scott, not at least until after you are out of office. Election time can't come soon enough," Lizzy said, a tear forming in the corner of her eye.

"Hang in there with me, Lizzy, just a few more months," Kelly replied, then wiped the tear away as it ran down her cheek.

"You promise?" Lizzy asked.

"Promise," Kelly said.

"Pinky swear?" Lizzy said teasingly, as she held out the little finger on her right hand.

Kelly smiled, reached up and interlocked the little finger on his right hand with hers. "Pinky swear," the lawman said, giving her a faint smile as he drifted off to sleep.

"I love you," Lizzy whispered as she bent over the bed and kissed Kelly softly on the forehead. "I'll be back to check on you in the morning." Then she walked away from his bedside and quietly closed the door.

February, 1867
Colorado City, Colorado Territory

Election night was a happy celebration, a night to thank the public servants for their past service and wish the new office holders best wishes in fulfilling the duties of their respective offices…But nobody was happier than Lizzy. She wondered if she might not be the happiest person in El Paso County, as she clung onto Kelly's left arm. This was the first time she could remember seeing him without his badge and gunbelt. As they joined the celebration in

Bancroft Park she could feel the weight of the Colt pocket pistol he carried in the shoulder holster he wore under his topcoat,

"Good evening Mrs. Meyers," Lizzy said, then added, "and Sheriff Meyers."

"Good evening, Lizzy," Bert Meyers replied, then nodded toward Kelly adding, "Mr. Kelly," with an emphasis on the Mister.

"Evening, Bert," Kelly replied, looking around at the peaceful crowd who had gathered to celebrate the election results. "Looks like you got things well in hand."

"Not all that hard, Scott," the new Sheriff replied, as he drew his new revolver, twirled it around forward twice and then backwards once before slipping it back into its holster. "You just gotta show those redskins and ruffians you mean business."

As soon as Sheriff Meyers's gun cleared its holster, Kelly instinctively took a half step forward and to the side, shielding Lizzy with his body, alarmed by the new Sheriff's careless gunplay.

"What's the matter, Mr. Kelly," Meyers said, "don't you trust me?"

"I've been around guns long enough to know they sometimes go off when you don't want them to," Kelly replied, unimpressed with Bert's fast-draw antics.

"Come on, dear," Mrs. Meyers said to her husband, "you'll scare someone with that. Besides, I'm thirsty and you promised me a glass of lemonade."

"Very well, dear," Bert replied to his wife. "You two have a nice night," the new Sheriff replied with a tip of his hat to Lizzy and a wink at the former sheriff.

As Sheriff Meyers and his wife walked away, Kelly watched him puff up his chest to show off his new badge to Robert Finley. Robert Finley had completed his first term as County Treasurer

and had been elected to serve a one year term as County Asses-
sor. Irving Howbert, who was only nineteen years of age, had been
elected to replace Robert Finley as County Treasurer. Robert Finley
smiled, tipped his hat to Mrs. Meyers, then approached Kelly and
Lizzy.

"Hope our new Sheriff lives long enough to grow into the job,"
Finley said to his friend Scott Kelly, pointing over his shoulder with
his thumb toward the county's new Sheriff.

"Heard you sold the sawmill," Kelly said, wanting to change the
subject away from politics.

"Yes," Finley replied, "Jerome Weir and C.T. Judd have wanted to
buy me out for some time now, almost since we got here, and made
me a fair offer."

"Well," Kelly replied, "they certainly know the lumber business,
and ain't afraid of hard work. They should make a go of it."

"With the War over now," Lizzy said, "along with all the growth
that's going to be brought in by the Kansas and Pacific Railroad
when it reaches Denver City, statehood can't be far behind."

"Well it does concern me some," Finley replied, pausing a moment to look into Kelly's knowing eyes, "that General Palmer chose
to run that railroad route on the most direct route to Denver City,
smack across the northern edge of the Cheyenne Arapaho Indian
Reserve. Tall Bull, Warchief of the Dog Soldiers, warned the government, 'If you run the iron horse across my homeland, I will be your
enemy for life.'"

"I met Tall Bull once. He struck me as a man of his word," Kelly
acknowledged somberly.

"I'm glad Tall Bull wasn't at Sand Creek," Finley acknowledged,
nodding his head toward Irving Howbert, who was talking with the
attorney from Fountain, John Clay Brown and his wife Alvira. "We

had our hands full as it was. Had it not been for Sergeant Brown and Corporal Howbert there," Finley said, "well, Company G would not have been anywhere's near ready for a fight during a winter campaign."

"I do wish President Lincoln could have lived long enough to see the country coming back together again," Lizzy said.

"I understand John Wilkes Booth was confirmed to be a member of the KGC," Kelly commented, "as were Dr. Samuel Mudd, David Herold, George Atzerodt and Lewis Powell."

"Come on Scott and Robert, we can't do anything about that, 'sides most of them were hanged with Mary Surratt," Lizzy said. "Let's go congratulate Irving Howbert on his election."

Three Days Later
Kelly Homestead, North of the Garden of the Gods

Kelly looked up from the doorway he was framing on his new horse barn to see Lizzy and her Chinese assistant coming up the lane in a small cart being pulled by a donkey. Lizzy was dressed in bib overalls, suitable for digging, but in Kelly's eyes, he had never seen a more beautiful woman. She jumped down from the cart, lifted a basket effortlessly from the back of the wagon and smiled happily as she waved for him to come join her, pointing to the shade of a cottonwood tree that stood at the base of a tall red sandstone column.

"I brought you a basket for lunch, Mr. Kelly," she said with an emphasis on the Mister.

"Thank you, Miss Hill," Kelly said, as he took her by her narrow waist and kissed her softly on the cheek.

Lizzy wiped the sweat away that he left on her skin with a smile; she loved his scent and everything about this man she intended to marry.

"Marcus Foster dropped by the house early this morning." Lizzy said as she opened the basket and handed Kelly a ham sandwich. "He has been busy putting up a house on one of the two eighty-acre sections of land he bought from you down on Fountain Creek. That would have been a wonderful place for our ranch, but here in this canyon, well this has to be the most spectacular location for a home as anywhere on the planet."

"I agree," Kelly said, taking a bite of the sandwich and then looking at the natural beauty that surrounded them. He swallowed, then added, "I've always thought this was a canyon suitable for a queen and her castle."

Lizzy smiled at the thought, and then said, "Marcus said he was hoping you had time to go out on another mountain expedition now that you're retired from public office."

"Maybe after I get the foundation staked out for the workshop over there, tailor made with enough space for a certain young archeologist..."

Lizzy looked to where Kelly was pointing at the base of another tall red rock formation.

Lizzy clapped her hands excitedly, "That's exactly what I told him!" Lizzy said with an approving smile. "Will you be coming by for supper after church Sunday?"

"Yes ma'am!" Kelly replied warmly.

"Maybe I'll sit next to you on the pew...and maybe, we can talk to Reverend Howbert after the sermon?!"

Kelly smiled and nodded his head knowingly in agreement. Lizzy hugged him excitedly, jumped up and started skipping off toward the cart.

"See you at the church, Mister Kelly!" Lizzy smiled as she hopped effortlessly into the cart next to her young Chinese assistant, grabbed the reins and drove the cart back down the tree covered lane.

"Yes, you will, Miss Hill!" Kelly said softly and waved as the donkey drawn cart pulled out of sight and took another savory bite out of the thickly cut honey-cured ham sandwich.

Three hours later Kelly looked up from driving the last foundation stake into the ground, wiped the sweat from his brow with his bandana and saw Charlie riding up the trail toward him as fast as his old buckskin mare could trot.

"Sheriff Kelly!" Charlie shouted. "Whoa Jenny," he said as he pulled the ancient horse to a stop, then slid effortlessly to the ground before running over to the former lawman.

"Sheriff, it's…" the excited teenager began, before being cut off mid-sentence.

"Charlie," Kelly interrupted, "I told you I'm not the Sheriff anymore."

"But it's the Big Tooth Jim Gang!" Charlie shouted, still out of breath, pointing toward Colorado City, then added, "They done killed two Mexican girls and shot their father!"

"Well, don't tell me, go tell Sheriff Meyers," Kelly said, with his hands on his hips, "I told you I'm not the Sheriff anymore."

"But, Sheriff," Charlie tried to explain, "Bert done quit!"

Half an Hour Later
County Office Building, Colorado City, Colorado Territory

"Three Days!" Kelly said in frustration to the three El Paso County Commissioners huddled together in the small county office building. "He only lasted three damn days!?"

"Said, 'They're too rough for me,'" Commissioner Cromwell replied. "Then he tossed the sheriff's badge on the desk and just walked away."

"Told me they done stole his new Colt revolver and his horse," Commissioner Sprague added, as M.S. Beach walked through the door.

"Lucky they didn't kill him too! They supposedly killed upwards of thirty people," M.S. Beach said, "They're called the Big Tooth Jim Gang."

"Anybody get a good look at them?" Kelly asked.

"I seen 'em," Commissioner Bley replied as he picked up the badge. "Three of 'em rode out of town; a white man, a Mexican and a half-breed Negro. Their leader, this Big Tooth Jim fella, is a huge, hideous looking man, stands at least six foot four, two hundred and seventy pounds, with big ears that stick straight out and two enormous brown stained teeth that protrude out of his mouth and curve upwards...kinda looks like walrus tusks."

"Word is this Big Tooth Jim fella wears a metal plate hanging from a cord tied around his neck," Commissioner Cromwell explained. "The papers up in Denver City reported this outlaw gang was said to be headed toward the New Mexico Territory, robbing and killin' folks along the way."

"The Indians say he is a man that can't be killed," added M.S. Beach.

"Come on, Kelly," Commissioner Bley pleaded, holding out the sheriff's badge in the palm of his hand, "you gotta accept this. There's no one else with your special kind of...well, special talent."

"Look," Kelly said firmly, "IF I do this I am not serving a whole term! You men need to be finding someone else with...this kind of special talent."

"You ain't going after them alone, are you Kelly?" Commissioner Sprague asked.

Reluctantly accepting the badge Kelly replied, "No, I'll take Dan Gassenger along as my deputy."

"Kelly," Beach commented with concern, "Scott, this is Big Tooth Jim…and he's got at least two other killers riding with him. Don't you think a posse is more what you need?"

"Of what?! Merchants and farmers with pitchforks? We saw where that got us. Dan's a sure shot and reliable. He'll be all the help I'll need…we gotta get on their trail now and ride hard. If they get past the Red River we'll never find em," Kelly said as he paused, pinned the badge back onto his vest where it had been the past five years. As he opened the front door he looked back and said, "but, I'm telling you gentlemen right here and now, I'm not doing another four-year term, so you all need to start planning on holding a mid-term election and make sure you got someone who'll last more than three days!" Then he slammed the door.

Manhunt - Day 2
Arkansas River, Colorado Territory

"That looks like the same three horses," Deputy Gassenger said, pointing to the three sets of horses' tracks leading up the muddy bank headed south, away from the Arkansas River.

"Agreed," Sheriff Kelly acknowledged, "looks like they're still riding pretty hard."

"You stop long enough to tell Lizzy good-bye afore you rode out?" Gassenger asked.

"Didn't have time," Kelly acknowledged with regret. "I left a note for her with Reverend Howbert, she's expecting me in church tomorrow morning. Hoping she'll understand." Kelly said as he rose up in the stirrups and pointed to the south. "This here road is the Taos Trail, sometimes called the Trappers Trail, 'cause it was used by all the Mountain Men to take their furs to trade in Taos, where they usually spent their winters. The trail crosses over the Sangre de Cristo Pass, and then turns south at Fort Garland, crosses the San Luis Valley and enters into the northern New Mexico Territory."

"You thinking Big Tooth Jim and his gang are headed for Taos?" Gassenger asked, peering off in the distance to the southwest.

"We'll know soon enough," Kelly replied. "Once they hit Huerfano Butte they'll either cross the Huerfano River or turn west, following the left bank of the Huerfano River toward El Badito."

"El Badito?" Gassenger replied, "If I remember my Spanish well enough, that means Little Ford or Crossing."

"Your memory serves you well, Dan," Sheriff Kelly acknowledged, slowing his horse to a halt so it could catch it's breath. "That crossing has been used for hundreds of years by the Ute and that's where Juan Bautista de Anza crossed with his troops after killing the Comanche War Chief, Cuerno Verde, along with a bunch of his warriors…somewhere there toward the base of the Wet Mountains," the Sheriff concluded, pointing toward the tree-covered mountains to their right.

Feeling their horses were rested well enough to proceed, the Sheriff urged his mount forward with his heels, something he rarely had to do with Marengo. God, how he missed that horse! Watching the Spanish Peaks coming closer into view, Kelly was reminded of his first encounter with Chief Ouray, and wondered how he and his People and Thundercloud were getting along with the continuing encroachment from the settlers and the ongoing Cheyenne Wars.

Reaching the Huerfano River Deputy Gassenger pointed to

the three sets of horse tracks leading into the river. "Looks like they crossed here."

"Let's make sure they come out on the other side and they're not just trying to throw us off their trail," Kelly said, as his horse waded into the cold water and lowered its head to drink.

"Looks like they came out over there. I'd say they can't be more than half a day ahead of us," Gassenger said, pointing to the three sets of horse tracks that they had been following for over a hundred miles. "But look it here," he said, pointing to the tracks in the mud, "looks like that last pony may of thrown a shoe."

"Probably got sucked off in the river bottom," Kelly acknowledged, looking down to make sure all four horseshoes were still attached to his horse's hooves. "I'm thinking they'll stop in Trinidad for supplies and may get that horse shod, unless they steal another one along the way. Then they'll head up and over Raton Pass, likely by-passing the Maxwell Toll Road so as they wouldn't be seen. If we ride hard, don't stop for supplies in Trinidad and take Maxwell's Toll Road, we should overtake them before they cross the Red River. C'mon, let's ride!"

As Sheriff Kelly and Deputy Gassenger broke their horses into a gallop, they barely noticed the beauty of the Spanish Peaks off to their right. They rode hard past the cutoff toward La Veta Pass and didn't acknowledge the terrain as it changed to flat, parched red rock and scattered low-lying juniper trees. They did notice that the third set of horse tracks, the one with the missing shoe on the right front hoof, had been replaced.

"You think they stopped at that ranch over there to get that shoe fixed?" Gassenger asked, as they rode past the entrance to a modest homestead a half mile off the trail to the west.

"Don't know," Kelly replied, taking special note to where the homestead was located to the west of a stacked rock cairn that appeared to have been intended as a property boundary, "but this might give us a chance to close the gap on them a little. Let's ride on."

The two lawmen didn't stop in Trinidad, the last town in the Colorado Territory, before picking up the outlaws' trail again as it headed toward the top of Raton Pass just a few miles to the south.

"That pile of horseshit," Deputy Gassenger said, pointing to the ground ahead of their two horses, "is definitely more fresh than any we seen so far."

"Noticed that," Kelly said in agreement, "looks like they stopped in Trinidad. I'd say we can't be more than an hour or two behind them now and if they by-passed the Toll Road we might catch up with 'em by nightfall."

Manhunt - Day 4
Raton Pass, Southern Colorado Territory

Approaching the entrance for Maxwell's Toll Road Sheriff Kelly pulled up his horse to a halt and waited for the man walking toward them. "Afternoon" the Sheriff said with a nod of his head.

"Can I help you, Sheriff?" Lucien Maxwell asked, after introducing himself and nodding at the badges on the two lawmen's coats.

"Sheriff Kelly, come down from El Paso County," the Sheriff explained. "This here is Deputy Gassenger and we're after Big Tooth Jim and his gang of cutthroats."

"Well, they didn't come through here, maybe they rode around my tollgate," Maxwell said, "but you're welcome to ride ahead to see for yourselves. I've heard of you, Sheriff Kelly,"

Maxwell explained, as he lifted the wooden gate for the toll road, "There'll be no toll for any lawman on my road, it's mighty good to meet you two."

"Nice to meet you, Lucien. Heard you rode with Kit Carson?" Kelly replied.

"That I did. You know him?" Maxwell asked.

"Never met him, but a Ute friend of mine named Ouray speaks highly of him."

"Then I'd say your friend is a good judge of character."

"Any word on Big Tooth Jim?"

"Word is he's killed upwards of thirty-five men, besides women and children,...two young girls 12 and 14 years old...he ties up the men he robs, beats 'em to death, rapes the women, drives off their cattle and horses. He's a brutish thug. They're callin themselves the 'Terror of the Rockies'. Ah, Kelly..." Maxwell said pausing as he searched for the right words, "Kelly," he began again looking the Sheriff in the eye, "no man ever went out after that fella and came back alive. They say he wears a metal plate around his neck; he's mean as they come. You'll know him when you see him...he's hard to miss, leaves dead men where ever he goes. Plenty of others have shot at this fella, Sheriff. Why, he's not even in Colorado anymore; he's certain to be outta your jurisdiction by now. There'd be no shame in you turning back..."

Sheriff Kelly interrupted firmly, "I may know where they're headed, and if we don't stop them now the killin will surely go on; he and his gang gotta be put down. Thank you for the free toll, Mr. Maxwell."

The El Paso County Sheriff and his brave deputy turned their horses south and rode over the pass into the vast New Mexico Territory in pursuit of the Terror of the Rockies.

"God speed, Sheriff Kelly," Lucien Maxwell said as the two lawmen rode out of sight.

Manhunt - Day 5
Rocky Arroyo, New Mexico Territory

The sun, hot and heavy, had turned to a warm orange, casting long shadows across the ground. Kelly looked down at the narrow dirt trail to see where the three sets of tracks led into the trees ahead. He pulled up on the reins and stopped his horse.

"Whoa," Kelly said softly.

"Yep, that looks like the same three horses," Deputy Gassenger acknowledged in agreement. "They'll be looking for a place to camp down for the night." Pointing toward some large boulders ahead, said, "That's where I'd be headed to camp if I were them."

"I'd do the same," Kelly said in concurrence. "Let's get these horses staked down out of sight and wait till nightfall to make our way into those juniper trees. We might get lucky enough in the moonlight to see if we can find where they're camped."

"Hope my stomach doesn't start growling again," Deputy Gassenger commented. "I finished off the last of my beef jerky midafternoon."

"Here," Kelly said, reaching into his saddlebag and sharing half of his last piece of buffalo jerky with his deputy. "With any luck at all, those fellas up there will be well supplied from their stopover in Trinidad and might not be needin' much of anything to eat tomorrow."

Two hours after mid-night, the overhead clouds in the night's sky started to part. As the two lawmen crept slowly forward, they grew increasingly appreciative of the moonlight being cast down from a cloudless night sky and a three-quarters crescent moon.

"Dew is starting to form up," Kelly observed, feeling the damp brush against his pant legs. "If we come across their camp, we best be thinking about rotating our ammunition throughout the night…can't afford a misfire with just the two of us against the three of them."

"Agreed," Deputy Gassenger acknowledged. "How do you want this to go down?"

"Here's the way I see this playing out," Kelly explained. "We get in close as we can without being seen. Hopefully we'll find some high ground, where the sun will come up behind our backs, wait there 'til sunrise. When their camp starts to awake, I'll shoot Big Tooth Jim first, before he can put on that metal plate we keep hearing about. You shoot whoever is closest to you and then we both shoot the one bandit that's left. That sound good to you?"

"Sounds like as good a plan as the next to me," Deputy Gassenger acknowledged thoughtfully.

"Course, you know," Kelly added with a slight smile, "no plan ever survives first contact with the enemy."

"That's reassuring," Gassenger said with a quiet laugh, "you learnt that fightin' Injuns?"

"No, Major Robert E. Lee always said that," Kelly acknowledged respectfully, adding, "down Mexico way in '47. Shame how the War Between the States is all he and so many of our other young officers who served bravely during the Mexican-American War, will ever be remembered by."

"I never heard you talk about them or that War before. You becoming nostalgic on me in your old age Sheriff?" Deputy Gassenger whispered, trying to lighten the mood as they spotted a small campfire, about two hundred yards ahead, off in the distance in the clearing of some trees near a small stream.

257

"No," Sheriff Kelly replied quietly, as he knelt down on the ground, "just acknowledging how only twenty years ago this here land was in Mexico, and twenty years before that it was part of the Spanish Empire."

"Three different countries in just one lifetime," Gassenger whispered. "I never thought of it that way. A lot can happen in one person's life. Anything you'd do differently?"

"Yes," the Sheriff replied with a wry smile, "I'd have stopped back in Trinidad for some provisions."

Deputy Gassenger smiled and shook his head in agreement, adding, "Don't go gettin' me thinking about food again."

"From here on we're only using hand signals," the Sheriff instructed. "Let's go put an end to these three worthless lives and make the world a safer place."

The lawmen made good use of the short rocky outcropping, located just fifty feet to the east of the outlaws' camp. The Sheriff would have preferred the rocks to be a little taller so they could stand up to stretch their legs during the night, but kneeling behind the rocks, with their rifles resting over the top, provided a natural support plus cover and concealment. Most importantly, they were appreciative that when the sun would come up in the east, it would be at their backs, making it difficult for the three outlaws to see them when the shooting commenced.

The lawmen quietly rotated the ammunition in their Henry repeating rifles and Colt revolvers throughout the night, hoping to ensure the dew in the morning air wouldn't cause a misfire. As the dawn's first light approached, the camp slowly came to life. It was still too dark to differentiate colors, especially skin colors, but it looked like the black outlaw was the first to get up. He walked over to relieve himself and check on the horses. Then, judging from the large sombrero he put on his head, the lawmen assumed the Mexican was the second man to roll out of bed. He began stirring the red coals of the campfire back to life as the first man walked back over to the campfire and sat down on a rock, facing their direction.

The two hungry lawmen were envious as they watched as the first two outlaws poured themselves a cup of steaming hot coffee. Even fifty feet away from the fire they could smell bacon frying in the pan over the campfire. Finally, they saw the third outlaw toss back his blanket and from a sitting position, stretch his arms above his head. The hulk of a man slowly stood up to his complete height. He was a big man, at least 6 foot 4 inches in height and 270 pounds was not an exaggeration. Towering above the other two outlaws sitting around the campfire, the lawmen watched as this huge man stretched with one arm and scratched his ass with the other.

As Big Tooth Jim patted his protruding belly, he broke wind and growled menacingly at the Mexican outlaw, "Hurry up with breakfast! I'm starving here!"

Sheriff Kelly, holding his Henry rifle tightly against his right shoulder, looked down the barrel and slowly took aim at a spot between the big man's shoulders. Kelly glanced over to confirm his deputy was in position to fire, and then brought the front sight into focus, took a deep breath and held it for a beat. As Kelly slowly released the air from his lungs, he counted softly aloud, "One… two…three," and gently squeezed the trigger until it fired.

"POW!" the rifle roared to life. Kelly watched the big man's body jerk suddenly as the bullet struck him square in the back, right where he had aimed between the shoulder blades. The man's body arched backwards and torqued slightly to the right as blood spurted out of his chest. Big Tooth Jim seemed almost suspended in midair for a second, frozen at the moment of impact, and then he dropped to his knees in the dirt and rolled over to one side, dead.

Almost instantaneous to the Sheriff's shot going off, Kelly heard the shot from Deputy Gassenger's rifle. Kelly watched as Dan's bullet struck the black outlaw in the middle of the chest, sending him backward and sprawling him out onto the ground. Kelly cocked the level action on his rifle, then took aim at the Mexican who had stood up, his gun drawn from its holster with one hand, as he had placed his other hand above his eyes trying to shield the early morning sun from his eyes. Before Kelly could pull the trigger a second shot went off from Deputy Gassenger's rifle.

"CRACK!" the shot to his right rang out. Kelly watched the Mexican outlaw's head snap back violently and his body staggered a few feet to the left of the fire before it dropped to the ground. The two lawmen waited patiently and watched for any movement from the three outlaws. Hearing no sounds at all, and seeing no movement from the outlaws' bodies, the two lawmen waited two or three minutes before they slowly stood up from behind the rocks and drew their Colt revolvers.

"Nice shooting," Kelly said to his deputy.

"Let's hope so," Gassenger replied as the two lawmen slowly crept forward.

Approaching the camp, the two lawmen saw the three outlaws were dead, just where they fell. Dan's first bullet went right through the black outlaw's heart and his second shot pierced the Mexican gang member's right eye, exiting the back of his head. Noticing the metal plate hanging around the saddle horn of the saddle where Big Tooth Jim had slept, Kelly held it up by the cord and found it had been lined with rubber and covered with dust.

"Doesn't look like this had been worn in days," Kelly commented.

"He must've been feeling like they was safe this far out in the New Mexico Territory," Dan commented as he inspected the metal breast plate, then began searching through the pockets of the two men he had just killed.

Sheriff Kelly bent over Big Tooth Jim's body, and after confirming for certain he was dead, began searching his pockets for any cash or other valuables. When the lawmen had recovered everything of value from the outlaws, they kicked their dead bodies over into the rocky arroyo and watched as the bodies rolled down the dusty embankment.

Sitting down at the campfire, Deputy Gassenger tossed the coffee on the ground from the two tin cups the outlaws had been drinking out of, poured two fresh cups of steaming hot coffee and handed one to the Sheriff.

"Hope you're not too particular who you're drinking after," he said with a smile.

Kelly accepted the hot cup of coffee with a smile, "Bacon smells 'bout done."

As the two lawmen finished the outlaws' breakfast and searched their saddlebags, Sheriff Kelly pulled out his white handkerchief and spread it out across a flat rock. He counted out the money he had taken from Big Tooth Jim, nearly $2000 in silver and gold coins, and laid the money in the middle of the handkerchief along with a man's silver pocket watch and a gold wedding ring. Deputy Gassenger did the same with the money he had collected from the other two outlaws, putting the total amount of cash at just over $2400.

"You think the commissioners might allow us a ten percent reward?"

"One would hope," the Sheriff replied thoughtfully. "Let's put out this fire, round up their horses and be on our way."

One Week After Manhunt Began
Judge Stone's Ranch, El Paso County, Colorado Territory

Judge Stone answered the knock on the door to find Marcus Foster standing there. "Hello Marcus, what can I do for you?"

"Well, Sir," Marcus began, "I'm wondering if maybe you or Lizzy heard any news from Scott Kelly. We was supposed to have gone on an elk hunt up Ruxton Creek day before yesterday and I haven't heard from him at all."

"I'm afraid we haven't heard from him either, Marcus," Judge Stone replied.

"Well…he was supposed to be retired when we made the plan. I suppose it might take more than a day or two to catch the 'Terror of the Rockies'…is Lizzy holdin' up okay?"

"Holdin' up as well as can be expected…but a friendly face might do her some good," Judge Stone replied.

Marcus nodded his head in understanding and followed Judge Stone through the ranch house and out to a yard between the house and the barn. There, sitting on the ground, Marcus found Lizzy. It was obvious she had been crying.

"Lizzy, Marcus Foster is here to see you again, my dear," Judge Stone said, then turned to leave the two alone under the shade of a tree.

"Oh Marcus," Lizzy said, wiping the tears from her eyes on the back of her sleeve. "Please excuse me, I must look a mess."

Marcus sat down on the ground beside her, then put his hand

on top of hers supportively. "I think you look as beautiful as ever, Lizzy."

"He promised he wouldn't do this anymore, Marcus. He's just chasing a ghost and every new outlaw seems to wear it's face. I wish he was more like you, Marcus." Lizzy said as she squeezed his hand. "He just can't say no..." Lizzy said with a quiet sniffle, adding, "just left me a note with Reverend Howbert, saying he'd he back soon as he can."

Marcus put his arm around Lizzy's shoulder; she rested her head against his chest.

Later that Afternoon
North of Trinidad, Colorado Territory

Sheriff Kelly and Deputy Gassenger turned west off the road at the rock cairn and led the outlaws' three horses toward the small homestead that stood in the shadow of the Spanish Peaks to the west. As they pulled up in front of the isolated cabin they had passed a few days before, a lone woman stepped outside onto the front porch, a Sharps rifle in hand.

"Evenin' ma'am," Sheriff Kelly began.

"Evenin'," the frontier woman replied, relaxing her grip on the rifle as she noticed the badges on the men's outer coats.

"Name's Scott Kelly, ma'am. I'm the Sheriff up in El Paso County. This here's my deputy, Dan Gassenger."

Deputy Gassenger tipped his hat to the lady, as the door to the cabin opened slightly, revealing the presence of three young children standing inside.

"To what do I owe this visit?" she asked, taking notice of the three horses being led by Deputy Gassenger, nodding in recognition at the bay in the middle as it nickered upon hearing the sound of her voice.

Sheriff Kelly began, "We understand Big Tooth Jim and his gang have been by this way a couple days back."

The woman appearing angry and depressed replied, "Don't know no names, but some highway men shot my husband and my oldest boy, both dead. Stole our best horse, there," she nodded at the bay, then continued telling of her painful ordeal. "They done drove off our milking cow, shot our dog, took everything of value we had...to be honest Sheriff, I don't know how we'll get on now. We can't get any sleep. I'm deathly afraid they might be comin' back..."

"I'm terribly sorry to hear about your loss ma'am," the Sheriff replied.

"That's very kind of you, Sheriff," the woman acknowledged as the three young children stepped outside and stood on the front porch around their mother.

"You should know," Deputy Gassenger replied, "we done killed 'em. They're all three dead now...They'll not be coming back. I'll put these three horses they was a riding over there in your corral."

"God be praised," the frontier woman said with relief, "and you did this?"

"Well, ma'am," Sheriff Kelly tried to explain, as he pulled out the white handkerchief tied at the top with a leather strap. "It's just what we do," he said as he handed the small white bundle to her.

"Oh my," she replied, opening up the handkerchief to see the money, pocket watch and wedding ring wrapped inside. "This is my wedding ring, and my husband's pocket watch, but all this money don't belong to us. We never had this much money ever all at one time."

"Well, we recognize it won't bring your husband or son back," the Sheriff acknowledged, "but maybe it'll help git you back on your feet again."

The Sheriff tipped his hat to the lady as she hugged her children and watched the two lawmen ride away.

Turning north back on the main road, the Sheriff turned to his deputy riding beside him, "Sorry Dan, looks like I done gave away any chance of a reward coming our way."

"That's okay Sheriff; she needs the money more'n us. It was her, wasn't it? The tracks. You knew all along that the horse with the shoed right hoof was stolen from her, didn't you?"

"Figured that's what went down here, from reading the tracks. When we get back I'll put in a claim to the County Commissioners. Maybe they'll pay us for the ammunition we used, anyways. Let's see…I fired one round, how many bullets did you fire?"

"Two."

"So that's ten cents for me. You got twenty cents a comin'. That's three dead outlaws for thirty cents. I'd say's they'd be getting their money's worth."

"Reckon so," the Deputy replied, as the two lawmen galloped off toward the north.

Two Weeks After Manhunt Began
Judge Stone's Ranch, El Paso County, Colorado Territory

It was nearly dark when Kelly knocked on the front door of Judge Stone's ranch house. He could hear muffled voices coming from inside, one he believed to be Lizzy's. The front door finally cracked open, but not far enough for him to step inside. Judge Stone was standing there and spoke first, "Scott. So glad you made it back safely, son…M.S. Beach told us you been asked to take a second term and who you done rode off after and all."

"Seems there was some unfinished business, but, I told the Commissioners I wouldn't serve the entire term...I was hoping to talk to Lizzy about that."

"I'll let her know you're here son," Judge Stone said, then closed the door.

Kelly stood alone on the front porch for several minutes, concern mounting as time rolled on, then slowly he turned to leave.

The front door creaked open again, just a few inches, to where he could see Lizzy's face; it was drawn and pale.

"Scott..." she tried to explain, "I just...I don't think I can do this anymore...just give me some time to think."

Then Lizzy closed the door.

Crestfallen, Kelly turned and walked away.

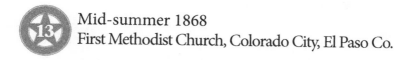 Mid-summer 1868
First Methodist Church, Colorado City, El Paso Co.

"You may kiss your bride," Reverend Howbert said, as Marcus lifted the veil above Lizzy's face and softly kissed her smiling lips.

"Ladies and gentlemen, may I introduce Mr. and Mrs. Marcus A. Foster," Reverend Howbert announced, concluding the wedding ceremony.

The happy couple locked arms and slowly walked down the aisle to the handsome carriage waiting outside; the team of spirited horses being held by Charlie Stone. The audience slowly followed the newlyweds outside and cheered as the carriage, decorated with brightly colored flowers, pulled away from the church. People chatted happily to one another as they streamed slowly away from the small Methodist church.

"Look, there's Mr. and Mrs. Robbins, let's go over to greet them," Mrs. Spielman said to her husband David, hanging onto his arm as they walked off to the east side of the church. The two ladies embraced and began chatting about their families, as their husbands walked slowly behind nodding politely at the other couples.

After the ceremony had concluded, David Spielman had followed Tom Robbins to where their hats had been hung on the rack to the side of the front doors, but neither had spoken to one another. Tensions between the two men had emerged during their previous discussion a few days earlier, centering on the escalating Indian raids. Now, as they waited for their wives, the two men it seemed would have to speak. Tom Robbins held out his hand toward David's outstretched hand and shook hands passively.

"Thomas, it's a beautiful morning, let's not let this unpleasantness come between us any further. It's a good day meant to be enjoyed among family and friends," David said, hoping to smooth things as the two men shook hands.

"David," Tom replied, avoiding eye contact, "not sure what's good about it."

"Well, after all, it was a nice wedding and is a beautiful summer day," David commented as they paused behind their wives. Neither of the ladies appeared in any hurry to leave.

"Not much round here to celebrate, if'n you was ta ask me." Tom Robbins griped, "Whole country's been at war with itself, going on over three years now, since Col. Chivington's troops punished Black Kettle's people on Sand Creek, and yet all people is talking about these days is this so-called Cheyenne War that keeps dragging on with no end in sight."

"Oh, come on, Tom," Mary Robbins said to her husband, "don't start in on that again. Business is picking up and the boys are growing up strong and healthy. There's much for us to celebrate, including this beautiful Indian summer day," trying to shake her husband out of his sour mood.

"How old are the boys now Mary?" Mrs. Spielman asked trying to support Mary's attempt to get their conversation back on a more positive note.

"George just turned eleven and Franklin is eight now," Mary replied with a warm smile.

"Tom," David said, "I been meaning to talk with you again that maybe you should reconsider running your range cattle in with my herd down along Fountain Creek. I already spoke with Judge Stone and he's going to ask Charlie to move their cattle in with mine. The boys and your cattle might be much less vulnerable that way."

"I will do no such thing," Tom quipped, "I done told you once, I'm tired of hearing all this talk about Indian attacks over here and Cheyenne Dog Soldiers over there!"

David Spielman continued, "Papers up in Denver City reported Henrietta Dietemann and her five-year old son, John, were killed along Comanche Creek in Douglas County, by the Cheyenne and Arapahoes back on August 27th and Mr. Teachout claimed 125 horses were stolen from his ranch on September 1st by twenty-five Indians. Their horse herd was driven north along Monument Creek, away from the Teachout Ranch, which as you know is located just six miles north of here."

"It's all nonsense, just rumors and folks more interested in submitting false depredation claims to the federal government, just trying to get rich. Those redskins know they done been whopped and they ain't coming back this way ever again."

"We don't know that, Tom," Mary said, "I would feel..."

"I done made up my mind," Tom interrupted firmly, "You women folk can fort up at Anway Hotel 'til mid-winter if you want, but right now I got work to do." With that Tom Robbins turned abruptly, put on his hat and stomped away.

Two Weeks Later
Spielman Homestead, Monument Creek, El Paso County

"You been in the house here all along?" Robert Love asked excitedly as he burst through the front door.

"Yes," David Spielman replied, setting the newspaper aside and getting up from his nap.

"Didn't you see the Indians?" Robert asked.

"No," David replied, "I had the New York Tribune over my face, whilst I was nappin there behind the door. Guess they didn't see me."

"Lucky thing, you might not be alive right now! Come," Robert said stepping hurriedly outside, "if you climb up on the roof you can see them for yerself."

"There they go!" David shouted pointing to the southeast across Monument creek from atop his roof. "Must be eight or ten of 'em!"

"There's more across the creek there, probably forty or fifty in total. I'm going to ride over to Colorado City to warn them," Robert said as he mounted his horse.

"Wait up," David shouted as he climbed down from the roof and started toward the nearby corral. "I'll get my pony and ride with you to town.

Approaching the corral, David stopped abruptly to see the gate standing open on an empty corral.

"Damn it all," David cursed, as he kicked the dirt, "I just bought that pony from A.M. White yesterday!" He shouted as Robert turned and galloped away to the south, down the right bank of Monument Creek. "Damned Injuns!" David muttered, shaking his fist in the air off to the south where he last saw the

Indians riding. Reluctantly, David Spielman began walking alone toward Colorado City where his hired man, David Wright, had already relocated Mrs. Spielman, along with their oxen and family's most valuable possessions.

A few minutes later, Charlie Stone spotted the Cheyenne and Arapaho warriors, riding south on the opposite side of Monument Creek. He had only a split second to decide; should he try to warn George and Frank Robbins or ride toward the safety of Colorado City. "Come on Jenny," Charlie shouted to his old buckskin mare, "let's go!"

George was the first to spot Charlie Stone galloping toward him, shouting and waving his hat in the air trying to get their attention. When George saw Charlie was being chased by more than a dozen Indians, he shouted to his younger brother, "Come on Frankie, we gotta git outta here!" George grabbed a handful of mane and jumped on the back of their father's plow horse, held out his left arm and extended his left foot for his younger brother to use as a step to climb aboard. Charlie had taught the Robbins boys this quick mount for two riders and they had practiced the technique countless times over the summer, just in case of this eventuality, but their old plow horse was no match for the swift ponies ridden by Tall Bull's Dog Soldiers. The boys hadn't ridden more than a hundred yards when Frankie looked back to see Charlie fall from his horse.

"George," Frank said to his brother, sitting on the horse in front of him, "they done got Charlie!"

"Don't watch, Frankie," George said to his little brother.

"George, I'm scared," Frankie said to his brother, closing his eyes and pressing his face deep against his big brother's back.

"Hang on Frankie," George said, kicking the horse beneath

him for all he was worth.

"They're gaining on us," Frankie said, hearing the Dog Soldier's war whoops closing in behind them, squeezing his arms tighter around his brother's waist, making it hard for him to breathe.

"Just hang on," George said, clutching his left hand tightly over Frank's hands, clamping his brother's hands tight against the front of his own chest.

"Ugh!" Frankie shouted as he felt the arrow enter his back. "They got me, Georgie!"

"I know," George replied, "they got both of us."

Looking down at the arrow that had penetrated his back, Frankie saw the arrow had exited the front of his chest and was stuck in his brother's back, pinning the two boys together.

A Dog Soldier wearing a white hat rode up along the left side of their old horse and struck Frankie on the left side of his head with a warclub. When Frank slid off the right side of their pony's back, since the two boys were pinned together by the arrow, he dragged his older brother down with him to the ground. When their bodies hit the hard dirt, the force of the impact caused their two bodies to separate, and then dozens of more arrows pierced their slim bodies. Within seconds, swarms of Dog Soldiers descended on the two brothers. Mercifully, eleven year old George and eight year old Frank were both dead before the real carnage began.

When Jerome Weir found the body of Charlie Everhart Stone, he was sickened to his stomach at the senseless mutilation of Charlie's body. Not only had the seventeen year old been scalped, he had so many arrows sticking out of his body that he looked like an oversized pincushion. What angered Jerome Weir the most was the Indians had evidently placed their guns within a few inches of Charlies face and shot out both of his eyes. Weir had lived around Indians long enough to know this atrocity was intended to deprive the victim of his use of sight in the afterlife, causing the victim to wander through eternity without the benefit of sight. This was a despicable act of violence and these savages needed to be held accountable by someone.

A quarter mile to the west, coming over the brow of a low hill west of Monument Creek, David Spielman stopped dead in his tracks. He spotted his two oxen on the other side of the hill, still hitched to the wagon but clearly unattended. "They have surely got Wright this time," David said to himself aloud. After retrieving his oxen he turned the wagon toward Colorado City and a short distance later, saw another wagon approaching carrying Judge Stone, Ora Bell and one or two others.

"You had better go to town at once," Judge Stone said. "The report has gone on ahead of you that you were killed. You see Charlie or the Robbins boys this morning?"

"Yes," David replied, "I seen them further down on Monument Creek from my place, tending cattle earlier this morning, near where Judge Baldwin been a grazing his sheep. I fear those Injuns were headed their way Judge!"

Most of the townsfolks later theorized Charlie Stone could have made it safely back to Colorado City, but after seeing the war party bearing down on him, everyone knew the seventeen year old cowboy would have felt it was his duty to warn the younger Robbins boys. A sheep herder named Judge Baldwin, not because he was a real judge like Judge Stone, but because he had once judged a sheep contest, was shot by the same Indians. Judge Baldwin survived being scalped as he had already been scalped once before, during some misadventure in South America. Apparently

Indians believed it bad medicine to scalp a man who had survived being scalped in the past. Judge Baldwin claimed it was Tall Bull who he had seen, leading the Dog Soldiers, when he was attacked and dozens of his sheep were killed just for spite.

When Judge Stone and the other men brought the bodies of his beloved son Charlie and the Robbins boys into town, the bodies of the three boys were laid out in the old log building that had initially served as Doc Garvin and M.S. Beach's cabin. Kelly had been building a barn on the land he owned north of the Garden of the Gods. By the time word reached him, the hostile Indians were long gone. When Kelly rode into Colorado City, he found Judge Stone sitting on the front porch of the log cabin, his face buried deep in his hands. Kelly walked slowly inside to see where the bodies of the three boys were placed on public display to eliminate any doubt the threat of Indian attacks should be taken seriously. The old cowboy hat that Kelly had given Charlie had been placed over his head and face to conceal where he had been scalped.

As Kelly stepped outside onto the front porch, Judge Stone was still sitting on the wooden step, staring at the ground. Kelly placed his hand on his shoulder momentarily, and then, having no place else to go, slowly walked across the dirt street toward Lucy Maggard's boarding house. Lucy had been washing dishes in her kitchen and watching people coming and going in and out of the log cabin all morning long, paying respects to the dead and their families. This was the saddest affair their small little town had ever witnessed. When she saw Scott Kelly walking toward her cabin, she wiped her hands on a kitchen towel, brushed back her hair and remembered ever so briefly how he used to hold her when they danced the night away. That seemed like a lifetime ago, in fact it was for Charlie and the Robbins boys.

Lucy greeted Kelly on her front porch, "How are you, Scott?"

"Ahhh, Lucy," Kelly replied, "hard times."

"I'm so sorry what happened, I know how much Charlie meant to you and how much you meant to Charlie. You've worked so hard Scott. You've protected this town as best you could. No one else could've done any better."

"Thank you Lucy," Kelly said, as he held her in his arms for a moment. "I wasn't able to protect everyone, Lucy. Not George Smith...not Marengo,...not Charlie. I fear that young man will leave a hole in my heart that can never be mended."

"I know," Lucy said as she patted the strong man on the back, both fighting back tears.

"I couldn't even protect Lizzy. Not really. Not in the end. I'm still not sure how I could've done anything differently."

"No one could've saved all those people, Scott. And you've saved so many others. You saved Lizzy too, by letting her go when you did. I know how much it hurts when you let someone that you love go."

"When Tall Bull and his Dog Soldiers decided to murder unarmed women and children, well they've crossed the line. This has become personal. I'll be riding out after them within the hour and won't be back until Tall Bull's dead, or I am." Kelly said, releasing his grip, "Not sure how long I'll be gone this time, I guess as long as it takes."

"You can't go after them by yourself Scott, that's suicide," Lucy said worriedly, "can't you take Robert Finley, Anthony Bott and Irving Howbert and some of the other Free Masons from the Lodge with you?"

"No," Kelly said thoughtfully, "those are all good men, but they need to stay here and protect the town with Sheriff Mason. When I was Sheriff, I stood by and watched brave men march off to Glorieta Pass, and later to Sand Creek, while I stayed here. Now, I have to leave, Lucy… the Dog Soldiers won't stop as long as Tall Bull is their leader, and Tall Bull won't stop until he's dead."

"I know these Dog Soldiers have to be stopped, but you can't do it alone or with just one deputy. Not like you used to, Scott, there's too many of them."

"I know Lucy, I'll try to join up with some of Colonel Shoup's men, if I can find them," Kelly replied as he looked back across the street to where Judge Stone was being joined by his wife, Lizzy and Marcus Foster. "I just didn't know who else to tell I was leaving."

"Scott," Lucy said softly as Kelly turned to leave, "I won't be here when you get back."

Kelly looked at Lucy in surprise. Unsure what to say, he waited for her to explain.

"It's too dangerous here," Lucy explained, "Denver's the Territorial Capitol now. That's where my business and I should be."

Kelly took Lucy's hand in his, "Ya know, my own Mama died when I was two… It was nice to feel that I was with family, when I was here, with you."

"Oh, Scott," Lucy said, trying harder to hold back her tears, "I always believed in you, and I will miss you … dearly."

Kelly kissed the back of her hand and then turned and walked away.

The little school in Colorado City was closed so that all of the schoolchildren could be paraded single-file through the log building to view the three mutilated bodies, two of the victims were their fellow classmates. Eleven year old Hattie Trout would remember for the rest of her life, hiding behind her older sister as they were marched passed the boys' dead bodies. She later wrote, "Going over with my sister to see the bodies. Everyone was flocking there so terrified and grieved over it. Oh they were a terrible sight, scalped and speared and they had placed their guns to their eyes and blew them out and faces and neck all powder burnt... Oh those were terrible times for everyone, so filled with fear and dread...The Indians also stampeded stock. The trail where they crossed Sand Creek...was a mile wide."

Hattie Trout went on to write things no eleven year old should know about. "Different tribes of Indians scalp differently. Some just took a very round piece of scalp; others took all over just leaving a few hairs in the front of the ears. The Indians at that time attacked an old man by the name of Baldwin but found he had been scalped before so left him to die, as they thought, but he lived many years after that and finally met death by falling into a vat in an old slaughter house."

Fall 1869
El Paso House Hotel, Colorado City, Colorado Territory

"General Palmer," Irving Howbert said to the distinguished looking man sitting alone in the dining room reading the Colorado City Journal weekly newspaper, "may I introduce Scott Kelly? Scott, this is General William Jackson Palmer."

The shorter man stood and extended his hand toward the former lawman, "Sheriff Kelly," extending the former County Sheriff the courtesy of using his title, a lifetime privilege shared by the military and those who have held political office. "It's a pleasure to meet you, I've heard so much about you and your time here in public office."

"It's a pleasure to meet you as well, General," Kelly said as he shook the other man's hand. "I have heard much about you as well."

"Won't you please join me for breakfast?" the congenial Civil War General in the dark suit said, adding, "Mr. Howbert, you are welcome to join us for breakfast, as well."

"Thank you sir," Irving Howbert replied, handing General Palmer a folded legal size bundle of papers. "But if you gentlemen are no longer in need of my services, I will excuse myself and see if I can locate one or two other property owners for you to meet before your stagecoach departs for Denver City at the top of the hour."

"Thank you Irving," General Palmer replied, glancing over the legal papers briefly, and seeing Scott Kelly's signature at the bottom of the last page of the deed, transferring ownership of the land located in the canyon north of the Garden of the Gods. "Looks like you have everything in order, as usual," General Palmer replied, handing Kelly a small bundle, "One thousand dollars cash, is that your understanding of our agreement as well, Mr. Kelly?"

"That is correct," Kelly replied, tucking the thick bank envelop deeply into his inside coat pocket.

"Don't you want to count it?" the General asked, nodding his head toward the bundle in Kelly's pocket.

"No Sir. If I can't trust you General Palmer, a Congressional Medal of Honor recipient, then well, we're all in serious trouble," Kelly replied with a nod of respect to the younger man.

"Very well then, I thank you, for your trust Sheriff Kelly," the General replied. "Please join me for breakfast, won't you? I would very much like to hear more about this beautiful countryside of yours."

"Gentlemen," Irving Howbert said as he began to leave, "I will leave you to enjoy your breakfast. I'm sure you will find you two have much in common."

"Thank you," both men said as the young El Paso County Clerk and Recorder left the dining hall and stepped outside onto Colorado Avenue.

"Coffee?" General Palmer asked, holding up a silver coffee urn and offering to pour its steaming contents into the blue porcelain cup sitting before Kelly.

"Please," Kelly replied, as he unfolded his cloth napkin and placed it across his lap.

"Tell me, Sheriff," Palmer said, now that the two men were alone, "as I intend to bring my family and a number of personal friends here over the next few years, do you believe the threat of hostile Indian attacks is behind us now, out here in the Colorado Territory?"

"I believe so," Kelly began, waiting patiently for the young Chinese woman to place their breakfast plates in front of them before continuing, "at least by the Cheyenne and Arapaho tribes in any organized fashion. With the killing of Black Kettle by General Custer's 7th Cavalry at the Battle of Washita River last November, the hostiles' ability to remain on the warpath has been severely impeded. Then with the killing of Tall Bull at the Battle of Summit Springs in July, well, most all of the Dog Soldiers' war chiefs are now gone."

"Were you there when Tall Bull was killed?"

"No, I was involved in a series of smaller skirmishes with some of Colonel Shoup's men, Colonel Shoup had already left the Territory, living in Idaho I believe, but most of the Cavalry men I rode with had previously fought under his command at one time or another."

"Do you feel the Ute are a threat?"

"No, they're generally a peaceful people. But make no mistake, the Ute can be fierce warriors if backed into a corner, and some of their leaders are real firebrands, but as long as Chief Ouray is alive, and no overzealous Indian Agent gets out of hand, I see no reason why the Whiteman and Ute cannot live peacefully among one another for many decades to come. Whenever they make their way back here to the Garden of the Gods next spring, you may want to let them know they're welcome to cut out a few of your cattle to butcher. Game is just not as plentiful as it used to be and a man may do a lot of things he wouldn't normally do to feed his hungry family. To the Ute, like most Indians I met out West here, their tribe is their family. You treat the Ute men, and their families, with respect and they will treat you and yours with respect."

"That's reassuring," the General replied, taking Kelly's words to heart. "Once my Denver & Rio Grande Railroad reaches the depot here for the Fountain Colony I'm planning to build, I intend to build a castle on the land I bought from you north of the Garden of the Gods for my wife, Mary Lincoln 'Queen' Mellen Palmer, in what I will call Queen's Canyon."

"I always felt that canyon was deserving of a queen and a castle," Kelly replied reflectively.

"What about you Sheriff, what are your plans?"

"I've always wanted to see the Pacific Ocean. Who knows, maybe I'll buy some land there in the Sierra Nevada Mountains and build a ranch along the Sacramento River."

"You think you might get back into law enforcement or run for political office again?"

"I hope not," Kelly said with a chuckle, "I've always said becoming Sheriff for El Paso County was the best and the worst decision I ever made in my life. Don't get me wrong, I wouldn't trade the privilege of being the Sheriff for El Paso County for love or money, but there's a certain price you, and those who you care for most, pay when you pin on a badge; not dissimilar to what you may have experienced when you put on your military uniform."

"I understand you fought during the Mexican-American War," Palmer replied, lightly buttering a piece of sourdough toast.

"I did, I suspect we may know some of the same men; men who know both service and sacrifice."

"I understand General Sherman was through here a while back," Palmer replied.

"Yes, but just overnight. He was headed south toward the Rosita Road, on his way to inspect the troops at Fort Garland, but he didn't want to be bothered with local Indian matters."

"Did you speak with him?" Palmer asked.

"No, I was busy catching up with a couple counterfeiters. They were staying in a hotel in Canon City, so I wasn't here at the time when General Sherman came through. The local townsfolk appointed Reverend William Howbert to speak for them, but I'm told the Reverend left their meeting with the clear understanding that Sherman shared General Sheridan's belief that, 'the only good Indian he'd ever seen was a dead Indian.'"

"That sounds more like Phil Sheridan than William Tecumseh Sherman," Palmer replied, wiping his neatly trimmed mustache with his white cloth napkin before continuing. "Sherman has always been one to embrace his commanding officer's orders as if they were his own and after Sherman's 'March to the Sea', where they cut a swatch across the breadbasket of the South; well, no soldier understood better than Generals Sherman and Sheridan how to eliminate their enemies ability to wage war."

"True. General Sherman's decision to eliminate the 'Commissary of the Plains', as he referred to buffalo, was the last nail in the coffin forcing a bitter end to the Cheyenne Wars. Sherman had seen firsthand how the Plains Indians could use every part of the American Bison to provide everything they needed to sustain their tribe. When buffalo hunters like Buffalo Bill Cody began to wipe out the vast buffalo herds that once numbered in the millions, well, the sun was about to set on the last of the Plains Indians."

"I understand you had a hand in some of the fiercest fighting, riding alongside Colorado's First Cavalry Regiment," General Palmer said as he finished the last of his breakfast and refreshed their coffee cups.

"I was there, at the end," Kelly acknowledged, not accustomed to speaking about his experiences in Mexico or on the High Plains. "There were many men, on both sides, who exhibited extraordinary heroism in defense of their people and cultural way of life. No different than what I suspect you witnessed fighting against the Confederacy."

"Likely the same in every battle of every war." Palmer replied introspectively, "Please continue."

"In one of the last skirmishes we fought in, a few months ago just northwest of Spruce Mountain in Douglas County, twenty-nine Dog Soldiers inadvertently rode into a box canyon. They were in a veritable ambush, there being no outlet to the canyon. They all fought desperately. Their Warchief had shaved his head and painted his face blue, just like the rest of them, with white bear claws streaming down their cheeks. This Dog Soldier wore the red sash around his waist, which was tied to his lance, identifying himself as the Warchief. When he dismounted and drove his lance into the ground he demonstrated to the other warriors that he would go no farther, and that this place was where he intended to fight to the death, and he did. I rode down on him and shot him from just a few feet away, twice through the heart, hopin' like hell he was Tall Bull, but he wasn't. He was a courageous warrior; I still see his defiant face when I close my eyes to sleep. He expected me to dismount and fight him on his terms, but when I saw he wasn't Tall Bull, I killed him and went after more Dog Soldiers to kill. It sounds heartless now, but I was so mad when I saw their numbers were diminishing, I was afraid the soldiers would kill them all and I wouldn't get to kill any more of 'em. My horse's reins were shredded to pieces and an arrow pierced my boot, but it never even broke the skin. The Indians lost seven horses–horses that had been stolen from a nearby ranch. Six soldiers were killed. We managed to kill their entire band of warriors. They fought bravely to the last man."

General Palmer sat quietly for a few moments; comparing mentally the picture Kelly had painted in his own mind to the many running horse battles he had fought with his cavalrymen during the Civil War.

Finally, Scott Kelly broke their silence, "The problem, as I saw it for the Indians, at least here in the Southwest, was they never changed their tactics. For hundreds, perhaps even thousands of years, war had been a very personal affair, fought intimately one on one. Their Warchiefs would lead his warriors to the battle; but from the beginning of the battle to the end, the fighting was one warrior against another. If you survived you fought the next warrior, one at a time. Then, when the Spanish brought the speed and mobility of the horse and the lethality of the gun from Europe, and deployed them effectively here in combat, well, under the right leadership, even the fierce Comanche couldn't withstand the fighting strength of the Spanish Empire."

General Palmer nodded knowingly, and then commented, "I studied the early Spanish maps and English transcriptions from Governor Juan Bautista de Anza's 1779 Campaign against the Comanche Warchief Cuerno Verde, which I understand means Green Horn, referencing the green buffalo horn affixed to the headdress he wore into battle. Anza's twenty-seven day campaign journal details how Anza led six hundred Spanish soldiers north from Santa Fe and how he was joined enroute by two hundred Ute and Jicarilla Apache warriors."

"I am told," Kelly explained, "that Anza's troops were led by the Ute, who had been victimized by the Comanche for years, across South Park and around to the north of Pikes Peak, then down the Ute Pass where they attacked and destroyed the Comanche base camp at the confluence of Fountain and Monument Creeks, but Cuerno Verde wasn't in camp at the time."

"The journal describes," Palmer continued, "that Cuerno Verde had led two hundred and fifty of his most fierce warriors on a raid at Taos, where he lost several warriors, and it was on their return trip that they clashed with Anza's forces somewhere south of the Arkansas River at the base of the Wet Mountains. When I was surveying the route for the Denver and Rio Grande I noticed a mountain peak north of the Spanish Peaks named Cuerno Verde, which is near where the final battle must have taken place. Anza's journal describes how Cuerno Verde rode into a rocky arroyo,

284

followed by his son, his Medicine Man who had declared himself immortal, his four subchiefs and at least ten of his elite guard. The Spanish held the high ground and cut off any avenue of escape or path for reinforcements. The Comanche in that arroyo soon found they were trapped, similar to your experience with the Dog Soldiers. They too fought bravely, using the same tactics they'd always used, but they failed to realize they were in over their heads."

"The Caballeros, Spanish cowboys, refer to someone who is in over their heads or simply inexperienced as a 'Green Horn,'" Kelly explained.

"I have heard that expression," Palmer said, "but didn't know where it came from until now; there is much that can be learned from history. Well, Sheriff, looks like my stage just pulled up out front. I'd best be going. There's no doubt El Paso County is better off because you were here; thank you for your service and your sacrifice," General Palmer said as he lifted his coffee cup in a quiet salute.

"And to you General, for your service and sacrifice as well," returning the gesture with his cup, "I have no doubt the Pikes Peak Region will benefit greatly from your leadership."

"There must be countless memories you leave behind," General Palmer commented, as the two men stood up from the table and made their way outside.

"There are," Kelly acknowledged, deep in thought, "most good, some not so much."

"Well, if you ever find yourself out this way again Sheriff, please stop by and say hello," the General replied.

Shaking hands, Kelly nodded at General Palmer and said, "Not sure I'll ever be coming back this way, but if I ever do I will certainly stop by to pay my respects."

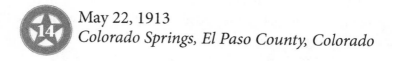
May 22, 1913
Colorado Springs, El Paso County, Colorado

"Welcome to Colorado Springs, Scott." Anthony Bott said, greeting Kelly warmly as he stepped down from the train onto the wooden platform.

"Thank you," Kelly replied fondly, as the two men shook hands, "it's nice to be back."

"It must feel rather odd, being back here after more than forty years," Bott said as he led the way to his horse drawn carriage waiting at the north end of the long wooden platform.

"In some ways yes," Kelly replied as he placed his bag in the back of the carriage, then climbed aboard to sit next to his friend on the buckboard, "but strangely, in other ways it feels as if I never left."

"Colorado Springs wasn't even here when you rode out," Bott commented, steering the carriage east up the hill and away from the train depot, and then turning the horses south on Cascade Avenue. Noticing Kelly was looking up at Pikes Peak, he stopped the buggy on the wide street in front of the Antlers Hotel. The twin towers on both ends of the hotel perfectly framed Pikes Peak in the distance "… but she's still here," he concluded with a nod toward the snowcapped purple mountain.

"And just as majestic as ever," Kelly replied as he gazed admiringly up at the peak that stood to the west. "Wasn't sure I'd ever see her again; but she's just as beautiful as the first time I laid eyes on her over a half century ago."

"That she is," Bott replied. "Come, let's make our way over to Colorado City and get you settled in at my place. Olivia will have supper waiting when we get there."

"Sounds wonderful, Anthony. Don't remember when I last had a home cooked meal; but, I don't want to be a burden on you or Olivia. It might be a couple weeks yet 'til they're ready for me to move in down at the Myron Stratton Home."

"No burden at all, 'sides it shouldn't be more than a few weeks."

"I appreciate you and Irving making arrangements for me to have a job there so as I could earn my keep, I just wouldn't feel right accepting charity."

"Well, I know they're looking forward to having you as their night watchman."

"That's quite a legacy Winfield Scott Stratton left in his will; leaving nearly all his fortune to establish and maintain a home for orphans and poor older folks. I've wondered about the name, the Myron Stratton Home. Do you happen to know who Myron Stratton was?"

"Yes I do, Myron Stratton was Winfield's father. He was a successful ship builder and taught his son his carpentry skills. Winfield also became an expert draftsman."

The two friends watched as an electric trolley passed northbound and rang its bell as it crossed the wide street. "Stratton bought the Colorado Springs Transit Railway," Bott said, nodding to the electric trolley going in the opposite direction, "back in '01. He renamed it the Colorado Springs & Interurban Railway Co., and donated it to the City, along with money to build the U.S. Post Office Building, the Mining Exchange Building and the El Paso County Office Building."

"I read where it's a magnificent building," Kelly said, seeing his friend's head nod in agreement. "I'll have to take a tour when I stop in next week...have to change my voter registration back to El Paso County. I remember the first time I registered back in '61, when I was appointed Sheriff, I wasn't sure if I was even a U.S. citizen or not back then, so I applied for citizenship at the same time."

"Yes, Winfield Scott Stratton and General Palmer were both very generous to the citizens of Colorado Springs. Palmer built Colorado College, Glockner Hospital and donated land for all our beautiful city parks," Bott said, turning the horse and buggy west up Colorado Avenue. "You ever meet Stratton? He got here in 1868 I believe."

"I remember meeting young Winfield a few times," Kelly replied, "before I headed off to California. He was just twenty years old, as I recall, when he arrived here, but he was a hard worker, pretty much like most all the rest of us back then. What do you suppose made Winfield more successful than most of the rest of us; you suppose he was just luckier than we were in striking it rich?"

Anthony thought about Kelly's question for a minute or two before offering his opinion. "Well luck might have had something to do with it, but I remember he educated himself at the Colorado School of Mines in Golden, then at Colorado College here in

Colorado Springs. He may have been more persistent than most. Every summer, for seventeen years in a row, he roamed the mountains beyond Pikes Peak. After falling asleep one night he claims he was visited by an angel who showed him in a dream where to dig. Legend says the next morning Stratton walked right to where that angel told him to dig and struck it rich. That was on the 4th of July, 1891. That's why he filed his claim under the name of the Independence Mine."

"That reminds me," Kelly replied, "are you and Olivia going to the El Paso Pioneer Association's Fourth of July dance at the Antlers Hotel?"

"No, Olivia's not much into dancing these days, bad knees and all, but you're welcome to borrow the horse and buggy if you'd like."

"Thank you, I appreciate your offer. Would you mind if I borrowed your horse and buggy for a couple hours tomorrow afternoon? I have a couple old friends I'd like to visit."

"Not at all Scott, Laura Belle's yours to borrow any time."

"Laura Belle? You named your horse after a Lady of the Evening?'

"Yes, but don't tell Olivia," Bott said, "She thinks Laura Belle was my Sunday School Teacher."

"Can't image where she might a got that idea," Kelly said, glancing to his friend sitting beside him on the buckboard, with a twinkle in his eye and a sly smile spreading across his bearded face.

Morning May 23, 1913
Carnegie Public Library, Colorado City

Scott Kelly walked down the narrow stairs leading from Anthony Bott's comfortable home, located above his business on the ground level. It was midmorning when Kelly stepped out onto the concrete sidewalk, having enjoyed catching up with Anthony over a long breakfast that morning. Kelly looked both ways down Colorado Avenue, trying to avoid being run over by one of the horseless carriages carrying people busily in both directions. Kelly had been suffering from stomach cancer and heart disease for months and his doctors suggested he might breathe better at a lower altitude. He had seen a motorcar several times before in Ouray, Colorado, watching out the hospital windows to the street below, although he had never ridden in one.

To Kelly's way of thinking, these noisy motor carriages, belching clouds of thick, grey smoke into the air, seemed a poor replacement for a team of well-trained horses, or even a team of raucous elk named Thunder and Buttons. Kelly watched another motorcar driving down the street approaching from his left and just as it drove passed him it backfired. POW! The loud noise startled Kelly and a team of horses pulling a coal wagon across the street. Kelly's right hand shot up instinctively to grab his right side, clutching his ribs where Johnny Salingo's bullet had struck him so many years ago, right here on this very street. Kelly felt for Uncle Doug's birthday coin, still tucked away in his vest pocket, attached to the watch with the horsehair chain. He pulled the silver pocket watch from his left vest pocket, as he had done countless times before, flipped the case open and glanced at the hands still permanently fixed at thirty-six minutes past two. A single moment frozen forever in time, painfully seared into his mind.

Kelly closed the case to the pocket watch, sealing more painful memories back away into the tiny box in the back of his mind, at least temporarily, and slipped the watch Lizzy had given him for Christmas a lifetime ago back into his left vest pocket. A young couple, perhaps in their twenties, was walking down the sidewalk and had seen Kelly jump when the motorcar backfired. They were trying to suppress their laughter, seeing how the old man had been startled by the noise. Kelly tipped his hat to the young couple as they passed, pretending not to hear as they snickered behind his back.

"Kids," Kelly thought to himself, as he shifted his attention to the problem at hand; how was he going to cross this busy street without getting run over. Seeing a break in traffic, Kelly walked briskly north across Colorado Avenue and without stopping, glanced to his right, across 25th Street to where M.S. Beach and Doc Garvin's log cabin had been relocated in Bancroft Park. Kelly quickened his pace, trying to distance himself from the memory of Charlie Everhart Stone's cold body lying inside, next to the two Robbins boys. Kelly stared straight ahead, focusing on his destination, the ornate tan building a half block ahead across Pikes Peak Avenue. Walking up the wide steps into the lobby of the Carnegie Public Library, he smiled briefly at the middle-aged lady with the brown hair pulled up in a bun behind the front desk and retrieved a copy of the Colorado Springs Gazette Telegraph from the newspaper rack.

Kelly made his way over to a comfortable red leather chair in a corner, settled in and marveled at the beautiful library, built by the generosity of a Scottish immigrant, the son of poor parents, who had become one of the richest men in America. This library was but one of hundreds that had been built across the country, paid for by Andrew Carnegie. Kelly opened the paper and read an article about how two brothers, Wilbur and Orville Wright, had taught themselves to fly and were now teaching the rest of the world how to fly. Another article told of how President Woodrow

Wilson had recently triggered the explosion of the Gamboa Dike, concluding construction of the Panama Canal, linking the Atlantic Ocean to the Pacific. Another article documented the opening of the Woolworth Building in New York City, declaring that with fifty-seven stories, it was now the tallest building in the world.

Holding the newspaper up to the morning light shining through the tall window, Kelly turned the page to the local section and read the headline, followed by a column: "First El Paso County Sheriff Visiting Here: Scott Kelly, one of the region's early pioneers and a member of the colony that settled in Colorado City, is visiting friends here for the first time in almost 40 years. He is the guest of Anthony Bott, one of the founders of Colorado City. Kelly was the first Sheriff of El Paso County, and was a terror to all law breakers within his jurisdiction. In the early days he sold what later became known as the Glen Eyrie property to General William J. Palmer for $1,000, investing the money in a ranch in the San Joaquin Valley, California. He learned a short time later that his property was near the headquarters of a band of horse thieves and road agents, and soon left that part of the country. During the last quarter of a century Kelly has made his home in Ouray, Colo. He expects to spend several days in Colorado City and the Pikes Peak region looking up old friends."

Afternoon May 23, 1913
Evergreen Cemetery, Colorado Springs, Colorado

"Hello General," Kelly said softly, as he placed the flowers on the grave below the stone marker. "I told you if I ever made it back I'd stop by and say hello. I regret I didn't make it back a little sooner. I would have enjoyed talking with you over breakfast, one last time." He placed his hand on top of the stone marker and knelt onto one knee then read the engraved lettering, "William Jackson Palmer, Born Kinsale Farm Delaware, Sept 17, 1836, Died Glen Eyrie Colorado March 13, 1909." Glancing at the other stone grave marker, located on the raised rectangular terrace, he stood and walked closer to where he could read the name, "Mary Lincoln 'Queen' Mellon Palmer" and saw the year of death was 1894. "I hope you and your queen enjoyed at least a few happy years together in your castle. May you both rest in peace."

Returning to the carriage, Kelly climbed in and drove the buggy one block to the south and two blocks to the east where he again dismounted and retrieved another small batch of yellow roses from the back of the wagon. He walked just a few feet east of the roadway, before spotting the large stone grave marker bearing the name "Finley". He walked closer, and removed his hat when he was close enough to read the inscription, "Grace, daughter of Robert & A.A. Finley, Born May 11, 1878, Died Jan. 11, 1897."

"Hello Grace, I knew your father," Kelly said, doing the math in his head. He was saddened to realize Robert Finley's only child had died when she was just nineteen years of age. Kelly turned his attention to the freshly dug grave, located just a few feet away to his right, "There you are Robert, figured you'd be close by." He knelt beside the modest gray grave marker, touched the stone marker and read the inscription, "Father Robert Finley 1830-1913."

Kelly laid the flowers atop the fresh mound of dirt, "Looks like I just missed you, too, my friend; I'm so sorry I didn't make it back a few months ago. I would have enjoyed seeing you once more." Kelly stood up, brushed the dirt from his pants leg and read the inscription on the matching grave marker located next to Robert's: "Mother Alvira A. Finley 1840 -" the date of death left open. "I can't imagine what grief you must have experienced in your life Alvira, losing your husbands John Clay Brown and Robert Finley, and then your nineteen year old daughter Grace. Perhaps there is some comfort in knowing you were loved by two good men in your life and from what I hear of your daughter, the name you and Robert chose for her, fit her well."

Turning his attention back to Robert's grave, Kelly clasped his hands together and said a short prayer, then placed his hat back on his head. "You did well my friend, you earned the respect of many friends and felt the love of a good woman, and even though you had to endure unimaginable heartache, losing your only child, I envy how your life turned out; yours was a life worth living. As you may know, I never married, nor had any children, least none that I know of, but I had felt the love of a good woman once, and felt the loss of a good horse and friends, young and old. Maybe that's what this old world is all about; it is about having to have endured the heartache from the loss of a loved one, so you could understand the depths of emotions separating our greatest happiness from our deepest sorrows. I pray our losses in this life are only temporary and we will be reunited with our loved ones again in the afterlife."

Reflecting back on his memories of when Robert Finley, John Brown, Anthony Bott and Irving Howbert first brought Freemasonry to the Pikes Peak region, and founded El Paso Lodge Number 13, the thirteenth Lodge of Masons in Colorado, Kelly respected how Robert Finley had taken his vow to care for the widows and orphans of fellow Free Masons to heart. Kelly knew he could have become a member of the lodge. All he had to do was ask, having been told Masons are prohibited from asking another man to join a Lodge. He knew and respected that all

Masonic brothers had taken a pledge to keep the secrets of their fellow Masons, but there were those two exceptions: murder and treason.

"That could have been problematic," Kelly thought to himself as he walked back toward the carriage, enjoying the sunshine on his face and the aroma of roses by the thousands that adorned the beautiful cemetery. He paused once again to gaze up at Pikes Peak standing to the West. "Can't imagine a more beautiful place to be buried," Kelly said as he climbed aboard the carriage and retrieved the horse's reins. "Come on, Laura Belle, let's go check on the progress being made on our new home south of town. Can't be staying with Mr. and Mrs. Bott forever now, can we?"

Late-June, 1913
Garden of the Gods, north of Colorado City

Scott Kelly pulled back on the reins, drawing the carriage to a halt along Camp Creek in front of the red Gateway Rocks. "Whoa, Laura Belle, we best wait here 'til they finish getting their pictures took." He stepped gingerly down from the wagon and watched patiently as Tod Powell, the photographer, arranged the fifty or so people up into two rows, the men standing behind the women who were seated on the ground. Many of the Ute men were wearing headdresses and several tipis were visible in the background.

"Alright now, everyone hold perfectly still," Tod instructed as he held the powder flash pan up high and ducked his head beneath the black hood of the large box camera.

"POOF!" the black powder in the pan above the camera flashed as people slowly started to resume talking and mingle about.

Kelly approached the photographer, busily packing up his camera equipment, and said, "That ought to make for a grand photograph."

"And an historic one, I should think," Tod Powell replied. "That Ute Chief, Buckskin Charlie, riding off over there, told me when he hired me that this will be the last Shan Kive for the Ute. His People wanted this moment and this sacred place of theirs to be remembered." Putting his camera carefully into the back of the buggy, the photographer nodded his head toward Kelly then said, "If you'll pardon me sir, I don't mean to be rude but I must rush back to my studio in Colorado Springs to develop my glass plate; if this photo didn't come out, I'll have to come back out here first thing in the morning. Otherwise they'll all be gone by midmorning."

Kelly watched as the photographer drove away in his buggy toward Colorado Springs, and then turned back to see a young Ute man leading an older Ute woman his way; she looked to be in her seventies. They were being followed by a big old, white dog.

The young Ute man stopped in front of Kelly. His face looked familiar, but the older man waited for the young Ute man to speak first. "Excuse me, Sheriff Kelly. My step-mother, Chipeta wishes to speak to you."

Kelly looked into the eyes of the older Indian woman. Her eyes clouded grey with cataracts, but he recognized the Ute woman he had not seen in over forty years, "White Singing Bird. You are as lovely as ever."

Chipeta smiled to hear him use her Ute name. She moved forward and touched Kelly's face and traced his smile of recognition with her finger tips. She placed her right hand on his chest, over his heart, and felt with her left hand down his chest to where she located the horsehair watch chain she had braided from the hair of Marengo and Thundercloud's tails.

"Mique," Chipeta said softly, the Ute word for hello, "how are you Scott Kelly? It is good to see you again. My husband came to me this morning in my prayers. He said you would be here this day."

Kelly replied, "Ouray always seemed to know things the rest of us didn't; but, tell me who is this young man standing beside you who reminds me so much of my old friend?"

"This is Ouray's lost son, Patron."

Kelly shook the young man's hand, "My God son. It is good to finally meet you!"

Patron smiled as Chipeta explained, "We kept our eyes open for a long time, before we saw him…before my eyes dimmed. He was raised by the Arapaho after being abducted along the Platte River from our buffalo hunting camp when he was a boy."

"Ouray was a good father, and he loved you very much; it is well you are back among your Ute family," Kelly replied.

"I have two families now," Patron explained, "one Ute, the other Arapaho."

"You are fortunate Patron," Kelly commented, "As one grows older they find the importance of family. I miss your father, he was my friend."

Chipeta, her right her hand still resting on Kelly's chest, above his heart, said softly, "You will see him again, and soon…he wants you to have this." Chipeta removed her hand from Kelly's chest and reached her hand deep into the bottom of a embroidered buckskin bag she carried slung over her left shoulder, and handed Kelly the old Spanish folding knife that Ouray and Kelly had traded back and forth several times in their younger days.

Kelly, examining the knife, saw that only a small portion of the gold crest of Queen Isabella remained attached to the now well-worn handle. "Towaoc" Kelly replied, the Ute word for thank you.

Chipeta, smiling, with Patron at her side, turned, her task now complete, and walked away, without a word of goodbye. Kelly recalled there was not a word for goodbye in Ute. Kelly thought of his friend Ouray explaining, "I see you now, and I will see you again, either in this life or the next." Thinking he would see his friend again brought a warm smile to his face.

Kelly watched as the old, white dog followed closely behind Chipeta and Patron, the three walking down the winding dirt trail, the old dog wagging his fluffy white tail, and then just before they walked out of sight, the white dog stopped and looked back momentarily at Kelly. The old man and old dog made eye contact and as Kelly raised his right hand and whispered, "Farewell my friend." The white dog barked once in acknowledgement, "woof" and then trotted off to catch up with Chipeta and Patron.

Kelly walked back to the horse and carriage he had borrowed from Anthony Bott, then rubbed Laura Belle's forehead. Laura Belle nickered as Kelly pulled a sugar cube from his vest pocket and held it out in the flat of his hand, under the horse's soft nose. "There's much the rest of us could learn from the Ute, if we were willing to listen and they were willing to speak," Kelly said to Laura Belle, who happily accepted the sugar cube he held out in the flat palm of his weathered hand. "The Ute believe you have a spirit Laura Belle, and all dogs have a spirit, and everything created by the Creator has a spirit; what do you say to that, Laura Belle?" The horse remained silent, savoring the taste of the sugar cube dissolving in her mouth. Kelly decided it was time to leave and struggled as he climbed aboard the buggy.

Turning back one last time to savor the view, the tipis erected in front of the red rocks, standing beneath the snow capped mountain the Ute called Tava, Kelly watched as a small wisp of smoke rose up from one of the tipis. He wondered if the smoke might be from Chipeta's tipi, and imagined her stirring the coals back to life with a stick as she prepared a noonday meal for Patron and her extended Ute family, or any hungry or injured passersby. He recalled the aroma of the warm broth and taste of her delicious turkey soup and the bitterness of the pine sap tea she prepared for him, as she nursed him back to health in the painful days after he lost his Marengo. There was no doubt in Kelly's mind that Ouray and Chipeta had saved his life when Hank Way shot Marengo out from under him; God, how he missed that horse.

"Giddy up, Laura Belle," Kelly said, "we'll both be ready for a nap when we get back to town."

As Kelly rode away from the Garden of the Gods in the slow-moving horse drawn carriage, making his way back to Colorado City, he closed his eyes and imagined what it might feel like to ride Marengo again in the afterlife. To gallop alongside Ouray, riding a few feet away on Thundercloud, so close you could reach out and touch them. To feel the wind rush across your face, look down to see the ground passing beneath the horse's pounding hooves. Oh, what he wouldn't give, just one last time, to feel the rhythm of that magnificent gray horse running beneath him; horse and rider moving as one. Anticipating one another's thoughts, sharing the moment, the exhilaration of the chase; the sheer joy of freedom!

Bump! Kelly felt the jolt of the carriage coming to a stop, and opened his eyes to see he was already back in Colorado City. Kelly looked down to find he was still holding the reins; however, as with most horses, Laura Belle knew her way back to the barn. She didn't need him to show her the way. The former lawman sighed heavily, locked his memories back into the dark box he kept sealed in the recesses of his mind, and then stepped down from the carriage, thinking he might just as well have been riding in the back of the carriage like a twenty-five pound sack of potatoes.

July 4th, 1913
Antlers Hotel, Colorado Springs, Colorado

The 1913 Independence Day Pioneers Ball was in full swing when Scott Kelly entered the spacious ballroom of the Antler's Hotel. A large band was playing an unfamiliar tune as he glanced around at the happy faces, not recognizing anyone at all that he knew. Perhaps he shouldn't have come, he thought to himself, and not for the first time that evening, somewhat embarrassed to see how much younger everyone was, by several decades. "Do I look as old to them as they look young to me?" he wondered as he considered leaving, but just then the band struck up a familiar tune, The Yellow Rose of Texas. How he loved to dance, he thought, longing to step foot once again onto the dance floor.

Kelly glanced around at the few single women present, maybe three or four across the way without an escort. He continued searching their faces for someone who looked as if they wanted to dance as much as he did, and spotted a pretty young lady swaying her body to the rhythm of the song. He approached the lovely young lady, bowed and was thrilled when she accepted his invitation to dance. The senior residents of El Paso County knew Kelly's reputation to thrill a crowd with his dance steps. He twirled the young lady around and looked into her smiling face; suddenly, her face seemed to almost transform in front of him and she looked almost exactly like Lizzy. The Antler's Grand Ballroom of 1913 seemed to be magically transformed back in time to the smaller more intimate space of the El Paso Hotel as it existed back in 1864. The large band shrank to a smaller three-piece string band, as the other couples cleared the dance floor, they watched in amazement as Kelly led the beautiful young woman around the dance floor. He felt as if he was dancing with Lizzy again!

Then, as the song came too soon to an end, the beautiful young woman in his arms spoke, "You are a most graceful dancer, Mr. Kelly."

Instinctively, Kelly bowed to his partner, kissed the back of her hand and when he looked back up Lizzy's face faded away. "Coming from a beautiful young lady like you, I take that as a very grand compliment. You look very much like a young lady I used to know...tell me, what is your name?"

"My name is Charlotte," the pretty young woman replied as she blushed.

"I was surprised you didn't have a partner."

"Oh...mama say's I'm too shy...so thank you for asking me."

"How do you know my name?"

"Why, everyone knows who you are, Sheriff Kelly! My grandmother tells me you were quite the hero when she was young. She said all the girls were silly over you and that all the men called you friend."

"Did she, now?! Truth is, I was hard to know..."

"Why's that, Mr. Kelly?"

"Well, I guess when you live as long as I have, and pause to look back at your life, well there's some things you're maybe not real proud of."

"Well sir, from everything I ever heard from Granny, she always said Sheriff Kelly lived the life of an honorable lawman.

She said you tracked down horse thieves and killed outlaws and murderers, cattle rustlers and stagecoach robbers, you even conquered an evil man who everyone called the 'Terror of the Rockies'—she said he had teeth like a Smilodon...a big saber-toothed cat! She said you were the bravest man she's ever known."

"My goodness, child, who was your grandmother?"

Pointing to a graceful woman in her seventies, Charlotte said, "She's right over there..."

Kelly turned to where the young woman was pointing and saw the woman she was pointing to in the crowd was Lizzy. Although she was no longer a young woman, she was as beautiful as the last time he saw her and he felt his heart begin to race.

"Come," Charlotte said, escorting Kelly over to where her grandmother stood watching, "Granny will want to say hello."

A thousand emotions flooded through Kelly's mind as he approached the woman whose love he had once known. She was standing alone. "Where was Marcus?" he wondered to himself, ashamed of the answer he hoped he would hear, *"Oh, he died a few years ago..."*

When Kelly stopped in front of Lizzy he found he was speechless, still spellbound in her presence. He accepted the graciousness of her warm embrace. Fortunately, she spoke first, so he didn't have to, "Hello, Scott, I heard you were back in town. I see you haven't lost a step."

"Hello, Lizzy," he replied, trying to contain his excitement, "you're just as beautiful as the first time I laid eyes on you."

"I'll let Grandpa know you'll be along in a moment," Charlotte said, leaving Kelly and her Grandmother alone.

"Grandpa?" Kelly asked, looking at Lizzy.

"I know, I suppose it's hard to think of Marcus as a Grandfather, or me as a Grandmother, but here we are. You'll have to come to dinner Sunday, after church. I'll ask Charlotte to coordinate your visit; she works for the local newspaper and wants very much to ask your permission to interview you for a local history piece she has been working on as of late."

"I would be honored to come to your and Marcus's home for dinner and be interviewed anytime by your granddaughter. She looks so very much like you."

"Charlotte and her sister both live with us; they have been so focused on their careers, they've not taken husbands yet, not sure they ever will. But Marcus and I love having them with us and we will be looking forward to hearing all about what you've accomplished since we last saw you, what some forty years ago, when you rode off into the sunset?"

"Not much to tell," Kelly said, trying to process the full range of emotions he was feeling, "I will look forward to dinner on Sunday."

October, 1913
Alamo Park, Colorado Springs,

"This seat taken?" the older gentleman asked as he and his wife approached the park bench where Kelly sat waiting for the next electric trolley car to take him back to the Myron Stratton Home.

"Please, join me," Kelly said, as he reluctantly scooted over, not sure how a gentleman could refuse. Kelly retrieved his knife from his pants pocket and extended the folding blade without looking. He subconsciously rubbed his thumb across the edge of the blade, testing the sharpness of the blade. He pulled a red apple from his coat pocket and cut a slice, offering it to the elderly couple sitting next to him on the bench.

"Oh, no thank you," the man replied, answering for himself and his wife, "is this where we catch the trolley?"

"It is," Kelly replied, as he wiped the juice from the apple on his pant leg and returned the knife to its proper place in his right coat pocket. Subconsciously he pulled the silver pocket watch from his left vest pocket and popped open the case.

"Thank you," the woman said, answering for herself and her husband, and then she nodded at the pocket watch in Kelly's hand. "How long until it arrives, do you know?"

Kelly glanced down at the hands, "Don't rightly know," he replied, and then felt compelled to explain, holding up his watch, "Afraid it broke, long ago. Been fixed on 2:36 now for more than forty years".

"Sentimental value," the woman acknowledged knowingly.

"Yes…suppose so. You in town visiting?" Kelly asked, intending to change the subject.

"We are!" The man answered, glanced up at Pikes Peak and then added, "Beautiful here!"

"I'm just back here myself." Kelly commented.

"Were you born out this way?" the woman asked politely.

"No I came here from Maine, originally," Kelly replied, unsure why he said Maine instead of giving his standard reply as vaguely saying he was "from back east."

"Well now! That's where we're from!" the man said.

"You don't say?!" Kelly replied, wondering if the man was making a joke.

"Houlton." The woman said.

"What?" Kelly asked, wondering how she could have guessed he was from Houlton.

"We're from Houlton," the man explained.

"Can't be!" Kelly said somewhat astonished that this couple sitting beside him was from his hometown. "Well now, that's where I am from! I never met anyone out West here who was from Houlton."

"Even out here it can be a small world!" the man commented, looking down the street to see if the trolley car was approaching.

"Might we have anyone in common?" the woman asked politely.

"Oh, it was so long ago," Kelly said, returning his pocket watch to his left vest pocket; then traced the braided horsehair watch chain with his fingers to confirm it was still attached to the fifty cent piece tucked away in his right vest pocket. "My Uncle Doug lived there, but he must be long gone by now. My sister is Katherine Kelly."

"Well now," the woman said, "we know Katherine and Emitt! Everyone does. Katherine was a Kelly before she married Emitt. They run the mercantile in Houlton!"

"Emitt?" Kelly asked, trying to make certain he heard her correctly.

"Why Katherine and Emitt Catsby, of course," the man replied.

"Emitt…" Kelly repeated to himself, beginning to realize the man he thought he had killed seventy-three years ago was still alive!

Late November, 1913
Village Inn Restaurant, Colorado Springs

"Thank you for meeting me for lunch Sheriff Kelly," Charlotte said as she flipped open the cover of her reporter's narrow spiral bound notebook. "I just want to make sure I have all the details correct before I approach my publishers about your story."

"My pleasure Charlotte," Kelly said, "but you don't have to pay for lunch."

"My editor approved the expenditure, which doesn't happen all that often," Charlotte said, as she handed the waitress a five dollar bill. "You may keep the change," she added with a pleasant smile.

"Well, please thank your editor for me," Kelly said, wiping his whiskers with the cloth napkin.

"I wanted to ask, when you lived in the cabin on the mountainside near Ouray for over twenty years," Charlotte asked, as she looked into the pale blue eyes of the older man who sat across from her, "didn't you ever get lonely?"

"Well, I didn't exactly live alone," he said with a twinkle forming in his eyes, "I had a cow and a cat to keep me company."

Charlotte laughed, made a note on her notepad, then asked, "What happened to them?"

"I was in the hospital in Ouray for over two months, when I returned home something had killed the cow, might a been a grizzly I'm guessin' by the way the carcass had been turned nearly inside out. I suspect the cat must a figured out on his own that I wasn't coming back and struck out to find better quarters."

Checking her notes, carefully written on several pages of her notebook, Charlotte said, "I believe I have everything here, the mining claim you filed in Leadville in the 1870's, the shootouts with the Salt Lake Jim and Hank Way Gangs, and the capture of the bank robber Jim Clarke, and how you and your deputy chased the Big Tooth Jim Gang down into the New Mexico Territory in the 1860's. Oh, here's one thing I know my editor is going to ask me, so I had better be prepared with an answer; why didn't you give Big Tooth Jim and his two outlaw gang members a chance to surrender?"

"Well, one thing I learned was to shoot first, otherwise you get shot."

"Besides getting shot once, and having your horse shot out from under you twice, you had a remarkable six years serving as El Paso County's first sheriff," the report asked, "Please tell me, what is it that you are most proud of?"

"I can say I never hit the back trail," the lawman replied.

Charlotte wrote that comment in her notebook, then looked up. "I know many of my readers are going to want to know, so I apologize if this comes across as too personal, but well, you were known to be quite popular with the ladies, and I know from first-hand experience how you are a natural on the ballroom floor; so, tell me, Sheriff Kelly, how was it that you never married?"

Kelly thought about her question for a moment, one that he had contemplated a thousand times himself, and then replied, "Well, truth is, the woman I loved married someone else."

"I see. That fact seemed to be well known by my grandparents," Charlotte replied as she wrote his answer down in her notebook. Sensing the subject of her interview was suddenly anxious to conclude their discussion, Charlotte added, "I have one final question I just have to ask, if you don't mind. My grandparents told me how excited you were when you told them the man you thought you had killed back in Maine, when you were fourteen, was still alive. What was that like for you to learn that after seventy-three years, the young man you thought you had killed, your sister's fiancé, was still very much alive and that you wouldn't have had to run away from home after all?"

"Well," Kelly said thoughtfully, "I'm glad to know that before I go over yonder my hands are clean."

December 30, 1913
Myron Stratton Home, Colorado Springs

Lightning cracked outside the frosted window, "Snow lightning," Marcus said to Lizzy, seeing how she had jumped when it cracked. "It's rather unusual from what I read," he added trying to comfort her as she sat in the rocking chair beside the bed.

"He was dancing just like the old days, at Thanksgiving," Lizzy said, looking down at Kelly's face, illuminated by the dim candle light.

"They say he was out on the night watch during the snow storm a few weeks back," Marcus said. "You know Scott, wouldn't come inside 'til he finished his rounds. You'd never know he was battling stomach cancer and heart problems as it was. Doesn't take long with pneumonia, not at his age, least that's how the doctor explained it," Marcus concluded, as he parted the beige window curtain to see outside. "Looks like the undertaker from D.F. Law's is here."

Marcus held the door open for the undertaker, dressed in a black suit. The man made his way solemnly inside, "Hello, I am Mr. Urich."

"I'm M.A. Foster, this is my wife, Lizzy Foster. We live over on Cheyenne Road, sorry to get you out on such a blistery cold morning. This here is Scott Kelly."

"I'm told Mr. Kelly was our first Sheriff," Mr. Urich said, removing his hat and walking over to the bed where he could feel for a pulse. "Any idea when he died?"

"The nursing staff here at the home said he had been doing

poorly since catching pneumonia making his rounds during the blizzard, but he supposedly ate a good meal last night. Everyone assumed he was on the mend; obviously that was not the case," Marcus replied, helping Mr. Urich with the details for the death certificate.

"Rankin Scott Kelly, Age 87, Single, White, Male," Mr. Urich read aloud, as he filled in the death certificate. "Would either of you happen to know where Mr. Kelly was from and his profession, when he wasn't serving in elected office?"

"He was from Maine and he was a brick and stone mason," Marcus replied, adding, "When he wasn't serving as our sheriff."

Mr. Urich turned his attention to the personal effects on the nightstand and counted the money aloud, "Seven dollars and thirty-six cents, not counting the fifty-cent piece with the bullet hole through it. Not sure that's worth anything, like it is, being shot through like that and all."

"If that's not enough to cover his burial expenses, please let us know," Marcus said.

"I don't suspect that will be a problem," Mr. Urich replied. "From what I hear, Sheriff Kelly had many friends here with the El Paso County Pioneers Association. Covering his remaining funeral expenses shouldn't be a problem."

"What do you suppose I should do with these?" Mr. Urich said; pointing to the old Spanish knife on the bedside, next to the pocket watch.

Lizzy picked up the old pocket watch that once belonged to her step-father. She opened the case to see the crystal face was cracked and the space that once held her tintype was empty. She closed the watch case, held the braided horsehair chain up to her nose briefly, and then handed the watch with the coin attached to the undertaker. "Bury these with him," Lizzy directed, as she stood up to leave. "Tuck the pocket watch into his left vest pocket, the coin with the bullet hole in it in his right vest pocket and the knife in his right coat pocket."

"Very well," Mr. Urich replied. "Mr. Foster, would you mind lending me a hand retrieving the gurney from the hearse?"

"Not at all," Marcus said, as he followed the undertaker outside.

"Is that your big white dog out there?" the undertaker asked of Marcus as they started toward the front door.

"We don't own a dog," Marcus answered as he buttoned his topcoat to go outside.

"Did Mr. Kelly own a dog?" the undertaker asked as he opened the front door.

"No," Marcus replied, "not anymore."

"When I pulled up it came right up to the hearse and sat down in the snow. Looked like it was waiting for someone, I thought it might have been you he was waiting for," the undertaker commented as he stepped outside and looked to where he had parked his hearse. "Looks like it's gone now, t'was was a huge dog, part Mastiff I believe. Guess it wandered off."

Lizzy slowly followed the two men to the door and stopped at the doorway to look back at the body of the man she had once hoped with all her heart to marry. "Goodnight Scott," Lizzy whispered as silent tears fell down her cheeks. Then she slowly turned away, stepped out into the cold morning air and closed the door.

Evergreen Cemetery Chapel, Colorado Springs

Knowing this was a historic moment, Charlotte Foster respectfully spoke with dozens of the town's people who attended the reception following Sheriff Kelly's funeral. She captured the thoughts of several of the early pioneers in her notepad, then spotted M.S. Beach retrieving his hat and making his way down the front steps toward his carriage parked in front of the small stone chapel.

"Excuse me, Mr. Beach," Charlotte began, walking quickly alongside the man who she respected for having helped found Colorado City in 1859. "You knew Sheriff Kelly. Please tell me, how do you think he should be remembered?"

M.S. Beach paused to look around at the hundreds of grave markers. Many of the people buried nearby were also some of El Paso County's earliest pioneers. After a moment of quiet reflection he replied, "People should remember Sheriff Kelly, our first lawman, as a man who was straight and strong and true."

People react differently when confronted by violence; most would choose to run from danger. Some men, whether driven by revenge or a sense of duty, or perhaps both, run toward danger. Rankin Scott Kelly was one of those who were first to respond to confront danger head-on, to ride toward the sound of the guns. And like most people who have confronted evil and survived, most chose not to talk much about the violence they have confronted, except on a rare occasion and generally then only to another warrior, who like themselves, stared evil in the eye and witnessed atrocities unimaginable to most people living in a civilized society.

Acknowledgments

I want to express my sincere appreciation to everyone who contributed to the success of this book—thank you! While there isn't room to list everyone by name, I would be remiss if I didn't mention a few special contributors beginning with Gina Scalzi. I had the good fortune of meeting Gina at one of my talks and book signings. Afterwards she offered to help me write a screenplay about Sheriff Kelly. It was through the months-long collaboration on the screenplay with Gina that the characters and plot for this novel truly developed. Thank you, Gina, for your efforts to help ensure the service of the first lawman in the Pikes Peak Region is not forgotten. Next, I must thank my family and friends who supported me throughout the writing of this second publication on Sheriff Kelly. My wife Brenda and daughter, Laynie, for listening to my countless hours discussing the life and times of Sheriff Kelly—thank you! To my sisters Vicki Pullen and Tammy Bodycomb, my Aunt Betty Davis, and friends, Ginger Hipsky, Judy Kilgore, Heidi Wigand-Nicely, Elizabeth

Taylor, Vern Kuykendall, Phil Tinsley and Karen Rhodes, I truly appreciated your careful review, editing and final proofreading of my manuscrip—thank you for contributing your time and talents to make this book shine. Finally, I want to thank Susie Schorsch, with the Old Colorado City Historical Society, who published my first nonfiction Sheriff Kelly book and provided invaluable support for the production of Sheriff Kelly's historical fiction novel. To my writing coach Toni Robino, thank you for seeing something worthwhile in my writing and for your determination to make me a better writer, and to Donald Kallaus, Rhyolite Press LLC, for the book layout, cover design and production of this the first novel under the Circle Star Publishing Imprint.

John Wesley Anderson

About the Author

John Wesley Anderson served as the 26th elected sheriff of El Paso County, Colorado (1995-2003). One of John's lifelong heroes was his uncle Harold "Red" Davis who served as the 24th elected sheriff (1979-1983). Both men enjoyed long law enforcement careers and both retired from the Colorado Springs Police Department prior to serving as sheriff. John has always had a passion for history, particularly the history of the American West. In 2017 John published his nonfiction book *Rankin Scott Kelly, First Sheriff of El Paso County, Colorado Territory (1861–1867)* and co-authored a screenplay with Gina Scalzi, based on this historical fiction novel. John lives with his wife, Brenda, their daughter Laynie, a rescue cat named Jay Catsby and a rescued dog named Puck, in northern El Paso County, Colorado.

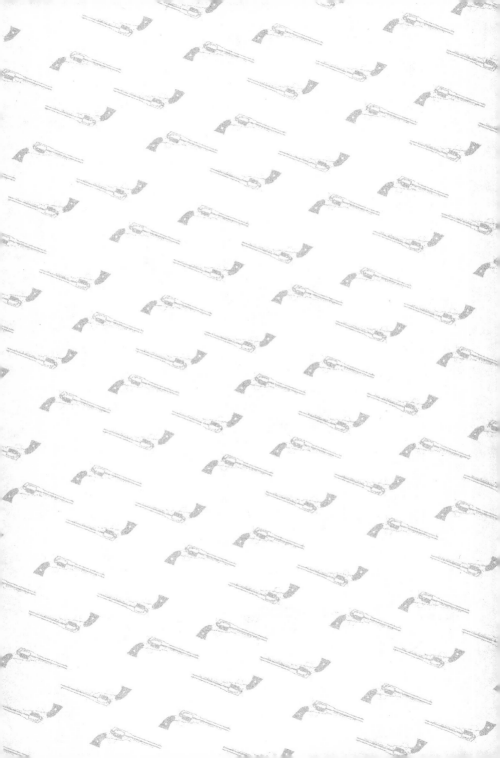